tiger's curse

A *New York Times* Bestseller
A *USA Today* Bestseller
A *Publishers Weekly* Bestseller
A Parents' Choice Award Winner

"A sweet romance and heart-pounding adventure. I found myself cheering, squealing and biting my nails—all within a few pages. In short, *Tiger's Curse* is magical!"

—Becca Fitzpatrick, *New York Times* bestselling author of *Hush, Hush*

"The hot new romance-adventure series of 2011 . . ."

—*Teen Magazine*

"The way Colleen weaves Indian culture, Hinduism, and her own made-up fairy tale into an action-packed love story is captivating."

—MTV.com's *Hollywood Crush* blog

PRAISE FOR OTHER BOOKS IN THE SERIES:

tiger's quest

A *New York Times* Bestseller
A *USA Today* Bestseller
A *Publishers Weekly* Bestseller
A Parents' Choice Award Winner

"Forget vampires and werewolves, tigers are the new hottest thing. The second book in Houck's Tiger's Curse series features a love triangle, passion and nonstop action. It's a guaranteed page-turner with a huge twist at the end that will leave you breathless."

—*RT Reviews*

". . . shocking, heart-rending, soul-tearing . . ."

—*Kirkus Reviews*

tiger's voyage

A *New York Times* Bestseller
A *USA Today* Bestseller

"Epic, grand adventure rolled into a sweeping love story . . ."
—Sophie Jordan, author of *Firelight*

"An epic love triangle that kept me eagerly turning the pages!"
—Alexandra Monir, author of *Timeless*

". . . high adventure ensues. As in *Tiger's Curse* and *Tiger's Quest*, this story is part action-adventure and part romance . . . the novel will satisfy the saga's fans, who will be delighted by the prospect of a fourth volume."
—*Booklist*

tiger's destiny

A *New York Times* Bestseller
A *USA Today* Bestseller

"Ablaze with fiery passions—and sheets of actual fire, too—this conclusion to the Tiger's Curse quartet brings Oregon teenager Kelsey and the two Indian were-tiger princes who have divided her heart through a climactic battle to a final, bittersweet mate selection. . . .[Readers] are sure to be left throbbing and misty-eyed."

—*Kirkus Reviews*

"Kelsey, Ren, and Kishan return in this final volume in Houck's popular Tiger's Curse series. [Houck] tells a good story that will appeal to both action-adventure and romance fans."

—*Booklist*

tiger's curse

tiger's curse

by COLLEEN HOUCK

For Jamie,
Bhagyashalin! May you be
endowed with luck!!
Colleen Houck

SPLINTER

New York

SPLINTER
NEW YORK

An Imprint of Sterling Publishing
1166 Avenue of the Americas
New York, NY 10036

ISBN 978-1-4549-0249-2

Sanskrit lettering by Hema Pendikatla.

Designed by Katrina Damkoehler.

Library of Congress Cataloging-in-Publication Data

Houck, Colleen.
Tiger's curse / by Colleen Houck.
  p. cm.
Summary: Seventeen-year-old Oregon teenager Kelsey forms a bond with a circus tiger who is actually one of two brothers, Indian princes Ren and Kishan, who were cursed to live as tigers for eternity, and she travels with him to India where the tiger's curse may be broken once and for all.
  ISBN 978-1-4027-8403-3
  [1. Tigers--Fiction. 2. Blessing and cursing--Fiction. 3. Immortality--Fiction. 4. Orphans--Fiction. 5. Circus--Fiction. 6. India--Fiction.] I. Title.
  PZ7.H81143Tig 2011
  [Fic]--dc22

2010033191

Distributed in Canada by Sterling Publishing
c/o Canadian Manda Group, 664 Annette Street
Toronto, Ontario, Canada M6S 2C8

For information about custom editions, special sales, and premium and corporate purchases, please contact Sterling Special Sales at 800-805-5489 or specialsales@sterlingpublishing.com.

Manufactured in the United States of America
Lot #:
10 12 14 16 18 20 19 17 15 13 11 9
09/15

For the Lindas in my life.
One gave me the motivation to write
and the other gave me the time.
Both I call sister.

contents

the tiger

by William Blake

Tiger! Tiger! burning bright
In the forests of the night,
What immortal hand or eye
Could frame thy fearful symmetry?

In what distant deeps or skies
Burnt the fire of thine eyes?
On what wings dare he aspire?
What the hand dare seize the fire?

And what shoulder and what art,
Could twist the sinews of thy heart?
And when thy heart began to beat,
What dread hand and what dread feet?

What the hammer? what the chain?
In what furnace was thy brain?
What the anvil? what dread grasp
Dare its deadly terrors clasp?

When the stars threw down their spears,
And watered heaven with their tears,
Did he smile his work to see?
Did he who made the Lamb make thee?

Tiger! Tiger! burning bright
In the forests of the night,
What immortal hand or eye
Dare frame thy fearful symmetry?

the curse

The prisoner stood with his hands tied in front of him, tired, beaten, and filthy but with a proud back befitting his royal Indian heritage. His captor, Lokesh, looked on haughtily from a lavishly carved, gilded throne. Tall, white pillars stood like sentinels around the room. Not a whisper of a jungle breeze moved across the sheer draperies. All the prisoner could hear was the steady clinking of Lokesh's jeweled rings against the side of the golden chair. Lokesh looked down, eyes narrowed into contemptuous, triumphant slits.

The prisoner was the prince of an Indian kingdom called Mujulaain. Technically, his current title was *Prince and High Protector of the Mujulaain Empire*, but he still preferred to think of himself as just his father's son.

That Lokesh, the raja of a small neighboring kingdom called Bhreenam, had managed to kidnap the prince was not as shocking as who was sitting beside Lokesh: Yesubai, the raja's daughter and the prisoner's fiancée, and the prince's younger brother, Kishan. The captive studied all three of them but only Lokesh returned his determined gaze. Beneath his shirt, the prince's stone amulet lay cool against his skin, while anger surged through his body.

The prisoner spoke first, struggling to keep the betrayal out of his voice, "Why have you—my soon-to-be-father—treated me with such . . . *inhospitality?*"

Nonchalant, Lokesh affixed a deliberate smile on his face. "My dear prince, you have something I desire."

"*Nothing* you could want can justify this. Are our kingdoms not to be joined? Everything I have has been at your disposal. You needed only to ask. Why have you done this?"

Lokesh rubbed his jaw as his eyes glittered. "Plans change. It seems that your brother would like to take my daughter for *his* bride. He has promised me certain remunerations if I help him achieve that goal."

The prince turned his attention to Yesubai, who, with cheeks aflame, assumed a demure, submissive pose with her head bowed. His arranged marriage to Yesubai was supposed to have ushered in an era of peace between the two kingdoms. He had been away for the last four months overseeing military operations on the far side of the empire and had left his brother to watch over the kingdom.

I guess Kishan was watching a little bit more than just the kingdom.

The prisoner strode fearlessly forward, faced Lokesh, and called out, "You have fooled us all. You are like a coiled cobra that has been hiding in his basket, waiting for the moment to strike."

He widened his glance to include his brother and his fiancée. "Don't you see? Your actions have freed the viper, and we are bitten. His poison now runs through our blood, destroying everything."

Lokesh laughed disdainfully and spoke, "If you agree to surrender your piece of the Damon Amulet, I might be persuaded to allow you to live."

"To live? I thought we were bartering for my bride."

"I'm afraid your rights as a betrothed husband have been usurped. Perhaps I haven't been clear. Your brother will have Yesubai."

The prisoner clenched his jaw, and said simply, "My father's armies would destroy you if you killed me."

Lokesh laughed. "He certainly would not destroy Kishan's new family. We will simply placate your dear father and tell him that you were the victim of an unfortunate accident."

He stroked his short, stippled beard and then clarified, "Of course, you understand, that even should I allow you live, I will rule *both* kingdoms." Lokesh smiled. "If you defy me I will forcibly remove your piece of the amulet."

Kishan leaned toward Lokesh and protested stiffly, "I thought we had an arrangement. I only brought my brother to you because you swore that you would *not* kill him! You were to take the amulet. That's all."

Lokesh shot out his hand as quickly as a snake and grabbed Kishan's wrist. "You should have learned by now that I *take* whatever I want. If you would prefer the view from where your brother is standing, I would be happy to accommodate you."

Kishan shifted in his chair but kept silent.

Lokesh continued. "No? Very well, I have now amended our former arrangement. Your brother *will* be killed if he does not comply with my wishes, and *you* will never marry my daughter unless you hand over your piece of the amulet to me as well. This private arrangement of ours can easily be revoked, and I can have Yesubai married to a different man—a man of *my* choosing. Perhaps an old sultan would cool her blood. If you want to remain close to Yesubai, you will learn to be submissive."

Lokesh squeezed Kishan's wrist until it cracked loudly. Kishan didn't react at all.

Flexing his fingers and slowly rolling his wrist, Kishan sat back, raised a hand to touch the engraved amulet piece hidden underneath his own shirt, and made eye contact with his brother. An unspoken message passed between them.

The brothers would deal with each other later, but Lokesh's actions meant war, and the needs of the kingdom were a priority for both.

Obsession pumped up Lokesh's neck, throbbed at his temple, and settled behind his black, serpentine eyes. Those same eyes dissected the prisoner's face, probing, assessing for weakness. Angered to the point of action, Lokesh jumped to his feet. "So be it!"

Lokesh pulled a shiny knife with a jeweled hilt from his robe and roughly yanked up the sleeve of the prisoner's now filthy, once-white Jodhpuri coat. The ropes twisted on his wrists and he grunted in pain as Lokesh drew the knife across his arm. The cut was deep enough that blood welled up, spilled over the edge, and dripped onto the tiled floor.

Lokesh tore a wooden talisman from around his neck and placed it beneath the prisoner's arm. Blood trickled from the knife onto the charm, and the engraved symbol glowed a fiery red before pulsing an unnatural white light.

The light shot toward the prince with groping fingers that pierced his chest and clawed its way through his body. Though strong, he wasn't prepared for the pain. The captive screamed as his body suddenly became inflamed with a prickly heat and he fell to the floor.

He reached out with his hands to brace himself, but he managed only to scratch feebly on the cold, white tile of the floor. The prince watched helplessly as both Yesubai and his brother attacked Lokesh, who shoved both back viciously. Yesubai fell to the ground, hitting her head hard on the dais. The prince was aware that his brother was near, overtaken by grief as the life drained from Yesubai's limp body. Then he was aware of nothing except the pain.

kelsey

I was standing on a precipice. Technically, I was just standing in line at a temp job office in Oregon, but it felt like a precipice. Childhood, high school, and the illusion that life was good and times were easy were behind me. Ahead loomed the future: college, a variety of summer jobs to help pay for tuition, and the probability of a lonely adulthood.

The line inched forward. I'd been waiting for what seemed like hours trying to get a lead on a summer job. When it was finally my turn, I approached the desk of a bored, tired job placement worker who was on the phone. The woman gestured me closer and indicated that I should sit down. After she hung up, I handed her some forms and she mechanically began the interview.

"Name, please."

"Kelsey. Kelsey Hayes."

"Age?"

"Seventeen, almost eighteen. My birthday's coming soon."

She stamped the forms. "Are you a high school graduate?"

"Yes. I graduated just a couple of weeks ago. I plan on attending Chemeketa this fall."

"Parents' names?"

"Madison and Joshua Hayes, but my guardians are Sarah and Michael Neilson."

"Guardians?"

Here we go again, I thought. Somehow explaining my life never got easier.

"Yes. My parents are . . . deceased. They died in a car accident when I was a freshman."

She bent over some paperwork and scribbled for a long time. I grimaced, wondering what she could be writing that was taking so long.

"Miss Hayes, do you like animals?"

"Sure. Umm, I know how to feed them . . ." *Is anyone lamer than me? Way to talk myself out of being hired.* I cleared my throat. "I mean, sure, I love animals."

The woman didn't really seem to care about my response, and she handed me a posting for a job.

NEEDED:
A TEMPORARY WORKER FOR TWO WEEKS ONLY

DUTIES INCLUDE: TICKET SALES,
FEEDING THE ANIMALS, AND
CLEANING UP AFTER PERFORMANCES.

Note: Because the tiger and dogs
need to be cared for 24/7, room and board
are provided.

The job was for the Circus Maurizio, a small family-run circus at the fairgrounds. I remembered getting a coupon for it at the grocery store and I'd even considered offering to take my foster parents' kids, Rebecca, who is six years old, and Samuel, who is four, so that Sarah and Mike could have some time to themselves. But then I lost the coupon and forgot all about it.

"So, do you want the job?" the woman asked impatiently.

"A tiger, huh? Sounds interesting! Are there elephants, too? Because I have to draw the line at scooping up elephant droppings." I giggled quietly at my own joke, but the woman didn't so much as crack a smile. Since I had no other options, I told her that I would do it. She gave me a card with an address and she instructed me to be there the next day by 6:00 a.m.

I wrinkled my nose. "They need me at six in the morning?"

The worker just gave me a look and shouted "Next!" at the line shuffling behind me.

What had I gotten myself into? I thought as I climbed into Sarah's borrowed hybrid and headed home. I sighed. *It could be worse. I could be flipping burgers tomorrow. Circuses are fun. I just hope there are no elephants.*

Living with Sarah and Mike was okay for the most part. They gave me a lot more freedom than most other kids' parents, and I think we have a healthy respect for each other—well, as least as much as adults can respect a seventeen-year-old anyway. I helped babysit their kids and never got into trouble. It wasn't the same as being with my parents, but we were still a family of sorts.

I parked the car carefully in the garage and headed into the house to find Sarah attacking a mixing bowl with a wooden spoon. I dropped my bag on a chair and went to get a glass of water.

"Making vegan cookies again, I see. What's the special occasion?" I asked.

Sarah jammed the wooden spoon into the dense dough several times as if the spoon were an icepick. "It's Sammy's turn to bring treats for his playdate."

I stifled a snigger by coughing.

She narrowed her eyes at me shrewdly. "Kelsey Hayes, just because your mother was the best cookie baker in the world doesn't mean I can't make a decent treat."

"It's not your skills I doubt, it's your ingredients," I said, picking up a jar. "Substitute nut butter, flax, protein powder, and agave. I'm surprised you don't put recycled paper in those things. Where's the chocolate?"

"I use carob sometimes."

"*Carob* is not chocolate. It tastes like brown chalk. If you're going to make cookies, you should make—"

"I know. I know. Pumpkin chocolate chip or double chocolate peanut butters. They're really bad for you, Kelsey," she said with a sigh.

"But they taste *so* good."

I watched Sarah lick a finger and continued. "By the way, I got a job. I'm going to be cleaning up and feeding animals at a circus. It's at the fairgrounds."

"Good for you! That sounds like it will be a great experience," Sarah perked up. "What kind of animals?"

"Uh, dogs mostly. And I think there's a tiger. But I probably won't have to do anything dangerous. I'm sure they have professional tiger people for that stuff. But I do have to start really early and will be sleeping there for the next two weeks."

"Hmmm," Sarah paused contemplatively. "Well we're just a phone call away if you need us. Would you mind taking the brussels sprouts casserole a la 'recycled newspaper' out of the oven?"

I set the stinky casserole in the center of the table while she popped her cookie sheets in the oven and called the kids to dinner. Mike came in, set down his briefcase, and kissed his wife on the cheek.

"What's that . . . smell?" he asked suspiciously.

"Brussels sprouts casserole," I answered.

"And I made cookies for Sammy's playgroup," Sarah announced proudly. "I'll save the best one for you."

Mike shot me a knowing look that Sarah caught. She snapped her dishtowel at his thigh.

"If that's the attitude you and Kelsey are bringing to the table then the two of you get cleanup duty tonight."

"Aw, honey. Don't be mad." He kissed Sarah again and wrapped his arms around her, trying his best to get out of the task.

I took that as my cue to exit. As I snuck out of the kitchen, I heard Sarah giggle.

Someday, I'd like a guy to try and talk himself out of cleanup duty with me in the same way, I thought and smiled.

Apparently, Mike negotiated well because he got put-the-kids-to-bed duty instead of cleanup, while I was left to do dishes on my own. I didn't mind really but as soon as I was done, I decided it was my bedtime too. Six o'clock in the morning was going to come awfully early.

Quietly, I climbed the stairs to my bedroom. It was small and cozy, with just a simple bed, a mirrored dresser, a desk for my computer and homework, a closet, my clothes, my books, a basket of different colored hair ribbons, and my grandmother's quilt.

My grandmother made that quilt when I was little. I was very young, but I remember her stitching it together, the same metal thimble always on her finger. I traced a butterfly on the worn-out, raggedy-at-the-corners quilt, remembering how I had snuck the thimble out of her sewing kit one night just to feel her near me. Even though I was a teenager, I still slept with the quilt every night.

I changed into my pajamas, shook my hair free from its braid, and brushed it out, flashing back to how mom used to do it for me while we talked.

Crawling under my warm covers, I set my alarm for, *ugh*, 4:30 a.m. and wondered what I could possibly be doing with a tiger so early in the

morning and how I would survive the three-ring circus that was already my life. My stomach growled.

I glanced at my nightstand and the two pictures I kept out. One picture was of the three of us: Mom, Dad, and me at a New Year's celebration. I had just turned twelve. My long brown hair had been curled but in the picture it drooped because I'd thrown a fit about using hairspray. I'd smiled in the shot, despite the fact that I had a gleaming row of silver braces. I was grateful for my straight white teeth now, but I'd absolutely hated those braces back then.

I touched the glass, placing my thumb briefly over the image of my pale face. I'd always longed to be svelte, tan, blond, and blue eyed but I had the same brown eyes as my father and the tendency toward chubbiness of my mother.

The other was a candid shot of my parents at their wedding. There was a beautiful water fountain in the background, and they were young, happy, and smiling at each other. I wanted that for myself someday. I wanted someone to look at me like that.

Flopping over on my stomach and stuffing my pillow under my cheek, I drifted off thinking about my mom's cookies.

That night, I dreamed I was being chased through the jungle, and when I turned to look at my pursuer, I was startled to see a large tiger. My dream self laughed and smiled and then turned and ran faster. The sound of gentle, padded paws raced along after me, beating in time with my heart.

2

the circus

My alarm startled me out of a deep sleep at 4:30 in the morning. It would be warm outside today, but not *too* hot. Oregon almost never got too hot. An Oregon governor must have passed a law a long, long time ago that said Oregon had to always have moderate temperatures.

It was dawn. The sun still hadn't climbed over the mountains, but the sky was already brightening, changing the clouds to pink cotton candy in the eastern horizon. It must have drizzled rain last night because I could smell an appealing fragrance in the air—the scent of wet grass and pine mingled together.

I hopped out of bed, turned on the shower, waited till the bathroom turned good and steamy, and then jumped in and let the hot water pound my back to wake up my sleepy muscles.

What exactly does one wear to a circus job? Not knowing what was appropriate, I tugged on a short-sleeved T-shirt and a good pair of work jeans. Then, I slipped my feet into tennis shoes, toweled dry my hair, and wove it into a quick French braid that I tied off with a blue ribbon. Next, I applied some lip gloss, and voilà, my circus primping was complete.

Time to pack. I figured I wouldn't need to bring much, just a couple of things to make me comfortable since I would only be at the circus for two weeks and could always make a pit stop at home. I rifled through my closet and selected three outfits, which were organized by color and hung neatly, before pulling open my dresser drawers. I grabbed a few sock balls, which were also meticulously arranged by color, and shoved everything into my trusty school backpack. Then I stuffed in some pens and pencils, a few books, my journal, some toiletries, my wallet, and the pictures of my family. I rolled up my quilt, stuffed it in the top, and jiggled the zipper until it shut.

Slinging my backpack over my shoulder, I headed downstairs. Sarah and Mike were already awake and eating breakfast. They woke up insanely early every day to go *running*. That was just crazy, and at 5:30 a.m. they were already done.

I mumbled, "Hey, good morning, guys."

Mike said, "Hey, good morning back. So, are you ready to start the new job?"

"Yeah. I get to sell tickets and hang around a tiger for two weeks. Great, huh?"

He chuckled. "Yep, sounds pretty great. More interesting than Public Works anyway. Want a lift? I drive right past the fairgrounds on my way into town."

I smiled at him. "Sure. Thanks, Mike. I'd love a ride," I replied.

Promising to call Sarah every few days, I grabbed a granola bar, quickly forced myself to gulp down half a glass of their soy milk—barely containing my gag reflex—and headed out the door with Mike.

At the fairgrounds, a big, blue sign posted on the street advertised upcoming events. A large slick banner read

POLK COUNTY FAIRGROUNDS
WELCOMES THE
CIRCUS MAURIZIO
FEATURING THE MAURIZIO ACROBATS
AND THE FAMOUS DHIREN!

Here we go. I sighed and started walking along the gravel path toward the main building. The central complex looked like a large airplane or military bunker. The paint was cracked and peeling in places, and the windows needed to be washed. A large American flag snapped and rolled in the breeze as the chain it was attached to clinked softly against the metal flagpole.

The fairground was an odd cluster of old buildings, a small parking lot, and a dirt path that wound between everything and around the border of the grounds. A pair of long, flatbed trucks were parked alongside several white canvas tents. Circus posters hung everywhere; there was at least one large poster on every building. Some featured acrobats. Some had pictures of jugglers.

I didn't see any elephants and breathed a sigh of relief. *If there had been elephants here, I probably would have smelled them already.*

A torn poster fluttered in the breeze. I caught the edge and smoothed it out against the post. It was a picture of a white tiger. *Well, hello there!* I thought. *I hope they have just one of you . . . and that you don't particularly enjoy eating teenage girls.*

Opening the door to the main building, I walked inside. The central hub had been converted into a one-ring circus. Tiers of faded red stadium chairs were stacked against the walls.

Chatting in the corner was a couple of people. A tall man, who looked like he was in charge, was off to the side, writing on a clipboard and inspecting boxes. I made a beeline for him across the black springy floor and introduced myself, "Hi, my name's Kelsey, your two-week temp."

He looked me up and down while chewing on something, and then spat on the floor. "Go around back, out those doors, and turn to your left. A black and silver motor home is parked out there."

"Thanks!" The tobacco spit disgusted me, but I managed to smile at him anyway. I made my way to the motor home and knocked on the door.

"Jus' a minute," a man's voice yelled. The door opened unexpectedly

fast, and I jumped back in surprise. A man in a dress robe towered over me, laughing heartily at my reaction. He was very tall, dwarfing my five-foot, seven-inch frame, and he had a rotund potbelly. Black, curly hair covered his scalp, but the hairline ended just a little bit past where it should be. Smiling at me, he reached up to shift his hairpiece back into place. A thin black mustache with both ends waxed to thin points stuck straight out from either side of his upper lip. He also had a tiny square goatee patch on his chin.

"Don't be-a intimadated at my appearance," he insisted.

I dropped my eyes and flushed. "I'm not intimidated. It just seems I caught you by surprise. I'm sorry if I woke you."

He laughed. "I like de surprises. It keeps me-a young and a most handsome man."

I giggled but stopped quickly after remembering this was probably my new boss. Crow's feet surrounded his twinkling blue eyes. His skin was tan, which showed off his toothy, white smile. He seemed like the kind of man who's always laughing at a private joke.

In a booming theatrical voice, with a strong Italian accent, he asked, "And who might you be, young lady?"

I smiled nervously. "Hi. My name's Kelsey. I was hired to work here for a couple of weeks."

He leaned over to grasp my hand. His completely enfolded mine and he shook it up and down enthusiastically enough to make my teeth rattle. "Ah, *Fantastico*! How propitious! Welcome to the Circus Maurizio! We are a little, how you say, short-handed, and need some *assistenza* while we are in your *magnifica città*, eh? *Splendido* to have you! Let us get a started *immediatamente*."

He glanced over at a cute young blonde girl about fourteen years old who was walking by. "Cathleen, take this *giovane donna* to Matt and *informare* him I *desideri*—that I wish him to work with her together. He's

incaricato to teach her today." He turned again to me. "Nice to meet you, Kelsey. I hope you *piacere*, ah, *enjoy*, working here at our *piccola tenda di circo!*"

I said, "Thanks, it was nice to meet you too."

He winked at me, then turned around, went back inside his motor home, and closed the door.

Cathleen smiled and led me around the back of the building to the circus's sleeping quarters. "Welcome to the big—er, well, small top! Come on, follow me. You can sleep in my tent if you want. There are a couple of extra cots in there. My mom, my aunt, and I all share a tent. We travel with the circus. My mom's an acrobat and my aunt is, too. Our tent's nice, if you can ignore all the costumes."

She led me into her tent and to a vacant cot. The tent was spacious. I stowed my backpack under an empty cot and looked around. She was right about the costumes. They were hanging everywhere—racks and racks of them. Lace, sparkles, feathers, and spandex covered every corner of the tent. There was also a lit mirrored table with makeup, hairbrushes, pins, and curlers strewn haphazardly over every square inch of the surface.

We then found Matt, who looked to be about fourteen or fifteen. He had brown hair, an average short haircut, brown eyes, and a happy-go-lucky grin. He was trying to set up a ticket stand by himself—and failing miserably.

"Hey, Matt," Cathleen said as we grabbed the bottom of the booth to help him.

She was blushing. How cute.

Cathleen continued, "Um, this is Kelsey. She's here for two weeks. You're supposed to show her the ropes."

"No problem," he replied. "See ya around, Cath."

"See ya." She smiled and flounced away.

"So, Kelsey, I guess you get to be my sidekick today, huh? Well, you'll love it," he said, teasing me. "I run the tickets and souvenir booths, and I'm the trash collector and stock boy. I basically do everything around here that needs to get done. My dad's the circus animal trainer."

"That's a cool job." I replied and joked, "It sounds better than a trash collector anyway."

Matt laughed. "Let's get going then," he said.

We spent the next few hours hauling boxes, stocking the concession stand, and preparing for the public.

Ugh, I'm out of shape, I thought as my biceps protested and tried to unionize against me.

Dad always used to say, "Hard work keeps you grounded" whenever Mom would come up with a massive new project like planting a flower garden. He was infinitely patient, and when I complained about the extra work, he'd just smile and say, "Kells, when you love someone, you learn to give and take. Someday that will happen to you too."

Somehow, I doubted this was one of those situations.

When everything was ready, Matt sent me over to Cathleen to pick out and change into a circus costume—which turned out to be gold, glittery, and something I normally wouldn't have touched with a ten-foot pole.

This job better be worth it, I muttered under my breath and crammed my head through the shiny neckline.

Donned in my new sparkly getup, I walked out to the ticket booth and saw that Matt had put up the price board. He was waiting for me with instructions, the lock box, and a ring of tickets. He had also brought me a sack lunch.

"It's show time. Chow down quick because a couple of buses of summer camp kids are on their way."

Before I could finish eating, the camp children descended upon me in a raucous, violent flurry of little bodies. I felt like tiny buffalo were stampeding over me. My customer service-like smile probably looked more like a frightened grimace. There was nowhere for me to run. They were all around me—each one clamoring for my attention.

The adults approached, and I asked them hopefully, "Are you all paying together or separately?"

One of the teachers responded, "Oh, no. We decided to let each child buy a ticket."

"That's great," I muttered with a fake smile.

I began selling the tickets, and Cathleen soon joined me until I heard the music of the performance begin. I sat there for about twenty minutes more, but nobody else came in, so I locked the money box and found Matt inside the tent watching the show.

The man I'd met earlier that morning was the ringleader. "What's his name?" I whispered to Matt.

"Agostino Maurizio," he replied. "He's the owner of the circus, and the acrobats are all members of his family."

Mr. Maurizio brought out the clowns, acrobats, and jugglers, and I found myself enjoying the performance. Before long, though, Matt elbowed me and motioned to the souvenir stand. Intermission was going to start soon: time to sell balloons.

Together we blew up dozens of multicolored balloons with a helium tank. The kids were in a frenzy! They ran to every booth and counted out their coins so they could spend every penny.

Red seemed to be the most popular balloon color. Matt took the money while I inflated the balloons. I'd never done it before, and I popped a few, which startled the kids, but I tried to make the loud pops into a joke by shouting, "Whoopsie!" every time it happened. Pretty soon, they were yelling, "Whoopsie!" along with me.

The music began again, and the kids quickly filed back to their

seats, clutching their assorted purchases. Several of the kids had bought glow-in-the-dark swords and were waving them around, threatening each other gleefully.

As we sat down, Matt's dad came into the ring to do his dog show. Then the clowns came out again and played various tricks on audience members. One threw a bucket of confetti over the kids.

Great! I probably get to sweep all that up.

Next, Mr. Maurizio came back out. Dramatic safari hunting music began, and the circus lights extinguished quickly, as if they had been mysteriously blown out. A spotlight found the announcer in the center of the ring. "And now . . . the highlight of our *programma*! He was taken from the harsh, wild *giungla*, the jungles, of India and brought here to America. He is a fierce hunter, a *cacciatore bianco*, who stalks his prey in the wild, waiting, watching for the right time, and then, he . . . *springs* into action! *Movimento!*"

While he was talking, men brought out a large, round cage. It was shaped like a giant upside-down bowl with a chain-link fence tunnel attached to one side. They set it in the middle of the ring and clamped locks onto metal rings embedded in cement blocks.

Mr. Maurizio continued. He roared into the microphone, and the kids all jumped in their seats. I laughed at Mr. Maurizio's theatrics. He was a good storyteller. He proclaimed, "This *tigre* is one of the most *pericoloso*—dangerous—predators in the entire world! Watch our trainer carefully as he risks his life to bring you . . . Dhiren!" He jerked his head toward the right, and then he ran out of the ring as the spotlight moved over to the canvas flaps at the end of the building. Two men had pulled out an old-fashioned animal wagon.

It looked like the kind of wagon on a box of animal crackers. It had a white, curvy gilt-edged top, big black wheels painted white around the edges, and ornamental carved spokes that were painted gold. Black metal bars on both sides of the wagon curved in an arch at the top.

A ramp from the wagon door was attached to the chain-link tunnel, as Matt's dad entered the cage. He set up three stools on the side of the cage opposite from where he stood. He had changed into an impressive golden costume and brandished a short whip.

"Release the tiger!" he commanded.

The doors opened, and a man standing by the cage prodded the animal. I held my breath as an enormous white tiger emerged from the cage, trotted down the ramp, and into the chain-link tunnel. A moment later, it was in the big cage with Matt's father. The whip cracked, and the tiger jumped up onto a stool. Another crack and the tiger stood on its hind legs and pawed the air with its claws. The crowd erupted into applause.

The tiger leapt from stool to stool while Matt's father kept pulling the stools farther and farther away. On the last leap, I held my breath. I wasn't sure if the tiger would make it to the other stool, but Matt's father encouraged it. Gathering itself, it crouched low, assessed the distance carefully, and then leapt across the breach.

Its entire body was airborne for several seconds, with its legs stretched out ahead and behind. It was a magnificent animal. Reaching the stool with its front paws, it shifted its weight, and landed its back feet gracefully. Turning on the small stool, it rotated its large body with ease, and sat, facing its trainer.

I clapped for a long time, totally in awe of the great beast.

The tiger roared on command, stood on its hind legs, and batted its paws in the air. Matt's father shouted another command. The tiger jumped down from the stool and ran around the cage in a circle. The trainer circled as well, keeping his eyes centered on the animal. He kept the whip just behind the tiger's tail, encouraging it to keep moving.

Matt's dad gave a signal and a young man passed a large ring though the cage—a hoop. The tiger leapt through the hoop, then quickly turned around and jumped back through again and again.

The last thing the trainer did was put his head inside the tiger's mouth. A hush fell on the crowd and Matt stiffened. The tiger opened its mouth impossibly wide. I saw its sharp teeth and leaned forward feeling concerned. Matt's father slowly moved his head closer to the tiger. The tiger blinked a few times, but it held still, and its powerful jaws gaped even wider.

Matt's dad lowered his head all the way inside the animal's mouth, fully within the chomping area of the tiger's maw. Finally, he slowly brought his head out. When his head was completely free and he had moved away, the crowd erupted in cheers, while he bowed several times. Other handlers appeared to help take down the cage.

My eyes were drawn to the tiger, which was now sitting on one of the stools. I saw it moving its tongue around. It was scrunching up its face as if it smelled something funny. It almost looked like it was gagging, like a cat does when it has a hairball. Then it shook itself and sat there calmly.

Matt's dad brought his hands up, and the crowd cheered loudly. The whip cracked again, and the tiger quickly jumped off the stool, ran back through the tunnel, up the ramp, and into its cage. Matt's dad ran out of the ring and stepped behind the canvas curtain.

Mr. Maurizio dramatically shouted, "The Great Dhiren! *Mille grazie!* Thank you so much for coming to see the Circus Maurizio!"

As the tiger's cage was wheeled away before me, I had a sudden urge to stroke its head and comfort it. I wasn't sure if tigers could show emotion, but for some reason I felt like I could sense its mood. It seemed melancholy.

Just at that moment, a soft breeze wrapped around me carrying the

scent of night blooming jasmine and sandalwood. It completely overwhelmed the strong aroma of hot buttered popcorn and cotton candy. My heart beat faster as goosebumps shot down my arms. But as quickly as it came, the lovely scent disappeared and I felt an inexplicable hole in the pit of my stomach.

The lights came up and the kids started stampeding out of the arena. My brain was still slightly foggy. Slowly, I got up and turned around to stare at the curtain where the tiger had disappeared. A faint trace of sandalwood and an unsettled feeling lingered.

Huh! I must have hypersensitivity disorder.

The show was over, and I was officially crazy.

the tiger

The kids rushed out of the building in a screaming mob. A bus started up in the parking lot. As it noisily shook itself awake rumbling, hissing, and puffing air out of its exhaust pipe, Matt stood up and stretched. "Ready for the real work now?"

I groaned, feeling the soreness in my arm muscles already. "Sure, bring it on."

He started cleaning the debris off the seats, as I followed behind to push them against the wall. When that was done, he handed me a broom. "We've got to get the whole area swept up, pack everything into the boxes, and then store them all away again. You get started, and I'll turn in the money boxes to Mr. Maurizio."

"No problem."

I started moving slowly across the floor, pushing the broom in front of me. I wound forward and back, like a swimmer doing laps, as I methodically swept up the rubbish. My mind wandered back to the acts I had seen. I loved the dogs the best, but there was something compelling about the tiger. My thoughts kept drifting back to the big cat.

I wonder what it's like up close. And why does it smell like sandalwood? I didn't know anything about tigers except what I had seen late at night on the Nature Channel and in old issues of *National Geographic*. I'd never been that interested in tigers before, but then again, I'd never worked in a circus before either.

I'd almost finished sweeping by the time Matt came back. He bent to help me scoop up the giant mound of trash before we spent a good hour packing up boxes and hauling them back to storage.

When this was done, Matt told me that I could have an hour or two off until it was time to join the troupe for dinner. I was eager to have a little time to myself, so I hurried back to the tent.

I changed clothes, wiggled into an only slightly uncomfortable place on my cot, and pulled out my journal. As I nibbled on my pen, I reflected on the interesting people I had met here. It was obvious that the circus folk considered each other family. Several times, I noticed people stepping in to help, even if it wasn't their job. I also wrote a bit about the tiger. The tiger really interested me. *Maybe I should work with animals and study that in college*, I reflected. Then I thought about my extreme dislike of biology and knew I'd never make it in that field.

It was almost time for dinner. The delectable aroma coming from the big building made my mouth water.

This was nothing like Sarah's vegan cookies, I thought. *No, it had the homey feel of Grandma's biscuits and gravy.*

Inside, Matt was setting up chairs around eight long folding tables. One of the tables was set up with Italian takeout. It looked fantastic. I offered to help, but Matt brushed me aside.

"You worked hard today, Kelsey. Relax, I got this," he said.

Cathleen waved me over. "Come sit by me. We can't start eating until Mr. Maurizio comes in to make the evening announcements."

Sure enough, the moment we sat down, Mr. Maurizio strolled dramatically into the building. "*Favoloso* performance, everyone! And a most *eccellente* job to our newest salesperson, eh? Tonight is a celebration! *Mangiate*. Fill your plates, *mia famiglia!*"

I giggled. *Huh. He plays the part all the time, not just for the show.*

I turned to Cathleen. "I guess that means we did a good job, right?"

She answered, "Yep. Let's eat!"

I waited in line with Cathleen, and then picked up my paper plate and filled it with Italian green salad, a big scoop of spinach-and-cheese-stuffed shells covered in tomato sauce, parmesan chicken, and, not having enough room on my plate, popped a warm breadstick into my mouth, grabbed a bottle of water, and sat down. I couldn't help but notice the large chocolate cheesecake for dessert, but I wasn't even able to finish the dinner I had on my plate. Sighing, I left the cheesecake alone.

After dinner, I moved to a quiet corner of the building and called to check in with Sarah and Mike. When I hung up, I approached Matt, who was putting all the leftovers into the fridge. "I didn't see your dad at the table. Doesn't he eat?"

"I took him a plate. He was busy with the tiger."

"How long has your dad been working with the tiger?" I asked, eager to learn more about the impressive cat. "According to the job description, I'm supposed to help out with the tiger somehow."

Matt shoved aside a half empty bottle of orange juice, wedged a box of takeout food next to it, and shut the refrigerator. "For the past five years or so. Mr. Maurizio purchased the tiger from another circus, and they had bought it from another circus before that. The tiger's history wasn't well documented. Dad says the tiger will perform only the standard tricks and refuses to learn anything new, but the good news is that it's never given him a problem. It's a very quiet, almost docile beast, as far as tigers go."

"So what do I have to do to it? I mean, am I really supposed to feed it?"

"Don't worry. It's not that hard as long as you avoid the big teeth," Matt joked. "I'm kidding. You'll just be bringing the tiger's food back and forth from building to building. See my dad tomorrow. He'll give you all the info you need."

"Thanks, Matt!"

There was about an hour left of light outside, but I had to get up early again. After showering, brushing my teeth, and changing into my warm flannel pj's and slippers, I hurried back to my tent and got cozy under my grandma's quilt. Reading a chapter in my book made me drowsy, so I quickly fell into a deep sleep.

The next morning after breakfast, I hurried to the kennel and found Matt's dad playing with the dogs. He looked a lot like an adult version of Matt, with the same brown hair and brown eyes. He turned to me as I approached and said, "Hello. It's Kelsey, right? I understand you'll be my assistant today."

"Yes, sir."

He shook my hand warmly and smiled. "Call me Andrew or Mr. Davis, if you prefer something more formal. The first thing we need to do is take these feisty little critters for a walk around the grounds."

"Sounds easy enough."

He laughed. "We'll see."

Mr. Davis gave me enough leashes to hook to five dogs' collars. The dogs were an interesting assortment of mutts including a beagle, a greyhound mix, a bulldog, a Great Dane, and a little black poodle. The animals bounced around everywhere, getting the leashes all twisted around each other—and me. Mr. Davis leaned over to help and then we started off.

It was a beautiful morning. The woods were fragrant, and the dogs were very happy, jumping about and pulling me in every direction except the one I wanted to go. They kicked up rustling pine needles and

leaves and exposed bare brown soil as they sniffed every square inch of the terrain.

As I unwound a dog from a tree I asked Mr. Davis, "Do you mind if I ask you some questions about your tiger?"

"Not at all. Ask away."

"Matt said that you guys didn't know much about the history of your tiger. Where did you get him from?"

Matt's dad rubbed a hand over the stubble on his chin and said, "Dhiren came to us when Mr. Maurizio purchased it from another small circus. He wanted to liven up the acts. He figured that I worked well with other animals, so why not tigers. We were very naïve. It usually requires extensive training to work with the big cats. Mr. Maurizio was insistent that I try and, fortunately for me, our tiger is very tractable.

"I was extremely unprepared to take on an animal of that size though I stayed and traveled with the other circus for a while. Their trainer taught me how to handle a tiger, and I learned how to care for it. I'm not sure I could have dealt with any of the other cats they were selling.

"They tried to get me interested in one of their very aggressive Siberians but I quickly realized that she wasn't for us. I negotiated for the white cat instead. The white was more even tempered and seemed to like working with me. To tell you the truth, our tiger seems bored with me most of the time."

I pondered this information as we silently walked down the trail for a while. Untangling the dogs from another tree, I asked, "Do white tigers come from India? I thought they came from Siberia."

Mr. Davis smiled. "Many people think they're from Russia because the white coat blends in with the snow, but Siberian tigers are larger and orange. Our cat is a Bengal or Indian tiger."

He looked at me thoughtfully for a moment and asked, "Are you ready to help me with the tiger today? The cages have safety latches, and I will be supervising you at all times."

I smiled, remembering the sweet scent of jasmine at the end of the tiger's performance. One of the dogs ran around my legs, trapping me and breaking the reverie for a moment.

"I would really enjoy that, thanks!" I replied.

After finishing our walk, we put the dogs back in the kennel and fed them.

Mr. Davis filled the dogs' trough with water from a green hose. He looked over his shoulder and said, "You know, tigers could be completely wiped out in the next ten years. India has already passed several laws against killing them. Poachers and villagers are mostly responsible. Tigers generally avoid humans, but they are responsible for many deaths in India every year and sometimes people take matters into their own hands."

Then, Mr. Davis gestured that I should follow him. We headed around the corner of the building to a large barn that was painted white with blue trim. He opened the wide doors for us to enter.

The bright sun filtered in and warmed the area, spotlighting the dust particles that flew around as Mr. Davis and I walked past. I was surprised at how much light shone in the two-level building despite there being only two high windows. Wide beams rose high overhead and arched across the ceiling; the walls were lined with empty stalls that held bales of hay stacked up to the ceiling. I followed him as he approached the beautiful animal wagon that had been a part of the performance yesterday.

He picked up a large jug of liquid vitamins and said, "Kelsey, meet Dhiren. Come here, I want to show you something."

We approached the cage. The tiger, who had been dozing, lifted its head and watched me curiously with bright blue eyes.

Those eyes. They were mesmerizing. They stared right into me, almost as if the tiger was examining my soul.

A wave of loneliness washed through me, but I struggled to lock it back into the tiny part of me where I kept such emotions. I swallowed thickly and broke eye contact.

Mr. Davis pulled a lever on the side of the cage. A panel slid down, separating the side of the cage near the door from Dhiren. Mr. Davis opened the cage door, filled the tiger's water dish, added about a quarter-cup of liquid vitamin, and closed and locked the door. Then, he pushed the lever to raise the panel in the cage again.

"I'm going to do some paperwork. I want you to get the tiger's breakfast," Mr. Davis instructed. "Head back to the main building and go back behind the boxes. You'll see a large refrigerator there. Take this red wagon with you to carry the meat from the fridge back here. Then take another package out of the freezer and put it into the fridge to thaw. When you return, put the food into Dhiren's cage just like I did with the vitamins. Be sure to close the safety panel first. Can you manage that?"

I grabbed the wagon handle. "No problem," I said over my shoulder as I headed back to the door. I found the meat quickly and returned in a few minutes.

I hope that safety door holds, or I'll be what's served for breakfast, I thought as I pulled the lever, dished up the raw meat into a wide bowl, and slid it carefully into the cage. I kept a wary eye on the tiger, but it just sat there watching me.

"Mr. Davis, is that a female or a male tiger?"

A noise came from the cage, a deep rumble from the tiger's chest. I turned to look at the tiger. "What are you growling at *me* for?"

Matt's dad laughed. "Ah, you've offended him. He's very sensitive, you know. In answer to your question, *he* is a male."

"Hmm."

After the tiger ate, Mr. Davis suggested I watch the tiger practice his performance. We closed the barn doors and slid the wooden beam down to lock them in place just to make sure the tiger couldn't escape. Then I scrambled up the ladder to the loft to watch from above. If anything went wrong, Mr. Davis had instructed me to climb out the window and return with Mr. Maurizio.

Matt's father approached the cage, opened the door, and called Dhiren out. The cat looked at him and then put his head back on his paws, still sleepy. Mr. Davis called again. "Come!"

The tiger's mouth opened in a giant yawn and his jaws gaped wide. I shuddered looking at the huge teeth. He stood up and stretched his front legs and then his back legs one at a time. I chuckled to myself for mentally comparing this large predator with a sleepy housecat. The tiger turned around and trotted down the ramp and out of the cage.

Mr. Davis set up a stool and cracked the whip, instructing Dhiren to jump up onto the stool. He got the hoop and had the tiger practice jumping in and out of it for several minutes. He leapt back and forth, running through the various activities with ease. His movements were effortless. I could see the sinewy muscles moving under his white and black striped fur as he went through the paces.

Mr. Davis seemed to be a good trainer, but there were a couple of times that I noticed the tiger could have taken advantage of him—but didn't. Once, Mr. Davis's face was very close to the tiger's extended claws, and it would have been very easy for the tiger to take a swipe, but instead, he moved his paw out of the way. Another time, I could have sworn Mr. Davis had stepped on his tail, but again, he just growled softly and moved his tail aside. It was very strange, and I found myself even more fascinated by the beautiful animal, wondering what it would feel like to touch him.

Mr. Davis was sweating in the stuffy barn. He encouraged the tiger to return to the stool, and then placed three other stools nearby and had him practice jumping from one to the other. Finishing up, he led the cat back to its cage, gave him a special jerky treat, and motioned for me to come down.

"Kelsey, you'd better head on over to the main building and help

Matt get ready for the show. We have a bunch of senior citizens coming in today from a local center."

I climbed down the ladder. "Would it be okay if I bring my journal in here to write sometimes? I want to draw the tiger's picture in it."

He said, "That's fine. Just don't get too close."

I hurried out the building, waved at him, and shouted, "Thanks for letting me watch you. It was really exciting!"

I rushed back to help Matt just as the first bus pulled into the parking lot. It was completely the opposite from the day before. First, the woman in charge bought all the tickets at once, which made my job much easier, and then all the patrons shuffled slowly into the ring, found their seats, and promptly fell asleep.

How could they sleep through all the noise? When intermission came, there wasn't much to do. Half of the attendees were still asleep, and the other half were in line for the restroom. Nobody really bought anything.

After the show, Matt and I cleaned up quickly, which gave me a few hours for myself. I ran back to my cot, pulled out my journal, a pen and pencil, and my quilt and walked over to the barn. I pulled open the heavy door and turned on the lights.

Strolling toward the tiger's cage, I found him resting comfortably with his head on his paws. Two bales of hay made a perfect chair with a backrest; my quilt spread over my lap warmed me as I opened my journal. After writing a couple of paragraphs, I began to sketch.

I'd taken a couple of art classes in high school and was fairly decent at drawing when I had a model to look at. I picked up my pencil and looked at my subject. He was looking right at me—not like he wanted to eat me, it was more like . . . he was trying to tell me something.

"Hey, Mister. What are you looking at?" I grinned.

I started my drawing. The tiger's round eyes were wide-set and a brilliant blue. He had long, black eyelashes and a pink nose. His fur was a soft, creamy white with black stripes radiating away from his fore- head and cheeks, all the way down to the tail. The short, furry ears were tilted toward me, and his head was resting lazily on his paws. As he watched me, his tail flicked back and forth leisurely.

I spent a lot of time trying to get the pattern of stripes right because Mr. Davis had told me that no two tigers had the same stripes. He said that their stripes were as distinctive as human fingerprints.

I continued to speak to him while drawing. "What's your name again? Ah, Dhiren. Well, I'll just call you Ren. Hope that's alright with you. So how's your day been? Did you enjoy your breakfast? You know, you have a very handsome face, for something that could eat me."

After a quiet pause with the only sounds being the scratch of my pencil and the deep rhythmic breathing of the large animal, I asked, "Do you like being a circus tiger? I can't imagine it's a very exciting life for you, being stuck in that cage all the time. I know *I* wouldn't like it very much."

I fell quiet for a while and bit my lip as I shaded in the stripes of his face. "Do you like poetry? I'll bring in my book of poems and read to you sometime. I think I have one about cats you might like."

I looked up from my drawing and was startled to see that the tiger had moved. He was sitting up, his head bent down toward me, and he was staring at me steadily. I started to feel a little bit nervous. *A large cat staring at you with great intensity can't be a good thing.*

Right then, Matt's dad strolled into the building. The tiger slumped down onto its side, but kept his face turned toward me, watching me with those deep blue eyes.

"Hey, kid, how're you doing?

"Umm, I'm fine. Hey, I have a question. Doesn't he ever get *lonely* by himself? Haven't you tried to, you know, find him a girl tiger?"

He laughed. "Not for him. This one likes to be alone. The other circus said they tried to produce offspring by breeding him with a white female in heat at the zoo, but he wouldn't have it. He stopped eating, so they pulled him out of there. I guess he prefers bachelorhood."

"Oh. Well, I'd better get back to Matt and help him out with the dinner preparations." I closed my journal and gathered my things.

As I strolled back to the main building, my thoughts were drawn to the tiger. *Poor thing. All alone with no girl tiger and no tiger cubs. No deer to hunt and stuck in captivity.* I felt sorry for him.

After dinner, I helped Matt's dad walk the dogs again and got settled in for the night. I put my hands under my head and stared at the tent ceiling, thinking some more about the tiger. After tossing and turning for about twenty minutes, I decided to go visit the barn again. I kept all the lights off in the building except the one near the cage and went back to my hay bale with my quilt.

Because I was feeling sentimental, I had brought a paperback copy of *Romeo and Juliet.*

"Hey, Ren. Would you like me to read to you for a while? Now Romeo and Juliet don't have any tigers in their story, but Romeo does climb a balcony, so you just picture yourself climbing a tree, okay? Wait a second. Let me create the proper setting."

The moon was full so I turned off the light and decided the moonlight coming through the two high windows brightened the barn sufficiently to read by.

The tiger's tail thumped the wooden base of the wagon. I turned on my side, made a pillow of sorts from the hay, and started reading aloud. I could just make out his profile and see his eyes shining in the shadowy light. I started getting tired and sighed.

"Ah. They don't make men like Romeo anymore. Maybe there never has been such a man. Present company excluded, of course. I'm sure

you're a very romantic tiger. Shakespeare sure wrote about dreamy men, didn't he?"

I closed my eyes to rest them a little and didn't wake up until the next morning.

From that moment on, I spent all my free time in the barn with Ren, the tiger. He seemed to like me being there and always perked his ears up when I started reading to him. I bugged Matt's dad with question after question about tigers until I was sure he felt like avoiding me. He appreciated the work I did though.

Every day, I got up early to take care of the tiger and the dogs, and every afternoon I wandered in to sit near Ren's cage and write in my journal. In the evenings, I would bring my quilt and a book to read. Sometimes, I'd pick out a poem and read it out loud. Other times, I just talked to him.

About a week after I had started working there, Matt and I were watching one of the shows as usual. When it was time for Ren to perform, he seemed to act differently. After trotting down the tunnel and entering the cage, he ran around in circles and paced back and forth several times. He kept looking out at the audience as if he was searching for something.

Finally, he froze as still as a statue, and stared right at me. His tiger eyes locked with mine, and I couldn't turn my head away. I heard the whip crack several times, but the tiger stayed focused on me. Matt elbowed me, and I broke eye contact.

"That's really strange," Matt said.

I asked him, "What's wrong? What's going on? Why is he looking at us?"

He shrugged. "It's never happened before. I don't know."

Ren finally turned away from us and began his normal routine.

After the show was over and I had finished cleaning up, I went to visit Ren, who was pacing in his cage. When he saw me, he sat down, settled himself, and placed his head on his paws. I walked up to the cage.

"Hey, Ren. What's going on with you today, Mister? I'm worried about you. I hope you aren't getting sick or something."

He rested quietly, but kept his eyes on me and followed my movements. I approached the cage slowly. I felt drawn to the animal and couldn't seem to block out a very strong, dangerous compulsion. It was almost a tangible pull. Maybe it was because I felt we were both lonely or maybe it was because he was such a beautiful creature. I don't know the reason, but I wanted—I *needed*—to touch him.

I knew it was risky, but I wasn't scared. Somehow, I *knew* that he wouldn't hurt me, so I ignored the red-alert bells dinging in my head. My heart began beating very fast. I took another step closer to the cage and stood there for a moment, shaking. Ren wasn't moving at all. He just continued to look at me calmly with his vivid blue eyes.

I slowly reached my hand out toward the cage, stretching just my fingertips to his paw. I made contact and touched his soft, white fur with the tips of my fingers. He exhaled a deep sigh, but other than that he didn't move. Feeling braver, I placed my whole hand on top of his paw, petted it, and traced one of his stripes with my finger. The next thing I knew, his head moved toward my hand. Before I could pull my hand out of the cage, he licked it. It tickled.

I withdrew my hand quickly. "Ren! You scared me! I thought you were going to bite off my fingers!" I tentatively held out my hand near the cage again, and his pink tongue darted out between the bars to lick my hand. I let him lick a few more times, and then headed over to the sink and washed the tiger saliva off.

Returning to my favorite spot by the hay bale, I said, "Thanks for not eating me."

He huffed quietly in response.

"What would you like to read today? How about that cat poem I promised you?"

I sat down, opened my poetry book, and found the right page. "Okay, here goes."

I AM THE CAT
by Leila Usher

In Egypt, they worshiped me
I am the Cat.
Because I bend not to the will of man
They call me a mystery.
When I catch and play with a mouse,
They call me cruel,
Yet they take animals to keep
In parks and zoos, that they may gape at them.
They think all animals are made for their pleasure,
To be their slaves.
And, while I kill only for my needs,
They kill for pleasure, power and gold,
And then pretend to a superiority!
Why should I love them?
I, the Cat, whose ancestors
Proudly trod the jungle,
Not one ever tamed by man.
Ah, do they know
That the same immortal hand
That gave them breath, gave breath to me?
But I alone am free
I am THE CAT.

I closed my book and gazed reflectively at the tiger. I imagined him proud and noble, racing through the jungle on a hunt. I suddenly felt very, very sorry about his situation. *It can't be a good life, performing in a circus, even if you have a good trainer. A tiger isn't a dog or a cat to be somebody's pet. He should be free in the wild.*

I stood up and walked back over to the tiger. Hesitantly, I reached my hand into his cage to pat his paw again. Immediately, his tongue flew out to lick my hand. I laughed at first and then sobered. Slowly, I moved my hand up to his cheek and stroked the soft fur. Then, feeling brave, I scratched him behind his ear. A deep vibration rumbled in his throat, and I realized he was purring. I grinned and scratched his ear some more.

"Like that, do you?"

I pulled my hand out of the cage, slowly again, and watched him for a minute, deliberating on what had happened. He had an almost human expression of melancholy on his face. *If tigers have souls, and I believe they do, I imagine his to be a lonely and sad one.*

I looked into those big blue eyes and whispered, "I wish you were free."

the stranger

two days later, I found a tall, distinguished man dressed in an expensive black suit standing next to Ren's cage. His thick, white hair was cut short, and he had a closely trimmed beard and mustache. His eyes were dark brown, almost black, and he had a long, aquiline nose and an olive complexion. The man was alone, talking softly, and definitely looked like he did not belong in a barn.

"Hello? Can I help you?" I queried.

The man whipped around quickly, smiled at me, and replied, "Hello! You must be Miss Kelsey. Allow me to introduce myself. My name is Anik Kadam. It is a pleasure to make your acquaintance." He pressed his hands together and bowed.

And I thought chivalry was dead.

"Yes, I'm Kelsey. Is there something I can do for you?"

"Perhaps there *is* something you can do for me." He smiled warmly and explained, "I would like to speak to the owner of your circus about this magnificent animal."

Confused, I replied, "Sure, Mr. Maurizio is in the back of the main building in the black motor home. Do you want me to take you there?"

"No need to trouble yourself, my dear. But, thank you kindly for the offer. I will go and see him immediately."

Turning, Mr. Kadam left the barn, quietly shutting the door behind him.

After checking Ren to make sure he was okay, I said, "Now *that* was strange," I said. "I wonder what he wanted. Maybe he has a thing for tigers." I hesitated for a moment, and then reached my hand through the cage bars. Amazed at my own boldness, I stroked his paw briefly and then began to get his breakfast ready.

Speaking over my shoulder, I said, "It's not every day a person sees a tiger as handsome as you are, you know. He probably just wants to compliment you on your performance."

Ren huffed in response.

I decided to grab a bite to eat myself and headed toward the main building—only to discover a flurry of unusual activity. People were gathered together, gossiping in small, scattered groups. I snatched a chocolate chip muffin and a bottle of cold milk and cornered Matt.

"What's going on?" I mumbled around a big bite of my muffin.

"I'm not exactly sure. My dad, Mr. Maurizio, and another man are in a serious meeting, and we were told to put a hold on our daily activities. We were instructed to wait here. We're *all* wondering what's going on."

"Hmm." I sat and ate my muffin, listening to the wild theories and speculations of the troupe.

We didn't have to wait long. A few minutes later, Mr. Maurizio, Mr. Davis, and Mr. Kadam, the stranger I'd met earlier, walked into the building.

"*Sedersi*, my friends. Sit. Sit!" Mr. Maurizio said with a beaming smile. This man, Mr. Kadam, has made me the most happy of men. He has made an offer to purchase our belov'd *tigre*, Dhiren."

There was an audible gasp in the room as several people jostled in their seats and softly whispered to one another.

Mr. Maurizio continued, "Now, now . . . *fate silenzio*. Shh, *amici miei*. Let me finish! He wishes to take our *tigre* back to India to the Ranthambore National Park, the great *tigre* reserve. Mr. Kadam's *denaro* will provide for our troupe for two years! Mr. Davis is in *d'accordo* with me and also feels that the tiger will be assuredly happier there."

I glanced at Mr. Davis, who solemnly nodded.

"It's agreed we will finish the shows for this week, and then the *tigre* will go with Mr. Kadam *con l'aereo*, by airplane, to India, while we will move on to our next city. Dhiren will stay with us this last week until we make the *grandioso* finale next Saturday!" the ringleader concluded and thumped Mr. Kadam on the back.

The two men turned and disappeared out of the building.

All at once, the hushed crowd started moving around quickly and began talking with each other. Silently, I watched them as they darted back and forth among the different groups like a flock of chickens at feeding time, scuttling in and out of the crowd and pecking for tidbits of information and gossip. They spoke in excited tones and patted each other's backs, murmuring animated congratulations that their next two years on the road were already paid for.

Everybody was happy except me. I sat there holding the remainder of my muffin in my limp hand. My mouth was still hanging open, and I felt frozen to my chair. After I pulled myself together, I got Matt's attention.

"What does this mean for your dad?"

He shrugged. "Dad still has the dogs, and he's always had an interest in working with miniature horses. Now that the circus has more money, maybe Dad can get Mr. Maurizio to purchase a couple that he could start training."

He walked off while I pondered the question, *what does this mean for me?* I felt . . . distressed. I knew that this circus gig would end soon anyway, but I'd put it out of my mind. I would really miss Ren. I didn't realize how much until that very moment. Still, I was happy for him. I sighed and chided myself for getting too emotionally involved.

Despite feeling happy for my tiger, I also felt gloomy knowing I'd miss visiting and talking to him. The rest of that day, I kept busy to keep my mind off it. Matt and I worked all afternoon, and I didn't have time to see Ren again until after dinner.

I hurried to my tent, grabbed my quilt, journal, and a book, and ran over to the barn. Finding my favorite spot, I sat down with my legs stretched out in front of me.

"Hey, Ren. Pretty big news for you, huh? You're going back to India! I really hope you'll be happy there. Maybe you can find yourself a pretty female tiger."

I heard a "harrumph" sound come from the cage and thought for a minute. "Hey, I hope you still know how to hunt and stuff. Well, I guess being on a reserve they'd keep an eye on you so you don't waste away."

I heard a noise coming from the back of the building and turned to see that Mr. Kadam had entered. I sat up a little straighter and felt a little self-conscious for being caught talking to a tiger.

"I am sorry to interrupt you," said Mr. Kadam. He glanced from the tiger to me, studied me carefully, and then stated, "You seem to have . . . affection for this tiger. Am I right?"

I answered unguardedly, "Yes. I enjoy spending time with him. So do you go around India rescuing tigers? That must be an interesting job."

Smiling, he replied, "Oh, it's not my main job. My true job is managing a large estate. The tiger is an item of interest for my employer and he's the one who has made the offer to Mr. Maurizio." He found a stool, placed it across from me, and sat down, balancing his tall body on the short stool with a natural ease I would not have expected from an older man.

I asked him, "Are you *from* India?"

"Yes," he replied. "I was born and raised there many years ago. The main holdings of the estate that I manage are there also."

I picked up a piece of straw and wrapped it around my finger. "Why is this owner so interested in Ren?"

His eyes twinkled as he glanced at the tiger briefly and then asked, "Do you know the story of the great Prince Dhiren?"

I shook my head. "No."

"Your tiger's name, *Dhiren*, in my language means 'strong one.'" He tilted his head and gazed at me thoughtfully. "A rather famous prince carried the same name, and he had quite an interesting history."

I grinned. "You are evading my question and rather successfully too. But I love a good story. Can you remember it?"

His eyes fixed on something far off in the distance, and he smiled. "I think I can." His voice changed. Losing its crisp cadence, Mr. Kadam's words took on a rounded, musical tone and he began, "Long ago, there was a powerful king of India who had two sons. One he named Dhiren. The two brothers received the best education and military training.

"Their mother taught them to love the land and all the people who lived there. She often took the boys to play with underprivileged children because she wished for them to learn what their people needed. This contact also taught them to feel humility and to be grateful for the advantages they had. Their father, the king, taught them how to rule the kingdom. Dhiren, in particular, grew up to be a brave and fearless military leader as well as a sensible administrator.

"His brother was also very brave, strong, and clever. He loved Dhiren, but, at times, he felt the piercing stab of jealousy in his heart, for despite being successful in all of his training, he knew that Dhiren was destined to be the next king. It was only natural for him to feel this way.

"Dhiren had a knack for impressing people easily with his acumen,

intelligence, and personality. A rare combination of charm and modesty embodied in the prince made him an outstanding politician. A person of contradictions, he was a great warrior as well as a renowned poet. The people loved the royal family and looked forward to many peaceful and happy years under Dhiren's reign."

I nodded, fascinated by the story, and asked, "What happened to the brothers? Did they battle each other for the throne?"

Shifting on the stool slightly, he continued, "King Rajaram, Dhiren's father, arranged a marriage between Dhiren and the daughter of a ruler from a neighboring kingdom. The two kingdoms had lived in peace for many centuries but in recent years small skirmishes had broken out on the borders with increasing frequency. Dhiren was pleased with the alliance not only because the girl, whose name was Yesubai, was very beautiful, but also because he was wise enough to know that the union would bring peace to his land. They were formally engaged while Dhiren was away inspecting the troops in another part of the kingdom. During that absence, his brother began to spend time with Yesubai, and soon they fell in love with each other."

The tiger snorted loudly and thumped his tail against the wooden floor of his cage a few times.

I glanced over at him, concerned, but he seemed fine. "Shh, Ren," I admonished. "Let him tell the story."

He put his head on his paws and watched us.

Mr. Kadam continued. "He betrayed Dhiren so he could have the woman he loved. He bartered with a prodigious and evil man who captured Dhiren on his journey home. As a political prisoner, Dhiren was dragged along behind a camel and paraded through the enemy's town where the people threw stones, sticks, muck, and camel dung at him. He was tortured, his eyes were plucked out of their sockets, the hair was shaved off his head, and eventually his body was torn apart into pieces and thrown into the river."

I gasped. "How horrible!"

Mesmerized by the story, I was bursting with questions, but I held back, wanting him to finish. Mr. Kadam focused his gaze on my face and continued gravely, "When his people learned what had happened, a great sorrow spread across the land. Some say that Dhiren's people went down to the river and pulled out the torn pieces of his body to give him a proper funeral. Others say that his body was never found.

"Hearing of their beloved son's death, the king and his wife, heavy with misery, lapsed into a deep despair. Soon, both of them departed from this life. Dhiren's brother ran away in shame. Yesubai took her own life. The Mujulaain Empire was thrown into dark shadows of morass and disarray. With the authoritative voice of the royal family gone, the military took over the kingdom. Eventually, the evil man who had killed Dhiren captured the throne but only after fifty years of terrible war and bloodshed."

As he finished his story, there was a tangible silence. Ren's tail rustled in his cage, which snapped me out of my reverie.

"Wow," I responded. "So, did he *love* her?"

"Of whom are you speaking?"

"Did Dhiren love Yesubai?"

He blinked. "I . . . don't know. Many marriages were arranged in those days, and love often wasn't a consideration then."

"That's a very sad sequence of events. I feel sorry for everyone, except for the bad guy, of course. A great story, though a bit bloody. An Indian tragedy. It reminds me of Shakespeare. He would have written a great play based on that tale. So, Ren is named after that Indian prince?"

Mr. Kadam raised his eyebrow and smiled. "It would appear so."

I looked over at the tiger and grinned. "See, Ren, you're a hero! You're one of the good guys!" Ren pricked his ears forward and blinked his eyes, watching me. "Thanks for sharing that story with me. I will definitely be writing about that in my journal."

I tried to pull him back to my original question, "But, it still doesn't explain why your employer is interested in tigers."

He cleared his throat while looking at me obliquely, stalling for a moment. For someone so eloquent, he fumbled awkwardly through his next words. He answered, "My employer has a special connection with this white tiger. You see, he feels he is to blame for the tiger's imprisonment—no, that is too harsh a word—for his capture. My employer allowed himself to be ensnared in a situation that led to the tiger being caged and sold. He has followed the tiger's whereabouts for the last few years, and now he's finally in a position to make amends."

"Huh. That's very interesting. It was *his* fault that Ren was captured in the first place? It's very kind of him to continue to be concerned about an animal's welfare like that. Please thank him for what he's doing for Ren."

He bowed his head toward me in acknowledgment, then, hesitating, fixed a somber gaze on me and queried, "Miss Kelsey, I hope it's not too forward of me to ask, but I need someone to accompany the tiger on his journey to India. I will not be able to tend to his daily needs or even travel with him for the entire journey. I have already asked Mr. Davis if he could accompany Dhiren, but he must stay here with the circus." He leaned forward on the stool and gestured slightly with his hands. "I would like to offer *you* that job. Would you be interested?"

I stared at his hands for a moment, thinking that a man such as he should have long, tapered, manicured fingers, but his fingers were thick and calloused, like a man accustomed to hard labor.

Mr. Kadam leaned forward. "The tiger is already used to you, and I can pay a good wage. Mr. Davis suggested you as a likely candidate and he mentioned that your temporary employment here is almost at an end.

If you choose to accept the job, I can assure you that my employer would appreciate having someone who can care for the tiger better that I can. The entire trip should take about a week, but I have been instructed to pay for your entire summer. I know that doing this for me will take you away from your home and delay your search for a new position elsewhere, so you will be duly compensated."

"What exactly would I have to do? Wouldn't I need a passport and other paperwork done?" I asked.

He inclined his head toward me. "I can, of course, arrange all the preliminaries for the trip. The three of us would fly to Mumbai, what you might still call Bombay. Upon arrival, I must stay in town on business, and you would then continue to accompany the tiger on the drive to the reserve. I will hire drivers and loaders to assist you on the journey. Your primary responsibility will be to care for Ren, feed him, and see to his comfort."

"And then . . . ?"

"The journey over land is about ten to twelve hours one way. After you arrive at the reserve, you would stay there for a few days to ensure he is acclimating well to his new environment and comparative freedoms. I would purchase a return plane ticket from Jaipur, so that you will be able to ride the Jaipur tour bus that goes from the reserve to the airport, then fly to Mumbai and home from there, making your return trip a little bit shorter."

"So it would be about a week altogether?" I asked.

He replied, "You can choose to either fly back home immediately or, if you like, you may stay on vacation in India for a few days and enjoy touring before you go home. Rest assured, I would provide for all of your travel as well as any other necessary accommodations along the way."

I blinked and stammered, "That's a very generous offer. Yes, my position here at the circus is almost at an end, and I would have to start looking for a new job very soon."

I bit my lip and started pacing, mumbling indecisively to myself as much as to him. "India's very far away. I've never been out of the country before, so the idea of it is both exciting and scary at the same time. Can I think about it and let you know? When do you need for me to give you an answer?"

"The sooner you say yes, the sooner I can make the necessary arrangements."

"Alright. Let me call my foster parents and talk with Mr. Davis to see what they think about all this, and then I'll let you know for sure."

Mr. Kadam nodded and mentioned that Mr. Maurizio knew how to contact him when I was ready to inform him of my decision. He also said that he would be around the circus for the rest of the afternoon finalizing paperwork.

With jumbled thoughts, I grabbed my things and walked back to the main building. *India? I've never been to a foreign country before. What if I can't communicate with anyone? What if something bad happens to Ren while he's under my care?*

Despite all the *what ifs* that were rolling around my brain, a part of me was seriously contemplating Mr. Kadam's offer. It was very tempting to spend a little more time with Ren, plus I'd always wanted to visit a foreign country. I could have a mini summer vacation and be paid too. Also, Mr. Kadam didn't strike me as one of those creepy men with bad intentions. In fact, he seemed trustworthy and grandfatherly.

I decided to ask Mr. Davis's opinion and found him teaching the dogs a new trick. He confirmed that Mr. Kadam had offered him the same job and that he'd been tempted to do it.

"I think it would be a great experience for you. You're terrific with animals, especially with Ren. If that's something you think you'd like to focus on in a future career, then you should consider it. The job would look good on a résumé."

Thanking him, I decided to call Sarah and Mike, who wanted to meet Mr. Kadam, check his credentials, and find out what kinds of safety measures he planned to use. They suggested throwing an impromptu birthday party for me at the circus so they could celebrate with me and meet Mr. Kadam at the same time.

After taking some time to think about the pros and cons, I felt my excitement for the trip melt away my nerves. *I really would like to go to India and see Ren settled on the tiger reserve. It would be an opportunity to do something that I'd never get the chance to do again.*

I walked back to the tiger cage and found Mr. Kadam already there. He was alone and appeared to be talking quietly to the tiger again.

I guess he likes talking to tigers as much as I do.

Just inside the door, I paused. "Mr. Kadam? My foster parents would like to meet you and wanted me to invite you to my birthday celebration tonight. They are bringing cake and ice cream after the evening performance. Can you come?"

His face lit up with a radiant, delighted smile. "Wonderful! I would love to come to your party!"

"Don't get too excited. They're likely to bring soy ice cream and gluten-free, sugar-free cupcakes." I laughed.

After speaking to him, I called my family to finalize the plans.

Sarah, Mike, and the kids came early to watch the show and were thoroughly impressed with Ren's performance. They loved meeting everyone. Mr. Kadam was polite and charming and told them that it would be impossible to accomplish his task without my help.

"I assure you that we will be in constant communication and Kelsey can call you at any time," he said.

Mr. Davis later added his two cents. "Kelsey is more than capable of doing the job as Mr. Kadam defines it. It's essentially the same thing she's been doing at the circus for the past two weeks. Plus it will be a great experience. I wish I could go myself."

We all had a great time, and it was fun having a circus party. Sarah even brought normal cupcakes and my favorite brand of ice cream. It might not have been a typical eighteenth birthday, but I was content to just be with my foster family, my new friends at the circus, and my carton of Tillamook Mudslide.

After the festivities, Sarah and Mike pulled me aside and reminded me to touch base with them often during my trip to India. They could see on my face that I was determined to go, and they immediately felt as comfortable with Mr. Kadam as I did. I hugged them excitedly and went to share the good news.

Mr. Kadam beamed a happy smile and said, "Now, Miss Kelsey, it will take me approximately one week to arrange the transportation. I will also need to obtain a copy of your birth certificate from your guardians and arrange traveling papers for both the tiger and yourself. My plan is to leave tomorrow morning and return as soon as I have the necessary documents."

Later, as he prepared to leave, Mr. Kadam walked over to shake my hand and held it for a minute, saying, "Thank you very much for your help. You have assuaged my fears and given hope to a disillusioned old man that has anticipated only calamity and disappointment." He squeezed my hand, patted it, and stepped quickly out the door.

With the day's excitement behind us, I went to visit Ren. "Here. I snuck in a cupcake. Probably not on your tiger diet, but you might as well celebrate too, huh?"

He gently took the cupcake from my outstretched hand, swallowed it in one gulp, and then started licking frosting off my fingers. I giggled and went to wash my hand.

"I wonder what Mr. Kadam was talking about. Calamity? Assuaged fears? He's a bit dramatic. Wouldn't you agree?"

I yawned and scratched him behind the ear, grinning as he leaned his head into my palm. "Well, I'm sleepy. I'm going to bed. We'll have a fun trip together, won't we?"

Stifling another yawn, I made sure he had enough water, then turned off the lights, shut the door, and headed to bed.

The next morning, I got up early to check on the tiger. I opened the doors and headed down to his cage, but found the door was open. He wasn't there!

"Ren? Where are you?"

I heard a noise behind me and turned around to find him lying on a pile of hay *outside* his cage.

"Ren! How on earth did you get out? Mr. Davis is going to kill me! I'm sure I locked your cage door last night!"

The tiger got up and shook himself, getting most of the hay off his fur, and walked lazily over to me. It was then I realized I was alone in a barn with an uncaged tiger. I was scared out of my mind, but it was too late to head back out of the barn. Mr. Davis taught me never to look away from big cats, so I stuck out my chin, put my hands on my hips, and sternly ordered him back to his cage. The odd thing was that he seemed to understand what I wanted him to do. He walked past me, rubbed his side against my leg, and . . . obeyed! He padded slowly over to the ramp, flicked his tail back and forth while watching me, and was up and through the door in two great leaps.

I hurried over to close the door and, when it finally shut, let out a long breath. After getting his water and food for the day, I set off in search of Mr. Davis to break the news.

Mr. Davis took it pretty well considering that a tiger was loose. He was surprised that I was more concerned for Ren's safety than my own.

He assured me that I'd done the right thing and was even impressed by how I'd handled it calmly. I told him that I would be more careful and make sure that the cage was always latched properly. Still, I was certain that I hadn't inadvertently left the cage unlocked.

The next week sped by in a blur. Mr. Kadam didn't reappear until the evening of Ren's last performance. He approached and asked if he could meet with me after dinner.

"Sure, I'll meet you at one of the tables over dessert," I replied.

The mood was one of celebration. When I saw Mr. Kadam enter the building, I gathered up my paper, pencil, and two dishes of ice cream and then sat down across from him.

He began by spreading out various forms and documents for me to sign.

"We will be driving the tiger in a truck from here to the Portland airport. From there we will board a cargo plane, which will fly us to New York City, pass over the Atlantic Ocean, and continue on to Mumbai. When we arrive in Mumbai, I will be leaving Ren in your capable hands for a few days while I tend to some business in the city.

"I have arranged for a truck to meet us at the Mumbai airport. You and I will supervise the workers who will be loading Ren from the airplane into the truck. A driver has been assigned to take both of you all the way to the reserve. Preparations have also been made for you to stay at the reserve for a few days. Then, you may return to Mumbai at your convenience in preparation for your trip home. I will be providing you traveling money, more than enough for any emergency."

I took notes in a frenzy, trying to copy down all of his instructions.

"Mr. Davis will help prepare Ren and will also load him onto the truck tomorrow morning. I suggest that you pack a bag for yourself that includes any personal items that you might wish to bring along. I will be

sleeping here tonight, so you may borrow my rental car and go home to gather your things, as long as you return here by early morning. Do you have any immediate questions?"

"Well, I have about a billion of them, but most of them can wait until tomorrow. I guess I'd better go home and get packed."

He smiled warmly and placed his car keys in my hand. "Thank you once again, Miss Kelsey. I look forward to our journey together. I will see you in the morning."

I smiled back and said goodnight. I went back to my tent to gather my things and visited briefly with Matt, Cathleen, Mr. Davis, and Mr. Maurizio. I had only spent a short amount of time at the circus, but I had already grown fond of them.

After wishing them luck and saying good-bye, I stopped by Ren's cage to say goodnight. He was sleeping already, so I left him alone and walked out to the parking lot.

There was only one car parked—a beautiful silver convertible. I looked at the key fob and read "Bentley GTC Convertible."

Holy cow. You have got to be kidding me. This car must be worth a fortune! Mr. Kadam trusts me to drive this?

I approached the car timidly and clicked the unlock button on the key chain. The car's headlights blinked at me. I opened the door, slid into the soft, buttery leather seats, and ran my hand over the elegant, pronounced stitching. The dashboard looked ultramodern, with handsome instrument controls and displays in a silvery metallic color. It was the most luxurious car I'd ever seen.

I started the engine and jumped as it roared to life. Even someone like me, with no real knowledge of cars, could tell that this car was fast. I sighed in pleasure as I realized that it also included heated massage seats. I arrived home in just a few short minutes, groaning in disappointment that I lived so close to the fairgrounds.

Mike insisted that a Bentley needed to be parked in the garage. He eagerly moved his old sedan out to the street and parked it next to the garbage cans. The poor reliable car was thrust out the door like an old house cat while the brand new kitten got a soft pillow on the bed.

Mike ended up spending several hours in the garage that night cooing over and petting the convertible. I, on the other hand, spent my evening figuring out what to bring to India. I did my laundry, packed a large bag, and spent some time hanging out with my foster family. The two kids, Rebecca and Sammy, wanted to hear all about my two weeks at the circus. We also talked about the exciting things I might see and do in India.

They were good people, a good family, and they cared about me. Saying good-bye was hard, even though it was only temporary. Technically, I was an adult, but I was still nervous about traveling so far alone. I hugged and kissed the two kids. Mike soberly shook my hand and gave me a half hug for a long minute. Then I turned to Sarah, who pulled me into a tight embrace. We were both teary-eyed afterward, but she assured me that they would always be just a phone call away.

That night, I quickly slipped into a deep sleep and dreamed of a handsome Indian prince who happened to have a pet tiger.

the plane

the next morning, I awoke with great energy and felt positive and enthusiastic about the trip. After showering and a quick breakfast, I grabbed my bag, hugged Sarah again because she was the only one awake, and ran out to the garage. Sliding into the Bentley, I found it as delicious as I remembered.

I pulled into the fairgrounds parking lot and stopped next to a medium-sized cargo truck. The vehicle had a thick windshield, very big wheels, and tiny doors that required climbing a step to reach them. It looked like a monster truck past its prime, but, instead of being put out to pasture, it had been recruited into the cargo business. Behind the cab was a flatbed with a boxy steel frame draped with gray canvas.

The ramp was down in the back: Mr. Davis was already loading Ren into the cage. Ren wore a thick collar around his neck, which was firmly attached to a long chain that Mr. Davis and Matt both gripped tightly. The tiger seemed very calm and unruffled despite the chaos going on around him. In fact, he watched me while waiting patiently for the men to prepare the truck. Finally, they were ready, and with a command from Mr. Davis, Ren quickly catapulted up into the crate.

Mr. Kadam took my bag and slung the strap over his shoulder. He asked, "Miss Kelsey, would you like to ride in the truck with the driver or would you like to accompany me in the convertible?"

I looked at the monster cargo truck and quickly made my decision, "With you. I'd never pick a monster flatbed over a sleek convertible."

He laughed in agreement before placing my bag in the trunk of the Bentley. Knowing it was time to go, I waved good-bye to Mr. Davis and Matt, climbed back into the convertible, and buckled my seatbelt. Before I knew it, we were cruising along I-5 behind the truck.

Talking was difficult over the wind, so I just leaned my head back against the soft, warm leather and watched the scenery go by. We were actually driving at a leisurely pace—fifty-five mph, about ten miles per hour under the speed limit. Curious onlookers slowed their cars to stare at our little convoy. The traffic became heavier near Wilsonville where we quickly caught up to the morning commuters who'd passed us earlier.

The airport was about twenty miles farther on Highway 205, a small highway that sat like a teacup handle on I-5. The truck in front of us turned onto Airport Drive and then pulled off on a side street and stopped behind some large hangars. Several cargo planes were lined up and being loaded. Mr. Kadam wove between people and equipment and came to a halt near a private plane. The name on the side read Flying Tiger Airlines, and it sported the image of a running tiger.

I turned to Mr. Kadam, nodded my head toward the plane, and said, "Flying Tiger, huh?"

He grinned. "It's a long story, Miss Kelsey, and I will tell you all about it on the plane." Pulling my bag out of the trunk, he handed the keys to a man standing by who promptly got into the gorgeous car and drove it off the tarmac.

We both watched as several burly men lifted the tiger's crate with a motorized pallet jack and expertly transferred him into the plane's large, custom cage.

Satisfied that the tiger was secure and comfortable, we climbed up the plane's portable staircase and stepped inside.

I was amazed at the opulence of the interior. The plane was decorated in black, white, and chrome, which made it look sleek and modern. The black leather seats were exceptionally cozy looking, a far cry from the cabin seats on commercial jets, *and* they fully reclined!

An attractive Indian flight attendant with long, dark hair gestured to a chair and introduced herself. "My name is Nilima. Please, go ahead and take your seat, Miss Kelsey." She had an accent similar to Mr. Kadam's.

I asked, "Are you from India too?"

Nilima nodded and smiled at me as she fluffed a pillow behind my head. Next, she brought me a blanket and a variety of magazines. Mr. Kadam sat in the roomy chair across from me. He waved away the attendant and strapped himself in, foregoing the pillow and blanket.

I had flown in a plane only a couple of times before on vacations with my family. During the actual flight, I was usually pretty relaxed, but the takeoffs and landings made me anxious and tense. The sound of the engines probably bothered me the most—the ominous roar as they came to life—and the pushed-back-in-your-chair feeling as the plane left the earth always made me queasy. The landings weren't fun either, but I was usually so excited to get off the plane and move around that I just wanted to be done with it.

This plane was definitely different. It was luxurious, wide open, and had plenty of legroom and comfy leather reclining chairs. It was so much nicer than flying coach. Comparing this to a regular plane was like comparing a soggy, stale French fry you find under a car seat with a giant baked potato with salt rubbed into the skin and topped with sour cream, crumbled bacon, butter, shredded cheese, and sprinkled with fresh-cracked black pepper. *Yep, this plane was loaded.*

All this luxury, coupled with the beautiful convertible car, made me wonder about Mr. Kadam's employer. He must be someone *very* rich and powerful in India. I tried to think of who it might be, but I couldn't even fathom a guess.

Maybe he's one of those Bollywood actors. I wonder how much money they make. No, that can't be it. Mr. Kadam has been working for him a long time, so he's probably a very old man now.

The plane had built up speed and taken off while I was pondering Mr. Kadam's mystery employer. I hadn't even noticed! Maybe it was because my chair was so soft that I just sank back into it when the plane ascended, or maybe it was because the pilot did an exceptional job. Perhaps it was a little of both. I looked out the window and watched the Columbia River grow smaller and smaller until we passed through the cloud cover and I couldn't see land anymore.

After about an hour and a half, I'd read a magazine cover to cover and finished the Sudoku puzzle as well as the crossword. I set down my magazine and looked at Mr. Kadam. I didn't want to pester him, but I had tons of questions.

I cleared my throat. He responded by smiling at me over his news magazine. Of course, the first thing that came out of my mouth was the question I cared the least about. "So, Mr. Kadam, tell me all about Flying Tiger Airlines."

He closed his magazine before setting it down on the table. "Hmm. Where to begin? My employer used to own, and I used to run, a cargo airline company called Flying Tiger Airlines Freight and Cargo or Flying Tiger Airlines for short. It was the largest major trans-Atlantic charter company in the 1940s and 1950s. We provided service to almost every continent in the world."

"Where did the name Flying Tiger come from?"

He shifted slightly in his seat. "You already know that my employer has a fondness for tigers, so it was that, coupled with the fact that a few of the original pilots had flown 'tiger' planes during WWII. You might remember that they were painted like tiger sharks to look fierce in battle.

"In the late '80s, my employer decided to sell the company. But he kept one plane, this one, for personal use."

"What is your employer's name? Will I get to meet him?"

His eyes twinkled. "Most assuredly. He will introduce himself when you land in India. I am certain he would like to converse with you." He shifted his gaze to the back of the plane for a moment and then back to me. Smiling with an encouraging expression, he added, "Are there any other questions?"

"So you're kind of like his vice president?"

The Indian gentleman laughed. "Suffice it to say, he is a very wealthy man who trusts me completely to handle all of his business dealings."

"Ah, so you're the Mr. Smithers to his Mr. Burns."

He quirked an eyebrow at me. "I'm afraid I don't understand your reference."

I blushed and waved a hand. "Never mind. They're characters on *The Simpsons*. You've probably never seen the show."

"I'm afraid I haven't. Sorry, Miss Kelsey."

Mr. Kadam seemed slightly uncomfortable or nervous when talking about his boss, but he enjoyed talking about planes, so I encouraged him to continue. I wiggled in my seat and shifted. Kicking off my shoes, I sat cross-legged in the chair and asked, "What kind of cargo did you transport?"

He visibly relaxed. "Over the years, the company transported quite a collection of interesting cargo. For example, we won the contract to convey Aquatic World's famous killer whale, as well as the torch from the Statue of Liberty. Most of the time, though, the cargo was quite mundane. We transported things such as canned goods, textiles, and packages, quite a variety of things, really."

"How on earth do you fit a whale into an airplane?"

"One flipper at a time, Miss Kelsey. One flipper at a time."

Mr. Kadam's face remained serious. I laughed hard. Wiping a tear from the corner of my eye, I asked, "So you ran the company?"

"Yes, I spent a lot of time developing Flying Tiger Airlines. I very much enjoy aviation." He gestured to the aircraft. "What we're riding in here is called an MD-11, a McDonnell Douglas. It's a long-range craft, which is necessary when traveling across the ocean. The body is spacious and comfortable, as you might have noticed. It has two engines mounted under the wings, and a third engine is located in the back at the base of the vertical stabilizer. Of course, the interior is built for comfort and relaxation, and we employ the pilot, ground crew, as well as other staff to ensure security."

"Hmm, sounds . . . sturdy."

He leaned forward a bit in his seat and spoke enthusiastically, "Though this plane is an older model, it still provides for a very swift journey." He began numbering its features on his fingers, "It includes a stretched fuselage, a large wingspan, a refined airfoil on the wing and tail plane, and brand new engines.

"The flight deck features the most modern conveniences—electronic instrument panels, dual flight management, GPS, central fault display—and it also has automatic landing capability for bad-weather conditions. Of course, we also kept our original company name and logo on the side, which you identified when we boarded."

He had become eagerly spirited during his technical ruminative. I'm sure it all meant *something*, but what exactly, I had no idea. The only thing I got out of it was that it was a pretty darn good plane and sounded like it had three engines.

He must have figured out that I had no clue what he was talking about because he looked at my perplexed face and chuckled. "Perhaps we should discuss something else, eh? What if I share some tiger myths from my homeland?"

I nodded enthusiastically, urging him to go on. I drew my legs to the side and tucked them into my chair. Then I pulled my blanket up to my chin and leaned back into my pillow.

Mr. Kadam's intonation changed as he went into storytelling mode. His English articulation dropped off, and his brisk accent became more pronounced, the words more melodic. I enjoyed listening to the cadence of his rhythmic voice.

"The tiger is considered the great protector of the jungle. Several Indian myths say the tiger has great powers. He will bravely combat great dragons but he will also help simple farmers. One of his many tasks is to tow rain clouds with his tail, ending drought for humble villagers."

"I'm very interested in mythology. Do the people of India still believe in these tiger myths?"

"Yes, especially in the rural areas. But, you will find believers in all parts of the country, even among those who consider themselves a part of today's modern world. Did you know that some say that a tiger's purrs will stop nightmares?"

"Mr. Davis said that tigers can't purr. He told me that big cats that growl and roar can't purr, but sometimes I swear Ren purrs."

"Ah, you are correct. Modern science says that a tiger cannot produce the sound identified as a purr. Several of the larger cats make a pulsating noise, but it isn't quite the same as the purr of a housecat. Still, there are some Indian myths that speak of a tiger purring. It's also said that a tiger's body has unique healing properties. This is one of the reasons why they are regularly hunted and killed and their bodies mutilated or sold for parts."

He leaned back in his chair, relaxing. "In Islam, it is believed that Allah will send a tiger to defend and protect those who follow him faithfully, but he will also send a tiger to punish those he considers traitors."

"Hmm, I think if I were Islamic I would run away from it, just to be on the safe side. I wouldn't know if it's coming to punish or to protect."

He laughed. "Yes, very wise of you. I confess, I have adopted somewhat of the same fascination that my employer has for tigers, and I have studied numerous texts regarding the mythology of Indian tigers, in particular."

He trailed off for a moment, lost in thought, and his eyes glazed over. His index finger rubbed at a spot on his open collar, and I noticed he was wearing a small, wedge-shaped pendant on a chain that was half-tucked inside his shirt.

As his focus turned back to me, he quickly dropped his hand to his lap and continued, "Tigers are also a symbol of power and immortality. They are said to vanquish evil through various means. They are called life givers, sentinels, guardians, and defenders."

I straightened my legs and angled my head back into the pillow. "Are there any damsel-in-distress type tiger myths?"

He considered, "Hmm, yes. In fact, one of my favorite stories is about a white tiger that sprouts wings and saves the princess who loves him from a cruel fate. Carrying her on his back, they relinquish their corporeal forms and become a single white streak journeying into the heavens, eventually joining the stars of the Milky Way. Together they spend eternity watching over and protecting the people of Earth."

I yawned sleepily. "That's really beautiful. I think that one's my favorite too." His soft, melodic voice had relaxed me. Despite my best efforts to stay awake and listen, I was falling asleep.

He continued steadily, "In Nagaland, they believe that tigers and men are related, that they are brothers. There is one myth that begins, 'Mother Earth was the mother of the tiger and also of man. Once the

two brothers were happy, loved each other, and lived in harmony. But a feud began over a woman, and Brother Tiger and Brother Man fought so wildly that Mother Earth could no longer tolerate their quarrel and had to send them both away.

"'Brother Tiger and Brother Man left the home of Mother Earth and emerged from a very deep, dark passage said to be a pangolin's den. Living together inside the earth, the two brothers still fought every day, until eventually they decided it would be better to live separately. Brother Tiger went south to hunt in the jungle, and Brother Man went north to farm in the valley. If they stayed away from each other, then both were content. But, if one encroached upon the other's territory, fighting began anew. Many lifetimes later, the legend still holds true. If the descendants of Brother Man leave the jungles in peace, Brother Tiger will also leave us in peace. Still, the tiger is our kin, and it is said that if you stare into a tiger's eyes long enough, you will be able to recognize a kindred spirit.'"

My eyelids were drooping against my wishes. I wanted to ask what a pangolin's den was, but my mouth wouldn't move and my eyelids felt so heavy. I made one last effort to stay awake by shifting up in my seat a little bit, forcing my eyes open.

Mr. Kadam looked at me thoughtfully. "A white tiger is a very special kind of tiger. It is immitigably drawn to a person, a woman, who has a powerful sense of self-conviction. This woman will possess great inner strength, will have the insight to discern good from evil, and will have the power to overcome many obstacles. She who is called to walk with tigers—"

I fell asleep.

When I awoke, the chair across from me was empty. I sat up and looked around, but I didn't see Mr. Kadam anywhere. Unbuckling my seatbelt, I headed off to find the restroom.

Opening a sliding door, I walked into a surprisingly large bathroom. This was not at all like the small boxy bathrooms in a regular plane. The lights were recessed in the walls and they softly illuminated the special features of the room. The bathroom was decorated in copper, cream, and rust colors, which were more to my liking than the modern austere look of the plane's cabin.

The first thing I noticed was the shower! I opened the glass door to peer inside. It had beautiful rust- and cream-colored tiles set in a lovely pattern. There were mounted pumps full of shampoo, conditioner, and soap. The copper showerhead was detachable, and a simple squeeze turned it on and off, similar to a kitchen sink sprayer. I figured this design would help to use less water, which wouldn't be in abundance on a plane. A thick cream-colored rug covered the beautiful tiled floor.

Off to the side two vertical cubbies, set into the wall, were filled with soft, alabaster towels held in place with a copper bar. Another wide compartment sported a silky soft, fully lined robe that felt like cashmere. It hung from a copper bar. Just under that, another smaller alcove held a pair of cashmere slippers.

A deep sink, shaped like a skinny rectangle, had a pump on each side of the copper faucet. One was full of creamy soap and the other with a sweet lavender lotion.

I finished up in the bathroom, almost hating to leave it, and headed back to my comfy seat. Mr. Kadam had returned, and Nilima, the flight attendant, brought us a delightful-smelling lunch. She had arranged a table between us and set it for two. What made our table unique were the slight depressions designed to hold all of our dinnerware. Our plates sat in short, round grooves specially made to fit them. There was a little thumbnail on one side so that the attendant could lift them in and out easily. Our glasses rested in slightly deeper grooves, and there was even

a small vase full of short-stemmed yellow roses set in its own hollowed out space.

Nilima lifted the warmer covers off our plates to set free the delicious aroma of fish.

She said, "Today's lunch is crusted hazelnut halibut with buttered asparagus, garlic mashed potatoes, and a lemon tart for dessert. What would you like to drink?"

"Water with some lemon," I responded.

"I'll have the same," said Mr. Kadam.

We enjoyed our lunch together. Mr. Kadam asked me many questions about Oregon. He seemed to have an unquenchable thirst for learning new facts and asked me about everything from sports, which I know almost nothing about, to politics, which I know absolutely nothing about, to the flora and fauna of the state, which I know a lot about.

We talked about what high school was like, my experiences at the circus, and about my hometown: the salmon runs, the Christmas tree farms, the farmer's markets, and the blackberry bushes that were so common, people actually considered them weeds. He was easy to talk with, a great listener, and I felt comfortable with him. The thought crossed my mind that he would make a wonderful grandpa. I never got a chance to know either of mine. They died before I was born, as did my other grandma.

After we finished our lunch, Nilima returned to clear our plates, and I watched how she removed the table. As she pushed a little button, a small, quiet motor sounded. The legless rectangular table tilted up until it was flush to the wall and then slid into the paneling. As the table settled, she let go of the button and instructed us to buckle up because we'd be arriving in New York soon.

The descent was as smooth as the takeoff, so I made it a point after we landed to meet the pilot and tell him that he was exceptionally

gifted. Mr. Kadam had to translate for me because the pilot didn't speak English other than basic flight words. As we refueled for the journey to Mumbai, I visited with Ren.

After making sure he had enough to eat and drink, I sat down on the floor next to his cage. He sauntered over and collapsed down on the floor right next to me. His back was stretched along the length of the cage with his striped fur sticking out through the bars tickling my legs, and his face next to my hand.

I laughed at him, leaned over to stroke the fur on his back, and recounted some of the tiger myths that Mr. Kadam had shared with me. His tail kept flicking back and forth, in and out of the cage bars.

Time flew by quickly, and the plane was soon ready to take off again. Mr. Kadam was already strapping in. I quickly patted Ren's back and returned to my chair as well.

We took off, and Mr. Kadam warned me that this would be a long flight, about sixteen hours, and also that we would lose a day on the calendar. After we reached the proper cruising altitude, he suggested that I might like to watch a movie. Nilima handed me a list of all the movies they had available, and I picked the longest one on the list: *Gone with the Wind.*

She moved to the bar area, pushed a button on the wall, and a large white screen quietly slid out from the side of the bar. My chair turned around easily to face the screen and it even reclined with a foot-rest, so I made myself comfortable and passed the time with Scarlett and Rhett.

When I finally got to, "After all, tomorrow *is* another day," I stood up and stretched. I looked out the window to see it was black outside. It only felt like 5:00 p.m., but I guessed it was probably 9:00 p.m. in our current time zone.

Nilima bustled over and returned the movie screen to its resting place, and then she began setting up the table again.

"Thank you so much for these delicious meals and thank you for the wonderful service," I told her appreciatively.

"Yes, thank you, Nilima." Mr. Kadam winked at her, and she inclined her head slightly and left.

I shared an amiable dinner once again with Mr. Kadam. This time we talked about his country. He told me all kinds of interesting things and described fascinating places in India. I wondered if I would have time to see or do any of those things. He spoke of ancient Indian warlords, mighty fortresses, Asian invaders, and horrible battles. When he talked, I felt like I was there seeing and experiencing it for myself.

For dinner, Nilima served us stuffed chicken Marsala with grilled zucchini and a salad. I felt a little better eating more vegetables, but then she brought out chocolate lava cakes for dessert.

I sighed. "Why does everything so bad for you always taste so dreamy?"

Mr. Kadam laughed. "Would you feel better if we shared one?"

"Sure," I grinned, cut my lava cake in half, and scooped his portion onto a clean plate Nilima had brought out.

I licked the hot fudge sauce off my spoon. *Life, well . . . at least today anyway, was good. Very good. I could learn to live like this.*

For the next couple of hours we talked about our favorite books. He liked the classics like I did, and we had a great time revisiting memorable characters: Hamlet, Captain Ahab, Dr. Frankenstein, Robinson Crusoe, Jean Valjean, Iago, Hester Prynne, and Mr. Darcy. He also introduced me to a couple of Indian characters that sounded interesting like Arjuna, Shakuntala, and Gengi from Japanese literature.

Stifling a yawn, I went back to check on Ren again. I reached through the bars to pet his head and scratched him behind the ear.

Mr. Kadam watched me and said, "Miss Kelsey, are you not afraid of this tiger? You don't believe that he will hurt you?"

"I think he *can* hurt me, but I know he *won't* hurt me. It's hard to explain, but I feel safe with him, almost like he's more of a friend than a wild animal."

Mr. Kadam didn't seem alarmed, only curious. He spoke softly to Nilima for a moment.

She approached me, inquiring, "Are you ready to sleep for a while, Miss?"

I nodded, and she showed me where my bag had been stowed. Picking it up, I set off for the bathroom. I wasn't gone for very long, but she'd been very busy.

There was now a curtain dividing the area, and she'd set up a pullout couch that became a snug bed with satin sheets and thick, soft pillows. A recessed light with a button was set into the wall right next to the bed. The plane was darkened, and she told me that Mr. Kadam would be on the other side of the curtain if I needed anything.

I quickly checked the tiger's cage. He watched me drowsily through slit eyes with his head on his paws.

"Goodnight, Ren. See you in India tomorrow."

Too tired to read, I climbed under the soft, silky covers, turned off the light, and let the drone of the engines lull me to sleep.

The smell of bacon woke me up. I peeked around the corner and saw Mr. Kadam seated, reading the paper with a glass of apple juice on the table in front of him. He looked at me over the paper. I saw that his hair was slightly wet and that he was already dressed for the day.

"Best attend your morning ablutions, Miss Kelsey. We will be arriving soon."

I grabbed my bag and headed for the luxurious bathroom. I took a quick shower, soaping through my hair with the fragrant rose-scented shampoo. When finished, I wrapped my hair with a thick towel and

pulled on the cashmere robe. I sighed deeply and let myself bask in the soft fabric for a moment while I decided what to wear. I chose a red blouse with jeans and brushed my hair back into a ponytail, tying it with a red ribbon. Hurrying back to Mr. Kadam, I sunk down in the leather chair while Nilima brought me a hot plate of bacon, eggs, and toast.

I ate the eggs, nibbled on the toast, and drank some orange juice, but decided to save my bacon for Ren. As Nilima stowed the bed and the table from breakfast, I wandered over to the cage with my treat. Trying to tempt him, I held out a piece through the cage. He came over, very gently bit the edge, pulled it out of my hand, and then swallowed it down in one gulp.

I laughed. "Gee, Ren, you've got to chew it. Wait, do tigers chew? Well, at least eat it slower. You probably never get a treat like this." I held out the other three pieces one by one. He gulped them all down and then shot his tongue through the bars to lick my fingers.

I laughed quietly and went to the bar to wash my hands. Then I cleaned up all my belongings and stowed my bag in the overhead compartment. I'd just finished when Mr. Kadam approached. He pointed out the window and said, "Miss Kelsey, welcome to India."

mumbai

I gazed out the window as we flew over the ocean and into the city. I guess I hadn't really expected a modern city, and I was amazed by the hundreds of tall, white, uniform buildings spread out before me. As we circled the large, half-moon-shaped airport, the plane's wheels drop in preparation for our landing.

The sleek aircraft bounced twice and settled down to hug the runway. I whirled in my chair to see how Ren was doing. He was standing up expectantly but, other than that, he seemed alright. I felt a rush of exuberant energy as we taxied across the runway and came to a stop on the outskirts of the airstrip.

"Miss Kelsey, are you ready to disembark?" Mr. Kadam asked.

"Yes. Just let me grab my bag."

I slung it over my shoulder, stepped out of the plane, and skipped quickly down the steps to the ground. Deeply inhaling the wet, sultry air, I was surprised to see a gray sky. It was warm and humid but tolerable.

"Mr. Kadam, isn't it usually hot and sunny in India?"

"This is the monsoon season. It's almost never cold here, but we do get rain in July and August and, on occasion, a cyclone."

I handed him my bag and strolled over to watch some workers attempt to load Ren. This was a much different operation than it had

been in the United States. Two men attached long chains to his collar while another man affixed a ramp onto the back of a truck. They got the tiger out of the plane okay, but then the man closest to Ren pulled on the chain too tightly. The tiger reacted fast. He roared angrily and half-heartedly swiped his paw at the man.

I knew it was dangerous for me to approach, but something pushed me forward. Thinking only of Ren's comfort, I walked over to the frightened man, took the chain from him, and motioned for him to back away. He seemed grateful to be relieved of the responsibility. I spoke soothing words to the tiger, patted his back, and encouraged him to walk with me to the truck.

He responded immediately and walked beside me as docile as a lamb, dragging the heavy chains behind him on the ground. At the ramp, he stopped and rubbed his body against my leg. Then he jumped up into the truck, quickly turned around to face me, and licked my arm.

I stroked his shoulder affectionately and murmured to him softly, calming him while my hand moved gently over his collar and detached the heavy chains. Ren looked over at the men who were still standing frozen in the same place with stunned expressions, snuffed out his displeasure at them, and growled softly. While I was giving him water, he rubbed his head along my arm and kept his eyes trained on the workers as if he was my guard dog. The men began talking very fast to one another in Hindi.

I closed the cage and locked it while Mr. Kadam walked over to the men and spoke quietly. He did not seem surprised by what had happened. Whatever he said had reassured the men because they began moving around the area again, making sure to give the tiger a wide berth. They swiftly rounded up equipment and moved the plane into a nearby hangar.

After Ren was secured in the truck, Mr. Kadam introduced me to the driver, who seemed nice but very young, even younger than me.

Showing me where my bag was stowed, Mr. Kadam pointed out another bag that he had purchased for me. It was a large black backpack with several compartments. He unzipped a few to show me some of the items he had placed inside. The back zipper pocket contained a sizeable amount of Indian currency. Another pocket held travel documents for Ren and me. Snooping, I opened another zipper and found a compass and a lighter. The main part of the bag was stocked with energy bars, maps, and bottles of water.

"Um, Mr. Kadam, why did you include a compass and a lighter in the bag, not to mention some of these other items?"

He smiled and shrugged, zipping up the compartments and placing the bag on the front seat. "You never know what things might come in handy along the journey. I just wanted to make sure that you are fully prepared, Miss Kelsey. You also have a Hindi/English dictionary. I have given the driver instructions, but he doesn't speak much English. I must take my leave of you now." He smiled and squeezed my shoulder.

I suddenly felt vulnerable. Continuing the journey without Mr. Kadam left me anxious. It felt like the first day of high school all over again—if high school was one of the biggest countries in the world and everyone spoke a different language. *Well, I'm on my own now. Time to act like a grown-up.* I tried to reassure myself, but fear of the unknown was chomping away inside me and chewing a hole through my stomach.

I asked pleadingly, "Are you sure you can't change your plans and travel with us?"

"Alas, I cannot attend you on your journey." He smiled reassuringly. "Don't fret, Miss Kelsey. You are more than able to care for the tiger, and I have meticulously arranged every detail of your trip. Nothing will go wrong."

I gave him a weak smile, and he took my hand, enfolded it in both

of his for a moment, and said, "Trust me, Miss Kelsey. All will be well with you." With a twinkle in his eye and a wink, he left.

I looked at Ren. "Well, kid, I guess it's just you and me."

Impatient to start and finish the trip, the driver called back through the cab of the truck, "We go?"

"Yes, we go," I responded with a sigh.

When I climbed in, the driver stepped on the gas and never, *ever* took his foot off the pedal. He raced out of the airport and in less than two minutes was winding quickly through traffic at frightening speeds. I clutched my door and the dash in front of me. He wasn't the only insane driver though. Everybody on the road seemed to think 130 kilometers per hour, or, according to my travel guide, 80 mph in a crowded city, with hundreds of pedestrians, was not quite fast enough. Hoards of people dressed in bright, vibrant colors moved in every direction past my window.

Vehicles of every description filled the streets—buses, compact cars, and some kind of tiny, boxy car with no doors and three wheels sped by. The boxy ones must have been the local taxis because there were hundreds of them. There were also countless motorcycles, bicycles, and pedestrians. I even saw animals pulling carts full of people and produce.

I guessed that we were supposed to be driving on the left side of the road, but there seemed to be no distinct pattern or even white stripes to mark the lanes. There were very few lights, signs, or signals. Cars just turned left or right whenever there was an opening and sometimes even when there wasn't. Once, a car drove right at us on a collision course and then turned away at the last possible second. The driver kept laughing at me every time I gasped in fear.

I gradually became desensitized enough to start to take in the sights that were speeding by, and, with interest, I saw countless multicolored markets and vendors selling an eclectic variety of wares. Merchants sold

string-puppets, jewelry, rugs, souvenirs, spices, nuts, and all manner of fruits and vegetables out of small buildings or street carts.

Everyone seemed to be selling something. Billboards showed advertisements for tarot cards, palm reading, exotic tattooing, piercing, and henna body-painting shops. The entire city was a hurried, wild, vibrant, and touristy panorama with people of all descriptions and classes. It looked like there was not one square inch of the city that was unoccupied.

After a harrowing drive through the busy city, we finally made it to the highway. At last, I was able to relax my grip a bit—not because the driver was moving slower, in fact, he had sped up—but because the traffic had dropped off considerably. I tried to follow where we were going on a map, but the lack of road signs made it difficult. One thing I did notice though was that the driver missed an important turn onto another freeway that would lead us up to the tiger reserve.

"That way; go left!" I pointed.

He shrugged and waved his hand at me dismissing my suggestions. I grabbed my dictionary and tried frantically to look up the word *left* or *wrong way*. I finally found the words *kharābī rāha*, which meant *wrong road* or *incorrect path*. He gestured to the road ahead with his index finger and said, "Fast drive road." I gave up and let him do what he wanted. It was *his* country after all. I figured he knew more about the roads than I did.

After driving for about three hours, we stopped at a tiny town called Ramkola. Calling it a town would be overemphasizing the size of the place because it boasted only a market, a gas station, and five houses. It bordered a jungle, which was where I finally found a sign.

YAWAL WILDLIFE SANCTUARY
PAKSIZAALAA YAWAL
4 KM

The driver got out of the truck and started to fill the tank with gas. He pointed to the market across the street and said, "Eat. Good food."

I grabbed the backpack and went to the rear of the truck to check on Ren. He was sprawled out on the floor of the cage. He opened his eyes and yawned when I approached but stayed in his inert position.

I walked to the market and opened the peeling squeaky door. A little bell rang announcing my presence.

An Indian woman dressed in a traditional sari emerged from a back room and smiled at me. "*Namaste.* You like food? Eat something?"

"Oh! You speak English? Yes, I would love some lunch."

"You sit there. I make."

Even though it was lunch for me, it was probably dinner for them because the sun was low in the sky. She motioned me over to a little table with two chairs that was set next to the window, and then she disappeared. The store was a small, rectangular room that housed various grocery products, souvenirs depicting the wildlife sanctuary nearby, and practical things such as matches and tools.

Indian music played softly in the background. I recognized the sounds of a sitar and heard the tinkling of bells but couldn't identify the other instruments. I glanced through the door where the woman had passed and heard the clatter of pans in her kitchen. It looked like the store was the front of a larger building and the family lived in a house attached to the back.

In surprisingly fast time, the woman returned, balancing four bowls of food. A young girl followed in behind her bringing even more bowls of food. It smelled exotic and spicy. She said, "Please to eat and enjoy."

The woman disappeared into the back, while the young girl started to straighten shelves in the store as I ate. They hadn't brought me any silverware, so I spooned up some of each dish with my fingers, remembering to use my right hand following Indian tradition. *Lucky Mr. Kadam had mentioned that on the plane.*

I recognized the basmati rice, *naan* bread, and *tandoori* chicken, but the other three dishes I'd never seen before. I looked over at the girl, inclined my head, and asked, "Do you speak English?"

She nodded and approached me. Motioning with her fingers, she said, "Little bit English."

I pointed to a triangular pastry filled with spicy vegetables. "What is this called?"

"This *samosa.*"

"What about this one and this?"

She indicated one and then the other: "*Rasmalai* and *baigan bhartha.*" She smiled shyly and bustled off to work on the shelves again.

As far as I could tell, the *rasmalai* were balls of goat cheese dipped in a sweet cream sauce, and the *baigan bhartha* was an eggplant dish with peas, onions, and tomatoes. It was all very good, but a bit too much. When I was finished, the woman brought me a milkshake made with mangoes, yogurt, and goat's milk.

I thanked her, sipped my milkshake, and let my eyes drift to the scene outside. There wasn't much of a view: just the gas station and two men standing by the truck talking. One was a very handsome young man dressed in white. He faced the store and spoke with another man who had his back toward me. The second man was older and looked like Mr. Kadam. They seemed to be having an argument. The longer I watched them, the stronger my conviction became that it *was* Mr. Kadam, but he was arguing hotly with the younger man, and I couldn't picture Mr. Kadam ever becoming angry like that.

Huh, that's weird, I thought and tried to catch a few words through the open window. The older man said *nahi mahodaya* often, and the younger man kept saying *avashyak* or something like that. I thumbed

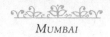

through my Hindi dictionary and found *nahi mahodaya* easily. It meant *no way* or *no, sir*. *Avashyak* was harder because I had to figure out how to spell it, but I eventually found it. That word meant *necessary* or *essential*, something that *must be* or *has to happen*.

I walked to the window to get a better look. Just then, the young man in white looked up and saw me staring at them from the window. He immediately ceased his conversation and stepped out of my line of vision, around the side of the truck. Embarrassed to be caught, but irresistibly curious, I made my way through the maze of shelves to the door. I needed to know if the older man really was Mr. Kadam or not.

Grabbing the loose door handle, I twisted it and pushed it open. It squeaked on rusty hinges. I walked across the dirt road and over to the truck, but still, I didn't see anyone. Circling the truck, I stopped at the back and saw that Ren was alert and watching me from his cage. But the two men and the driver had disappeared. I peeked into the cab. No one was there.

Confused, but remembering I hadn't paid my bill, I crossed the street and went back into the store. The young girl had already cleared away my dishes. I pulled some bills from the backpack and asked, "How much?"

"One hundred rupees."

Mr. Kadam had told me to figure out money by dividing the total by forty. I quickly calculated she was asking for two dollars and fifty cents. I smiled to myself as I thought about my math-loving dad and his quick division drills when I was little. I gave her two hundred rupees instead, and she beamed happily.

Thanking her, I told her the food was delicious. I picked up my backpack, opened the squeaky door, and stepped outside.

The truck was gone.

7

the jungle

How could the truck be gone?

I ran out to the gas pump and looked both ways down the dirt road. Nothing. No dust cloud. No people. Nothing.

Maybe the driver forgot about me? Maybe he needed to get something and is coming back? Maybe the truck was stolen and the driver is still around here somewhere? I knew none of these were likely scenarios, but they made me feel hopeful—if only for a minute.

I walked around to the other side of the gas pump and found my black bag lying in the dust. I rushed over to it, picked it up, and checked inside. Everything seemed to be in order.

Suddenly, I heard a noise behind me and whirled around to see Ren sitting by the side of the road. His tail twitched back and forth while he watched me. He looked like a giant abandoned puppy wagging his tail hoping someone would claim him and take him home.

I muttered, "Oh, no! This is just great! 'Nothing will go wrong,' Mr. Kadam said. Ha! The driver must have stolen the truck and let you out. What am I going to do now?"

Tired, scared, and alone, my mom's words of advice came flooding back: "bad things sometimes happen to good people"; "the key to happiness is to try to make the best of, and be thankful for, the hand we're dealt," and her all-time favorite, "when life gives you lemons, make lemon meringue pie." Mom had tried and practically given up having kids—and then I came along. She always said that you never know what's going to be right around the corner.

So, I focused on the positives. First, I still had all my clothes. Second, I had my traveling papers and a bag full of money. That was the good news. The bad news, of course, was that my ride was gone and a tiger was on the loose! I decided the first order of business was to secure Ren. I went back to the store and bought some jerky snacks and a long length of rope.

With my newly acquired fluorescent-yellow rope, I walked outside and tried to get my tiger to cooperate. He'd moved off several paces and was now heading for the jungle. I ran after him.

The sensible thing would have been to go back to the store, borrow a phone, and call Mr. Kadam. He could send some people, professional-type people, to catch him. But I was far from thinking sensibly at this point. I was afraid for Ren. I had absolutely no fear of him for myself, but what if others panicked and used weapons to subdue him? I also worried that even if he escaped, he couldn't survive in the jungle. He wasn't used to hunting on his own. I knew it was utterly foolish, but I chose to follow my tiger.

I begged, "Ren, come back! We need to get some help! This isn't your reserve. Come on, I'll give you a nice treat!" I waved the jerky snack in the air, but he kept moving. I was weighed down with Mr. Kadam's backpack and my bag. I could keep up with him but the extra weight was too much for me to overtake him.

He wasn't moving very quickly, but he always managed to keep several paces ahead of me. Suddenly, he loped off and darted into the jungle. My backpack bobbed heavily up and down as I chased after him. After about fifteen minutes of pursuit, sweat was trickling down my face, my clothes were stuck to my body, and my feet were dragging like heavy stones.

As my pace slowed, I entreated again, "Ren, *please* come back. We need to go back to the town. It's going to be dark soon."

He ignored me and began winding through the trees. He'd stop to turn and look at me every so often.

Whenever I thought I'd finally catch him, he'd accelerate and leap ahead a few feet, causing me to chase after him again. I felt like he was playing a game with me. He was always just out of reach. After following Ren for another fifteen minutes and still not catching him, I decided to take a break from my pursuit. I knew I'd traveled far from town, and the light was dimming. I was totally lost.

Ren must have realized that I wasn't following him anymore because he finally slowed, turned around, and ambled guiltily back over to me. I glared at him.

"Figures. The minute I stop, you come back. I hope you're happy with yourself."

Tying the rope to his collar, I turned around in a circle and carefully studied each direction to try to get my bearings.

We had traveled deep into the jungle, looped in and out of trees, and twisted and turned numerous times. I realized, with great despair, that I'd lost all sense of direction. It was twilight, and the dark canopy of trees overhead blocked out the little sun we had left. A choking fear settled inside me, and I felt a wave of icy, nibbling cold slither slowly down my spine. It shot wintry streams down my arms and legs and poked out my skin in spiky goose bumps.

I twisted the rope around my hands nervously and grumbled at the tiger. "Thanks a lot, Mister! Where am I? What am I doing? I'm who-knows-where in India, in the jungle, at night, with a tiger on a rope!"

Ren sat down quietly beside me.

My fear overwhelmed me for a minute, and I felt as if the jungle was closing in. All the distinctive sounds rushed to clatter and wrestle with my frightened mind, attacking my common sense. I imagined creatures stalking me, their glassy, hostile eyes watching and waiting to pounce. I looked up and saw angry monsoon clouds surging, quickly swallowing up the early evening sky. A stiff, numbing wind whipped through the trees and swirled around my rigid body.

After a couple of moments, Ren got up and moved ahead, gently pulling my tense body along with him. I reluctantly followed. I laughed nervously and madly for a moment because I was letting a tiger lead me through a jungle, but I figured there was no point in *me* trying to lead the way. I had no idea where we were. Ren continued walking on some unseen path, pulling me along behind him. I lost track of time, but my best guess was that we walked through the jungle for an hour, maybe two. It was very dark now, and I was scared and thirsty.

Remembering that Mr. Kadam had packed water in the bag, I unzipped the pocket and felt around for a bottle. My hand brushed against something cold and metallic. A flashlight! I turned it on and felt a bit of relief at having a beam of light to cut through the darkness.

In the shadows, the dense jungle appeared menacing, not that it wasn't equally as terrifying during the day, but my measly flashlight beam didn't penetrate very far, which made the situation even worse. When the thin moon appeared and dispersed its beams intermittently through the thick tree cover overhead, Ren's coat gleamed where the silvery light touched it.

I peered ahead, catching shiny glimpses of his body as he moved through the undulating, flickering patches of light. When the moon hid behind the clouds, Ren disappeared completely on the trail ahead. I turned my flashlight to him and saw prickly undergrowth scratching his silvery white fur. He responded to the thorns by roughly shoving the plants aside with his body, almost as if he were making a path for me.

After walking for a long time, he finally pulled me near a copse of bamboo that was growing near a large teak tree. He stuck his nose up in the air, smelling for who-knows-what and then wandered over to a grassy area and lay down.

"Well, I guess that means this is where we sleep for the night." I shrugged out of my backpack while grousing, "Great. No, really. It's a lovely choice. I'd give it four stars if it included a mint."

First, I untied the rope from Ren's collar, figuring that my trying to keep him from running away was moot at this point, and then crouched down and unzipped my bag. Pulling out a long-sleeved shirt, I tied it around my waist and got out two water bottles and three energy bars. I unwrapped two of the energy bars and held them out to Ren.

He carefully took one out of my hand and gulped it down.

"Should a tiger eat energy bars? You probably need something with more protein, and the only thing around here with protein is me, but don't even think about it. I taste *terrible*."

He quirked his head at me as if seriously considering it, then quickly swallowed the second energy bar. I opened the third and slowly nibbled on it. Unzipping another pocket, I found the lighter and decided to make a fire. Searching by flashlight, I was surprised to find a good amount of wood close by.

Remembering my Girl Scout days, I built a small fire. The wind blew it out the first two times, but the third time it took, making homey little crackling sounds.

Satisfied with my work and setting aside larger logs to add later, I moved the backpacks closer to the fire. Finding a plastic bag in the pack, I picked up a large curved piece of bark, shoved small chunks of wood on the ends, and lined the inside with the bag. I poured a bottle of water into it and carried my makeshift bowl over to Ren. He lapped it all up and kept licking the bag, so I poured in another bottle for him, which he also drank greedily.

I walked back to the fire and was startled by an ominous howl nearby. Ren jumped up at once and rushed off in a whirl, disappearing into the darkness. I heard a deep growling and then an incensed and vicious snarl. I stared gravely into the darkness between the trees where Ren had disappeared, but he soon returned unharmed and began rubbing his side on the teak tree. Satisfied with that tree, he moved on to another one, and another one, until he'd rubbed up against every tree that surrounded us.

"Gee, Ren. That must be some itch." Leaving him to his scratching, I plumped the softer bag with my clothes in it to use for a pillow and slipped my long-sleeved shirt over my head. I pulled out my quilt, hating to get it dirty but desperately needing the warmth and comfort it offered, and spread it out over my legs. Then I eased onto my side, tucked my hand under my cheek, stared at the fire, and felt fat tears slide down my face.

I started listening to the eerie sounds around me. I heard clicks, whistles, pops, and cracks everywhere, and started to imagine creepy crawly things burrowing in my hair and down into my socks. I shivered and tucked my quilt around me snugly, so that it covered every part of my body, and settled to the ground again wrapped up mummy-style.

That was much better, but then I imagined animals creeping up behind me. Just as I began to roll onto my back, Ren lay down right next to me, snuggled his back against mine, and began to purr.

Grateful, I wiped the tears off my cheeks and was able to tune out the night sounds by listening to Ren's purr, which later changed into deep, rhythmic breathing. I inched a little closer to his back, surprised to find that I could sleep in the jungle after all.

A bright ray of sun hit my closed eyelids, and I slowly cracked them open. Not remembering where I was for a minute, I stretched my arms

up over my head, only to cringe in pain as my back rubbed against the hard ground. I also felt a heavy weight on my leg. I looked down to see Ren, eyes squeezed tightly shut in sleep, with his head and one paw draped over my leg.

I whispered, "Ren. Wake up. My leg is asleep."

He didn't budge.

I sat up and shoved his body lightly. "Come on, Ren. Move!"

He growled softly but stayed put.

"Ren! I mean it! *Mooove!*" I shook my leg and shoved him harder.

He finally blinked open his eyes, yawned a giant, toothy tiger yawn, and then rolled off my leg and onto his side.

Standing up, I shook out my quilt, folded it, and tucked it into the bag. I also stamped out the ashes from the fire to make sure nothing was still burning.

"Just so you know, I *hate* camping," I complained loudly. "I'm not so much appreciating that there's no bathroom out here. 'Nature calls' while walking in the jungle is on my list of least favorite things. You tigers, and men in general, have it so much easier than us girls."

I gathered up the empty bottles and wrappers and put them into the pack. The last thing I picked up was the yellow rope.

The tiger just sat there observing me. I decided to give up the pretense that I was the one leading him and stowed the rope away in the pack.

"Okay, Ren. I'm ready. Where are we heading off to today?"

Turning, he stalked off into the jungle again. He weaved his way around trees and undergrowth, over rocks and across small streams. He didn't seem to be in a hurry, and he even stopped for a break every once in a while, as if knowing I needed one. Now that the sun was out, the jungle was becoming quite steamy, so I took off my long-sleeved shirt and tied it back around my waist.

The jungle was very green and had a peppery kind of fragrance, much different than the forests of Oregon. The large deciduous trees were sparse and had graceful, willowy branches. The leaves were an olive-green color rather than the deep greens of the evergreens I was used to. The bark was dark gray and rough to the touch; where cracks formed, the bark peeled away and sloughed off in thin, flaky layers.

Flying squirrels leapt from tree to tree, and we often startled grazing deer. Smelling a tiger, they quickly bounced away on springy legs. I watched Ren to see his reaction, but he ignored them. I noticed another common tree that was more moderate in size and also had a papery bark, but where the bark split on this one, a sticky, gummy resin dripped down the trunk. I leaned against one to pick a pebble out of my shoe and spent the next hour trying to peel the goo off my fingers.

I'd just gotten it off when we weaved through a particularly dense undergrowth of tall grasses and bamboo and sent a flock of colorful birds into flight. I was so startled that I backed into another sap tree and got sticky sap all over my upper arm.

Ren stopped at a small stream. I pulled out a bottle of water and drank it all down. It was nice to have less weight in the backpack, but I was concerned about where I would get water from after my supply ran out. I supposed I could drink from the same stream as Ren, but I would put that off for as long as possible, knowing that my body wouldn't handle it as well as his.

I sat down on a rock and searched for another energy bar. I ate half of one and gave Ren the other half, plus another one. I knew I could survive on that many calories, but I was pretty sure Ren couldn't. He'd have to hunt soon.

Opening a pocket of Mr. Kadam's backpack, I found a compass. I pushed it into the pocket of my jeans. There was still money, the traveling papers, more water bottles, a first aid kit, bug spray, a

candle, and a pocketknife, but no cell phone, and my personal cell phone was missing.

Strange. Could Mr. Kadam have known that I would end up in the jungle? I thought about the man who looked like Mr. Kadam standing by the truck right before it was stolen and wondered aloud, "Did he *want* me to get lost out here?"

Ren wandered over to me and sat down.

"No," I said, looking into the animal's blue eyes. "That doesn't make any sense either. What reason could he possibly have for flying me all the way to India just to get me lost in the jungle? He couldn't have known you would lead me in here or that I'd follow you. He's not the type to deceive anyway."

Ren gaze shifted to the ground as if *he* felt guilty.

"I guess Mr. Kadam is just a really well-prepared Boy Scout."

After a brief rest, Ren got up again, walked off a few paces, and turned around to wait for me. Complaining, I dragged myself off the rock, and followed along behind him. Pulling out the bug spray, I gave my limbs a good spritz and squirted some on Ren for good measure. I laughed when he wrinkled his nose and a big tiger sneeze shook his body.

"So, Ren, where are we going? You act like you have a destination in mind. Personally, I'd like to get back to civilization. So if you could find us a town, I'd be most appreciative."

He continued to lead me on a trail that only he could see for the rest of the morning and into the early afternoon.

Checking my compass often, I figured out that we were traveling eastward. I was trying to calculate how many miles we'd walked when Ren burrowed between some bushes. I followed him to find a small clearing on the other side.

With great relief, I saw a small hut that sat right in the middle of the clearing. Its curved roof was covered with rows of canes tied close together that draped over the top of the structure like a blanket. Stringy fibers, tied into intricate knots, lashed large bamboo poles together to make walls, and the cracks were thatched with dried grasses and clay.

The hut was surrounded by a barrier of loose stones piled on top of each other to create a short wall about two feet high. The stones were covered in thick, verdant moss. In front of the hut, thin panels of stone were affixed to the wall and were painted with an indecipherable assortment of symbols and shapes. The shelter's doorway was so tiny that an average-sized person would have to bend over to enter. There was a line of clothing flapping in the wind, and a small flourishing garden was planted on the side of the home.

We approached the rock wall, and just as I was stepping over, Ren leapt over the barrier next to me. "Ren! You scared the stuffing out of me! Make a noise first or something, would you?"

We approached the small hut, and I steeled myself to knock on the tiny door, but then I hesitated, looking at Ren. "We need to do something about you first." I took the yellow rope out of my backpack and walked over to a tree on the side of the yard. He followed me haltingly. I beckoned him closer. When he finally came close enough, I slipped the rope through his collar and tied the other end to a tree. He didn't look happy.

"I'm sorry, Ren, but we can't have you loose. It would scare the family. I promise I'll be back as soon as I can."

I began walking over to the small house, but then froze in my tracks when I heard a quiet male voice behind me say, "Is this *really* necessary?"

Turning around slowly, I saw a handsome young man standing directly behind me. He looked young, in his early twenties. He was taller than me by a head and had a strong, well-developed trim body that was clothed in loose white cotton garments. His long-sleeved shirt

was untucked and carelessly buttoned, revealing a smooth, well-built golden-bronze chest. His lightweight pants were rolled at the ankles, emphasizing his bare feet. Glossy black hair swept away from his face and curled slightly at the nape of his neck.

His eyes were what riveted me the most. They were my tiger's eyes, the same deep cobalt blue.

Reaching out a hand, he spoke. "Hello, Kelsey. It's me, Ren."

an explanation

The man approached me carefully with his hands splayed out in front of him and repeated, "Kelsey, it's me, Ren."

He didn't appear fearsome, but my body tightened in apprehension nonetheless. Confused, I held my hand out in front of me in a futile attempt to halt his progress. "What? What did you say?"

He came closer, put his hand on his muscled chest, and spoke slowly. "Kelsey, don't run. I'm Ren. The tiger."

He turned over his hand to show me Ren's collar and the yellow rope coiled about his fingers. I looked behind him, and sure enough, the white cat was missing. I took a few steps back to put more distance between us. He saw my movement and immediately froze. The back of my knees hit the stone barrier. I stopped and blinked my eyes several times, not comprehending what he was telling me.

"Where's Ren? I don't understand. Did you *do* something to him?"

"No. I *am* him."

He began to approach me again, while I shook my head.

"No. You *can't* be."

I tried to take another step and almost fell backward over the wall. He reached me in the blink of an eye and caught my waist, steadying me.

"Are you alright?" he asked politely.

"No!" He was still holding my hand. I stared at it, imagining the tiger's paws.

"Kelsey?" I looked up into his startling blue eyes. "I am your tiger."

I whispered, "*No*. No! It's not possible. How could that *be*?"

His quiet voice was soothing. "Please, come inside the house. The owner is not at home right now. You can sit down and relax, and I will attempt to explain everything."

I was too stunned to argue, so I allowed him to guide me toward the hut. He clutched my fingers in his as if afraid that I would run back into the jungle. I didn't usually follow strange men around, but something about him made me feel safe. I knew with certainty that he wouldn't harm me. It was the same strong feeling I experienced with the tiger. He bowed his head to get through the door and stepped into the small hut, pulling me along behind him.

It was a one-room shelter with a small bed in one corner, a tiny window on the side wall, and a table with two chairs in another corner. A curtain was pulled back to reveal a small bathtub. The kitchen was just a sink with a water pump, a short counter, and some shelves with various canned food products and spices. Above our heads, the ceiling was strung with a hanging assortment of dried herbs and plants that filled the room with a sweet fragrance.

The man gestured that I should sit on the bed, then leaned against a wall and waited quietly for me to settle myself.

Recovering from the initial shock, I snapped out of my daze and assessed my situation. He was Ren, the tiger. We stared at each other for a moment, and I *knew* he was telling the truth. The eyes were the same.

I felt the fear in my body drain away while a new emotion rushed forward to fill the void: anger. Despite all the time I'd spent with him, he'd chosen not to share this secret with me. He'd led me through the jungle, apparently on purpose, and allowed me to believe that I was lost, in a foreign country, in the wilderness, alone.

I knew he'd never hurt me. He was a . . . friend, and I trusted him. But why hadn't he trusted *me*? He'd had plenty of opportunities to share this peculiar reality, but he hadn't.

Looking at him with suspicion, I irritably asked, "So, what *are* you? Are you a man who became a tiger or a tiger that turned into a man? Or are you like a werewolf? If you bit me, would I turn into a tiger too?"

He tilted his head with a puzzled expression on his face, but he didn't answer right away. He watched me with the same intense blue eyes as the tiger. It was disconcerting.

"Uh, *Ren*? I think I'd feel more comfortable if you moved a little farther away from me while we discuss this."

He sighed, walked calmly over to the corner, sat on a chair, and then leaned against the wall, balancing himself on the chair's two back legs. "Kelsey, I will answer all of your questions. Just be patient with me and give me time to explain."

"Alright. Explain."

As he gathered his thoughts, I scrutinized his appearance. I couldn't believe that this was my tiger—that the tiger I cared about was this man.

He didn't look very tiger-like, other than his eyes. He had full lips, a square jaw, and an aristocratic nose. He didn't look like any other man I'd ever seen. I couldn't place it, but there was something else, something cultured about him. He exuded confidence, strength, and nobility.

Even barefoot with nondescript clothing, he looked like someone powerful. And even if he weren't good looking—and he was *extremely* good looking—I still would have been drawn to him. Maybe that was the tiger part of him. Tigers always seem regal to me. They capture my attention. He was as beautiful a man as he was a tiger.

I trusted my tiger, but could I trust the man? I warily eyed him from the edge of the rickety bed, my doubts obvious on my face. He was patient, allowing me to boldly study him, and even seemed amused, as if he could read my thoughts.

I finally broke the silence, "Well, *Ren*? I'm listening."

He pinched the bridge of his nose between his thumb and forefinger, then slid his hand up through his silky black hair, mussing it in a distractingly attractive way.

Dropping his hand to his lap, he looked at me thoughtfully from under thick eyelashes. "Ah, Kelsey. Where do I begin? There's so much I need to tell you, but I don't even know where to start."

His voice was quiet, refined, and genial, and I soon found myself mesmerized by it. He spoke English very well with just a slight accent. He had a honeyed voice—the kind that sends a girl off into wistful daydreams. I shook off my reaction and caught him scrutinizing me with his cobalt blue eyes.

There was a tangible connection between us. I didn't know if it was simple attraction or something else. His presence was unsettling. I tried looking away from him to calm myself, but I ended up twisting my hands and staring at my feet, which were tapping the bamboo floor with jittery energy. When I looked back at his face, the side of his mouth was turned up in a smirk and one of his eyebrows was raised.

I cleared my throat weakly. "I'm sorry. What did you say?"

"Is it that hard to sit still and listen?"

"No. You just make me nervous, that's all."

"You weren't nervous around me before."

"Well, you don't look the same as you did before. You can't expect me to behave the same way around you now."

"Kelsey, try to relax. I would never harm you."

"Okay. I'll sit on my hands. Is that better?"

He laughed.

Whoa. Even his laugh is magnetic.

"Keeping still is something I had to learn while being a tiger. A tiger must lie motionless for long periods of time. It requires patience and for this explanation you will need some."

He stretched his powerful shoulders and then reached up to pull on the string of an apron hanging from a hook. He twisted it around his finger unconsciously and said, "I have to do this rather quickly. I only have a few minutes of each day when I can take human form—to be exact, only twenty-four minutes of each twenty-four-hour day—so, because I'll change into a tiger again soon, I want to make the most of my time with you. Will you let me have these few minutes?"

I took a deep breath. "Yes. I want to hear your explanation. Please go on."

"Do you remember the story of Prince Dhiren that Mr. Kadam told you at the circus?"

"Yes, I remember. Wait. Are you saying—?"

"That story was mostly accurate. I am the Dhiren that he spoke of. I was the prince of the Mujulaain Empire. It's true that Kishan, my brother, and my fiancée betrayed me, but the end of the story is a fabrication. I was *not* killed, as many people have been led to believe. My brother and I were cursed and changed into tigers. Mr. Kadam has faithfully kept our secret all of these centuries. Please don't blame him for bringing you here. It was my fault. You see, I . . . *need* you, Kelsey."

My mouth went suddenly dry, and I found myself leaning forward, barely sitting on the edge of the bed. I almost fell off. I quickly cleared my throat and readjusted my position on the bed, hoping he hadn't noticed.

"Uh, what do you mean you need me?"

"Mr. Kadam and I believe you are the only one who can break the curse. Somehow, you've already freed me from captivity."

"But, I didn't free you. Mr. Kadam's the one who purchased your freedom."

"No. Mr. Kadam was unable to purchase my freedom until you came along. When I was captured, I was no longer able to change into my human form or gain my freedom until something, or should I say *someone*, special came along. That someone special was you."

He curled the apron string around his finger, and I watched as he unwound it and began again. My eyes drifted back up to his face. It was turned toward the window. He appeared calm and serene, but I recognized underpinnings of sadness hidden from view. The sun shone through the window, and the curtain blew slightly in the breeze, causing sunlight and shadow to dance across his face.

I stammered, "Okay, what do you need me for? What do I have to do?"

He turned back to me and continued, "We came to this hut for a reason. The man who lives here is a shaman, a monk, and he's the one who can explain your role in all this. He wouldn't share anything further until we found you and brought you here. Even I don't know why you are the chosen one. The shaman also insists that he must speak with us alone. That's why Mr. Kadam was left behind."

He leaned forward. "Will you stay here with me until he returns and at least hear what he has to say? If you decide afterward that you wish to leave and return home, Mr. Kadam will arrange it."

I stared at the floor. "Dhiren—"

"Please call me Ren."

I blushed and made eye contact. "Okay, Ren. Your explanation is overwhelming. I don't know what to say."

Varying emotions flitted across his handsome face.

Who was I to reject a handsome man—I mean tiger. I sighed. "Alright. I'll wait and meet your monk, but I'm hot, sweaty, hungry, tired, in need of a good bath, and frankly, I'm not sure I even trust you. I don't think I could take another night of sleeping in the jungle."

He sighed in relief as he smiled at me. It was like the sun bursting through a raincloud. His smile filled me with golden bright happy rays. I wanted to close my eyes and bask in the warm glow.

"Thank you," he said. "I'm sorry that this part of the journey was uncomfortable for you. Mr. Kadam and I had a disagreement about luring you into the jungle. He thought we should just tell you the truth, but I wasn't sure if you would come. I thought that if you spent a little more time with me, you would learn to trust me, and I could reveal who I was in my own way. That was what we were arguing about when you saw us by the truck."

"So that was you! You should have told me the truth. Mr. Kadam was right. We could have avoided the entire jungle hike and driven here."

He sighed. "No. We would've had to cross through the jungle anyway. There's no way to drive into the sanctuary this deeply by car. The man who lives here prefers it that way."

I crossed my arms and muttered, "Well, you still should have told me."

He twisted the apron tie. "You know, sleeping outdoors isn't all bad. You get to stare up at the stars and cool breezes ruffle your fur after a hot day. The grass smells sweet and," he made eye contact with me, "so does your hair."

I blushed and grumbled, "Well, I'm glad *someone* enjoyed it."

He smiled smugly and said, "I *did*."

I had a quick flash of him as a man snuggled up next to me in the forest, imagined him resting his head on my lap while I stroked his hair, and decided to focus on the matter at hand.

"Well, listen, Ren, you're changing the subject. I don't appreciate the way you manipulated me into being here. Mr. Kadam should've told me at the circus."

He shook his head. "We didn't think you'd believe his story. He made up the trip to the tiger reserve to get you to India. We figured once you were here, I could change into a man and clarify everything."

I admitted, "You're probably right. If you had changed to a man there, I don't think I would have come."

"Why *did* you come?"

"I wanted to spend more time with . . . you. You know, the tiger. I would have missed him. I mean you." I blushed.

He grinned lopsidedly. "I would have missed you too."

I wrung the hem of my shirt between my hands.

Misreading my thoughts, he said, "Kelsey, I'm truly sorry for the deception. If there'd been any other way—"

I looked up. He hung his head in a way that reminded me of the tiger. The frustration and awkwardness I felt about him dissipated. My instincts told me that I should believe him and help him. The strong, emotional connection that drew me to the tiger tugged at my heart even more powerfully with the man. I felt pity for him and his situation.

Softly, I asked, "When will you change back into a tiger?"

"Soon."

"Does it hurt?"

"Not as much as it used to."

"Do you understand me when you are a tiger? Can I still speak to you?"

"Yes, I'll still be able to hear and understand you."

I took a deep breath. "Okay. I'll stay here with you until the shaman comes back. I still have a lot of questions for you though."

"I know. I'll try to answer them as best I can, but you'll have to save them for tomorrow when I'll be able to speak with you again. We can stay here for the night. The shaman should be back around dusk."

"Ren?"

"Yes?"

"The jungle frightens me, and this situation frightens me."

He let go of the apron string and looked into my eyes. "I know."

"Ren?"

"Yes?"

"Don't . . . leave me, okay?"

His face softened into a tender expression, and his mouth turned up in a sincere smile. *"Asambhava.* I won't."

I felt myself responding to his smile with one of my own when a shadow fell across his face. He clenched his fists and tightened his jaw. I saw a tremor pass through his body, and the chair fell forward as he collapsed to the ground on his hands and knees. I stood to reach out to him and was amazed to see his body morph back into the tiger form I knew so well. Ren the tiger shook himself, then approached my outstretched hand and rubbed his head against it.

9

a friend

I sat on the edge of the bed thinking about what Ren had shared with me. Looking at the tiger now, I thought, or perhaps hoped, that I might've actually imagined everything. *Maybe the jungle is causing me to hallucinate. Is all this real? Is there really a person underneath that fur?*

Ren stretched out on the floor and rested his head on his paws. He looked at me with his gorgeous blue eyes for a long moment, and at once, I knew that this was real.

Ren had said that the shaman wouldn't be back until dusk, which was still several hours away. The bed looked inviting. A nap would be nice, but I was filthy. I decided that a bath was the first order of business and went to investigate the tub, which needed to be filled old-school style—with a bucket.

I began the arduous task of pumping water into the bucket, dumping it into the tub, and starting all over again. It looked easier on television than it was in real life. I thought my arms were going to fall off after only three buckets, but I pushed through the ache knowing how good a bath would feel. My tired arms convinced me that a half bath was more than adequate.

I kicked off my tennis shoes and started to unbutton my shirt. I got about halfway down when I suddenly realized that I had an audience. I held my shirt together and turned around to find Ren watching me.

"Some gentleman you are. You're being as quiet as a mouse on purpose, aren't you? Well, I don't think so, Mister. You'd better sit outside until I'm done with my bath." I waved my arm in the air. "Go . . . keep watch or something."

I opened the door, and Ren slowly dragged his body outside. Quickly undressing, I stepped into the tepid water and began scrubbing away at my dirty skin with the shaman's homemade herbal soap. After soaping through my hair with the lemony sage bar and rinsing off, I lay back in the tub for a moment, thinking. *What have I gotten myself into? Why didn't Mr. Kadam tell me any of this? What are they expecting me to do? How long am I going to be stuck in the jungle in India?*

Questions whirled around in my mind, displacing any coherent thoughts. They tossed around, spinning into a cyclone of confusion. Giving up trying to make sense of it all, I climbed out, dried off, got dressed, and opened the door for Ren who had been lying with his back pressed against it.

"Okay, you can come back in now. I'm decent."

Ren wandered back in while I sat on the bed cross-legged and began combing the tangles out of my hair.

"Well, Ren, I'll sure be giving Mr. Kadam a piece of my mind after we get out of here. You're not off the hook yet either, by the way. I have a thousand questions so you'd better prepare yourself."

I braided my hair and tied a green ribbon around the tail. Tucking my arms behind my head, I lay down on the pillow and stared up at the bamboo ceiling. Ren put his head on the mattress near mine and looked at me with an apologetic tiger expression.

I laughed and patted his head, awkwardly at first, but he leaned in, and I overcame my shyness quickly.

"It's fine, Ren. I'm not mad, really. I just wish you two had trusted me more."

He licked my hand and lay down on the floor to rest while I turned on my side to watch him.

I must have drifted off to sleep because when I opened my eyes it was dark in the hut except for a lantern glowing softly in the kitchen. Seated at the table was an old man.

I sat up and rubbed the sleep out of my eyes, surprised that I'd slept so long. The shaman was busy picking the leaves off several plants spread out on the table. As I stood up, he beckoned me closer.

"Hallo, little lady. You sleep long time. Very tired. Very, very tired."

I walked to the table, followed by Ren. He yawned, arched his back, and stretched himself one leg at a time, then sat at my feet.

"You hungry? Eat. Good food, hmmm?" The shaman smacked his lips, "Very tast-ey." The little man stood up and scooped some aromatic, herby vegetable stew out of a bubbling pot on the wood stove. He added a piece of warm flatbread along the edge of the bowl, and came back to the table. Pushing the bowl toward me, he nodded satisfactorily and then sat down and continued stripping the leaves from the plants.

The stew smelled heavenly, especially after eating energy bars for a day and a half.

The shaman clucked his tongue. "What your name?"

"Kelsey," I mumbled, as I chewed.

"Kahl-see. You have good name. Strong."

"Thank you for the food. It's delicious!"

He grunted in response and waved his hand dismissively.

I asked him, "What's your name?"

"My name, uh, too immense. You call me Phet."

Phet was a small, brown, wrinkly man with a crown of wiry gray hair circling the back of his head. His shiny bald patch reflected the light of the lamp. He was dressed in a roughly woven, grayish-green wrap and sandals. The material was wound around his scrawny arms, and his bare legs stuck out below it from his knobby knees down. A sarong was thrown over his shoulder haphazardly, and I was surprised the flimsy garment even stayed on his thin frame.

"Phet, I'm sorry to barge into your home. Ren led me here. You see—"

"Ah, Ren, your tiger. Yes, Phet be acquainted with why you here. Anik say you and Ren coming, so, I go Suki Lake today for . . . preparation."

I scooped up some more stew as he brought me a cup of water. "Do you mean Mr. Kadam? Did he tell you we were coming?"

"Yes, yes. Kadam tell Phet." The shaman pushed aside his plants, making room on the corner of the table, and then picked up a little cage that held an exquisite tiny red bird. "Birds at Suki Lake are many, but this bird largely extraordinary."

He leaned over, clicked his tongue at the bird, and waggled his finger next to the cage. He started humming and spoke to it gaily in his native language. Turning his attention back to me, he said, "Phet linger all day capture. Bird sing be-u-ti-full song."

"Will he sing for us?"

"Who is knowing? Sometime bird *never* sing, whole lifetime. Only sing if special parson. Kahl-see is special parson?"

He laughed uproariously as if he'd made a fantastic joke. "Phet, what is the bird called?"

"He is Durga's hatchling."

I finished my stew and set the bowl to the side. "Who is Durga?"

He grinned. "Ah. Durga be-u-ti-full goddess, and Phet," gesturing to himself, "is willing low servant. Bird sing for Durga *and* one special woman." He picked up his leaves again and continued working.

"So you are a priest of Durga?"

"Priest edify other citizen. Phet exist alone. Serve alone."

"Do you like to be alone?"

"Alone is reasoned mind, hear things, see things. Added people is too many voice."

He had a good point. I don't mind being alone either. The only problem is that if you're always alone, you get lonely.

"Hmm. Your bird is very beautiful."

He nodded and worked quietly.

"May I help you with the leaves?" I asked.

He grinned widely, revealing a broken smile with several missing teeth. His eyes almost disappeared amid the deep brown wrinkles. "You want assist me? Yes, Kahl-see. Watch Phet. Follow. You try."

He held the stem of a plant and pulled downward with his fingers until he had stripped off all of the leaves. He handed me a branch with tiny leaves, which looked like a type of rosemary. I plucked off the fragrant green leaves and piled them up on the table. We worked companionably together for a while.

Apparently, he harvested the herbs for a living. He showed me the different plants that he'd collected and told me their names and what they were used for. He also had the dry collection, which was hanging from the ceiling, and he spent some time describing each one of those. Some of the names I was familiar with, but others I'd never heard of before.

The more interesting ones were arjuna, the ground bark of a tree used medicinally to aid circulation and digestion; turmeric, good for circulation as well but also provided aid to the respiratory system; and neem leaves, which did something to aid digestion. I didn't ask any detailed questions about that one.

Others were gotu kola, which smelled bitter and sweet. Phet said it gave long life and lots of energy. Brahmi leaves helped a person think better, and shatavari was a root good for female problems.

He stood on a little step stool, took down some of the dry plants, and replaced them with fresh ones, and then he got out a mortar and pestle. After teaching me how to crumble the herbs and grind them, he turned the job over to me so I could grind several different types.

Phet opened one jar that had hard, golden drops of resin inside. I smelled it and exclaimed, "I remember that smell from the jungle. It's that gummy stuff that drips from the tree, right?"

"Very good Kahl-see. It name olibanum. Come from Boswellia tree, but maybe you call frankincense."

"Frankincense? I always wondered what that was."

He took out a small chip and handed it to me. "Here, Kahl-see, taste."

"You want me to *eat* that? I thought it was a perfume."

"Take, Kahl-see, you try." He put a piece on his own tongue, and I followed suit.

It smelled spicy, and its flavor was sweet and warm. Its texture was like sticky gum. Phet chewed with his few teeth and grinned at me.

"Good taste, Kahl-see? Now breathe long."

"Breathe long?"

He demonstrated by sucking in a deep breath, so I did too. He thumped me on the back, which would have caused me to spit out the gum if it wasn't permanently stuck to my teeth. "You see? Good you stum-ack, good breathe, no worries." He handed me the small jar of frankincense. "You keep, good value meant for you."

I thanked him, and after placing the jar in my backpack, returned to the mortar and pestle.

He asked, "Kahl-see, you travel lengthy way, yes?"

"Oh, yes, a very long way." I told him about meeting Ren in Oregon and then journeying to India with Mr. Kadam. I also described the loss of the truck, our trek through the jungle, and ended with finding his home.

Phet nodded and listened intently. "And your tiger is not as always tiger. Am I correct in this saying?"

I looked at Ren. "Yes, you are correct."

"You wish to help the tiger?"

"Yes, I wish to help him. I'm angry that he tricked me, but I understand why he did." I ducked my head and shrugged my shoulders. "I just want him to be free." At that moment, the little red bird burst into a lovely song and continued to sing for the next few minutes.

Phet closed his eyes, listened with an expression of pure rapture, and hummed quietly along. When the bird stopped singing, he opened his eyes and looked at me with a delighted smile.

"Kahl-see! You very special! Joyful is my feeling! Phet to perceive song of Durga!" He got up gleefully and began bustling away all the plants and jars. "At the present, you must respite. Important sunrise is tomorrow. Phet must pray in the dark hours, and you necessity sleep. Embark on your traverse tomorrow. It's hard as difficult. In first light, Phet assist you in the company of tiger. Durga's secret to unveil. Now go drowse."

"I just had a long nap, and I'm not sleepy yet. Can't I stay with you and ask more questions?"

"No. Phet go pray. Necessary express thanks Durga in favor of unforeseen blessing. You essential slumber. Phet assemble brew expand Kahl-see sleep."

He placed several leaves into a cup and poured steaming water over them. After a minute, he handed the cup to me and indicated that I should drink it. It smelled almost like a peppermint tea with a hint of spice similar to cloves. I sipped it and enjoyed the flavor. He shooed me

over to the bed and sent Ren along with me. After dimming the lamp, he pulled a satchel over his shoulder, smiled at me, and left, closing the door quietly behind him.

I lay down on the bed thinking that sleep would be impossible, but before long I drifted off into a slumber that was comfortable, gray, and dreamless.

Early the next morning, Phet awakened me by clapping his hands together loudly. "Hallo, Kahl-see and fateful Ren. Phet is pray even as you sleeping. As a consequence, Durga makes miracle. You must awaken! Compose yourself and we converse."

"Okay, Phet, I'll hurry." I pulled the curtain around me and got dressed.

In the kitchen Phet was cooking eggs and had already set a large plate of them on the floor for Ren. I washed my hands with the herbal soap and sat down at the table, pulled out my braid, and finger combed through my wavy hair.

Ren stopped eating, gulped his mouthful of eggs, and watched me intently as I worked with my hair.

"Ren, stop staring at me! Eat your eggs. You're probably starving."

I tied my hair up in a ponytail, and he finally turned back to his food. Phet brought me a plate also. It had a small salad with a strange variety of mixed greens from his garden and a nice omelet. Then he sat down to talk to us.

"Kahl-see, I am favorable man at present. Durga exclaim to me. She *will* help you. Numerous year in the past, Anik Kadam pursue remedy to comfort Ren. I advise him Durga be partial to tiger, but no one can alleviate him. He ask me what can he do? That nighttime, Phet dream two tigers, one pale like moon, one black, night resembling. Durga speak softly my ear. She say only special girl can break curse. Phet know

girl is Durga's favored one. She struggle for tiger. I tell Anik: watch for goddess' special girl. I give indication—girl alone, brown hair, dark eyes. She be devoted to tiger, and her utterance are powerful like goddess melody. Help tiger be free again. I tell Anik: discover Durga's favored one and bring to me."

He placed his brown, crooked hands on the table and leaned closer to me. "Kahl-see, Phet perceive *you* are exceptional favored one of Durga."

"Phet, what are you talking about?"

"You are strong, beautiful warrior like Durga."

"Me? A strong, beautiful warrior? I think you have the wrong girl."

Ren growled low in his throat and Phet clicked his tongue. "No. Durga's hatchling sing for *you*. You are *accurate* girl! Do not thrust away destiny, toss away like weed! Is precious, costly flower. Patience. Wait time and bloom open."

"Okay, Phet, I'll try my best. What do I have to do? How can I break the curse?"

"Durga help you at Kanheri Cave. Use key to open chamber."

"What key?" I asked.

"Key is distinguished Mujulaain Empire Seal. Tiger knows. Find underground place in cave. Seal is key. Durga lead you to answer. Free tiger."

I started to tremble uncontrollably. This was too much to take in at once. Secret cave messages, being the favored one of an Indian goddess, and going off on a jungle adventure with a tiger? It was too much for me to accept. I felt overwhelmed. My mind kept screaming, *Not possible! Not possible! How did I get trapped in this bizarre situation? Oh, yeah. I volunteered.*

Phet watched me curiously. He put his hand on top of mine. It was warm and papery and calmed me instantly.

"Kahl-see, have faith in self. You strong woman. Tiger protect you."

I looked down at Ren, who was sitting on the bamboo floor watching me with a concerned expression. "Yes, I know he'll watch out for me. I do want to help him break the curse. It's just a little . . . daunting."

Phet squeezed my hand, and Ren lifted a paw to my knee. I swallowed my fear and pushed it to the back of my mind. "So, Phet, where do we go next? The cave?"

"Tiger know where to go. Follow tiger. Get Seal. Must hasten departure. Before you go, Kahl-see, Phet bestow you goddess mark and prayer."

Phet picked up a small arrangement of leaves we had picked through the night before. He waved them in the air around my head and down each of my arms while chanting softly. Then he pulled out a small leaf and touched it to my eyes, nose, mouth, and forehead. He turned to Ren and went through the same process.

Next, he stood and brought over a small jar filled with brown liquid. He took a thin twig that had been stripped of its leaves and lightly dipped it in the jar. Taking my right hand in his, he began to draw geometrical designs. The liquid had a pungent smell, and the swirls he drew reminded me of henna hand drawings.

When he was done, I turned my hand back and forth, admiring the skill it took to create the elaborate artwork. The patterns he drew covered the back of my right hand, as well as the palm and fingertips.

"What is this for?" I asked.

"This symbol powerful. The mark stay lots of days."

Phet gathered up all the leaves and twigs, threw them into the old cast-iron wood-burning stove, and stood over it for a moment to inhale the smoke. Then, he turned to me, bowing.

"Kahl-see, now time to depart."

Ren headed out the door. I bowed back to Phet and then hugged

him briefly. "Thank you for everything you've done. I really appreciate your hospitality and your kindness."

He smiled at me warmly and squeezed my hand. I grabbed my bag and backpack, ducked under the doorframe, and followed Ren outside.

Grinning, Phet came to the little door and waved good-bye.

10

a safe haven

Well, I guess that it's back to the jungle for us, eh, Ren?"

He didn't turn around to acknowledge my comment but kept treading slowly on ahead. I trudged along behind, thinking about all the questions I would ask when he changed back into a man again.

After walking for a couple of hours, we came upon a small lake. I guessed that this was the Suki Lake Phet had been talking about. There were, indeed, many birds here. Ducks, geese, kingfishers, cranes, and sandpipers dotted the water and the sandbanks looking for food. I even spied larger birds, maybe eagles or hawks of some type, circling overhead.

Our arrival disturbed a flock of herons, which took off in a brief frenzied flight and then settled again in the water on the far side of the lake. Little birds darted around everywhere in colors of green, yellow, gray, blue, and black with red chests, but I didn't see any of Durga's hatchlings.

Where the trees shaded the water, clusters of lily pads made good places for frogs to perch and rest. They watched us with beady yellow eyes and jumped into the water with a plop as we passed by. I saw more frogs swimming and darting among the other flowering water plants near the lake's shoreline.

I spoke as much to myself as to Ren, "Do you think there are any alligators or crocodiles in the lake? I know one of those is indigenous to America, but I can never remember which one is which."

He started walking alongside me, and I wasn't sure if that meant there *were* dangerous reptiles to watch out for or if he just wanted to keep me company. I let him walk between the lake and me just to be on the safe side.

The air was hot, and the jungle drooped, sagging under the heat. The sky was bright, with not one monsoon cloud to provide shade. I was sweating hard. Ren led us through the shade of the trees as much as possible to keep us cool and help make the trip a bit more bearable, but I was still miserable. While skirting the edge of the lake, he kept up a slow and steady pace that I could follow easily. Even so, I could feel blisters forming on my heels. I pulled sunscreen out of the backpack and dabbed it on my face and arms. My compass indicated that we were traveling north.

When Ren stopped to drink at a small stream, I discovered that Phet had packed lunch. It was a large green leaf wrapped around a ball of sticky white rice stuffed with spicy meat and vegetables. It was bit too spicy for my taste, but the plain rice helped staunch the heat. Finding two more leaf wraps in the backpack, I tossed them to Ren, who showed off by leaping up and catching them in the air. He, of course, gulped them down whole.

Hiking for about four more hours, we finally broke out of the jungle and onto a small road. I was happy to walk on the smooth pavement—at least until it started burning my soles. I could have sworn that the hot, black tar was melting the rubber on the bottom of my shoes.

Ren stuck his nose in the air, turned right, and marched alongside the road for a half mile or so until we came upon a brand new, metallic green Jeep SUV. It had tinted windows and a black hard top.

Ren stopped next to the Jeep and sat down.

I panted, took a long swig of water, and said, "What? What do you want me to do?"

Ren just stared blankly.

"Is it the car? You want me to get *in* the car? Okay, I just hope the owner doesn't get mad."

Pulling the door open, I found a note from Mr. Kadam on the driver's seat.

Miss Kelsey,

Please forgive me. I wanted to tell you the truth.

Here is a map with directions to Ren's home. I will meet you there.

The key is in the glove box. Don't forget to drive on the left side of the road.

The trip will take about an hour and a half. I hope you are safe.

Your friend,
Anik Kadam

I picked up the map and placed it on the passenger seat. Opening up the back door, I threw in the bags and pulled out another water bottle for the drive. Ren hopped up into the back and stretched out.

I swung into the driver's seat and popped open the glove compartment to find a small ring of the promised keys. The big one read *Jeep*. I started the engine and smiled gratefully as a rush of cold air blew in from the vents.

When I pulled out onto the small, vacant road, a little voice on a GPS device chirruped: "Drive fifty kilometers. Then turn left."

Staying on the left side of the road and gripping the wheel, I looked down at my hand. Despite sweating and wiping at my face constantly, Phet's ink design was still there, as permanent as a tattoo. I turned on the radio, found a station that played interesting music, and let it keep me company on the drive while Ren napped in the back.

Mr. Kadam's directions, in addition to the GPS unit, were easy to follow. There was almost no traffic along the route he had chosen, which was good, because every time a car passed me, I clutched the wheel nervously. I had just learned how to drive on the right side of the road, and switching sides was not easy. Driving on the "wrong" side of the road certainly wasn't covered in driver's ed.

After an hour, the directions said to turn onto a small dirt road. There was no name on the path, but the GPS beeped that we were at the right place, so I turned and entered deep jungle. We seemed to be in the middle of nowhere, but the road was maintained and the drive was smooth.

The sun was setting and the sky was turning dark, when the road opened up into a cobbled brightly lit drive that circled around a tall sparkling fountain. Flowers surrounded the fountain, and sitting behind it was the most gorgeous home I'd ever seen. It looked like a multi-million dollar mansion that might be found in the tropics or perhaps sitting on the shores of Greece. I imagined the perfect place for it would be on the peak of an island overlooking the Mediterranean Sea.

I parked, opened the doors, and marveled at the magnificent setting.

I exclaimed, "Ren, your home is amazing! I can't believe you own this!"

Grabbing my bags, I walked slowly up the paved stone walkway and admired the four-car garage. I wondered what types of vehicles were housed there. Beautiful tropical plants surrounded the home, turning the grounds into a lush paradise. I recognized plumeria flowers, bird-of-paradise, ornamental bamboo, tall royal palms, thick ferns, and leafy banana trees, but there were many others as well. A curved pool and hot tub were lit up on the side of the house, and a glittering fountain sprayed water from the pool into the air while rotating its patterns and colors.

The three-story house was painted white and cream. On the second floor was a covered, wraparound veranda with wrought iron balustrades, supported by cream-colored pillars. The upper floor featured tall, arched balconies while sparkling panoramic windows were the feature of the main floor.

When Ren and I approached the marble and teakwood entryway, I twisted the doorknob and found the door unlocked. The outside was warm and vibrant, reflecting the intense, bold colors of India. The inside was opulent and lovely, decorated in cooler shades of purple, green, and peacock blue.

We stepped into the wide, dramatic foyer. The entryway had vaulted ceilings, exquisite marble flooring, and a curved sweeping staircase with ornate ironwork balustrades. The room was capped by a dazzling crystal chandelier. Huge windows showcased the panoramic view of the surrounding jungle.

I slipped out of my sneakers, regretting how dirty they were, and crossed the foyer into a gentleman's library. Dark brown leather chairs, ottomans, and cozy couches were set atop a beautiful rug. A large globe stood in the corner, and the walls were lined with bookshelves. There was even a sliding ladder reaching up to the top shelves. A heavy desk sat to one side with a leather chair. It was meticulously neat and organized, immediately reminding me of Mr. Kadam.

A carved stone fireplace took up one wall. I couldn't imagine when a fireplace would ever be used in India, but it was a beautiful showpiece nonetheless. A golden vase full of peacock feathers picked up the teal, green, and purple accents of the throw pillows and rugs. I thought it was the most beautiful library in the world.

As we made our way into the house, I heard Mr. Kadam call out, "Miss Kelsey? Is that you?"

I had been determined to be upset with both him and Ren but discovered I couldn't wait to see him.

"Yes, it's me, Mr. Kadam."

I found him in Ren's large, stainless steel gourmet kitchen. It had a black marble floor, granite countertops, and double ovens, where Mr. Kadam had been busy preparing a meal.

"Miss Kelsey!" The businessman rushed toward me and said, "I'm so glad you are safe. I hope you aren't terribly angry with me."

"Well, I'm not too happy about how everything happened, but," I grinned at him and looked down at the tiger, "I blame this guy more than you. He admitted that you wanted to tell me the truth."

Mr. Kadam grimaced apologetically and nodded. "Please forgive both of us. We never intended to upset you. Come. I have prepared a meal."

He bustled back to the kitchen, pulled open the door to a room full of fragrant fresh and dried spices, and disappeared inside for several minutes. When he stepped out, he deposited his selections on the kitchen island and opened another small door to a deep, walk-in butler's pantry. I peeked inside and saw shelves full of fancy dishes and goblets including an impressive collection of silver. He pulled out two delicate china plates and two goblets and then set them on the table.

I closed the door. "Mr. Kadam, something's been bothering me."

He teased, "Only *one* thing?"

I laughed. "For now. I've been wondering, did you ever really ask Mr. Davis to come with you to take care of Ren? I mean, what would you have done if he'd said yes and I'd said no?"

"I did ask him, just to keep up appearances, but I also suggested subtly to Mr. Maurizio that it might be in his best interest to persuade Mr. Davis *not* to go. In fact, I offered him more money if he would insist Mr. Davis stay with the circus. As far as what to do if you had turned us down, I suppose we would have had to make you a better offer and keep trying until we found one you couldn't refuse."

"What if I still said no? Would you have kidnapped me?"

Mr. Kadam laughed. "No. If our offer had still been turned down, my next step would have been to tell you the truth and hope you believed me."

"Whew, that's a relief."

"*Then* I would have kidnapped you." He chuckled at his joke and turned his attention back to our dinner.

"That's not very funny, Mr. Kadam."

"I couldn't resist. Sorry, Miss Kelsey."

He led me out of the kitchen to a small breakfast nook. We sat at a round table next to a bay window that overlooked an illuminated swimming pool. Ren settled himself at my feet.

Mr. Kadam wanted to know everything that had happened to me since I'd last seen him. I told him about the truck, and found out that he paid the driver to leave me stranded. Then we talked about the jungle and Phet.

Mr. Kadam asked many questions about my conversations with Phet and was particularly interested in my henna design. He turned my hand over and closely examined the symbols on each side.

"So you *are* the favored one of Durga," he concluded, leaned back in his chair, and smiled.

"How did you know I was the right person? I mean, how did you know it was *me* who would be able to break the curse?"

"We were not really sure that you *were* the right person until you met Phet and he confirmed it. When Ren was in captivity, he could not alter his form. Somehow, you spoke the words that set him free. It allowed him to change to a man again and contact me. We hoped that you were the right person to break the curse, the one that we'd been searching for, Durga's favored one."

"Mr. Kadam, who is Durga?"

Mr. Kadam retrieved a small golden statuette from the other room and placed it delicately on the dinner table. It was a beautifully carved Indian goddess with eight arms. She was shooting a bow and arrow—and she was riding a tiger.

Touching a delicate carved arm, I said, "Please tell me about her."

"Of course, Miss Kelsey. In the language of the Hindus, *Durga* means 'invincible one.' She is a great warrior and considered the mother goddess of many of the other gods and goddesses of India. She has at her command many weapons and rides a magnificent tiger named Damon into war. A very beautiful goddess, she's been described as having long curly hair and a bright complexion that glows even brighter when she is engaged in battle. She's often dressed in cerulean robes, the color of the sea, and jeweled ornaments of carved gold, precious gemstones, and shiny black pearls."

I turned the statue. "What are the weapons she's holding?"

"There are several different depictions of her throughout India. In each one, Durga has a slightly different number of arms and array of weapons. This statue shows a trident, a bow and arrow, the sword, and a *gada*, which is similar to a mace or a club. She is also carrying a *kamandal*, or conch shell, a *chakram*, a snake, and armor with a shield. I have seen other drawings of Durga with a rope, a bell, and a lotus flower. Not only does Durga have multiple weapons at her disposal, but also she can manipulate lightning and thunder as well."

I picked up the statue and looked at it from different angles. The eight arms were fearsome. *Note to self: in a battle against Durga, run the other direction.*

Mr. Kadam continued, "The goddess Durga was born out of the river to help humanity in their time of need. She fought a demon, Mahishasur, who was half-human and half-buffalo. He terrorized the earth and the heavens, and no one could kill him. So Durga took the form of a warrior goddess to defeat him. She is also called *The Fair Lady* because of her great beauty."

Placing the statue back on the table, I said uncertainly, "Mr. Kadam, I don't mean to be disrespectful, and I hope I don't offend you, but I don't really believe in this kind of stuff. I think it's fascinating, but it seems too weird to be real. I feel like I'm stuck in some kind of Indian myth in *The Twilight Zone*."

Mr. Kadam smiled. "Ah, Miss Kelsey, don't worry. No offense taken. During my travels and my research trying to help Ren break the curse, I have had to open myself to new ideas and beliefs that I, too, had never considered before. What is real and what is not is for your heart to decide and for your heart to know.

"Now, you must be tired from your journey. I will show you to your room where you can rest."

He led me upstairs to a large bedroom decorated in plum and white with gold trim. A round vase of white roses and gardenias lightly perfumed the room. A four-poster bed with mounds of plum-colored pillows adorning it was set against the wall. Thick piled white carpet covered the floor. Beveled glass doors opened to the largest veranda I'd ever seen and overlooked the pool and fountain.

"It's lovely! Thank you, Mr. Kadam."

He nodded and left me, closing the door softly behind him.

I yanked off my socks and enjoyed walking barefoot on the plush carpet. Textured glass doors opened into a stunning bathroom bigger than Mike and Sarah's entire first floor. There was a white marble deep-plunge spa tub and a huge shower that could also function as a steam room. Soft plum-colored towels hung on a heated rack and glass bottles held soaps and bubble bath in lavender and peach fragrances.

Next to the bathroom was a walk-in closet with white padded changing benches, hutches, and drawers. One side was empty and the other side held a rack of brand new clothes still wrapped in cellophane. The dresser was also full of clothes. A whole wall was built just to hold shoes, but it was mostly empty. One new shoebox sat there waiting to be opened.

After a thoroughly relaxing shower and braiding my hair, I unpacked my few clothes and arranged them in the closet and the dresser. I set my makeup, compacts, hairbrush, and ribbons on a mirrored tray lying on the marble sink and rolled up the cord of my flat iron and stowed it in a drawer.

Dressed in pajamas, I scooted to the back of the bed and had just pulled out my poetry book when I heard a light tapping at the open veranda doors. I looked out at the veranda and my heart started pounding in my chest. A man was standing out there. I caught a flash of blue eyes—Ren, the Indian prince version. When I stepped outside, I noticed that his hair was wet, and he smelled wonderful, like waterfalls and the woods mixed together. He was so good looking that I felt even mousier than usual. As I walked toward him, my heart began to beat even faster.

Ren looked at me and frowned. "Why aren't you wearing the clothes I bought you? The ones in your closet and dresser?"

"Oh. You mean those clothes are for *me*?" I asked, confused and tongue-tied.

"I didn't . . . But . . . Why would you . . . How . . . Well, anyway, thank you. And thank you for the use of the beautiful room."

Ren smiled at me widely and almost knocked me off my feet. He took hold of a wisp of my hair that had come loose in the breeze, tucked it behind my ear, and said, "Did you like your flowers?"

I just stared at him, then blinked and managed to squeak out a tiny yes. He nodded, satisfied, and gestured to the patio chairs. I bobbed my head faintly and sucked in a breath as he took my elbow and guided me to a chair. After making sure I was comfortable, he moved to the chair opposite from me. I guess because I was just staring at him and couldn't come up with a coherent thought of my own, he began speaking.

"Kelsey, I know you have many questions for me. What would you like to know first?"

I was mesmerized by his bright blue eyes, which somehow sparkled even in the dark. Finally, I snapped out of it. I mumbled the first thought that came to mind: "You don't look like other Indian men. Your . . . your eyes look . . . different and . . ." I stammered lamely. *Why can't I get it together?*

Ren didn't seem to notice my total lack of sophistication.

"My father was of Indian descent, but my mother was Asian. She was a princess from another country who was betrothed to my father to become his bride. Plus, I'm more than three hundred years old, which might make a difference too, I suppose."

"More than three hundred years old! That means you were born in—"

"I was born in 1657."

"Right." I fidgeted. *Apparently, I find older men extremely attractive.* "Then why do you look so young?"

"I don't know. I was twenty-one when I was cursed. I haven't aged since then."

About a million questions popped into my mind and I suddenly felt the need to try to solve this puzzle.

"What about Mr. Kadam? How old is he? And how does Mr. Kadam's boss fit into this? Does he know about you?"

He laughed. "Kelsey. I'm Mr. Kadam's boss."

"You? *You* are his wealthy employer?"

"We don't really define our relationship that way, but what he said was more or less accurate. Mr. Kadam's age is more complicated. He's actually a bit older than me. He was once my man-at-arms and my father's trusted military advisor. When I fell under the curse, I ran to him and was able to change to a man long enough to tell him what had happened. He quickly organized things, hid my parents and our wealth, and has been my protector ever since."

"But, how can he still be alive? He should have died a long time ago."

Ren hesitated. "The Damon Amulet protects him from aging. He wears it around his neck and never takes off."

I flashed back to our plane ride and remembered catching a glimpse of Mr. Kadam's pendant. I shifted forward in my seat.

"Damon? Isn't that the name of Durga's tiger?"

"Yes, the name of Durga's tiger and the amulet are the same. I don't know much about the connection or the amulet's origins. All I know is that the amulet was broken into several parts a long time ago. Some say there are four pieces, each representing the basic elements, the four winds, or even the four points of the compass. Some say there are five or even more. My father gave me his piece, and my mother gave hers to Kishan.

"The man who placed the tiger's curse on me wanted our pieces of the amulet. That's why he double-crossed Kishan. No one is sure what kind of power the amulet would wield if all the pieces were reassembled. But he was ruthless and would stop at nothing to claim all the pieces and find out."

Ren continued, "Mr. Kadam wears my piece of the amulet now. We believe that the amulet's power has protected him and kept him alive all this time. Though he's aged, it has been, thankfully, very slow. He is a trusted friend who has given up much to help my family through the years. I can never repay my debt to him. I don't know how I would have survived all this time without him." Ren looked out across the pool and whispered, "Mr. Kadam cared for my parents until their deaths and watched over them when I couldn't."

I leaned over to place my hand on top of his. I could sense his sadness as he thought about his parents. His lonely ache filled me somehow and entwined with my own. He turned his hand over and began absentmindedly stroking my fingers with his thumb as he stared out at the landscape, wrapped in his own thoughts.

Normally, I would have felt awkward or embarrassed holding hands with a man I'd just met. Instead, I felt comforted. Ren's loss echoed my own, and his touch gave me a sense of peace. As I looked at his handsome face, I wondered if he felt the same way. I understood the sting of isolation. The counselors at school had said that I didn't mourn or grieve enough after my parents' death and that it prevented me from forming bonds with other people. I always shied away from deep relationships. I realized that in a way, we were both alone, and I felt great compassion for him in that moment. I couldn't imagine three hundred years without human contact, without communication, without anyone looking into my eyes and knowing who I am. Even if I had been uncomfortable, I couldn't have denied him that moment of human contact.

Ren shot me a warm, lazy smile, kissed my fingers, and said, "Come, Kelsey. You need to sleep, and my time is almost up."

He pulled me up so that I stood very close to him, and I almost stopped breathing. As he held my hand, I felt a slight tremor pass through the tips of my fingers. He pulled me along to my door, said a quick goodnight, bowed his head, and then was gone.

The next morning I investigated my new clothing options, courtesy of Ren. I was surprised to see that they were mostly jeans and shirts, modern clothes that American girls would wear. The only difference was that these were the bright, vivid colors of India.

I zipped open one cellophane bag in the closet and was amazed to find a silky blue Indian-style dress. It was detailed with tiny silver teardrop pearls all over the skirt and bodice. The dress was so beautiful I rushed to try it on.

The skirt slid smoothly over my head and down my arms to settle at my waist. It fit snugly at the top of my hips. From there, it fell to the floor in swirling, heavy folds—heavy because of the hundreds of pearls clustered at the bottom hem. The bodice was cap sleeved and also copiously beaded with pearls. It fit tightly and ended just above my belly button, which gave me two inches of waistline exposure all around. Normally, I would never wear midriff-exposing clothing, but this dress was stunning. I twirled around in front of the mirror feeling like a princess.

Because of the dress, I decided I would make an extra effort with my hair and makeup. I retrieved my seldom-used compact and brushed on blush, some dark eye shadow, and blue liner. I finished it off with mascara and a pink-tinted lip gloss. Then, I pulled out my braids from the night before and finger combed through the locks of hair, arranging them in soft curls down my back.

A sheer blue scarf came with the dress, and I draped it around my shoulders, not really knowing how to arrange it. I hadn't planned to wear the dress during the day, but once I had it on I couldn't bring myself to take it off.

Barefoot, I sashayed down the staircase and headed to breakfast.

Mr. Kadam was already in the kitchen, humming and reading an Indian newspaper. He didn't even bother to look up.

"Good morning, Miss Kelsey. There's breakfast for you on the kitchen island."

I flounced over, trying to get his attention, picked up my plate and a glass of papaya juice, and then conspicuously arranged my dress and sighed dramatically as I sat down across from him. "Good morning, Mr. Kadam."

He peeked at me from around the side of the newspaper, smiled, and then set the paper down. "Miss Kelsey! You look charming!"

"Thank you." I blushed. "Did you pick it out? It's lovely!"

He smiled at me with twinkling eyes. "Yes. It's called a *sharara*. Ren wanted you to have some more clothing, and I purchased it while in Mumbai. He asked me to acquire something special as well. His only instructions were 'beautiful' and 'blue.' I wish I could take all the credit for the selection, but I had a bit of help from Nilima."

"Nilima? The flight attendant? Is she your? I mean, are you—?" I stuttered, embarrassed.

He laughed at me. "Nilima and I do have a close relationship as you have guessed, but not the kind you're thinking of. Nilima is my great-great-great-great-granddaughter."

My jaw hit the floor in shock. "Your what?"

"She's my granddaughter with several greats added."

"Ren told me that you were a bit older than he was, but he didn't mention that you had a family."

Mr. Kadam folded his newspaper and sipped some juice. "I was married once, a long time ago, and we had a few children. Then they had children and so on. Of all my descendants, only Nilima knows the secret. For most of them, I am a distant, wealthy uncle who is always away on business."

"What about your wife?"

Mr. Kadam lost his smile and became thoughtful. "Life was very difficult for us. I loved her with all my heart. As time passed, she began to get older, and I did not. The amulet affected me profoundly in ways I didn't expect. She knew about my situation and claimed it didn't bother her."

He rubbed the amulet under his shirt. Seeing my interest, he pulled out a thin silver chain and showed me the wedge-shaped, green stone. At the top, there was a faint outline of a tiger's head. Glyphs ran down the outside circle, but Mr. Kadam said that he could only read part of one word.

With melancholy, he rubbed the amulet between his fingers. "My dear wife became old and very sick. She was dying. I took this amulet from around my neck and begged her to wear it. She refused, wrapped my fingers around it, and made me swear to never remove it again until my duty was fulfilled."

A small tear slipped out of the corner of my eye. "Couldn't you have forced her to wear it and maybe take turns?"

He shook his head sadly. "No. She wanted to follow the natural course of life. Our children were married and happy, and she felt it was time for her to move on to the next life. She was comforted knowing I would be around to care for our family."

Mr. Kadam smiled sorrowfully. "I stayed with her until she died and with many of my children and grandchildren after that. But, as the years passed, it became harder for me to bear seeing them suffer and die. Also, the more people who knew Ren's secret, the more danger he would be in, so I left them. I return to visit from time to time to check up on my descendants, but it's . . . difficult for me."

"Did you ever marry again?"

"No. I seek out one of my great-grandchildren to work for me every once in a while, and they're wonderful to me. Also, Ren was a good companion for me until his capture. I have not sought out someone to love since then. I don't think my heart could take saying good-bye again."

"Oh, Mr. Kadam, I'm so sorry. Ren was right; you have sacrificed many things for him."

He smiled at me. "Don't feel sad for me, Miss Kelsey. It is a time for celebration. *You* have come into our lives. And you being here makes me very happy." He took one of my hands in his, patted it, and winked at me.

I didn't really know what to say in response, so I just smiled back at him. Mr. Kadam let go of my hand, stood up, and began to wash the plates. I got up to help as Ren padded lazily into the room yawning widely as only a tiger could. I turned around and patted his furry head, only a little awkwardly.

"Good morning, Ren!" I said brightly, and then spun around to show off my outfit. "Thank you so much for the dress! It's quite beautiful, isn't it? Nilima did a great job picking it out."

Ren abruptly sat down on the floor, watched me twirl in my dress for a moment, and then got up and left.

"What's up with Ren today?" I asked.

Mr. Kadam turned while drying his hands on a towel. "Hmm?"

"Ren just took off."

"Who knows with tigers? Perhaps he is hungry. Excuse me for a moment, Miss Kelsey." He smiled at me and went after Ren.

Later, we both settled down in the lovely peacock room, which housed Mr. Kadam's amazing book collection. The books were stacked carefully on polished mahogany shelves. I picked out a book on India that was full of old maps.

"Mr. Kadam, can you show me where the Kanheri Cave is? Phet said that's where we need to go to speak to Durga to figure out how to get Ren out of this mess."

He opened the book and pointed to a map of Mumbai. "The cave is in the northern part of the city, in Borivali National Park, which now is called the Gandhi National Park. The Cave of Kanheri is a basaltic rock cave that has ancient writing chiseled on the walls. I have been there before, but I have never found an underground passage. Archeologists have been studying the cave for years, but still no one has yet found a prophecy written by Durga."

"What about the Seal that Phet spoke of? What is it?"

"The Seal is a special stone that has been in my care all of these years. I keep it safe with many of Ren's heirlooms in a bank vault. In fact, I must leave now to retrieve it. I will bring it to you tonight. It might be a good idea for you to call your foster parents today and let them know you're alright. You can tell them you are staying on in India through the summer as my apprentice in the business, if you like."

I nodded. I really did need to call them. Sarah and Mike were probably wondering if I'd been eaten by a tiger by now.

"I must also gather a few things from town that you will need to take with you on your journey to the cave. Please make yourself at home and rest. There is a luncheon and a dinner already prepared for you in the refrigerator. If you go for a swim, please wear sunscreen. It's kept in a cabinet near the pool, next to the towels."

Wandering back upstairs, I found my cell phone left on the dresser in my room. *Nice of him to give it back after the jungle incident.* I sat down in a gold velvety easy chair, called my foster parents, and had a long chat about the traffic, the food, and the people of India. When they asked about the tiger reserve, I evaded the question by saying that Ren was well taken care of. Mr. Kadam was right. The easiest way to explain my staying in India was that I was offered a position working as an intern for Mr. Kadam through the end of summer.

After I hung up with them, I located the laundry area and washed my clothes and my grandmother's quilt. Then, having nothing else to do, I explored every part of the house. The entire basement was a fully appointed gym, but not with modern exercise equipment. The floor was covered with a black cushioned mat. It was a daylight basement, so half of the room was built underground in the hillside and the rest was open to the sunlight with large floor-to-ceiling windows. A sliding glass door opened to a large deck that led out to the jungle. The back wall was paneled and smooth.

There was a button pad by the door. I pushed the top button, and a section of paneling flipped out to reveal an assortment of ancient weapons such as axes, spears, and knives of various lengths hanging in specially made compartments. I pushed the button again and it flipped shut. I pushed the second button, and it flipped open another section of wall that contained swords. I moved closer to inspect them. There were many different styles ranging from thin rapiers to heavy broadswords and one that was specially encased in glass. It looked like a samurai sword that I'd seen once in a movie.

Wandering back up to the first floor, I found a high-tech home theater with a state-of-the-art media system and reclining leather seats. Right behind the kitchen was a formal banquet-style dining room with marble floors, crown molding, and a glittering chandelier. Off to the side of the peacock library, I discovered a music room with a shiny black grand piano and a large sound system with hundreds of compact discs. Most of them looked Indian, but I also found several American singers, including Elvis Presley. A very old, odd-shaped guitar was hung on the wall, and there was a curved black leather couch set in the middle of the room.

Mr. Kadam's bedroom was also on the main floor, and his room looked a lot like the peacock room, full of polished wooden furniture and books. He also had a couple of beautiful paintings and a sunny

reading area. On the third floor, I found an inviting loft. It had a small set of bookshelves and two comfy reading chairs and overlooked the sweeping stairway.

I also found another large bedroom, a bath, and a storage room. On my floor, I found three more bedrooms, not including mine. One was decorated in rose colors for a girl, which I thought might be for Nilima when she came to visit. The second appeared to be a guest room, but the colors were more masculine. Almost all of the rooms had private baths.

Stepping into the last room, I saw glass doors that led out to my veranda. The decoration of this room was plain in comparison to the others. The furniture was dark polished mahogany, but there were no details or knickknacks. The walls were plain and the drawers empty.

Is this where Ren sleeps?

Spotting a desk set in the corner, I approached it and saw thick, cream-colored paper and an ink well with an old-fashioned fountain pen. The top sheet had a note written in beautiful calligraphy.

> *Kelsey Durgaa Vallabh*
>
> *Bhumi-ke-niche gupha*
>
> *Rajakiya Mujulaain Mohar*
>
> *Sandesha Durgaa*

A green hair ribbon that looked suspiciously like one of mine lay next to the ink bottle. I peeked in the closet and found nothing—no clothes, no boxes, and no possessions.

I went back downstairs and spent the rest of the afternoon studying

Indian culture, religion, and mythology. I waited until my stomach growled to eat dinner, hoping for some company. Mr. Kadam still hadn't returned from the bank, and there'd been no sign of Ren.

After dinner, I went upstairs and found Ren standing on the veranda again, looking at the sunset. I approached him shyly and stood behind him. "Hello, Ren."

He turned and openly studied my appearance. His gaze drifted ever so slowly down my body. The longer he looked, the wider his smile got. Eventually, his eyes worked their way back up to my bright red face.

He sighed and bowed deeply. "*Sundari.* I was standing here thinking nothing could be more beautiful than this sunset tonight, but I was mistaken. You standing here in the setting sun with your hair and skin aglow is almost more than a man can . . . fully appreciate."

I tried to change the subject. "What does *sundari* mean?"

"It means 'most beautiful.'"

I blushed again, which made him laugh. He took my hand, tucked it under his arm, and led me to the patio chairs. Just then, the sun dipped below the trees leaving its tangerine glow in the sky for just a few more moments.

We sat again, but this time he sat next to me on the swinging patio seat and kept my hand in his.

I ventured shyly, "I hope you don't mind, but I explored your house today, including your room."

"I don't mind. I'm sure you found my room the least interesting."

"Actually, I was curious about the note I found. Did you write it?"

"A note? Ah, yes. I just scribbled a few notes to help me remember what Phet had said. It just says seek Durga's prophecy, the Cave of Kanheri, Kelsey is Durga's favored one, that sort of thing."

"Oh. I . . . also noticed a ribbon. Is it mine?"

"Yes. If you'd like it back, you can take it."

"Why would you want it?"

He shrugged, looking embarrassed. "I wanted a memento, a token from the girl who saved my life."

"A token? Like a fair maiden giving her handkerchief to a knight in shining armor?"

He grinned. "Exactly."

I jested wryly, "Too bad you didn't wait for Cathleen to get a little older. She's going to be very pretty."

He frowned. "Cathleen from the circus?" He shook his head, "You were the chosen one, Kelsey. And if I had the option of choosing the girl to save me, I still would have picked you."

"Why?"

"A number of reasons. I liked you. You are interesting. I enjoyed listening to your voice. I felt like you saw through the tiger skin to the person underneath. When you spoke, it felt like you were saying exactly the things I *needed* to hear. You're smart. You like poetry, *and* you're very pretty."

I laughed at his statement. *Me, pretty? He can't be serious.* I was average in so many ways. I didn't really concern myself with current makeup, hairstyles, or fashionable, but uncomfortable, clothes like other teenagers. My complexion was pale, and my eyes were so brown that they were almost black. By far, my best feature was my smile, which my parents paid dearly for and so did I—with three years of metal braces.

Still, I was flattered. "Okay, Prince Charming, you can keep your memento." I hesitated, and then said softly, "I wear those ribbons in memory of my mom. She used to brush out my hair and braid ribbons through it while we talked."

Ren smiled understandingly. "Then it means even more to me."

When the moment passed, he continued, "Now, Kelsey, tomorrow we're going to the cave. During the day, there are many tourists, which means we'll have to wait until evening to look for Durga's prophecy. We'll be sneaking into the park through the jungle and traveling on foot for a while, so wear the new hiking boots that we bought for you, the ones in the box in your closet."

"Great. Nothing like breaking in new hiking boots on a trek through the hot Indian jungle," I teased.

"It shouldn't be that bad, and even new hiking boots should be better on your feet than your sneakers."

"I happen to like my sneakers, and I'm bringing them along just in case your boots blister my feet."

Ren stretched out his long legs and crossed his bare feet in front of him. "Mr. Kadam will pack a bag with things we might need. I'll make sure he leaves room for your sneakers. You'll have to drive us to Mumbai and to the park because I'll be back in tiger form. I know you don't like the traffic here. I'm sorry that you're burdened with this."

I muttered, "Not liking the traffic is an understatement. People don't know how to drive here. They're *crazy*."

"We can take back roads with the least traffic on the way, and we'll be driving only to the outskirts of Mumbai, not through the city as before. It shouldn't be too bad. You're a good driver."

"Ha, easy for you to say. You'll just sleep in the back the whole way."

Ren touched my cheek with his fingers and gently turned my face to his. "*Rajkumari*, I want to say thank you. Thank you for staying and helping me. You don't know what this means to me."

I mumbled, "You're welcome. And *rajkumari* means?"

He flashed me a brilliant white smile and deftly changed the subject. "Would you like to hear about the Seal?"

I knew he was avoiding answering, but acquiesced, "Okay, what is it?"

"It's a carved rectangular stone, about three fingers thick. The king always wore it in public. It was a symbol of the duties of the royal family. The Seal of the Empire has four words carved upon it, one on each side: *Viveka*, *Jagarana*, *Vira*, and *Anukampa* which translated loosely means 'Wisdom,' 'Vigilance,' 'Bravery,' and 'Compassion.' You'll need to bring the Seal with you when we go to the cave. Phet said it was the key that would open the passageway. Mr. Kadam will put it on your dresser before we leave."

I stood up, walked to the railing, and stared up at the budding stars. "I can't imagine the life that you came from. It's so different from what I know."

"You're right, Kelsey."

"Call me Kells."

He smiled and approached me. "You're right, *Kells*. It *is* different. I have much to learn from you. But, perhaps I can teach *you* a few things as well. For example, your scarf. . . . May I?"

Ren removed the shawl draped around my shoulders and held it out.

"There are many different ways to wear a *dupatta* scarf. One way is to arrange it across your shoulders as you did just now, or you can drape one end over your shoulder and the other across your arm as is the current style. Like this."

Wrapping it around his body, he turned around to show me, and I couldn't help but laugh. "And how do you know the current style?"

"I know lots of things. You'd be surprised." He pulled it off again, twisting the scarf another way. "You can also fold it across your hair, which is appropriate when meeting with your elders, as it shows respect."

I bowed low to him, giggled, and said, "Thank you for showing me the proper respect, Madam. And might I say you look lovely in silk."

He laughed and showed me a few more ways to wear it, each one funnier than the last. As he spoke, I found myself drawn to him. *He's so . . . attractive, charming, magnetic, compelling . . . captivating.* He was easy to look at, no question about that, but even if he weren't, I could still picture myself sitting happily beside him talking for hours.

I saw a tremor run through Ren's arm. He quieted his demeanor and took a step closer to me. "My favorite style, though, is the way you were wearing it earlier when you had it draped across both of your arms loosely. That way, I get the full effect of your exquisite hair tumbling down your back."

Wrapping the filmy fabric around my shoulders, he pulled the shawl and gently tugged me closer. He reached out, captured a curl, and wrapped the hair around his finger.

"This life is so different from what I know. So many things have changed." He let go of the shawl, but he kept hold of the curl. "But some things are much, *much* better." He let go of the curl, trailing a finger down my cheek, and gave me a little nudge back toward my room.

"Goodnight, Kelsey. We have a busy day tomorrow."

the cave of kanheri

The next morning, I woke to find the Mujulaain Empire Seal on the dresser. The beautiful, creamy stone had golden orange striations and hung from a soft ribbon. I picked up the heavy object to examine it more closely and immediately noticed the carved words that Ren had said meant "wisdom, vigilance, bravery, and compassion." A lotus flower bloomed on the bottom of the Seal. The detailing in the intricate design demonstrated highly sophisticated workmanship. It was lovely.

If he was as true to these words as Ren says he was, Ren's father must have been a good king.

For a minute, I let myself imagine an older version of Ren as king. I could easily envision him leading others. There was something about him that made me want to trust and follow him. I grinned wryly. *Women would follow him over a cliff.*

Mr. Kadam had served his prince for more than three hundred years. The idea that Ren could inspire a lifetime of loyalty was extraordinary. I set aside my speculations and looked at the centuries-old Seal again with awe.

I opened the bag Mr. Kadam had left and found it contained cameras, both digital and disposable, matches, a few handheld digging tools, flashlights, a pocketknife, glow sticks, paper with rubbing charcoal, food, water, maps, and a few other things. Several of the items were placed in waterproof plastic bags. I tested out the weight of the pack and found it surprisingly manageable.

I opened the closet, fingered my pretty dress again, and sighed. Slipping on some jeans and a T-shirt, I laced up my new hiking boots and grabbed my sneakers.

Downstairs, I found Mr. Kadam slicing mango for breakfast.

"Good morning, Miss Kelsey," he said and gestured to my neck. "I see you found the Seal."

"I did. It's very pretty, but a little bit heavy." I scooped some mango slices onto my plate and poured some homemade hot cocoa into a mug. "You've taken care of it all these years?"

"Yes. It's very precious to me. The Seal was actually made in China, not India. It was a gift given to Ren's grandfather. Seals that old are quite rare. It's made of Shoushan stone, which contrary to popular belief, is not a type of jade. The Chinese believed that Shoushans were brightly colored Phoenix eggs, found high in mountain nests. Men who risked their lives to locate and capture them received honor, glory, and wealth.

"Only the very richest of men had items carved from this type of stone. To receive one as a gift was a great honor for Ren's grandfather. It's a priceless heirloom. The good news for you, though, is that it's also considered good luck to own or wear something made from this type of stone. Perhaps it will help you on your journey in more ways than one."

"It sounds like Ren's family was very special."

"Indeed they were, Miss Kelsey."

We'd just sat down to a breakfast of yogurt and mango when Ren stalked into the room and put his head down on my lap.

I scratched his ears. "Nice of you to join us. I guess you're anxious to get moving today, huh? You must be excited that you're this close to breaking the curse."

He kept watching me intently as if impatient to leave, but I didn't want to rush. I pacified him by feeding him pieces of mango. Content for the moment, he sat down and enjoyed his treat, licking the juice from my fingers.

I laughed. "Stop it! That tickles!" He ignored me, moved up my arm, and licked me almost all the way up to my sleeve. "Ew, gross, Ren! Alright. Alright. Let's go."

I washed my arm off, took one last look at the view, and made my way out to the garage. Mr. Kadam was already outside with Ren. He took my bag from me, put it on the passenger seat, and then held open my door as I hopped into the Jeep.

"Be careful, Miss Kelsey," Mr. Kadam warned. "Ren will watch out for you, but there are many dangers ahead. Some we've planned for, but I'm sure you'll face many that I am unaware of. Use caution."

"I will. Hopefully, we'll be back very soon."

I rolled up the window and backed out of the garage. The GPS began beeping at me, telling me where to go. Once again, I felt a deep appreciation for Mr. Kadam. Ren and I would be truly lost without him.

The drive was uneventful. The traffic was very light for the first hour. It gradually began to pick up the closer we got to Mumbai, but by then I had almost gotten used to driving on the other side of the road. We drove for about four hours before I pulled to a stop at the end of a dirt road that bordered the park.

"This is where we're supposed to go in. According to the map, it'll take us two and a half hours to walk to the Cave of Kanheri." I checked my watch and continued, "That gives us about two hours to kill since we can't go in until nightfall when the tourists have gone."

Ren leapt out of the car and followed me into the park to a shady spot. Ren lay down on the grass, and I sat down next to him. At first,

I used his body as a backrest and then gradually relaxed against him, using his back as a pillow.

Staring up into the trees, I started talking. I told Ren about visits with my grandma, growing up with my parents, and the vacations we used to go on as a family.

"Mom was a nurse in a geriatric facility at first, but then she decided to stay home and raise me," I explained, thinking back with fond memories. "She made the best chocolate-chocolate chip and peanut butter cookies. Mom believed that showing your love meant making homemade cookies, which is probably why I was chubby as a kid.

"Dad was your average backyard-grilling-kind of dad. He was a math teacher, and I guess some of that rubbed off on me because I like math, too. We all loved reading, and we had a cozy home library. Dr. Seuss books were my favorite. Even now I can almost sense my parents near me when I pick up a book.

"When we traveled, my parents liked to stay at bed-and-breakfasts, where I'd get a room all to myself. We toured practically the whole state and saw apple farms and old mines, Bavarian-themed towns that served German pancakes for breakfast, the ocean, and the mountains. I think you'd easily fall in love with Oregon. I haven't traveled all over the world like you have, but I can't imagine a place more beautiful than my home state."

Later, I talked about school and my dreams to go to a university, though I couldn't afford more than a community college. I even spoke of my parents' car accident, about how alone I felt when it happened, and what it was like living with a foster family.

Ren's tail flicked back and forth, so I knew he was awake and listening, which surprised me because I figured he'd just go to sleep, bored with my chatter. Eventually, I trailed off, getting sleepy myself, and drowsed in the heat until I felt Ren stir and sit up.

I stretched. "Time to go already, huh? Okay, lead the way."

We trekked through the park for a couple of hours. It had a much more open feel than the Yawal Wildlife Preserve. The trees were spaced farther apart. Beautiful purple flowers covered the hills. But, when we got closer, I noticed that they were diminishing in the heat. I guessed that they sprung up briefly during the monsoon rains and would soon be gone.

We passed teak trees and bamboo, but there were other types I couldn't identify. Several animals darted across our path. I saw rabbits, deer, and porcupines. Looking up at the branches, I spied hundreds of birds in a variety of colors.

As we walked under a particularly dense group of trees, I heard strange, alarmed grunts and spotted rhesus monkeys swinging as high up as they could climb. They were harmless and familiar, but as we moved deeper into the park, I saw other, more fearsome creatures. I skirted a giant python that hung from a tree and watched us with black, unblinking eyes. Huge monitor lizards with forked tongues and long bodies scurried quickly across our path, hissing. Big, fat bugs buzzed around lazily in the air, bounced drunkenly off objects in flight, and then continued on their journey.

It was pretty but also creepy, and I was glad that I had a tiger nearby. Every once in a while, Ren would veer off the path and circle around in a way that made me think he was avoiding certain places or perhaps, I shuddered, certain *things*.

After about two hours of walking, we arrived at the edge of the jungle by the Kanheri Cave. The forest had thinned out, opening to a hill, bare of trees. Stone steps led up the hill to the entrance, but we were still too far away to see more than just a small glimpse of the cave. I started toward the steps, but Ren jumped in front of me and nudged me back toward the tree line.

"You want to wait a bit longer? Okay, we'll wait."

We sat down under the cover of some bushes and waited for an hour. Slightly impatient, I watched tourists emerge from the cave, make their slow way down the steps, and walk to a parking lot. I could hear them chattering as they left in their cars.

I remarked enviously, "Too bad we couldn't have driven in here. It sure would've saved us a lot of hassle. But, I guess people wouldn't understand why a tiger was following me around. Plus, the park ranger would be keeping tabs on us too, if we'd driven in."

Finally, the sun set, and the tourists left. Ren stepped forward carefully out of the trees and sniffed at the air. Satisfied, he began moving toward the stone steps that were cut into the rocky hill. The long climb up left me breathless by the time we reached the top.

Once inside the cave, we came upon an open stone bunker with rooms that reminded me of beehive cells. Each one was identical to the other. A stone block the size of a small bed was positioned on the left side of every room, and hollowed-out shelves were located on the back walls. A sign noted that this place used to be where the Buddhist monks lived and that the cave was part of a Buddhist settlement dating back to the third century.

Isn't it strange that we're looking for an Indian prophecy in a Buddhist settlement? I thought as we continued on. *But then again, everything about this adventure is a bit strange.*

Walking farther in, I noted long stone trenches connected by arches that ran from a central stone well and continued on—probably higher into the mountains. A sign read that the trenches were once used as an aqueduct to move water to the area.

Reaching the main room, I ran my hands over the deep grooves of the elaborately carved wall. Ancient Indian writing and hieroglyphics had been etched into the walls.

The remnants of a ceiling, still held up in some places by rock pillars, cast deep shadows over the area. Statues were carved into stone columns, and, as we walked through, I kept my eye on them just to make sure they didn't let the remainder of the roof come crashing down on top of us.

Ren continued making his way to the back of the main room toward the black gaping maw of the cave that led even deeper into the hill. I followed him and stepped through the opening and onto a sandy floor in a large, circular room. Pausing, I let my eyes adjust for a minute. The round room had many doorways. The light coming in was just enough to silhouette the opening, but it could not penetrate into any of the other corridors beyond and was quickly fading as the sunlight disappeared.

I pulled out a flashlight and asked, "What do we do now?"

Ren stepped over to the first shadowy doorway and disappeared into the darkness. Following him, I ducked into the small room. It was filled with stone shelves. I wondered if it might have been used as a library once. I wandered through and made my way to the back, hoping to see a giant sign that read: "Durga prophecy here!", when I felt a hand on my shoulder. I jumped at Ren's touch.

"Don't do that! Can't you give me some kind of warning first?"

"Sorry, Kells. We need to check each room for a symbol that looks like the Seal. You look high and I'll look low."

He squeezed my shoulder briefly and morphed back into his tiger form.

I shuddered. *I don't think I'll ever get used to that.*

We didn't see any carvings in the room, so we moved on to the next one and the next one. At the fourth doorway, we searched more carefully because the room was full of glyphs. We spent at least an hour in there. No luck in the fifth either.

The sixth chamber was empty. Not even a stone shelf graced the walls, but the seventh door was where we found a match. The opening led to a much smaller room than the others. It was long and narrow and had a couple of shelves similar to the other rooms. Ren found the engraving under one of the shelves. I probably would have overlooked it if I'd been searching alone.

He growled softly at me and stuck his nose up under the ledge.

"What is it?" I asked and bent down.

Sure enough, under the shelf on the wall in the back of the room was an engraving that matched the Seal exactly.

"Well, I guess this is it. Keep your fingers, er, claws crossed."

I removed the Seal from around my neck and pressed it into the carving, wiggling until I felt it click into place. I waited, but nothing happened. I tried twisting the Seal, and this time, I heard a mechanical whirring behind the wall. After a full turn, I felt resistance and heard a quiet pneumatic hiss. Dust blew out from the edges of the wall revealing that it wasn't a wall at all, but a door.

A deep, muffled rumble shook the wall as it slowly rolled back. I popped the Seal out, put it back around my neck, and aimed my feeble light through the door. I only saw more walls. Ren nudged me aside and entered first. I stayed as close to him as I possibly could and almost stomped on his paws a couple of times.

Shining my light on the wall, I found a torch hanging in a metal sconce. I pulled out matches and was surprised that the torch lit almost immediately. The flame brightened the corridor much more than my meager flashlight had.

We were at the top of a winding stairway. I peered cautiously over the edge into a dark abyss. Since the only way to go was down, I took the torch and started the descent. A clicking noise sounded behind us, and with a slight whoosh, the door closed, sealing us in.

I muttered, "Great. I guess we'll worry about how to get out later, then."

Ren just looked up at me and rubbed his head down my leg. I massaged the scruff of his neck, and we continued down the steps. He placed his body on the outside of the steps, which allowed me to hug the wall as we descended. I wasn't normally afraid of heights, but a secret passageway plus narrow stairs plus a dark abyss and no handrail equals freaking me out. I was very grateful that he took the more dangerous side.

We crept along slowly, and my arm began to ache from holding the torch. I shifted it to my other hand, careful not to dribble any hot oil onto Ren. When we'd finally reached the dusty bottom, another dark passageway gaped open before us. A short distance from its beginning, we came upon a fork leading in two different directions. I groaned.

"Fantastic. A maze. Which way do we go now?"

Ren stepped into one corridor and smelled the air. Then he moved to the other one and raised his head to sniff again. Moving back to the first one, he continued. I sniffed the air too, just to see if I could smell what he did, but the only thing I detected was an acrid, noxious sulfur-like odor. The bitter smell permeated the cavern and seemed to intensify with each turn we made.

We continued onward in the dark, twisting through the underground labyrinth. The torch cast a flickering light on the walls, creating scary shadows that danced in sinister circles. As we made our way through the tomblike maze, we frequently came upon open areas that branched off. Ren had to stop and smell each opening before choosing the one that he felt led us in the right direction.

Shortly after passing through one of the open areas, a terrifying sound shook the passage. A metallic hammering grated loudly and a sharp-spiked iron gate slammed to the ground right behind me. I spun around quickly and cried out in fright. Not only were we in an ancient dark maze, it was an ancient dark maze full of booby traps.

Ren moved up beside me and stayed very close, close enough for me to keep my hand on his neck. I dug my fingers into his fur and held on tight for reassurance. Three turns later, I heard a quiet hum emanating from one of the passageways ahead. The hum increased in volume the closer we walked.

Turning a corner, Ren stopped and looked directly ahead. His fur stood straight up and crackled against my fingers. I raised my torch to see why he had stopped and gripped his fur as I started shaking.

The corridor ahead was moving. Giant black beetles, as big as baseballs, were lazily crawling over one another, obstructing the entire passageway ahead. The strange aberrations seemed to limit their movements to the corridor directly ahead of us.

"Uh . . . Ren, are you sure we need to go down that direction? This other passageway looks a little better."

He took a step closer and, reluctantly, I took a step closer too. The bugs had shiny black exoskeletons, six hairy legs, quivering antennae, and two pointed mandibles on the front that clacked back and forth like sharp scissors. Some of the bugs cracked open thick black wings and hummed heavily as they flew to the opposite wall. The prickly legs of other bugs stuck to the ceiling.

I looked at Ren and gulped as he started forward, determined to go through the passage. He looked back at me.

"Okay, Ren, I'll do it. But this will really, *really* freak me out. I'm running the entire way, so don't expect me to wait for you."

I took a few steps back, tightened my grip on the torch, and began to sprint. Squishing my eyes to slits, I ran with my lips tightly closed, screaming in the back of my throat the entire way. I darted through the passage as quickly as possible and almost lost my balance a few times when my boots rolled across several bugs at once, crunching them. A horrible image flashed through my mind: landing in the hoard face down. I resolved to be more careful with my footing.

I felt like I was running on a giant roll of bubble wrap, and every step popped several giant, juicy bubbles. The beetles burst like ketchup packets and splattered green slime in every direction. This action, of course, disturbed the other bugs. Several of them took flight and started swarming around my body, landing on my jeans, shirt, and hair. I was able to bat them away from my face with my free hand, which was poked by their pinchers several times.

Finally making it to the other side, I began shaking my body in great convulsions to rid myself of any hitchhikers. I had to reach up and grab a couple that wouldn't detach, including one that was climbing up my ponytail. Then I began scraping my shoes against the wall and looked around for Ren.

He was running fast through the now-buzzing passageway, and with a great leap, landed next to me, shaking himself fiercely. Several bugs still clung to his fur, and I had to push them off with the butt of my torch. One of them had pinched his ear hard enough to make it bleed. Luckily for me, I'd made it through without any of them pinching me to the point of breaking skin.

"I guess it helps to wear clothes, Ren. They end up pinching your clothes instead of your skin. Poor tiger. You have squished bugs all over your paws. Yuck! At least I have the benefit of wearing shoes."

He shook each paw in turn, and I helped him pry bug bodies from between his toe pads. Shuddering one last time, I doubled my pace to put as much distance between the bugs and us as possible.

About ten turns later, I stepped onto a stone that sank into the ground. Freezing in place, I waited for the next booby trap to spring. The walls started to shake, and small metal panels slid back to allow sharp, spiky, metal barbs to emerge on both sides. I groaned. Not only were spikes sticking out of the walls, but also the trap was compounded by a slick black oil that poured out of stone pipes, covering the floor.

Ren changed into a man.

"There's poison on the tips of the spikes, Kelsey. I can smell it. Stay in the middle. There's enough room for us to pass through, but don't allow yourself to be even scratched by those barbs."

I took another look at the long pointy spikes and shivered, "But what if I slip?"

"Hold tightly on to my fur. I'll use my claws to anchor us as we go, and we'll go slowly. Don't rush through this one."

Ren changed back into a tiger. I adjusted my backpack and tightly gripped the scruff of his neck. He stepped gingerly into the pool of oil, testing it with one paw first. His paw slipped a little, and I watched as his claws emerged and sank through the oil and into the dirt floor. He forced them deep into the oily ground. After locking his leg, he then took another step and sank those claws in. Once that paw was firmly in place, he had to yank hard to get his other foot back up.

It was a painstakingly tedious process. Each deadly spike was placed at random intervals so I couldn't even get comfortable with a rhythm. I had to focus all my attention on them. There was one by my calf, then my neck, my head, my stomach. I started counting and stopped after fifty. My entire frame shook from clenching my muscles and moving stiffly for so long. All it would take was one second of slipped concentration—one wrong step and I'd be dead.

I was glad Ren was taking his time, because there was barely enough room for us to walk side by side. We only had about an inch of free space on either side of us. I planted each step carefully. Sweat dripped down my face. About halfway through, I screamed. I must have stepped into a particularly oily place because my boot slipped out from under me.

My knee buckled, and I staggered. This spike was aimed at chest height but luckily I twisted at the last second and my backpack took the spike instead of my arm. Ren froze in place, waiting patiently for me to right myself.

I panted and righted myself limb by trembling limb. It was a miracle I didn't end up impaled. When Ren made a whining sound, I patted his back.

"I'm fine," I reassured him.

I was lucky, very lucky. We continued on going even slower and finally emerged on the other end, shaky but safe. I collapsed on the dirt floor and groaned, rubbing my stiff neck.

"After the spikes, the bugs don't seem so bad anymore. I think I'd rather do the bugs again than that one."

Ren licked my arm and I petted his head.

After a brief rest, we went on. We walked through several more turns without event. I was just beginning to let my guard down when a noise set off again and a doorway sunk down behind us. Another doorway started descending ahead of us, and we ran for it but didn't make it. Well, Ren could have made it, but he wouldn't go through it without me.

A rushing sound started banging against pipes overhead, and a panel opened in the ceiling. A moment later, we were knocked to the floor by a flood of water that fell on top of us. It doused our torch and quickly began filling the chamber. The water was already up to my knees by the time I was able to stand. I yanked open a zipper and felt blindly. Finding a long tube, I gave it a snap, shook it, and the liquid inside began to glow. The color changed Ren's white fur yellow.

"What do we do? Can you swim? It'll go over your head first!"

Ren changed into a man. "Tigers can swim. I can hold my breath longer as a tiger than as a man."

The water was now up to our waists, and he quickly pulled me past the surging pipe and over to the door in front of us. By the time we reached it, I was floating. Ren dove under looking for a way out.

When his head popped back up, he shouted, "There's another Seal mark on the door. Try to insert the Seal and twist it like you did before!"

I nodded and took a deep breath. Diving under the water, I felt along the door for the mark. I finally found it, but I was running out of air. Struggling to the surface, I kicked hard, weighed down by the heavy backpack and the Seal around my neck. Ren reached down under the water, grabbed my bag, and yanked me to the surface.

We were floating near the ceiling now. We would drown any minute. I took a few deep breaths.

"You can do this, Kells. Try again."

I took another breath and yanked the Seal from around my neck. He let go of my bag, and I dove again, pulling myself down to the bottom of the door. I pressed the Seal into the groove and twisted it one way and the other, but it wouldn't budge.

Ren had changed back into a tiger and was now swimming down to me. His paws tore at the water, and the motion swept the fur back from his face, making him look scary, like a white striped sea monster. The grimace of pointed teeth didn't help. I was running out of air again, but I knew the chamber had filled and there were no more options.

I panicked and started to think the worst. *This was where I would die. I would never be found. No one would hold a funeral for me. What would it feel like to drown? It would be fast. It only takes a minute or two. My dead corpse would be bloated and swollen, floating next to Ren's tiger body forever. Would those awful bugs get in and nibble on me? That seemed worse than the dying, somehow. Ren could hold his breath longer. He'd watch me die. I wonder how he'd feel about that. Would he regret it? Would he feel guilty? Would he pound against the door himself?*

I fought against the desperation to swim to the top. There was no more top. There was no more air. Frustrated and terrified, I beat my fist against the Seal and felt a slight movement. I beat on it again, harder, and I felt a whoosh. The door finally began to rise, and the Seal fell out. I reached down desperately, just able to grab the ribbon between two fingers as the water spilled out of the door, taking us along with it.

The water dumped us into the next corridor and then slid down through drain holes, leaving the floor sopping and muddy. I gasped and coughed, sucking in deep breaths. I looked at Ren, laughed, and then coughed again. Even gagging, I still laughed.

"Ren," *giggle-cough*, "you look like a," *cough-cough-giggle*, "drowned cat!"

He must not have seen the humor in it. Ren huffed, walked right up next to me, and shook himself like a dog, spraying water and mud all over. His fur stood up everywhere in wet spikes.

I sputtered, "Hey! Thanks a lot! Well, I don't care. It's still funny."

I tried to squeeze all the water out of my clothes, slipped the Seal around my neck, and decided to check the cameras to make sure no water had seeped into the bags. I dumped the soggy contents of the bag onto the floor. The items fell into a muddy puddle that splashed my soaked clothes. Except for the soggy food, everything else looked well contained. Thanks to Mr. Kadam's foresight, all the cameras looked intact. "Well, we can't eat, but other than that, we're good."

I reluctantly got up again. Uncomfortable and soaked, I grumbled for at least the next ten minutes. My boots made squishing noises, and my wet clothes chaffed. "The bright side is that we washed off the bugs and the oil," I murmured.

When the light from the glow tube faded, I pulled a flashlight out of the backpack and shook it. It sloshed wetly inside, but it still worked. We took a few left turns and a right and came upon a long corridor, longer than any of the others had been. Ren and I started making our way through. About halfway along it, Ren stopped, jumped in front of me, and started forcing me to move backward—fast.

"Great! What is it now? Scorpions?"

At that moment, a great rumbling noise shook the tunnel. The sandy ground I had just been standing on collapsed. I scrambled backward as more of the floor crumbled and plunged down into a deep chasm. The quaking stopped suddenly, so I crawled to the edge to look down. Holding my flashlight over the edge didn't help much because I still couldn't see how deep the hole was.

Frustrated, I shrieked out to the hole, "Wonderful! Who do you think I am? Indiana Jones? Well, I think you should know that there ain't no whip in this bag!" I groaned and turned to Ren. Indicating the path across the chasm, I said, "And I suppose *this* direction is where we need to go, right?"

Ren bent his head down and peered into the rift. Then he walked back and forth along the edge, examining the walls and looking at the path that continued on the other side. I plopped down with my back to the wall, pulled out a water bottle from the bag, took a long drink, and shut my eyes.

I felt a warm hand touch mine.

"Are you okay?"

"If you mean am I injured, then the answer is no. If you mean am I 'okay' as in am-I-confident-I'm-still-sane, the answer is still no."

Ren frowned. "We have to find a way to get across the chasm."

"You're certainly welcome to give it a try." I waved him off and went back to drinking my water.

He moved to the edge and peered across, looking speculatively at the distance. Changing back to a tiger, he trotted a few paces back in the direction we had come from, turned, and ran at full speed toward the hole.

"Ren, no!" I screamed.

He leapt, clearing the hole easily, and landed lightly on his front paws. Then he trotted a short distance away and did the same thing to come back. He landed at my feet and changed back to human form.

"Kells, I have an idea."

"Oh, this I've got to hear. I just hope you don't plan on including me in this scheme of yours. Ah. Let me guess. I know. You want to tie a rope to your tail, leap across, tie it off, and then have me pull my body across the rope, right?"

He cocked his head as if considering it, and then shook his head. "No, you don't have the strength to do something like that. Plus, we have no rope and nothing to tie a rope to."

"Right. So what's the plan?"

He held my hands and explained. "What I'm proposing will be much easier. Do you trust me?"

I was going to be sick. "I trust you. It's just—" I looked into his concerned blue eyes and sighed. "Okay, what do I have to do?"

"You saw that I was able to clear the gap pretty well as a tiger, right? So what I need you to do is to stand right at the edge and wait for me. I'll run to the end of the tunnel, build up speed, and leap as a tiger. At the same time, I want you to jump up and grab me around my neck. I'll change to a man in midair so that I can hold onto you, and we'll fall together to the other side."

I snorted noisily and laughed. "You're kidding, right?"

He ignored my skepticism. "We'll have to time it precisely, and you'll have to jump too, in the same direction, because if you don't, I'll just hit you full power and drive us both over the edge."

"You're serious? You seriously want me to do this?"

"Yes, I'm serious. Now stand here while I make a few practice runs."

"Can't we just find another corridor or something?"

"There aren't any. This is the right way."

Reluctantly, I stood near the edge and watched him leap back and forth a few times. Observing the rhythm of his running and jumping, I began to grasp the idea of what he wanted me to do. All too quickly Ren was back in front of me again.

"I can't believe you've talked me into doing this. Are you sure?" I asked.

"Yes, I'm sure. Are you ready?"

"No! Give me a minute to mentally write a last will and testament."

"Kells, it'll be fine."

"Sure it will. Alright, let me take in my surroundings. I want to make sure I can record every minute of this experience in my journal. Of course, that's probably a moot point because I'm assuming that I'm going to die in the jump anyway."

Ren put his hand on my cheek, looked in my eyes, and said fiercely, "Kelsey, trust me. I will *not* let you fall."

I nodded, tightened the shoulder straps of my bag, and moved nervously to the edge of the chasm. Ren changed back into tiger form and ran all the way to the end of the tunnel. He crouched down and then surged forward in a rush of speed. A huge animal was charging, barreling toward me, and all my instincts said to run—run as fast as I could in the other direction. The fear of the chasm behind me dwindled in comparison to being run down by an animal of his size.

I almost shut my eyes in fear, but I pulled myself together at the last possible second, ran two steps, and hurtled my body into the void. Ren took a mighty leap at exactly the same time and I reached out to wrap my arms around his neck.

I desperately began clutching at his fur, sensing myself falling, and then felt arms grab me around my waist. He pulled me tightly to his muscled chest, and we rolled in the air so that he was under me. We hit the dirt floor on the other side of the chasm with a heavy thump that knocked the wind out of me as we bumped and skidded along for a bit on Ren's back.

I sucked a huge breath of air into my collapsed lungs. Once I could breathe again, I examined Ren's back. His white shirt was dirty and torn, and his skin was scratched and bleeding in several places. I took a wet shirt from the bag to clean his scratches, while removing little pieces of gravel embedded in his skin.

When I was finished, I grabbed Ren around the waist in a fierce hug. He wrapped his arms around me and pulled me close. I whispered against his chest quietly but firmly, "Thank you. But don't ever . . . ever . . . *ever* do that again!"

He laughed. "If I get results like this, I surely will do it again."

"You will *not!*"

Ren reluctantly let me go, and I began mumbling, complaining about tigers, men, and bugs. He seemed very pleased with himself for surviving a near-death experience. I could practically hear him chanting to himself: I overcame. I conquered. I'm a man, etc, etc. I smirked. *Men! No matter what century they're from, they're all the same.*

I checked to make sure I had everything I needed and then pulled out my flashlight again. Ren changed back into a tiger and moved in front of me.

We walked down a few more passageways and came upon a door etched with symbols. There was no knob or handle. On the right-hand side, about one third of the way down was a handprint with markings similar to mine. I looked down at my hand and turned it over. The symbols were a mirror image.

"It matches the drawing from Phet!"

I put my hand on the cold, stone door, lined it up with the drawing, and felt a warm tingling. Pulling my hand off, I looked at my palm. The symbols were glowing bright red, but strangely, my hand didn't hurt. I moved it back toward the door and felt the warmth build up again. Electric sparks began popping out between the door and my hand as

I moved closer. It looked like a mini lightning storm was occurring between my hand and the stone, and then I felt the stone move.

The door opened inward, as if pulled by invisible hands, and allowed us to pass. We walked into a large grotto that was glowing dimly from phosphorescent lichen growing on the stone walls. The center of the grotto housed a tall rectangular monolith with a small stone post set in front of it. I dusted off the stone post and saw a set of handprints—a right and a left. The right handprint looked the same as the one on the door, but the left one had the same markings that were on the back of my right hand.

I tried putting both hands on the stone block, but nothing happened. I put my right hand with the backside down on the left handprint. The symbols started glowing red again. Flipping my hand over, I placed it palm down on the right handprint and felt a more than a warm tingle this time. The connection crackled with energy, and heat poured out of my hand and into the stone.

I heard a deep rumbling at the top of the monolith and a wet sucking, slurping noise. Golden liquid spilled over the top of the edifice and poured down the four sides, pooling into a bowl-shaped basin at the bottom. The solution was reacting to something on the stone. The stone hissed and steamed as the liquid foamed, bubbled, and fizzed, eventually dribbling down into the basin.

After the hissing stopped and the steam cleared, I gasped in shock, seeing that glyph engravings had appeared on all four sides of the stone where none had been before.

"I think this is it, Ren. This is Durga's prophecy! This is what we have been looking for!"

I pulled out the digital camera and started taking pictures of the structure. Then I took some more with the disposable camera for good measure. Next, I grabbed the paper and charcoal and made a rubbing of the handprints on the stone and the door. I had to document every-thing so Mr. Kadam could figure out what it all meant.

I wandered around the monolith trying to make out some of the symbols and then heard a yelp from Ren. I saw him pick up his paw carefully and set it down again gingerly. The golden acid was seeping out of the basin in little rivulets and moving across the stone floor, filling in all the cracks. I looked down to see that my shoelace was steaming where it lay in a golden puddle.

We had both just leapt over to the sandy part of the floor when another great rumble shook the maze. Rocks began to fall from the high ceiling. They dropped to the stone floor and shattered into tiny pieces. Ren nudged me back against the wall, where I ducked down, sheltering my head. The shaking became worse, and with a deafening crack, the monolith split in two. It fell with a mighty boom to the floor and broke into large chunks. The golden acid bubbled through the broken basin and started to spread across the floor, slowly destroying the stone and everything else it touched.

Acid crept closer to us until there was no place for us to go. The doorway had been blocked, sealing us in, and there appeared to be no other way out. Ren got up, sniffed the air, and walked a short distance away. Standing up on his hind legs, he put his claws on the wall and started scratching furiously at something.

Approaching him, I saw that he had opened a hole and that there were stars on the other side! I helped him dig and pulled out rocks until the hole was big enough for him to leap through. After he was out, I tossed out my backpack and shimmied my way through until I fell out the other side and rolled across the ground.

At that moment, a huge boulder fell with a thunderous boom, sealing off the hole. The quaking slowed and then stopped. Silence descended in the dark jungle where we stood as a light, powdery dust filtered down from the air and fell gently upon us.

durga's prophecy

I got up slowly, dusted off my arms, and found my flashlight. I felt Ren's hand grasp my shoulder as he spun me around and looked me over.

"Kelsey, are you alright? Did you get hurt?"

"No. I'm fine. So, are we done here? The Cave of Kanheri was fun and all, but I'd like to go home now."

"Yes," Ren agreed. "Let's head back to the car. Stay very close to me. Animals that were sleeping when we came into the jungle are awake and hunting now. We must be careful." He squeezed my shoulder, morphed into tiger form again, and headed into the trees.

It appeared that we were on the far side of the cave, maybe a half mile behind it at the bottom of a steep hill. Ren led me around the hill to the stone steps where we had started so many hours ago.

I was actually happier walking through the jungle at night because I couldn't see all of the scary creatures that I was sure were watching us, but after about an hour and a half, I didn't even care if animals were watching me or not. I was so tired. I could barely keep my eyes open and my feet moving.

Yawning for about the hundredth time, I asked Ren again, "Are we there yet?"

He rumbled softly in a response, and then suddenly stopped, lowered his head, and peered into the darkness.

With eyes fixed on the jungle, Ren turned into a man. "We're being hunted," he whispered. "When I say run, go that way and don't look back . . . run!"

He pointed to my left and dashed into the dark jungle as a tiger. I soon heard an impressive, menacing roar shake the trees. Rousing my tired body, I began to sprint. I had no idea where I was or where I was going, but I tried to keep myself going in the direction he'd pointed. I moved quickly through the jungle for about fifteen minutes before slowing down. Breathing heavily, I stopped and listened to the sounds in the dark.

I heard cats, big cats, fighting. They were about a mile off, but they were loud. Other animals were quiet. They must have been listening to the fight too.

Heavy growls and roars echoed through the jungle. It sounded like more than two animals, and I started worrying about Ren. I walked for another fifteen minutes and listened carefully, trying to pick out Ren's sound from the other animals. All of a sudden, it became deathly quiet.

Did he drive them off? Is he safe? Should I go back and try to help him?

Bats fluttered overhead in the moonlight as I quickly backtracked my steps. I'd gone about a quarter mile in what I hoped was the right direction when I heard a popping, rustling noise in the bushes and saw a pair of yellow eyes stare at me from the darkness.

"Ren? Is that you?"

A shape emerged from the bushes and crouched down, watching me. It wasn't Ren.

A black panther was staring at me boldly, assessing my ability to fight back. I didn't move. I was sure that if I had, he would have sprung immediately. I stood up as tall as I could and tried to look too big to eat.

We watched each other for another minute. Then, the panther

sprung. One moment he was crouching, tail flicking back and forth, and the next he was quickly accelerating toward my face.

The panther's sharp claws were extended and glistened in the moonlight. Transfixed, I stood and watched the snarling cat's claws and gaping maw full of teeth draw closer to my face and neck. I screamed, drew my hands up to protect my head, and waited for claws and teeth to rip my throat out.

I heard a roar and felt a rush of air brush past my face and then . . . nothing. I cracked open my eyes and spun around looking for the panther.

What happened? How could he have missed me?

A flash of white and black rolled through the trees. It was Ren! He'd attacked the panther in mid-flight and pushed him out of my path. The panther growled at Ren and circled him for a moment, but Ren roared back and batted the panther across the face. The panther, not wanting to face a cat more than twice his size, growled again and ran off quickly into the jungle.

Ren's white-and-black shadowy form hobbled through the trees to me. There were bloody scratches all over his back, and his right paw was hurt, maybe broken, causing him to walk with a limp. For just a moment, he turned into a man and fell at my feet, panting. He reached for my hand.

"Are you hurt?" he asked.

I crouched down next to him and hugged his neck tightly, relieved we had both survived.

"I'm fine. Thank you for saving me. I'm so glad you're safe. Will you be able to walk?"

Ren nodded, gave me a weak smile, and returned to his white tiger form. With a lick of his paw, he snuffed and started walking.

"Okay. Then let's go. I'm right behind you."

Another hour of walking and we were back to the Jeep. Too tired to do anything else, we drank about a gallon of water each, folded the back seat down, and climbed in. I fell into a deep sleep with my arm draped over Ren.

The sun rose too quickly the car started to get hot. I woke up drenched in sweat. My entire body was sore and filthy. Ren was exhausted too, and still drowsy, but his scratches didn't look bad. In fact, they were surprisingly almost healed. My tongue was thick and fuzzy, and I had a terrible headache.

I groaned as I sat up. "Ugh, I feel terrible, and I didn't even have to fight panthers. A shower and a soft bed are calling my name. Let's go home."

Reaching into the backpack, I checked each of the cameras and the charcoal rubbings and secured them before I pulled the Jeep out into the morning traffic.

Upon our arrival, Mr. Kadam rushed out the door and began peppering me with questions. I handed him the backpack and walked zombie-like toward the house, mumbling, "Shower. Sleep."

I made my way up the stairs, peeled off my dirty clothes, and stepped into the shower. I almost fell asleep standing under the tepid water as it pounded my back, massaged my aches and pains, and washed away all the dried sweat and mud. Rousing myself to rinse my hair, I somehow managed to get out and blot myself dry. I slipped on my pajamas and fell into bed.

About twelve hours later, I woke up to a covered tray of food and realized I was starving. Mr. Kadam had outdone himself. A stack of fluffy crepes sat next to a plate of sliced bananas, strawberries, and blueberries. Strawberry syrup, a bowl of yogurt, and a mug of hot chocolate accompanied it. I pounced on my midnight snack. I ate every delicious crepe and then took my cocoa onto the balcony. I made a mental note to thank Mr. Kadam for being so wonderful.

It was the middle of the night and cool outside, so I snuggled into a cozy deck chair, wrapped my quilt around me, and sipped the hot cocoa. A breeze blew my hair into my face and when I reached up to push it aside, I realized with dismay that I had been so tired, I'd forgotten to comb it out after my shower. After finding my brush, I headed back to my comfy chair.

Brushing through my hair was usually bad enough after a shower. Letting it dry without brushing it was a terrible mistake. It was full of painful tangles, and I hadn't made much progress when the door at the end of the veranda opened and Ren walked out. I squeaked in alarm and hid behind my hair. *Perfect, Kells.*

He was still barefoot, but had on khaki pants and a sky-blue button-down shirt that matched his eyes. The effect was magnetic, and here I was in flannel pajamas with giant tumbleweed hair.

He sat across from me and said, "Good evening, Kelsey. Did you sleep well?"

"Uh, yes. Did you?"

He grinned a dazzling white smile and nodded his head slightly. "Are you having trouble?" he asked and watched my detangling progress with an amused expression.

"Nope. I've got it all under control."

I wanted to divert his attention away from my hair, so I said, "How's your back and your, um, arm, I guess it would be?"

He smiled. "They're completely fine. Thank you for asking."

"Ren, why aren't you wearing white? That's all I've ever seen you wear. Is it because your white shirt was torn?"

He responded, "No, I just wanted to wear something different. Actually, when I change to a tiger and back, my white clothes reappear. If I changed to a tiger now and then switch back to a man again, my current clothes would be replaced with my old white ones."

"Would they still be torn and bloody?"

"No. When I reappear, they're clean and whole again."

"Hah. Lucky for you. It would be pretty awkward if you ended up naked every time you changed."

I bit my tongue as soon as the words came out and blushed a brilliant shade of red. *Nice, Kells. Way to go.* I covered up my verbal blunder by tugging my hair in front of my face and yanking through the tangles.

He grinned. "Yes. Lucky for me."

I tugged the brush through my hair and winced. "That brings up another question."

Ren rose and took the brush out of my hand.

"What . . . what are you doing?" I stammered.

"Relax. You're too edgy."

He had no idea.

Moving behind me, Ren picked up a section of my hair and started gently brushing through it. I was nervous at first, but his hands in my hair were so warm and soothing that I soon relaxed in the chair, closed my eyes, and leaned my head back.

After a minute of brushing, he pulled a lock away from my neck, leaned down by my ear, and whispered, "What was it you wanted to ask me?"

I jumped.

"Umm . . . what?" I mumbled disconcertingly.

"You wanted to ask me a question."

"Oh, right. It was, uh—that feels nice."

Did I say that out loud?

Ren laughed softly. "That's not a question."

Apparently, I did.

"Was it something about me changing into a tiger?"

"Oh, yes. I remember now. You can change back a forth several times per day, right? Is there a limit?"

"No. There's no limit as long as I don't remain human for more than a total of twenty-four minutes in a twenty-four hour day." He moved on to another section of hair. "Do you have any more questions, *sundari*?"

"Yes . . . about the maze. You were following a scent, but all I could smell was nasty sulfur. Was that what you were following?"

"No. I was actually following a lotus flower scent. It's Durga's favorite flower, the same flower that's on the Seal. I figured that was the right way to go."

Ren finished with my hair, set the brush down, and then began lightly massaging my shoulders. I tensed again, but his hands were so warm and the massage felt so good, I sat back in my seat and started to slowly melt into a puddle.

From a place of utter tranquility, I slurred thickly, saying, "A lotus scent? How could you smell that with all the other noxious odors in there?"

He touched my nose with the tip of his finger. "It's my tiger nose. I can smell lots of things people can't." He squeezed my shoulders one last time and said, "Come on, Kelsey. Get dressed. We have work to do."

Ren circled around to the front of the chair and offered me his hand. I put mine in his and felt tingly, electric sparks shoot down my arm. He grinned and kissed my fingers.

Shocked, I asked, "Did you feel that too?"

The Indian prince winked at me. "Definitely."

Something about the way he said "definitely" made me wonder if we were talking about the same thing.

After I got dressed, I went downstairs to the peacock room, and found Mr. Kadam hunched over a large table stacked with various tomes. Ren, the tiger, was perched beside him on an ottoman.

I dragged another chair over to the table and shoved aside a large stack of books so I could see what Mr. Kadam was working on.

Mr. Kadam rubbed his tired, red eyes.

"Have you been working on this since we got home, Mr. Kadam?"

"Yes. This is fascinating! I've already translated the writing on the paper rubbing that you did, and I am now working on the pictures you took of the monolith." He handed me his notes.

दून्ढना नवदुर्गी पारितोषिकं
Dhundhana   navadurga   Paritoshikam
Seek   Durga's   Prize

चत्वारि भेन्ठा पञ्च बलिदानं देना
Chatvari   bhenta   pancha   balidanam   dena
Four   gifts   five   sacrifices

एक रूपान्तरं
Eka   Rupantaram
One   transformation

पशु भवति (मानुष:) मानुष्य
Pashu   phabana   (bhavati)   manushya
Beast   becomes   mortal

"Wow, you've been very busy!" I commented admiringly. "What do you think 'four gifts' and 'five sacrifices' means?"

"I am not completely sure," Mr. Kadam replied. "But, I think it might mean that your quest isn't over just yet. There may be more tasks that you and Ren need to complete before the spell can be broken. For example, I have finished translating one side of the monolith, and it indicates that you need to go somewhere else to obtain an object, a gift, that you'll give to Durga. You will need to find four gifts. My guess is that there's a different gift mentioned on each wall. I'm afraid you're only at the first step of this journey."

"Okay, so what does the first wall say?"

Mr. Kadam pushed a piece of paper toward me.

> For protection, seek her temple
> And take hold of Durga's blessing.
> Travel west and search Kishkindha
> Where simians rule the ground.
> Gada strike in Hanuman's realm;
> And hunt the branch that's bound.
> Thorny dangers grasp above;
> Dazzling dangers lie below,
> Strangle, ensnare, the ones you love—
> And trap in brackish undertow.
> Lurid phantoms thwart your route
> And guardians wait to bar your way.
> Beware once they begin pursuit
> Or embrace their moldering decay.
> But all of this you can refute
> If serpents find forbidden fruit
> And India's hunger satisfy . . .
> Lest all her people surely die.

"Mr. Kadam, what's Hanuman's realm?"

"I've been researching that," he replied. "Hanuman is the monkey god. His realm is said to be Kishkindha, or the Monkey Kingdom. There is great debate as to where Kishkindha was located, but the current thought is that the ruins of Hampi are most likely to be on, or near, ancient Kishkindha."

From the stack on the table, I pulled out a book that had detailed maps, found Hampi in the index, and thumbed through the pages. It was located in the bottom half of India in the southwestern region.

"Does that mean we have to go to Kishkindha, deal with a monkey god, and find a branch of some sort?"

Mr. Kadam answered, "I believe what you will be seeking is actually the forbidden fruit."

"As in Adam and Eve? Is that the forbidden fruit you're talking about?"

Mr. Kadam considered, "I don't think so. Fruit is a common enough mythological prize, symbolic of life. People need to eat, and we depend upon the fruits of the ground for sustenance. Often, different cultures of the earth celebrate fruit or the harvest in a variety of ways."

"Yes!" I responded. "Americans celebrate the harvest at Thanksgiving and display a cornucopia. Are there any stories in India regarding famous fruits?"

"I'm not sure, Miss Kelsey. The pomegranate is important to many Indian cultures, as well as to the Persians and Romans. I'll have to look more into that, but offhand, there's nothing else I can think of."

Mr. Kadam smiled and put his nose back into his translations.

Picking up a few books on Indian culture and history, I made my way over to a cozy chair and sat down with a lap-pillow to read. Ren hopped off the stool and curled up at my feet, actually, on top of my feet, keeping them toasty while Mr. Kadam continued to research at his desk.

I felt like I was back in my parents' library again. It felt natural to sit relaxing with these two, even though they were affected by unnatural elements. I reached down to scratch Ren behind his ear. He purred contentedly but didn't open his eyes. Then I shot a smile over at Mr. Kadam, even though he didn't see it. I felt happy and complete, as if I belonged. Setting aside my musings, I found a chapter about Hanuman and began to read.

"He is a Hindu god, who is the personification of devotion and great physical strength. He served his lord Rama by going to Lanka to find Rama's wife Sita."

Phew . . . too many names.

"He found that she had been captured by the Lanka king named Ravana. There was a great battle between Rama and Ravana, and, during that time, Rama's brother fell ill. Hanuman went to the Himalayan Mountains to seek an herb to help heal Rama's brother, but he couldn't identify the herb, so, instead, he brought back the entire mountain."

I wonder how he moved the mountain exactly. I hope we don't have to do that.

"Hanuman was made immortal and invincible. He is half-human and half-ape and is faster, quicker, and mightier than all other apes. The son of a wind god, Hanuman is still worshiped today by many Hindus who sing his hymns and celebrate his birth every year."

"Strong ape-man, mountain moving, and singing. Got it," I mumbled sleepily.

It was still the middle of the night, and I was feeling warm and tired despite my long rest earlier. I set my book down and, with Ren still curled at my toes, dozed for a while.

I left Mr. Kadam alone most of the next day, encouraging him to get some sleep. He'd stayed up all night, so I tried to move through the house quietly.

Later that afternoon, he visited me on the terrace. He smiled as we sat down.

"Miss Kelsey, how are you faring? These burdens you're facing must weigh very heavily on you, especially now that we know we have more journeys to take."

"I'm okay, really. What's a little bug juice between friends?"

He smiled, but then his expression became serious again. "If you ever feel pushed too far . . . I just . . . don't want to endanger you. You have become very important to me."

"It's alright, Mr. Kadam. Don't worry. This is what I was born to do, right? Besides, Ren needs my help. If I don't help him, he'll be stuck as a tiger forever."

Mr. Kadam smiled and patted my hand. "You're a very brave and courageous young lady. A finer lady I haven't met in a long, long time. I hope Ren sees how lucky he is."

I blushed and looked out at the pool.

He continued, "From what I have gathered so far, we need to go to Hampi next. That distance is entirely too far for the two of you to go alone. I will accompany you on the journey. We'll leave at first light tomorrow. I want you to rest as much as you can today. You still have a few hours of daylight left. You should relax. Perhaps take a swim. Do something for yourself."

After Mr. Kadam left, I thought about what he'd said. *A swim would be relaxing.*

Changing into a swimsuit, I slathered sunscreen over me as best I could and dove into the cool water.

I swam several laps and then flipped over on my back and looked up at the palm trees. They towered over the pool, and I lazily floated in and out of their shade. The sun had dipped down to tree level, but the air was still warm and pleasant. I heard a noise from the side of the pool and saw Ren lying at the edge watching me swim.

I ducked under the surface, swam up close to where he was, and then popped out of the water.

"Hey, Ren." I splashed him and laughed.

The white tiger just harrumphed at me, blowing out some air.

"Come on. Don't want to play, huh? Okay, suit yourself."

I swam several more laps and finally decided I'd better go in because my fingers had turned into wrinkled prunes. Wrapping a towel around my body and hair, I made my way up the steps to shower. I emerged from the bathroom to see Ren lying on the rug. There was a silvery blue rose on my pillow.

"Is this for me?"

Ren made a tiger noise that seemed to mean yes.

Crushing the flower to my nose, I inhaled the sweet fragrance deeply and flipped over on my stomach to look at the tiger at the side of my bed.

"Thank you, Ren. It's beautiful!" I kissed him on the top of his furry head, scratched him behind the ears, and laughed as he leaned into the scratch. "Would you like me to read you some more *Romeo and Juliet*?"

He lifted a paw and placed it on my leg.

"I guess that means yes. Okay, let's see. Where were we? Ah, Act II, Scene III. Enter Friar Lawrence and then Romeo."

We had just finished the scene when Romeo kills Tybalt when Ren interrupted.

"Romeo was a fool," Ren said, suddenly back in human form. "His big mistake was not announcing the marriage. He should have told both families. Keeping the marriage a secret will ruin Romeo. Secrets like that can be the downfall of any man. They're often more destructive than the sword."

Ren sat there quietly, wrapped in his own thoughts.

I asked softly, "Should I continue?"

He shook off his momentary melancholy and smiled. "Please."

I repositioned myself to sit up against the headboard and pulled a pillow on my lap. He changed back into a tiger and leapt up onto the foot of the bed. He stretched out on his side at the bottom of the huge mattress.

I started reading again. Every time I read something Ren didn't like, he flicked his tail in annoyance.

"Quit twitching, Ren! You're tickling my toes!"

That statement only inspired him to do it more. When I got to the end of the play, I closed the book and peeked at Ren to see if he was still awake. He was, and he'd changed back to a man again. He was still lying on his side at the foot of the bed with his head propped up on his arm.

I asked, "What did you think? Were you surprised at the ending?"

Ren considered his answer. "Yes and no. Romeo made some bad decisions throughout the entire play. He was more worried about himself than his wife. He didn't deserve her."

"Does the ending bother you that much? Most people focus on the romance of it, the tragedy that they could never be together. I'm sorry if you didn't like it."

Ren's thoughtful faced brightened. "On the contrary, I quite enjoyed it. I haven't had someone to talk with about plays or poetry in . . . well, since my parents died. I used to write poetry myself, in fact."

I admitted softly, "Me too. I miss having someone to talk with."

Ren's handsome face lit up in a warm smile, and I suddenly became preoccupied with a string on my sleeve. He hopped off the bed, picked up my hand, and bowed deeply.

"Perhaps I will read some of my poetry to you next time."

He flipped my hand over and pressed a soft, lingering kiss on my palm. His eyes twinkled with mischief. "I leave you with a holy palmer's kiss. Goodnight, Kelsey."

Ren quietly closed the door behind him, and I tugged the covers up to my chin. My palm still tingled where he'd kissed it. I smelled my rose again, smiled, and tucked it into the arrangement on my dresser.

Wiggling under my covers, I sighed dreamily and fell asleep.

waterfall

The next morning I got up and found a half-full backpack by my door with a note from Mr. Kadam. It said that I should pack three or four days' worth of clothes and to include my swimsuit.

The swimsuit, hung overnight, was dry now. I tossed it in my bag, included a towel for good measure, piled the rest of my things on top of that, and made my way downstairs.

Mr. Kadam and Ren were already in the Jeep when I hopped in. As soon as my seatbelt clicked, Mr. Kadam handed me a breakfast bar and a bottle of juice and sped off.

"What's the hurry?" I asked.

He answered, "Ren has added a detour to our trip and would like to stop somewhere on the way. The plan is to drop the two of you off for a few days and then return to pick you up later. After that, we will proceed to Hampi."

"What kind of a detour?"

"Ren would prefer to explain it to you himself."

"Hmm."

From the look on his face, I knew that no matter how I wheedled him, Mr. Kadam would not divulge any details. I decided to set aside my curiosity about the future and focus on the past instead.

"Since we're in for a long drive, why don't you tell me more about yourself, Mr. Kadam? What was your life like growing up?"

"Alright. Let me see. I was born twenty-two years before Ren in June 1635. I was an only child born to a military family of the Kshatriya caste. So, it was natural for me to be trained to enter the military."

"What's a Kshatriya caste?"

"India has four castes, or *varnas*, similar to different social classes: the Brahmins are teachers, priests, and scholars; the Kshatriyas are rulers and protectors; the Vaishyas are farmers and traders; and the Shudras are craft workers and servants. There are also different levels in each caste.

"People of different castes never mingled with one another during any part of their life. Their entire life was lived within their own group. Though officially outlawed for the last fifty years or so, the caste system is still practiced in several parts of the country."

"Was your wife from the same caste as you?"

"It was easier for me to continue my role as a retired soldier who was highly favored by the king, so the answer is yes."

"But was it an arranged marriage? I mean, you loved her, right?"

"Her parents arranged it, but we were happy together for the time allotted to us."

I stared at the road ahead of us for a moment and then glanced at Ren, who was napping in the back.

"Mr. Kadam, does it bother you that I ask so many questions? Don't feel like you have to answer all of them, especially if they're too personal or painful for you."

"I don't mind, Miss Kelsey. I enjoy talking with you." He smiled at me and changed lanes.

"Okay, then. Tell me a little bit about your military career. You must have fought some really interesting battles."

He nodded. "I started training when I was very young. I think I must have started at age four. We never went to school. As future military men, our entire young lives were devoted to being good soldiers, and all of our studies were in the art of warfare. There were dozens, perhaps even a hundred different kingdoms in India at the time. I was fortunate to live in one of the most powerful ones under a good king."

"What kinds of weapons did you use?"

"I was trained in all variety of weapons, but the first skill we were taught was hand-to-hand combat. Have you ever seen martial arts movies?"

"If you mean like Jet Li and Jackie Chan, then yes."

He nodded. "Fighters who were skilled in hand-to-hand combat were highly sought after. As a young man, I rose in rank quickly because of my skill in this area. No one was able to best me in sparring matches. Well, almost no one. Ren has beaten me on occasion."

I looked at him with surprise. "Mr. Kadam! Are you telling me you are a master of karate?"

"Something like that." He smiled. "I was never as good as the cele-brated masters who came to train us, but I picked up enough. I enjoy sparring, but my great skill is with the sword."

"I've always wanted to learn karate."

"During that time, we didn't call it karate. The martial arts that we used during warfare was less visually exciting. It emphasized overcoming your opponent as quickly as possible which often meant killing or striking a blow that would knock someone out long enough for you to escape. It wasn't as structured as you see it today."

"Gotcha, no *Karate Kid I*, skip ahead to *Karate Kid II*. Fights to the death it is. So, you and Ren are both trained in martial arts."

He smiled. "Yes, and he was very adept. As the future king, he studied the sciences, crafts, the arts, and philosophy, as well as many

other branches of knowledge known as the sixty-four arts. He was also trained in all manner of warfare, including the martial arts.

"Ren's mother was also well versed in the martial arts. She had been taught in Asia and insisted that her children be able to protect themselves. Experts were brought in, and our kingdom quickly became renowned for fighting in that medium."

For a minute, I allowed myself to get lost in the visual image of Ren doing martial arts. *Fighting without his shirt on. Bronze skin. Taut muscles.* I shook my head and berated myself. *Snap out of it, girl!*

I cleared my throat, "Umm, so what were you saying?"

"Chariots . . ." Mr. Kadam continued, not even noticing my brief lack of attention. "Most of the soldiers were in the infantry, and that's the area in which I started. I was trained in the use of the sword, the spear, the mace, as well as many other weapons before I moved on to chariots. By the age of twenty-five, I was in charge of the king's army. By the age of thirty-five, my job was to teach others, including Ren, and I was called to be the king's special military advisor and war strategist, particularly in the use of battle elephants."

"It's hard to imagine elephants in war. They seem so gentle," I reflected.

"Elephants were quite formidable in battle," Mr. Kadam explained. "They were heavily armored and carried an enclosed structure on their backs to protect archers. Sometimes we secured long daggers dipped in poison to their tusks which proved very effective in a direct assault. Just imagine facing an army with twenty thousand armored elephants. I don't believe we have that many elephants left in all of India now."

I could almost feel the ground shaking underfoot as I visualized thousands of battle-ready elephants descending on an army.

"How awful for you to have to be a part of all that bloodshed and destruction, and to think that was your whole life. War is a terrible thing."

Mr. Kadam shrugged. "War was different then than it is today. We followed a warrior's code, similar to Europe's code of chivalry. We had four rules. Rule One: You must fight with someone who has similar armor. We wouldn't fight a man who did not have the same amount of protective gear. This is similar to the concept of not using a weapon against an unarmed man."

He raised a second finger. "Rule Two: If your enemy can't fight any longer, the battle is over. If you've disabled your opponent and rendered him helpless, you must stop fighting. You *don't* finish him off.

"Rule Three: Soldiers do not kill women, children, the aged, or the infirm, and we do not injure those who surrender.

"And Rule Four: We do not destroy gardens, temples, or other places of worship."

"Those sound like pretty good rules," I commented.

"Our king followed Kshatriadharma, or the Law of Kings, which means that we could only fight in battles that were considered just, or righteous, and that had the approval of the people."

We both fell silent for a while. Mr. Kadam seemed wrapped in thoughts about his past, and I tried to understand the time he lived in. As he smoothly switched lanes again, I was impressed with his ease at driving in heavy traffic while he was so quietly reflective. The streets were crowded, and the drivers were zipping past at frightening speeds, but that didn't seem to leave any impression on Mr. Kadam.

Later, he turned to me and said, "I've made you sad, Miss Kelsey. I apologize. I didn't mean to upset you."

"I'm just sad that you had so much warfare in your life and that you missed out on so many other things."

Mr. Kadam looked at me and smiled. "Don't be sad. Remember that it was just one small part of my life. I have been able to see and experience more things than would normally have been possible for any man. I have seen the world change century after century. I have witnessed many terrible things, as well as many wonderful things. Also, remember that, even though I was a military man, we weren't constantly at war. Our kingdom was large and reputable. Though we trained for battle, we engaged in serious warfare only perhaps a handful of times."

"Sometimes I forget how long you and Ren have been alive. Not that I'm saying you're old or anything."

Mr. Kadam chuckled. "Indeed not."

I nodded and picked up a book to study more about Hanuman. It was fascinating to read the stories surrounding the monkey god. I was so immersed in my study that I was surprised when Mr. Kadam pulled over.

We grabbed a quick lunch, during which Mr. Kadam encouraged me to try some different types of curry. I discovered that I was not much of a curry fan, and he chuckled as I made faces at the spicy ones. I loved the naan bread though.

As we settled back into the car, I pulled out a copy of Durga's prophecy and began reading. *Snakes. That can't be a good thing. I wonder what type of protection or blessing Durga would give us.*

"Mr. Kadam, is there a temple of Durga near the ruins of Hampi?"

"Excellent question, Miss Kelsey. I had the same thought myself. Yes, there are temples to honor Durga in almost every city in India. She is a very popular goddess. I have found a temple near Hampi that we will visit. Hopefully, we'll find our next clue to the puzzle there."

"Hmm."

I went back to my study of the prophecy. *Mr. Kadam had said a gada was like a mace, or a club, so that means it's a weapon. Hanuman's realm. That means the ruins of Hampi, or Kishkindha. And then hunt the branch that's bound. Maybe it's the branch that holds the fruit. Thorny dangers and dazzling dangers? The thorns could be rose bushes or thorny vines maybe.*

"Mr. Kadam, any idea what dazzling dangers might be?"

"No. Sorry, Miss Kelsey, I can't think of anything. I've also been

pondering, 'Lurid phantoms thwart your route.' I've found no information on this, which makes me think we might have to interpret it literally. There might be spirits of some kind that try to stop you."

I gulped. "And what about the uh, serpents?"

"There are many dangerous serpents in India—the cobra, the boa, the python, water snakes, vipers, king cobras, and even some that fly."

That didn't sound good at all. "What do you mean fly?"

"Well, technically, they don't really fly. They just glide to other trees, like the flying squirrel."

I sank lower in my seat and frowned. "What an exceptional variety of poisonous reptiles you have here."

Mr. Kadam laughed. "Yes, we do indeed. It's something we've learned to live with, but, in this case, it sounds like the snake or snakes will be helpful."

I read the line again: *If serpents find forbidden fruit, and India's hunger satisfy . . . lest all her people surely die.*

"Do you think that what we do could somehow affect all of India?"

"I'm not sure. I hope not. Despite my centuries of study, I know very little about this curse or the Damon Amulet. It has great power, but as to how it could affect India, I haven't figured that out yet."

I had a slight headache, so I leaned my head back and closed my eyes. The next thing I knew, Mr. Kadam was nudging me awake.

"We're here, Miss Kelsey."

I rubbed my sleepy eyes. "Where?"

"We're at the place where Ren wanted to stop."

"Mr. Kadam, we're in the middle of nowhere surrounded by jungle."

"I know. Don't be afraid. You'll be safe. Ren will protect you."

"Why do those words always precede me wandering in the jungle with a tiger?"

He laughed lightly, grabbed my bag, and walked around to my door to open it for me.

I stepped out and looked up at him. "I'll have to sleep in the jungle again, won't I? Are you sure I can't go with you while he gets whatever it is he needs?"

"I'm sorry, Miss Kelsey, but in this case he will need you. It's something he can't do without you and may not even be able to do with you."

I groaned, "Right. And, you, of course, can't tell me what it is."

"It's not for me to tell. This is his story to share."

I muttered, "Fine. And you'll be back to pick us up when?"

"I will go into town and purchase a few items. Then I'll meet you back here in about three or four days. I may end up having to wait for you. He might not be able to find what he is searching for on the first couple of nights."

I sighed and glared at Ren. "Great. More jungle. Okay, let's get on with it. Please lead the way."

Mr. Kadam handed me a bottle of bug spray with sunscreen, placed some items in my backpack, and helped fit it onto my shoulders. I sighed deeply as I watched him pull away in the Jeep. Then I turned to follow Ren off into the jungle.

"Hey, Ren. How come I always have to follow you into a jungle? How about next time you follow me to a nice spa or maybe to the beach? How about that?"

He snuffed and kept on moving.

"Fine, but you owe me after this."

We walked the rest of the afternoon.

Later, I heard a rumbling noise ahead of us but couldn't figure out what it was. The farther we walked, the louder the noise grew. We walked through a grove of trees and into a small clearing. Finally, I saw the source of the sound. It was a beautiful waterfall.

A series of gray stones were spread out like steps onto a tall hill. The water foamed and flowed over each stone, plummeted down, and spread out like a fan falling to a wide turquoise pool below. Trees and small bushes with petite red flowers surrounded the pool. It was lovely.

As I approached one of the bushes, I noticed it looked like it was moving. At my next step, hundreds of butterflies took to the air. There were two varieties: one was brown with cream-colored stripes and the other was brownish-black with blue stripes and dots. I laughed and twirled around in a cloud of butterflies. When they settled again, several landed on my arms and my shirt.

I climbed a rock that looked out over the falls and studied a butterfly perched on my finger. When it flew off, I stood quietly watching the water tumble down. Then I heard a voice behind me.

"It's beautiful, isn't it? It's my favorite place in the entire world."

"It is. I've never seen anything like it."

Ren came up to me and nudged a butterfly from my arm to his finger. "These are called crow butterflies, and the others are blue tigers. The blue tigers are brighter and easier to spot, so they live with the crows for camouflage."

"Camouflage? Why do they need it?"

"The crows are inedible. In fact, they're poisonous, so other butter-flies try to mimic them to fool predators."

He took my hand and guided me a little way along a path by the falls. "We'll make camp here. Go ahead and sit down. I have something I need to tell you."

I found a flat place and set down the backpack. I pulled out a bottle of water and settled myself against a rock. "Okay, go ahead."

Ren began pacing back and forth and started speaking. "The reason we're here is because I need to find my brother."

I choked on my mouthful of water. "Your brother? I assumed he was dead. You haven't mentioned him at all, except that he was cursed with you. You mean he's still alive and lives here?"

"To be honest with you, I don't know if he's still alive or not. I assume he is because I am. Mr. Kadam believes that he still lives here in this jungle."

He turned and looked at the waterfall, and then sat down next to me, stretched out his long legs, and picked up my hand. He toyed with my fingers as he spoke, "I believe he's still alive. It's just a feeling I have. My plan is to search the area in ever-widening circles. Eventually, one of us will cross the other's scent. If he doesn't show up or if I can't catch his scent in a few days, we'll go back, find Mr. Kadam, and continue our journey."

"What do you need me to do?"

"Wait here. I'm hoping that if he won't listen to me, meeting you might convince him. Also, I hope that—"

"Hope what?"

He shook his head. "It's not important now." He squeezed my hand distractedly and jumped up. "Let me help you set up camp quickly before I begin my search."

Ren went off to look for firewood while I unrolled a small easy-to-set-up two-person tent strapped to the outside of the backpack. *Thank you, Mr. Kadam!* I zipped open the tent bag and spread it out on a patch of even ground. After a few minutes, Ren came over to help me. He already had a fire going and had a nice stack of wood to keep it ablaze.

"That was fast," I muttered jealously as I stretched the tent fabric over a hook.

He popped his head over the other side and grinned. "I was trained extensively on how to live outdoors."

"I guess."

He laughed. "Kells, there are many things that you know how to do that I don't. Like setting up this tent apparently."

I smiled. "Pull the fabric down over the hook on the stake."

We finished up quickly, and he dusted off his hands.

"We didn't have tents like these three hundred years ago. They look similar, but these are much more complicated. We just used wooden poles."

He walked up to me, tugged on my braid, and impulsively kissed my forehead. "Keep the fire going. It scares wild animals away. I'm going to circle the area a few times, but I'll be back before it gets dark."

Ren bounded off into the jungle as a tiger again. I tugged on my braid, thought about him for a minute, and smiled.

While I waited for him to come back, I looked through my backpack to see what Mr. Kadam had provided for dinner. *Ah, he outdid himself again—freeze-dried chicken and rice with chocolate pudding for dessert.* I poured some water from my bottle into a little pot and set it on a flat rock that I had pushed into the coals. When the water bubbled, I used a T-shirt as a pot holder and transferred the hot water to my dinner pouch. I waited several minutes for it to reconstitute, and then enjoyed my meal, which wasn't half bad actually. It sure was tastier than Sarah's tofu turkey at Thanksgiving.

The sky started to darken, and I decided I'd feel safer in my tent, so I climbed in and folded my quilt up to use as a pillow.

Ren returned shortly after that, and I heard him place more wood on the fire. He said, "No sign of him yet." Then he changed back to a tiger and settled himself at the tent opening.

I unzipped the tent and asked him if he would mind me using his back as a pillow again. He moved and stretched out as an answer. I scooted closer, laid my head on his soft fur, and wrapped my quilt around me. His chest rumbled rhythmically in a deep purr, which helped me to fall asleep.

Ren was gone when I awoke and returned around lunchtime as I was brushing out my hair.

"Here, Kells. I brought you something," he said unassumingly and held out three mangos.

"Thanks. Uh, dare I ask where you got them?"

"Monkeys."

I stopped in mid-brush. "Monkeys? What do you mean monkeys?"

"Well, monkeys don't like tigers because tigers eat monkeys. So, when a tiger comes around, they jump up in the trees and pummel the tiger with fruit or feces. Lucky for me today they threw fruit."

I gulped. "Have you ever . . . *eaten* a monkey?"

Ren grinned at me. "Well, a tiger does have to eat."

I dug a rubber band out of the backpack so I could braid my hair. "Ugh, that's disgusting."

He laughed. "I didn't really eat a monkey, Kells. I'm just teasing you. Monkeys are repellant. They taste like meaty tennis balls and they smell like feet." He paused, "Now a nice juicy deer, *that* is delectable." He smacked his lips together in an exaggerated way.

"I don't think I really need to hear about your hunting."

"Really? I quite enjoy hunting."

Ren froze into place. Then, almost imperceptibly, he lowered his body slowly to a crouch and balanced on the balls of his feet. He placed a hand in the grass in front of him and began to creep closer to me. He was tracking me, hunting me. His eyes locked on mine and pinned me to the spot where I was standing. He was preparing to spring. His lips were pulled back in a wide grin, which showed his brilliant white teeth. He looked . . . feral.

He spoke in a silky, mesmerizing voice, "When you're stalking your prey, you must freeze in place and hide, remaining that way for a long time. If you fail, your prey eludes you." He closed the distance between us in a heartbeat.

Even though I'd been watching him closely, I was startled at how

fast he could move. My pulse started thumping wildly at my throat, which was where his lips now hovered as if he were going for my jugular.

He brushed my hair back and moved up to my ear, whispering, "And you will go . . . hungry." His words were hushed. His warm breath tickled my ear and made goose bumps fan out over my body.

I turned my head slightly to look at him. His eyes had changed. They were a brighter blue than normal and were studying my face. His hand was still in my hair, and his eyes drifted down to my mouth. I suddenly had the distinct impression that this was what it felt like to be a deer.

Ren was making me nervous. I blinked and swallowed dryly. His eyes darted back up to mine again. He must have sensed my apprehension because his expression changed. He removed his hand from my hair and relaxed his posture.

"I'm sorry if I frightened you, Kelsey. It won't happen again."

When he took a step back, I started breathing again. I said shakily, "Well, I don't want to hear any more about hunting. It freaks me out. The least you could do is not tell me about it. Especially when I have to spend time with you outdoors, okay?"

He laughed. "Kelsey, we all have some animalistic tendencies. I loved hunting, even when I was young."

I shuddered. "Fine. Just keep your animalistic tendencies to yourself."

He leaned toward me again and pulled on a strand of my hair. "Now, Kells, there *are* some of my animalistic tendencies that you seem to like." He started making a rumbling sound in his chest, and I realized that he was *purring*.

"Stop that!" I sputtered.

He laughed, walked over to the backpack, and picked up the fruit. "So, do you want any of this mango or not? I'll wash it for you."

"Well, considering you carried it in your mouth all that way just for me. And taking into account the source of said fruit. Not really."

His shoulders fell, and I hurried to add, "But I guess I *could* eat some of the inside."

He looked up at me and smiled. "It's not freeze-dried."

"Okay. I'll try some."

He washed the fruit, peeled off the outside with a knife from the backpack, and sliced off segments for me. We sat next to each other and enjoyed the fruit. It was juicy and delicious, but I wouldn't give him the satisfaction of knowing how much I liked it.

"Ren?" I licked the juice from my fingers and took another piece.

"Yes?"

"Is it safe to swim by the waterfall?

"Sure. It should be safe enough. This place used to very special to me. I came here all the time to escape the pressures of palace life and to have time to be alone and think."

He looked at me. "In fact, you're the first person I've ever shown it to, other than my family and Mr. Kadam, of course."

I looked at the beautiful waterfall and began to speak quietly, "There are dozens of waterfalls in Oregon. My family used to take picnics by them. I think we saw most of the falls in the state. I remember standing close to one watching it with my dad while the cloud of spray slowly soaked us."

"Did any of them look like this one?"

I smiled. "Nope. This one's unique. My favorite time to visit was in the winter, actually."

"I've never seen a waterfall in the winter."

"It's beautiful. The water freezes as it falls down the craggy mountains. The smooth rocks around the falls become slick with ice, and, as more water pours over them, icicles start to grow. The spiky ice slowly swells

and lengthens as it creeps down the hill, stretching and crackling and breaking until the icy tips touch the water below in long, thick, twisted ropes. The water that's still moving seeps, dribbling over the icicles slowly and glazing it in shiny layers. In Oregon, the surrounding hills are lush with evergreens, and are sometimes tipped with snow."

He didn't respond.

"Ren?" I turned to see if he was still paying attention, and I found him studying me intently.

A slow, lazy smile lit his face. "That sounds very beautiful."

I blushed and quickly looked away.

He deliberately cleared his throat. "It sounds amazing, but cold. The water here doesn't freeze." He took my hand and laced our fingers together. "Kelsey, I'm sorry your parents are gone."

"Me too. Thanks for sharing your waterfall with me. My parents would have loved it here." I smiled at him and then jerked my head toward the jungle. "If you don't mind, I'd like a bit of privacy so I can change into my swimsuit."

He stood and bowed to me dramatically. "Never let it be said that Prince Alagan Dhiren Rajaram denied the request of a beautiful lady." He washed his sticky hands in the pool, changed to a tiger, and trotted off into the jungle.

I gave Ren some time to move off, slipped on my swimsuit, and dove into the water.

It was crystal clear, and it quickly cooled my hot, sweaty skin. It felt delicious. After swimming and exploring in the pond, I swam to the falls and found a rock to sit on just under the spray. I let the water pound over my body in icy cold blasts. Later, I scooted over to the sunny side of the rock and folded my legs up out of the water. Pulling my wet hair over my shoulder, I let the sun warm me.

I felt like a mermaid looking over her tranquil domain. It was so

peaceful and pleasant here. With the blue water, the green trees, and the butterflies fluttering here and there, it was like a scene right out of *A Midsummer Night's Dream*. I could even picture the fairies flitting from flower to flower.

Just then, Ren galloped out of the jungle and took a flying leap. All five hundred pounds of his white tiger body landed with a splat right in the middle of the pool, sending rippling waves over to lap against my rock.

"Hey," I said when he surfaced, "I thought tigers hated the water."

He paddled over to me and swam around in circles, showing me that tigers did know how to swim. Darting his big head under the falls, he swam behind them and over to my rock. Pulling himself up behind me, he violently shook out his fur like a dog. Water sprayed in every direction, including all over me.

"Hey, I was drying off!"

I slid back into the water and swam out to the center of the pool. He jumped in again too, and paddled around me in circles while I splashed him, laughing. He dove under me and stayed underwater for a long time. Finally, he surfaced, leapt on top of a rock, and jumped into the air to belly flop into the water right next to me. We played in the water until I started to get tired. Then I swam back over to the falls again and stood in the stream with my arms raised, letting the water fall all around me.

I heard a pop and a thump from above. A few rocks fell down in the water right next to me with a plop and a splash. As I quickly moved out of the falls, a rock thumped me on the back of my head. My eyelids fluttered and closed as my body slumped into the cool water.

tiger, tiger

Kelsey! *Kelsey!* Open your eyes!"

Someone was shaking me. Hard. All I wanted to do was fall back into the black peaceful sleep, but the voice was desperate, insistent.

"Kelsey, listen to me! Open your eyes, *please!*"

I tried to crack open my eyes, but it hurt. The sunlight was making the painful pounding in my head worse. *What an awful headache!* My mind finally started to clear, and I recognized our campground and Ren, who was kneeling next to me. His wet hair was slicked back, and he had an expression of concern on his beautiful face.

"Kells, how do you feel? Are you okay?"

I intended to answer him with a really good sarcastic retort, but, instead, I choked and began coughing up water. I inhaled a deep breath, heard a crackly wetness in my lungs, and began coughing some more.

"Turn on your side. It helps to get the water out. Here, let me help you."

He pulled me toward him so that I was resting on my side. I coughed up some more water. He took off his wet shirt and folded it. Then he gently lifted me and placed it under my sore head, which hurt too much to appreciate his . . . bronzed . . . sculpted . . . muscular . . . bare chest.

Well, I guess I must be okay if I can appreciate the view, I thought. *Sheesh, I'd have to be dead not to appreciate it.*

I winced as Ren's hand brushed against my head, shaking me from my reverie.

"You've got a major bump here."

I reached up to feel the giant lump on the back of my skull. I gingerly touched it and recalled the source of my headache. *I must have lost consciousness when the rock hit me. Ren saved my life. Again.*

I looked up at him. He was kneeling next to me with a look of desperation on his face, and his body was shaking. I realized that he must have changed to a man, dragged me out of the pool, and then remained by my side until I woke up. *Who knows how long I've been laying here unconscious.*

"Ren, you're in pain. You've been in this form too long today."

He shook his head in denial, but I saw him grit his teeth.

I pressed my hand on his arm. "I'll be okay. It's just a bump on the head. Don't worry about me. I'm sure Mr. Kadam has some aspirin tucked away in the backpack. I'll just take that and lie down to rest for a while. It'll be alright."

He trailed his finger slowly from my temple to my cheek and smiled softly. When he pulled back, his whole arm shook and tremors rippled under the surface of his skin. "Kells, I—"

His face tightened. He threw his head to the side, snarled angrily, and morphed to a tiger again. He softly growled, then quieted, and drew close beside me. He lay down next to me and watched me carefully with his alert blue eyes. I stroked his back, partly to reassure him and partly because it soothed me too.

I stared up through the dappled trees and willed my headache to subside. I knew that I would have to move eventually, but I really didn't want to. He purred softly, and the comforting sound actually

helped my headache. Sighing deeply, I got up, knowing that I'd be more comfortable if I changed my clothes.

I sat up delicately, slowly, while breathing deeply, hoping that by moving cautiously the nausea would dissipate and the world would stop spinning. Ren lifted his head, alert to my efforts.

"Thank you for saving me," I whispered as I stroked his back. I kissed the top of his furry head. "What would I do without you?"

Zipping open the backpack, I found a small box that contained a variety of medications, including aspirin. I popped a couple in my mouth and swallowed a mouthful of the bottled water. Pulling out my dry clothes, I turned to Ren. "Okay, here's the deal. I'd like to change back into my regular clothes, so if you would head off into the jungle again for a few minutes, I would appreciate it."

He growled at me, sounding a bit angry.

"I'm serious."

He growled louder.

I rested my palm against my forehead and held on to a nearby tree to steady my wobbly legs. "I need to change, and you are *not* staying here to watch me."

He huffed, stood, and growled softly like he was saying no, and stared me down. I stared right back and pointed to the jungle. He finally turned around, but then he padded into the tent and lay down on my quilt. His head faced inward while his tail twitched back and forth outside the opening.

I sighed and winced after turning my head too quickly. "I guess that's the best I'm going to get out of you, isn't it? Stubborn tiger." I decided that I could live with his compromise, but I kept an eye on his flicking tail as I changed my clothes.

I felt a little better for having on dry clothes. The aspirin had started working, and my head throbbed less, but it was still tender. I decided that I'd rather sleep than eat, so I skipped dinner but opted for hot cocoa.

Carefully making my way around our campsite, I added a couple of logs in the fire pit and put the water on to boil. Crouching down, I worked the fire for a while with a long branch to get it crackling again and got out a packet of hot chocolate mix. Ren watched every move I made.

I dismissed him. "I'm fine. Really. Go off on one of your scouting trips or whatever."

Ren just sat there stubbornly, twitching his tiger tail.

"I'm serious." I spun my finger in a circle. "Go circle the grounds. Look for your brother. I'll just gather some firewood and go to bed."

He still wouldn't move and made a noise that sounded slightly like a whining dog. I laughed and petted his head.

"You know, despite appearances, I'm usually pretty good at taking care of myself."

The tiger harrumphed and sat beside me. I leaned against his shoulder while mixing my hot chocolate.

Before the sun set, I gathered wood and drank a bottle of water. When I crawled into my tent, Ren followed me. He stretched out his paws, and I carefully positioned my head on them to cushion it. I heard a deep tiger sigh, and he settled his head next to mine. When I woke up the next morning, my head was still cushioned on Ren's soft paws, but I'd turned, buried my face in his chest, and had thrown my arm around his neck, cuddling him close like he was a giant stuffed animal.

I pulled away a little awkwardly. As I got up to stretch, I cautiously felt my lump and was happy to find it greatly reduced. I felt much better.

Famished, I broke out some granola bars and a package of oatmeal. I heated enough water over the fire again to pour into my oatmeal and make another cup of hot chocolate. After breakfast, I told Ren to head off on patrol and that I was going to wash my hair.

He waited for a while, watching my movements until he felt reassured, then took off, and left me to fend for myself. I grabbed a small bottle of biodegradable shampoo that Mr. Kadam had included for me; the soap smelled like strawberries. He'd even included conditioner.

Changing into my swimsuit, shorts, and sneakers, I hiked down to my sunning rock. Staying on the edge of the falls, well away from the place I'd been hit by falling rocks, I gently wet and soaped my hair. Leaning slightly into the sparkling water, I let it softly rinse out the bubbles. The cool water felt good on my sore head.

Moving over to the sunny side of the rock, I sat down to brush my hair. When I was done, I closed my eyes and turned my face toward the early morning sun, letting it warm me as my hair dried. This place was a paradise, no question about it. Even with a bump on the head and my dislike of camping, I could appreciate the beauty of my surroundings.

It was not that I didn't appreciate nature. In fact, I liked spending time outdoors with my parents when I was growing up. It was just that I always enjoyed sleeping in my own bed *after* appreciating nature.

Ren came back around midday and sat by me companionably while we ate our freeze-dried lunches. It was the only time I'd ever seen him eat as a man other than the mango fruit. Afterward, I rooted around in my bag for my book of poetry. I asked Ren if he'd like me to read to him.

He'd changed back into a tiger, and I didn't hear a growl or another type of tiger protest, so I grabbed my book of poetry and sat down with my back resting against a big rock. He padded over next to me and surprised me by morphing into a man. He flipped onto his back and laid his head in my lap before I could get a word in. Then he sighed deeply and closed his eyes.

I laughed and said, "I guess that means yes?"

Keeping his eyes closed, he mumbled, "Yes, please."

I flipped through my book to pick a poem to read. "Ah, this one seems appropriate. I think you'll like it. It's one of my favorites, and it's also written by Shakespeare, the same guy who wrote *Romeo and Juliet*."

I began reading and held the book with one hand while absent-mindedly stroking Ren's hair with the other.

SHALL I COMPARE THEE TO A SUMMER'S DAY?
by William Shakespeare

Shall I compare thee to a summer's day?
Thou art more lovely and more temperate.
Rough winds do shake the darling buds of May,
And summer's lease hath all too short a date.
Sometime too hot the eye of heaven shines,
And often is his gold complexion dimm'd;
And every fair from fair sometime declines,
By chance or nature's changing course untrimm'd;
But thy eternal summer shall not fade
Nor lose possession of that fair thou ow'st;
Nor shall Death brag thou wander'st in his shade,
When in eternal lines to time thou grow'st:
So long as men can breathe or eyes can see,
So long lives this, and this gives life to thee.

His voice was soft. "That was . . . excellent. I like this Shakespeare."

"Me too."

I was thumbing through the poetry book searching for another poem when Ren said, "Kelsey, perhaps I could share a poem of my country . . . with you."

Surprised, I set my book down. "Sure, I'd love to hear some Indian poetry."

He opened his eyes and stared up at the trees overhead. Capturing my hand, he twined my fingers through his and rested our hands on his chest. A slight breeze was blowing. It caused the leaves to dance and twist in the sun, weaving shadows and sunlight across his handsome face.

"This is an old poem of India. It's taken from an epic story that's been told for as long as I can remember. It's called the *Sakuntala* by Kalidasa."

> *Thy heart, indeed, I know not:*
> *but mine, oh! cruel, love*
> *warms by day and by night;*
> *and all my faculties are centered on thee.*
> *Thee, O slender maid,*
> *love only warms;*
> *but me he burns;*
> *as the day-star only stifles the fragrance of the night-flower,*
> *but quenches the very orb of the moon.*
> *This heart of mine,*
> *oh thou who art of all things the dearest to it,*
> *will have no object but thee.*

"Ren, that was very beautiful."

His eyes turned to my face. He smiled and reached a hand up to touch my cheek. My pulse quickened, and my face felt hot where he touched it. I became suddenly aware that my fingers were still twined in his hair, and my hand was resting on his chest. I quickly removed them and twisted them in my lap. He sat up slightly, leaning on one hand, which brought his beautiful face very close to mine. His fingers moved down to my chin and, with the lightest touch, he tilted my face so that my eyes met his intense blue ones.

"Kelsey?"

"Yes?" I whispered.

"I would like permission . . . to kiss you."

Whoa. Red alert! The comfortable feeling I was enjoying with my tiger just a few minutes before had disappeared. I became acutely nervous and prickly. My perspective swung 180 degrees. I was, of course, aware that a man's heart beat inside the tiger's body, but, somehow, I'd shifted that knowledge to the back of my mind.

Awareness of the prince burst into my conscious mind. I stared at him, astonished. He was, well, to be blunt, he was out of my league. I'd never even considered the possibility of a relationship with him, other than friendship.

His question forced me to acknowledge that my comfortable pet tiger was actually a virile, robust example of masculinity. My heart started hammering against my ribcage. Several thoughts went through my head all at once, but the dominant thought was that I would very much *like* to be kissed by Ren.

Other thoughts were creeping around at the edge of my consciousness too, trying to wiggle into the forefront. Thoughts like—*it's too soon—we barely know each other—and maybe he's just lonely*—spun through my mind. But, I clipped the threads of those thoughts and let them blow away. Stomping down on caution, I decided that I did want him to kiss me.

Ren moved just a smidgen closer to me. I closed my eyes, took a deep breath, and then . . . waited. When I opened my eyes, he was still staring at me. He really was waiting for permission. There was nothing, and I mean nothing I wanted more in the world at that moment than to be kissed by this gorgeous man. But, I ruined it. For some reason, I fixated on the word *permission*.

I nervously rambled, "What . . . umm . . . what do you mean you want my *permission*?"

He looked at me curiously, which made me feel even more panicky. To say I had no experience with kissing would be an understatement. Not only had I never kissed a boy before, I'd never even met a guy I *wanted* to kiss until Ren. So, instead of kissing him like I wanted to, I got flustered and started coming up with reasons to not do it.

I babbled, "Girls need to be swept off their feet, and asking permission is just . . . just . . . old-fashioned. It's not spontaneous enough. It doesn't scream passion. It screams old fogy. If you have to ask, then the answer is . . . no."

What an idiot! I thought to myself. *I just told this beautiful, kind, blue-eyed, hunk of a prince that he was an old fogy.*

Ren looked at me for a long moment, long enough for me to see the hurt in his eyes before he cleared his face of expression. He stood up quickly, formally bowed to me, and avowed softly, "I won't ask you again, Kelsey. I apologize for being so forward."

Then he changed into a tiger and quickly ran off into the jungle, leaving me alone to berate myself for my foolishness.

I shouted, "Ren, wait!" But it was too late. He was gone.

I can't believe I insulted him like that! He must hate me! How could I do that to him? I knew I only said those things because I was nervous, but that was no excuse. *What did he mean he would* never *ask me again? I* hope *he asks me again.*

I replayed my words over and over again in my mind and thought of all the things I could have said that would have given me a better result. Things like, "I thought you'd never ask" or "I was just about to ask you the same question."

I could have just grabbed the man and kissed *him* first. Even just a simple "Yes" would have done the trick. I could have said dramatically, "As you wish," "Kiss me. Kiss me as if it were the last time," or "You had me at hello." He'd never seen the movies, so why not? But, no. I had to go on and on about "permission."

Ren left me alone the rest of the day, which gave me plenty of time to kick myself.

Late in the afternoon, I was sitting on my sunning rock with my journal open, pen in hand, staring into space, utterly miserable, when I heard a noise in the jungle near our camp.

I gasped in shock as a large black cat emerged from the trees. It circled the tent and stopped to smell my quilt. Then it walked to the fire and sat there for a moment not afraid of it at all. After a few minutes, it loped off into the trees, only to come back into the clearing from the other side. I sat still, hoping it hadn't seen me.

It was much larger than the panther that had attacked me near the Cave of Kenhari. In fact, as it came closer to where I was sitting, I made out jet-black stripes on a dark, sable coat of fur. Bright, golden eyes scanned the camp, seemingly calculating. I'd never heard of a black tiger, but it was most certainly a tiger! It must not have seen me because, after circling our camp and sniffing the air a few times, the tiger disappeared back into the jungle.

Still, just to be safe, I sat on my rock for a long time to make sure it was gone for good.

After hearing nothing for a while, and feeling stiff, I decided it was safe to move. At the exact same second, a man stepped out of the jungle nearby. He boldly approached me, looked me slowly up and down, and said, "Well, well, well. We are full of surprises, aren't we?"

The man was dressed in a black shirt and pants. He was very

handsome, but in a darker, more swarthy way than Ren. His skin was antique-bronze, and his hair was ink-black, longer than Ren's, but also swept back from his face and slightly curled.

His eyes were gold with specks of copper. I tried to identify the color. I'd never seen anything like it before. They were like pirate gold—the color of gold doubloons. In fact, *pirate* was a good way to describe him. He looked like the kind of guy who might be found gracing the cover of a historical romance novel, playing the part of a dark lothario. As he smiled at me, his eyes crinkled slightly at the corners.

I knew immediately who I was looking at. This was Ren's brother. Both men were very handsome and had the same regal bearing. They were about the same height, but while Ren was tall, lean, and muscular, this man was heavier and brawnier, with more powerful arms. I thought he might take more after their father. While Ren, with his prominent Asian features—the slightly almond-shaped blue eyes and golden skin— surely took after his mother.

Strangely, I wasn't afraid, though I recognized an undercurrent of danger. It was almost as if the tiger part of him had overtaken the man.

I stated, "Before you say anything, I think you should know that I know who you are. *And* I know *what* you are."

He stepped forward and quickly closed the gap between us. Then he cupped my chin, lifting my face for his perusal.

"And *who* or *what* do you think I am, my lovely?"

His voice was very deep, smooth, and silky—like hot caramel. His accent was more pronounced than Ren's and he hesitated as if he hadn't used his voice in a long time.

"You're Ren's brother, the one who betrayed him and stole his fiancée."

His eyes tightened, and I felt a twinge of fear. He clicked his tongue, "Tch, tch, tch. Now, now. Where are your manners? We haven't even been properly introduced yet, and here you are making wild accusations against me. The unfortunate younger brother of this one."

He lifted a lock of my hair and rubbed it between his fingers before tilting his head. "I do have to give Ren credit. He always manages to surround himself with beautiful women."

I was about to step away from him when I heard a tremendous bellow from the trees and saw Ren crash through the camp and leap, snarling into the air. His brother quickly moved me to the side and then leapt also, changing into the black tiger I'd seen before.

Ren was beyond rage. He roared so loudly that I felt the vibrations of it quiver through my body. The two tiger bodies smashed together in the air with an explosive clap and fell hard to the ground. They rolled in the grass, clawed at each other's backs, and bit whenever they got a chance.

I scrambled as far off to the side as I could and ended up near the falls, behind some bushes. I tried to shout at them to stop, but the fighting was so loud that it drowned out my voice. The two big cats rolled apart and faced each other. They crouched close to the ground, tails twitching, ready to pounce. They began circling the fire, keeping it between them.

For the moment, they were growling menacingly and locked in a staring contest. I decided that this was the best time to intervene, when the claws were on the ground and not in the air. I approached the two tigers slowly, staying closer to Ren's side.

Mustering my courage, I entreated, "Please, stop it. Both of you. You're brothers. It doesn't matter what happened in the past. You need to talk to each other."

I implored Ren, "You were the one who wanted to seek *him* out. Now's your opportunity to talk, to tell him what you need to say."

I looked at Ren's brother. "And you. Ren's been a captive for many

years, and we're working on a way to help *both* of you. You should listen
to him."

Ren changed into a man. He said sharply, "You're right, Kelsey. I did
come out here to talk to him, but I see that he still cannot be trusted.
There's no . . . vestige of consideration in him. I should *never* have come
here."

"But, Ren—"

Ren moved in front of me and spat angrily at the black tiger.
"*Vasīyata karanā! Badamāśa!* I've been circling you for two days! You
had no right to come here when you *knew* I was gone! And you will
never touch Kelsey again if you know what's good for you!"

Ren's brother changed back to a man as well, shrugged his shoulders,
and said casually, "I wanted to see what you were protecting so fiercely.
You're right. I've been following you for two days, getting close enough
to see what you were up to, but staying far enough away so that I could
approach you on my terms. As for me staying here to listen to you, there
is nothing you could say that would hold any interest for me whatsoever,
Murkha."

Kishan rubbed his jaw and grinned as he traced the long scratches
left by his fight with Ren. He darted his eyes in my direction, and with
a cursory glance at his brother, added, "Unless, of course, you'd like to
talk about *her*. I'm always interested in your women."

Ren moved me back and responded with an outraged roar. Morphing
in midair, he attacked his brother again. The two rolled through the
camp biting and scratching, banging against trees and slamming down
on sharp rocks. Ren lashed out with a paw aimed for his brother, but he
hit a tree instead, leaving deep, jagged claw marks in the thick trunk.

The black tiger took off running into the jungle, with Ren chasing
after him. Their two angry roars echoed through the trees, frightening
a flock of birds that took off squawking. The fight continued as they

moved from one part of the jungle to another. I could follow their path by standing on my rock and watching the trees shake in the jungle and tracking the procession of irritated birds, rousted from their comfortable perches.

Ren finally barreled back into the campsite with his brother half riding his back, sinking in his claws and biting his neck. Ren stood up on his back legs and shook his brother off. Then he leapt up onto a large rock overlooking the pool and turned to face him.

Gathering himself, the black tiger leapt on top of Ren, who jumped up to block him. The move ended up pushing them both into the pool of water.

I stood at the side of the pool watching the fight. One tiger would explode from the water and pounce on the other, pushing him under. Claws raked faces, backs, and sensitive underbellies as the two large cats battered and mauled each other repeatedly. Neither one seemed to dominate the other.

Just when I thought they'd never stop, the fighting seemed to wane. The black tiger dragged his battle-weary body up out of the water, walked a few paces away, and collapsed on the grass. Panting heavily, he rested for a minute before starting to lick his paws.

Ren was next out of the water. He placed himself between his brother and me and buckled at my feet. Deep scratches covered his body and blood oozed from cuts that stood out sharply against his white fur. A nasty gash went from his forehead to his chin, slicing across his right eye and his nose. A large puncture wound from a bite on his neck seeped slowly.

I stepped around him and quickly retrieved the backpack. I dug through the bag until I found the first aid kit, popped it open, and took out a small bottle of rubbing alcohol and a large roll of gauze. My innate fear of blood and wounds was set aside as a natural protective instinct kicked in. I was more scared *for* them than *of* them and knew they needed help. Somehow, I found the courage.

Moving to Ren first, I flushed rocks and dirt out of the wounds with clean bottled water, and then I poured rubbing alcohol on the gauze and pressed against the worst of them. He didn't seem mortally wounded, as long as I could stop the bleeding, but there were several deep rips. On his side, the shredded skin was torn so badly it looked like it'd been through a meat grinder.

He softly growled as I moved from his back to his neck and cleaned the puncture wound. I took a large padded bandage from the kit, sprinkled rubbing alcohol on it, pressed it over the badly shredded section on his side, and put pressure on it to stop the bleeding. Ren softly roared at the sting while I grimaced in sympathy. I left the pad in place. Last, I cleaned his face and murmured reassuring words as I worked on his forehead and nose, careful to avoid the eye. It didn't look as bad as it did the first time I saw it. Maybe I was imagining it was worse than it was.

I did the best I could, but I was worried about infection, and I was seriously concerned about Ren's side and eye. A tear fell down my cheek as I pressed gauze against his forehead.

He licked my wrist as I worked. I stroked his cheek and whispered, "*Ren*, this is awful. I wish this hadn't happened. I'm so sorry. It must hurt terribly." A tear dropped and splashed on his nose. "I'm going to go take care of your brother now."

I wiped my eyes and retrieved another roll of gauze. I went through the same process with the black tiger. A particularly bad, gaping tear started at his neck and went down to his chest, so I spent a lot of time on that area. A bite on his back was deep and full of dirt and small pieces of gravel. It was bleeding profusely at first, which was probably a good thing because the blood helped to flush out the wound. I applied pressure for a few minutes, until the blood slowed enough that I was able to clean the bite. His back quivered, and he growled when I put rubbing alcohol on it.

I held the gauze over the wound, and more tears dribbled down my chin. I sniffed, "You could probably use stitches on that one." Addressing both tigers, I scolded softly, "You two will probably get an infection and your tails will fall off."

Kishan made a huffing noise that sounded suspiciously like laughter, which made me stiffen and get a little angry.

"I hope you both appreciate the fact that cleaning your wounds freaks me out. I hate blood. Also, for your information, *I* will decide who will or won't be touching me. I'm not some ball of string that gets tossed between you two cats. I'm also not the person you're really fighting about either. What happened between you two is long over and done with anyway, and I really hope you can learn to forgive each other."

Golden eyes looked into mine, and I explained, "The reason we came here is because Ren and I are trying to break the curse. Mr. Kadam's been helping us, and we have a good idea of where to start. We're going to be looking at a gift to offer Durga, and, in exchange, you both get to be men again. Now that you know why we're here, we can get back to Mr. Kadam and be on our way. I think both of you may need to go to a hospital."

Ren rumbled in his chest and started licking his paws. The black tiger rolled to his side to show me a long scratch that went from his neck down to his belly. I cleaned that one too. When I finished with him, I walked back to my bag and placed the bottle of rubbing alcohol inside. I wiped my eyes on my sleeve and jumped when I turned and found Ren's brother standing behind me as a man.

Ren got up, alert, and watched him carefully, suspicious of his brother's every move. Ren's tail twitched back and forth, and a deep grumble issued from his chest.

Kishan looked down at Ren, who had crept even closer to keep an eye on him, and then looked back at me. He reached out his hand, and when I placed mine in it, he lifted it to his lips and kissed it, then bowed deeply with great aplomb. "May I ask your name?"

"My name is Kelsey. Kelsey Hayes."

"Kelsey. Well, I, for one, appreciate all the efforts you have made on our behalf. I apologize if I frightened you earlier. I am," he smiled, "out of practice in conversing with young ladies. These gifts you will be offering to Durga. Would you kindly tell me more about them?"

Ren growled unhappily.

I nodded. "Is Kishan your given name?"

"My full name is actually Sohan Kishan Rajaram, but you can call me Kishan if you like." He smiled a dazzling white smile, which was even more brilliant due to the contrast with his dark skin. He offered an arm. "Would you please sit and talk with me, Kelsey?"

There was something very charming about Kishan. I surprised myself by finding I immediately trusted and liked him. He had a quality similar to his brother. Like Ren, he had the ability to set a person completely at ease. Maybe it was their diplomatic training. Maybe it was how their mother raised them. Whatever it was made me respond positively. I smiled at him.

"I'd love to."

He tucked my arm under his and walked with me over to the fire. Ren growled again, and Kishan shot a smirk in his direction. I noticed him wince when he sat, so I offered him some aspirin.

"Shouldn't we be getting you two to a doctor? I really think you might need stitches and Ren—"

"Thank you, but no. You don't need to worry about our minor pains."

"I wouldn't exactly call your wounds minor, Kishan."

"The curse helps us to heal quickly. You'll see. We'll both recover swiftly enough on our own. Still, it was nice to have such a lovely young woman tending to my injuries."

Ren stood in front of us and looked like he was a tiger suffering from apoplexy.

I admonished, "Ren, be civil."

Kishan smiled widely and waited for me to get comfortable. Then he scooted closer to me and rested his arm on the log behind my shoulders. Ren stepped right between us, nudged his brother roughly aside with his furry head, creating a wider space, and maneuvered his body into the middle. He dropped heavily to the ground and rested his head in my lap.

Kishan frowned, but I started talking, sharing the story of what Ren and I had been through. I told him about meeting Ren at the circus and about how he tricked me to get me to India. I talked about Phet, the Cave of Kanheri, and finding the prophecy, and I told him that we were on our way to Hampi.

As I lost myself in our story, I stroked Ren's head. He shut his eyes and purred, and then he fell asleep. I talked for almost an hour, barely registering Kishan's raised eyebrow and thoughtful expression as he watched the two of us together. I didn't even notice when he'd changed back into a tiger.

15

the hunt

t he sleek black tiger stared, its yellow eyes glittering with rapt attention, as I concluded my Cave of Kanheri highlights.

It was late into the night. The jungle, which had seemed so noisy during the day, was now silent except for the crackling of the logs on the fire. I played with Ren's soft ears. His eyes were still squeezed shut, and he was purring slightly, or perhaps, snoring would be more accurate.

Changing back into a man, Kishan looked at me reflectively and said, "It sounds very . . . interesting. I just hope you don't end up getting hurt in the process. It would be smarter of you to return to your home and leave us to our fate. This sounds like the start of a long mission and one rife with danger."

"Ren has protected me so far, and with two tigers watching over me, I'm sure I'll be fine."

Kishan hesitated. "Even with two tigers, things can go wrong, Kelsey. And . . . I don't plan on going with you."

"What? What do you mean? We know how to break the curse. At least the first step, anyway. Kishan, I don't get it. Why won't you help us . . . help yourself?"

Kishan shifted his weight and explained, "Two reasons. The first is

that I refuse to have any more deaths on my conscience. I've already caused too much pain in my life. The second is . . . well, I just don't believe we will be successful. I think you two and Kadam are just chasing ghosts."

"Chasing ghosts? I don't understand."

Kishan shrugged. "You see, Kelsey, I've become accustomed to life as a tiger. It's not a bad existence, really. Plus, I'm used to it. I've come to accept that this is my life now." He trailed off and got lost in his thoughts.

"Kishan, are you sure that it's not *you* who's chasing ghosts? You're punishing yourself by staying out here in the wild, aren't you?"

The younger prince stiffened. His golden eyes snapped back to me. His face grew cold and uncaring. I recognized shock and pain in his eyes. My abruptness hurt him deeply. It was as if I'd torn off a bandage carefully placed to cover the wounds of the past.

I put my hand over his and gently asked, "Kishan, don't you want a future for yourself or a family? I know what it feels like when someone you love dies. It's lonely. You feel broken, like you can never be whole again. You feel like they took a piece of you with them when they left.

"But you are not alone. There are people you can care for and who will care for you. People who will give you lots of reasons to go on living. Mr. Kadam, your brother, and me. There could even be someone else to love. Please come with us to Hampi."

Kishan looked away and continued softly, "I gave up wishing for things that will never be a long, long time ago."

I gripped his hand harder. "Kishan, please reconsider."

He squeezed my hand back and smiled. "I'm sorry, Kelsey." He stood up and stretched. "Now, if you and Ren insist on going on this long journey, he will have to hunt."

"Hunt?" I cringed. Ren hadn't been eating much from what I'd seen.

"He might have been eating enough for a human, but definitely not enough for a tiger. He's a tiger most of the time, and for him to be strong enough to protect you on this journey, he'll have to eat more. Something big, like a nice boar or a water buffalo."

I gulped. "Are you sure?"

"Yes. He's very thin for a tiger. He needs to bulk up. Get some protein."

I stroked Ren's back. I *could* feel his ribs.

"Okay, I'll make sure he hunts before we leave."

"Good." He bowed his head and grinned at me. He grasped my fingers in farewell and seemed reluctant to let them go. Finally, he said, "Thank you, Kelsey, for the very interesting chat."

With that, he changed back into the black tiger and loped off into the jungle.

Ren was still asleep with his head on my lap, so I sat quietly for a bit longer. I traced the stripes on his back and looked at his scratches. Where gaping rips had been only an hour ago, the skin had almost completely healed. The long scratch across his face and eye was gone. Not even a scar remained.

When my legs were completely numb from having Ren's weight on them, I shifted out from under his head and built up the fire again. He just rolled over on his side and continued sleeping.

That fight must have taken a lot out of him. Kishan is right. He does need to hunt. He's got to keep up his strength.

Ren slept as I puttered around the area restocking the woodpile and eating dinner.

Ready to sleep myself, I grabbed my quilt, wrapped it around my body, and lay down near him. His chest rumbled, but he never awoke;

he just rolled closer to me. Using his back as a pillow, I fell asleep looking at the stars.

I woke up in the late morning with my quilt twisted all around me. I looked around for Ren, but I didn't see him anywhere. The fire was ablaze, though, as if he'd just thrown logs onto it. I rolled onto my stomach to try to wiggle out of the quilt, only to gasp in pain as a tremor rippled across my back.

Reaching around and trying to rub my sore muscles, I groaned, "Too many nights sleeping on the hard ground and you wind up an old lady before your time." I gave up and lay back down.

I heard a soft footfall, and Ren stuck his nose into my face.

"Oh, don't mind me. I'm just going to lay here until my spine pops back into alignment."

He turned and began kneading my back with his tiger paws. I laughed painfully as I tried to suck air back into my lungs. He was like an extremely heavy kitten sharpening his claws on a human couch.

I squeaked out, "Thanks anyway, Ren, but you're too heavy. You're knocking the wind out of me."

His heavy tiger paws lifted off my back and were replaced by warm, strong hands. Ren began massaging my lower back, and my thoughts drifted back to the embarrassing kissing altercation. My face turned hot, and my body tensed, causing my back to spasm even more.

"Relax, Kelsey. Your back is full of knots. Let me work on it."

I tried to not think about Ren, and instead remembered my one and only massage from a middle-aged masseuse. It was actually painful, and I never went back for another one. The lady pushed too hard and dug her knuckles into my shoulder blades. I didn't want to say anything, so I just suffered through it. Each minute was torture. With every rub, I repeated the mantra "I hope it's over. I hope it's over."

Ren's massage was completely different. He was gentle and applied medium pressure with his palms. Rubbing in a circular pattern down my spine, he found the tight spots and worked the muscles until they were warm and loose. When he was finished with my back, he trailed his fingers up my spine, to the collar of my shirt, and began to massage my shoulders and neck, which shot little tingles all through my body.

Nimble fingers began at my hairline and pressed in little circles, working my neck. Then Ren increased the pressure using smooth strokes from my neck to my shoulders. Wrapping his fingers over the arch of my neck, he kneaded, squeezed, and compressed the muscles, easing away the aches and pains leisurely and methodically. Eventually, the pressure lightened until it was almost a caress. I sighed deeply, enjoying it immensely.

When he stopped, I carefully tested my back by sitting up. He got up and reached under my elbow to steady me as I stood up.

"Do you feel better, Kelsey?"

I smiled up at him. "Yes. Thank you so much."

I twined my arms around his neck and hugged him affectionately. His body seemed stiff. He didn't hug me back. I pulled away and saw that his lips were tight, and he wouldn't make eye contact.

"Ren?"

He pulled my arms from around his neck, held my hands in front of him, and finally looked at me. "I'm glad you feel better."

He moved away from me to the other side of the fire and changed into a tiger.

Not good, I thought. *What just happened? He's never acted cold to me before. He must still be mad at me about the kissing thing. Or maybe he's still upset about Kishan. I don't know how to fix this. I'm not good at talking about relationship stuff. What can I say to make it right?*

Instead of talking about us or our relationship or the non-kiss, which was obviously hanging in the air between us, I decided to change the subject. I cleared my throat.

"Uh, Ren? You need to go off on a hunt before we leave. Your brother said you needed to eat, and I think you should really consider it."

He just huffed and rolled on his side.

"I'm serious. I promised him you would, and . . . I'm not leaving the jungle with you until you go out to hunt. Kishan said that you're too thin for a tiger and that you need to eat a boar or something. You like hunting anyway, remember?"

Ren walked over to a tree and began rubbing his back against it.

I offered, "Do you have an itch on your back? I can scratch it for you. It's the least I could do after the massage you gave me."

The white tiger stopped twitching for a moment and looked at me, and then he dropped to the dirt and rolled over on his back, wrenching his body back and forth while his legs pawed the air.

Hurt that he would brush me off that way, I shouted, "You'd rather rub your back in the dirt than to have me scratch it for you? Fine! Do it yourself then, but I'm still not leaving until you hunt!" I spun around and grabbed the backpack, crawled into the tent, and zipped it up.

Half an hour later, I peeked out. Ren was gone. I sighed and began collecting firewood again to bulk up our supply.

I was dragging a heavy log over to the fire pit when I heard a voice coming from the forest. Kishan was leaning against a tree watching me. He whistled.

"Who knew such a small girl would have such big muscles?"

I ignored him and finished dragging the log, then dusted off my hands and sat down with a bottle of water.

Kishan sat down beside me, a little too close, and angled his legs in front of him. I offered him a bottle of water, and he took it.

"I don't know what you said, Kelsey, but whatever it was, worked. Ren is out hunting."

I grimaced. "Did he say anything to you?"

"Just that I was supposed to watch you while he was gone. A hunt can take several days."

"Really? I had no idea it would take that long." I hesitated, "So . . . he doesn't mind you staying here while he's gone?"

"Oh, he minds," he chuckled, "but he wants to make sure you're safe. At least he trusts me *that* much."

"Well, I think he's mad at both of us right now."

Kishan looked at me curiously with a raised eyebrow. "How so?"

"Um . . . let's just say we had a misunderstanding."

Kishan's face turned hard. "Don't worry, Kelsey. I'm sure that whatever he's upset about is foolish. He's very argumentative."

I sighed and shook my head sadly. "No, it's really all my fault. I'm difficult, a hindrance, and I'm a pain to have around sometimes. He's probably used to being around sophisticated, more experienced women who are much more . . . more . . . well, more than I am."

Kishan quirked an eyebrow. "Ren hasn't been around *any* women as far as I know. I must confess that I'm now exceedingly curious as to what your argument was about. Whether you tell me or not, I won't tolerate any more derogatory comments about yourself. He's lucky to have you, and he'd *better* realize it."

He grinned. "Of course, if you did have a falling-out, you're always welcome to stay with me."

"Thanks for the offer, but I don't really want to live in the jungle."

He laughed. "For you, I would even consider a change of residence. You, my lovely, are a prize worth fighting for."

I laughed and punched him lightly on the arm. "You, sir, are a major flirt. Worth fighting for? I think you two have been tigers for too long.

I'm no great beauty, especially when I'm stuck out here in the jungle. I haven't even picked a college major yet. What have I ever done that would make someone want to fight over me?"

Kishan apparently took my rhetorical questions seriously. He reflected for a moment, and then answered, "For one thing, I've never met a woman so dedicated to helping others. You put your own life at risk for a person you met only a few weeks ago. You are confident, feisty, intelligent, and full of empathy. I find you charming and, yes, beautiful."

The golden-eyed prince fingered a strand of my hair. I blushed at his assessment, sipped my water, and then said softly, "I don't like him being angry with me."

Kishan shrugged and dropped his hand, looking slightly annoyed that I'd steered the conversation back to Ren. "Yes. I've been on the receiving side of his anger, and I've learned not to underestimate his ability to hold a grudge."

"Kishan, can I ask you something . . . personal?"

He chuckled and rubbed his jaw. "I am at your service."

"It's about Ren's fiancée."

His countenance darkened, and he murmured tightly, "What do you want to know?"

I faltered for a moment. "Was she beautiful?"

"Yes. She was."

"Will you tell me a little about her?"

His face relaxed a little, and he stared off into the jungle. He ran a hand through his hair and mused, "Yesubai was bewitching. She was the most beautiful girl I'd ever seen."

He spoke quietly, "The last day I saw her, she wore a sparkling gold *sharara* with a tinkling jeweled belt, and her hair was coiled and twisted up with a golden chain. She dressed elegantly, arrayed as a bride in all

her finery, that day. That last image of her is something I will never forget.

"What did she look like?"

"She had a lovely, oval face, full pink lips, dark lashes and eyebrows, and the most amazing violet eyes. She was petite, only coming up to my shoulder. When her hair was down, she often covered it with a scarf, but it was smooth, silky, and black as a raven's wing. Her hair was so long it cascaded down her back to her knees."

I closed my eyes and pictured this perfect woman with Ren. The idea of it pierced me with an emotion I didn't know I could feel. It punctured my heart and ripped a gaping hole right through the center.

Kishan continued, "The minute I saw her, I knew that I wanted her. I would have no other but her."

I asked, "How did you two meet?"

"Ren and I were not allowed to engage in battle at the same time for fear that both of us would be killed, and then there would be no heir to the throne. So, while Ren was off in combat, I was stuck at home training with Kadam, learning about military strategy and working with the soldiers.

"One day, as I was returning home from weapons practice, I decided to take a detour through the gardens. There was Yesubai, standing near a fountain where she had just plucked a lotus blossom. Her scarf hung down around her shoulders. I asked her who she was, and she quickly turned around, covered her glorious hair and face, and looked at the ground."

I asked, "Is that when you realized who she was?"

"No. She curtsied, told me her name, and then ran off to the palace. I assumed that she was a visiting dignitary's daughter. When I returned to the palace, I immediately began asking about her and quickly found out that arrangements had been made for her to marry my brother! I was

insanely jealous. I was his second in everything. Ren was given all the things I wanted in life. He was the favorite son, the better politician, the future king, and now the man who would marry the girl I wanted."

He spat out, "He'd never even met her. I didn't even know that my parents were seeking a bride for Ren! He was only twenty-one, and I was twenty. I asked my father if he could alter the arrangement so that I could be Yesubai's betrothed instead. I reasoned that another princess could be found for Ren. I even offered to seek a bride for him myself."

"What did your father say?"

"He was totally focused on the war at that time. I told him that Ren wouldn't care either way, but father wouldn't even listen to my pleas. He insisted that the arrangements with Yesubai's father were irrevocable. He said that her father had insisted that she marry the heir to the throne so that she could become the next queen."

He stretched out his arms along the log we were resting against and continued, "She left a few days later and was taken by caravan to meet Ren, to sign documents, and go through the ceremony of betrothal. She stayed there with him for just a few hours, but the trip took a week. It was the longest week of my life. Then she returned to the palace to wait. For *him*."

His golden eyes pierced mine. "Three months she stayed in our palace waiting, and I tried to avoid her as best I could, but Yesubai was lonely and wanted company. She wanted someone to walk the grounds with her, and I reluctantly agreed, thinking I could keep my feelings in check.

"I told myself that she would be my sister soon and that it was okay to like her, but the more I got to know her, the more deeply I fell for her and the more resentful I became. One evening, as we were wandering the gardens, she admitted to me that she wished that *I* was her betrothed.

"I was exultant! Immediately, I tried to embrace her, but she put me off. She was very strict about following protocol. On our walks, she even had a chaperone follow us at a discreet distance. She implored me to wait, promising that we would figure out a way to be together. I was insanely happy and determined that I would do everything, anything, necessary to make her mine."

I reached over to hold his hand. He squeezed mine and then went on.

"She said that she had tried to put her feelings for me aside for the good of the family, for the good of the kingdom, but that she couldn't help but to love me. Me—not Ren. For the first time in my life, I was chosen above him. Yesubai and I were both very young and in love. When the date approached for Ren's return, she became desperate and insisted that I speak with her father. This was entirely improper, of course, but I was lovesick and agreed, determined to do anything to make her happy."

"What did her father say?"

"Her father agreed to give me her hand in marriage *if* I conceded to certain conditions."

I interjected, "That's when you arranged to have Ren captured, right?"

He winced. "Yes. In my mind, Ren was a hurdle I had to jump over in order to have Yesubai. I endangered him so that I could have her. In my defense, I was told that the soldiers were going to escort him to her father's palace and that we would make different arrangements regarding the betrothal. Obviously, things didn't go as planned."

I entreated, "What happened to Yesubai?"

He said softly, "An accident. She was struck and she fell, breaking her neck. I held her as she died."

I squeezed his hand. "I'm so sorry, Kishan." Though I wasn't sure I wanted to know, I decided to inquire anyway. "Kishan, I once asked

Mr. Kadam if Ren loved Yesubai. He never really gave me a straight answer."

Kishan laughed bitterly. "Ren loved the idea of her. Yesubai was beautiful, desirable, and would make a wonderful companion and queen, but he didn't really know her. In letters, he insisted on calling her Bai and wanted her to call him Ren. She hated that. She felt that only lower castes of people used nicknames. In all honesty, they didn't really even know each other."

At first, I felt relieved, but then I remembered Kishan's description of Yesubai. Not knowing a girl well didn't mean she wasn't desired or sought after. Ren could easily still be harboring feelings for his lost fiancée.

A slight tremor shot through Kishan's arm, and I knew his time as a man was up.

"Thanks for staying with me, Kishan. I have so many more questions. I wish you could talk with me longer."

"I'll stay here with you until Ren returns. Perhaps we can converse again tomorrow."

"I would like that."

The troubled man changed into the black tiger and found a nice spot for a nap. I decided to write in my journal for a while.

I felt awful about Yesubai's death. I turned to a blank page, but ended up drawing a picture of two tigers with a beautiful, long-haired girl in the middle. Sketching a line leading from the girl to each tiger, I sighed. It was hard to sort out your feelings on paper if you hadn't really sorted them out in your head yet.

Ren didn't return the rest of the day, and Kishan napped all afternoon. I walked past him noisily several times, but he kept on sleeping. I muttered, "So much for my big protector. I could walk off into the jungle and he'd never know it."

The big black tiger huffed slightly, probably trying to tell me that he knew what was going on, even if he was napping.

I ended up reading quietly the rest of the afternoon, missing Ren. Even when he was a tiger, I felt like he always listened to me and that he would talk with me if he could.

After dinner, I patted Kishan on the head and retreated to my tent to get some sleep. As I cushioned my head on my arms, I couldn't help but notice the big empty hole next to me where Ren always slept.

The next four days continued in the same pattern. Kishan stayed nearby, left on patrol a couple of times a day, and then returned to sit by me during lunch. After lunch, he changed to a man and allowed me to pester him with questions about palace life and the culture of his people.

On the morning of the fifth day, the routine changed. Kishan changed to a man right after I emerged from the tent.

"Kelsey, I'm worried about Ren. He's been gone a long time, and I haven't caught his scent on patrol. I suspect that he's had no luck on his hunt. He hasn't hunted since he was captured, which was more than three hundred years ago."

"Do you think he's hurt?"

"It's a possibility, but keep in mind that we heal quickly. There aren't many beasts here that would try to injure a tiger, but there are poachers and traps. I think I should go look for him."

"Do you think it'll be easy to find him?"

"If he's smart, he would have stuck to the river. Most of the herds congregate near the water. Speaking of food, I noticed you were getting low. Last night while you were sleeping, I met Mr. Kadam at his camp near the road and brought back more of those meal packages." He indicated a bag left by the tent.

"You must have carried that in your mouth the entire way. Thank you."

He grinned. "You are entirely welcome, my lovely."

I laughed. "Better to carry a backpack in your teeth over several miles than to have Ren sink his into your hide for letting me starve, eh?"

Kishan frowned. "I did it for you, Kelsey. Not him."

I put my hand on his arm. "Well, thank you."

He pressed his hand on top of mine. "*Aap ke liye.* For your sake, anything."

"Did you tell Mr. Kadam that we would be a bit longer?"

"Yes, I explained the situation to him. Don't worry about him. He's comfortably camped near the road and will wait as long as necessary. Now, I want you to pack up some water bottles and food. I'm taking you with me. I would leave you here, but Ren insists that you get into trouble if left alone."

He touched my nose. "Is that true, *bilauta*? I can't imagine an endearing young woman such as you getting into trouble."

"I don't get into trouble. Trouble finds me."

He laughed. "That much is obvious."

"Despite what you tigers think, I can take care of myself, you know," I said in a slightly sulky tone.

Kishan squeezed my arm. "Perhaps we tigers *enjoy* taking care of you."

Soon we set off on a trail that angled up toward the top of the falls. It was a slow but steady climb, and my legs started to protest as we neared the apex. He let me rest for a while at the top. I took in the view of the jungle and made out our little camp below in the small clearing.

We continued to follow the river until we arrived at a large tree trunk that had fallen across. It was stripped bare of branches, and the rushing water had peeled off the bark, leaving the trunk smooth but dangerous to walk on. The water was rushing, and every once in a while it splashed over the top of the makeshift bridge.

Kishan leapt up on the trunk and padded across. The tree bobbed up and down under his weight, but it seemed stable enough. He landed softly on the other side and then turned to watch me cross. Somehow, I mustered the courage and put one foot directly in front of the other. It was like walking on Mr. Maurizio's tightrope—with the added bonus of it being extra-slippery.

I yelled across nervously, "Kishan! Did you ever think that crossing this log just might be a little bit easier for a tiger with claws than for a girl with a heavy backpack wearing sneakers? If I fall in, I hope you're ready for a swim!"

Finally safe on the other side, I breathed a deep sigh of relief. We continued walking, and after about three miles, Kishan finally caught Ren's scent, which we followed slowly for another two hours. He let me get a good rest then while he took off to scout out Ren's location.

He returned a half an hour later and reported, "There's a large herd of black antelope in the clearing about a half mile away. Ren has been stalking them unsuccessfully for three days. Antelope are extremely fast. Usually a tiger would target a baby or an injured animal, but this group is only adults.

"They're edgy and jumpy because they know Ren is stalking them. The herd is sticking close together, which makes it hard for him to single one out. He's also been hunting for several days, so he's very tired. I'm going to lead you to a safe place downwind where you can stay and rest, while I help Ren with the hunt."

I agreed and shouldered my pack again. He led me through the trees to climb another large hill. Kishan stopped to sniff the wind several times along the way. After we'd climbed several hundred feet, he found a place for me to rest before setting off to help Ren.

After a while I was utterly and absolutely bored. I couldn't see much from where I was sitting.

I had already drunk an entire bottle of water and was starting to feel restless so I decided to walk around just a bit to get my bearings and explore the area. I carefully noted rock formations and used my compass to make sure I knew where I was.

Hiking farther up the hill, I spied a large rock jutting out over the tree line. The rock was flat on top and shaded by a large tree. I climbed up to it and was amazed with the view. I scrambled up higher, crossed my legs, and sat down. The river meandered lazily below, weaving back and forth at a sluggish pace a few hundred feet below me. I sat back against a tree trunk and enjoyed the breeze.

About twenty minutes later, a movement caught my attention. A large animal emerged from the trees below. Several more creatures followed. At first, I thought they were deer, but then I realized they were probably some of the antelopes that Kishan had been talking about. I wondered if they were from the same herd that Ren and Kishan were following. The tops of their bodies were sable colored while the bottom half was white. They had white chins and white rings circling their big brown eyes.

The bucks sported two long, twisted horns that stuck straight out from the top of their heads like television antennas. The larger males' horns were bigger and more tightly twisted than the smaller males'. The animals' hides ranged from light tan to dark brown.

They drank from the river, flicking their white tails back and forth. The bigger males kept watch while the others drank. The females were about five feet tall and the males, if their horn height was included, stood a foot or two taller. The longer I looked at their impressive horns, the more nervous I felt for Ren.

No wonder he's had a hard time catching one of them.

The herd seemed to relax, and some of the animals even started grazing. I scanned the trees for Ren, but I couldn't see him anywhere. I watched the herd for a long time. The animals were beautiful.

The attack came quickly. The herd stampeded. Kishan was a black streak racing across the landscape. He singled out a large male, who ran quickly in a different direction from the herd, which I figured was either his fatal mistake or an act of great bravery to lead the predator away from the group.

Kishan chased the antelope toward a copse of trees, leapt up on its back, dug his front claws into the sides of the animal, and nipped at its backbone. Just then, Ren shot out from the trees, came up alongside the animal, and bit its front leg. Somehow, the antelope twisted out from under Kishan, who fell off. The black tiger started circling around, looking for another opportunity to leap.

The antelope pointed its long horns at Ren, who paced back and forth. The animal remained focused, always protecting itself with its horns. Its ears twitched back and forth, listening for Kishan, who had slunk around behind it.

Kishan leapt up and swiped his claws at the animal's haunches. The power of the blow took the antelope down. Seeing an opportunity, Ren leapt in to bite at its neck. The antelope writhed and twisted, trying to get up, but the two tigers had the advantage.

Several times I thought the animal might escape. The antelope thrashed about and eventually managed to dart away a few paces. Panting, it watched the tigers slowly rise and approach. The antelope quivered with exhaustion and limped lamely as it waited for the next attack. The tigers slowly tackled it to the ground again.

I thought the whole process would be quick, but the hunt took much longer than I'd expected. It was as if Ren and Kishan were tiring the beast out, engaging it in a macabre dance of death. The tigers were moving wearily too. It seemed they saved their energy for the chase, burning up all their strength on that. The kill itself was an almost sluggish process.

The antelope struggled valiantly. It kicked out several times and caught both tigers with its hooves. The tigers clamped on with their jaws until the animal finally stopped moving.

When it was over, Ren and Kishan rested, panting heavily from the exertion. Kishan started eating first. I tried to look away. I wanted to, but I couldn't help myself. It was unspeakably fascinating.

Kishan braced his claws against the antelope and sunk his teeth deeply into its body. Using the force of his jaw, he ripped off a dripping chunk of steaming flesh. Ren followed suit. It was grisly, nauseating, and disturbing. It shot shivers down my spine, but I just couldn't tear my eyes away.

After the meal was done, the brothers moved slowly, as if drugged or sleepy, which made me wonder if it was similar to the post-turkey feeling on Thanksgiving Day. They lay near their meal, occasionally going back to lick at the juiciest parts. A black cloud of giant flies descended. There must have been hundreds in that swarm, all buzzing around the fresh kill.

As the insects surrounded them, I imagined the flies landing on the dead animal and Kishan and Ren's bloody faces. That's when I lost it and couldn't watch any longer.

I picked up my backpack and slid down the rough hill, covering the distance in just a few moments. I headed back to our original campsite more anxious about facing the two tigers than about getting lost. I wasn't sure I could face either Kishan or Ren after what I had just seen.

With only a couple hours of sunlight left, I set off at a brisk pace, made it back to the log, and crossed the river before the sun had set. I slowed during the last few miles. Darkness was falling, and rain clouds had moved in. Sprinkles hit my face, and the path grew wet and slippery, but the real downpour didn't hit until I was back at the campground.

I wondered if the rain was now falling on the tigers and figured that would probably be a good thing, so it could wash the blood off their faces and drive off the flies. I involuntarily shuddered.

At that moment, the idea of food disgusted me. I climbed into my tent and sang happy songs from *The Wizard of Oz* to get my mind off the disturbing images I'd just seen, hoping that it would help me fall asleep. It backfired on me, though, because after I fell asleep, I dreamed of the cowardly lion tearing chunks out of Dorothy.

kelsey's dream

orothy and Toto turned into other disturbing dreams. Alone and lost, I was running in the darkness. I couldn't find Ren, and something evil was chasing me. I had to get away. Strange, grasping fingers reached out to pull my clothes and hair. They scraped my skin and tried to drag me off the path. I knew if they did, they would ensnare and destroy me.

I turned a corner, entered a large room, and saw a dark, villainous man dressed in rich amethyst robes. He was standing over another man tied to a large table. I watched from a dark corner as he raised a sharp, curved knife into the air. The man chanted softly in a language I didn't understand.

Somehow, I knew I had to save his captive in the nightmare. I launched myself at the man with the knife and pulled on his arm, trying to wrestle the knife from his hand. My hand started to burn bright red, and sparks crackled.

"No, Kelsey! Stop!"

I looked down at the altar and gasped. It was Ren! His body was torn and bloody, and his hands were bound over his head.

"Kells . . . get out of here! Save yourself! I'm doing this so he can't find you."

"No! I won't let you! Ren, change into a tiger. Run!"

He shook his head frantically and said loudly, "Durga! I accept! Do it now!"

"What is it? What do you need Durga to do?" I said.

The man began chanting again loudly, and, despite my feeble efforts to stop him, he raised the blade and plunged it into Ren's heart. I screamed. My heart beat in sick rhythm with his. With each thud, his strength diminished. His damaged heart beat slower and slower until it stalled and finally stopped.

Tears rolled down my face. I felt a terrible, cutting pain. I watched Ren's lifeblood drip down the table and pool on the tiled floor. Slumping to the ground on my hands and knees, I choked on my emotions.

Ren's death was unbearable. If he was dead, then so was I. I was drowning in sorrow; I couldn't breathe. I didn't have any will left to drive me. There was no incentive, no voice urging me to fight back, to kick for the surface, to rise above the pain. Nothing could make me breathe or make me live again.

The room disappeared, and I was shrouded in blackness once again. The dream changed. I was wearing a golden dress and ornate jewelry. Seated on a beautiful chair on a high dais, I looked down to see Ren standing on the floor in front of me. I smiled at him and held out my hand, but Kishan grabbed it as he sat down beside me.

I glanced at Kishan, confused. He was smiling smugly at Ren. When I turned back to Ren again, his anger was white hot, and he glared at me with hatred and fiery contempt.

I struggled to free my hand from Kishan's grasp, but he wouldn't let me go. Before I could free myself, Ren changed into a tiger and ran into the jungle. I screamed after him, but he couldn't hear me. He *wouldn't* hear me.

Wind whipped the cream-colored drapes, and storm clouds rushed in, pushed along by the brisk wind. The clouds blanketed the trees and darkened the sky. Lightning struck in several places. I heard a mighty roar echo across the landscape. It was the impetus I needed. I wrenched my hand out of Kishan's and ran into the squall.

Rain began to beat the ground, slowing my progress as I searched for Ren. My beautiful golden sandals were stripped away, stuck in the thick mud created by the downpour. I couldn't find him anywhere. I pushed my dripping hair out of my eyes and shouted, "Ren! Ren! Where are you?"

A thunderbolt struck a nearby tree with a mighty boom. Fragments of bark shot out in every direction as the tree cracked, and the trunk twisted and splintered. It crashed down and pinned me to the ground with its branches.

"Ren!"

Muddy rainwater pooled under me. I carefully squirmed and twisted my bruised, aching body until I could slither out from under the tree. The golden dress was ripped and torn, and my skin was covered with bloody scratches.

I yelled again, "Ren! Please come back! I need you!"

I was cold and shaking, but I continued running through the jungle, tripping over roots and shoving aside gray, prickly undergrowth. Searching and yelling while running, I wove between trees looking for him. I forlornly begged, "Ren, please don't leave me!"

Finally, I spotted a white form loping through the trees and doubled my efforts to catch up to him. My dress caught on a thorny bush, but I fiercely dug my way through it, determined to reach him. I followed the path of lightning strikes in the jungle nearby.

I wasn't afraid of the lightning, though it hit close enough that I could smell burned wood. The lightning guided me to Ren. I found him lying on the ground. Large burn marks scorched his white fur where lightning bolts had repeatedly struck him. Somehow, I knew I had done it. I was the one responsible for his pain.

I stroked his head and the soft, silky fur of his neck and cried, "Ren, I didn't want this. How could this happen?"

He changed to a man and whispered, "You lost faith in me, Kelsey."

I shook my head in denial. Tears streaked down my cheeks. "No, I didn't. I wouldn't!"

He couldn't look me in the eyes. "*Iadala*, you left me."

I threw my arms around him desperately. "No, Ren! I'll never leave you."

"But you did. You walked away. Was it too much to ask you to wait for me? To believe in me?"

I sobbed forlornly. "But, I didn't know. I didn't know."

"It's too late now, *priyatama*. This time, I'm leaving you." He closed his eyes and died.

I shook his limp body. "No. No! Ren come back. Please come back!"

Tears mixed with rain and blurred my vision. I angrily brushed them from my eyes, and when I opened them again, I saw not just him but also my parents, my grandmother, and Mr. Kadam. They were all lying on the ground dead. I was alone and surrounded by death.

I cried and shouted over and over, "No! It can't be! It *can't* be!"

A black anguish seeped through my body. Thick and viscous, it oozed through my core and dribbled down my limbs. I felt so heavy, so full of despair, and so alone. I held onto Ren and rocked his body back and forth, unconsciously trying to comfort myself. But I found no relief.

Then, I wasn't alone anymore. I realized that it wasn't me rocking Ren, but someone else was rocking me, and holding me tightly. I became alert enough to know that I had been dreaming but the pain of the dream still engulfed me.

My face was wet with real tears and the storm had been real. Wind surged through the trees outside pushing a hard rain to beat against the canvas. A lightning bolt struck a nearby tree and briefly lit up my small tent. In the flash, I made out dark wet hair, golden skin, and a white shirt.

"Ren?"

I felt his thumbs wipe the tears from my cheeks. "Shh, Kelsey. I'm here. I'm not leaving you, *priya. Mein yaha hoon.*"

With great relief and a hiccupping sob, I reached up to wrap my arms around Ren's neck. He slid his body farther into the little tent to get out of the rain, pulled me onto his lap, and tightened his arms around me. He stroked my hair and whispered, "Hush now. *Mein aapka raksha karunga.* I'm here. I won't let anything happen to you, *priyatama.*"

He continued to soothe me with words from his native language until I felt the dream fade. After a few minutes, I was recovered enough to pull away, but I made a conscious choice to stay right where I was. I liked the feel of his arms around me.

The dream made me realize how alone I really felt. Since my parents had died, no one had held me like this. Of course, I hugged my foster parents and their kids, but no one had managed to break through my defenses—nor had I let anyone pull this depth of emotion from me in a long while.

That was the moment I knew that Ren loved me.

I felt my heart open to him. I already loved and trusted the tiger part of him. That part was easy. But, I recognized that the man needed that love even more. For Ren, it had been centuries—if ever. So, I held him close and didn't break apart from him until I knew he was out of time.

I whispered in his ear, "Thank you for being here. I'm glad you're a part of my life. Please stay in the tent with me. There's no reason for you to sleep outside in the rain."

I kissed his cheek and lay down again, spreading my quilt over me. Ren changed to a tiger and lay down next to me. I snuggled against his back and fell into a dreamless, peaceful sleep despite the storm raging outside.

The next day I awoke, stretched, and crawled out of the tent. The sun had evaporated the rainwater and turned the wet jungle into a steamy sauna. Branches and leaves torn off in the storm littered the campground. A sopping wet moat full of ashy, gray water surrounding charred black lumps of wood was all that remained of our roaring fire.

The waterfall was rushing faster than usual, pushing sodden pieces of flotsam into the now muddy pool.

"No bath today," I greeted Ren, who'd changed into a man.

"It doesn't matter anyway. We're heading out to meet Mr. Kadam. It's time we resumed our journey," he replied.

"But what about Kishan? There is no way you can convince him to come with us?"

"Kishan's made his position clear. He wishes to remain here, and I'm not going to beg him. Once he's made up his mind, he rarely changes it."

"But, Ren—"

"No buts."

He approached me and tugged lightly on my braid. Then he smiled and kissed my forehead. What passed between us during the storm had repaired the emotional rift that had put us at odds, and I was happy that he was my friend again.

"Come on, Kells. Let's pack up."

It took only a few minutes to get the tent rolled up and everything stowed in the backpack. I was relieved to get back to Mr. Kadam and civilization, but I didn't like leaving things with Kishan this way. I didn't even get a chance to say good-bye.

On the way out, I swept past the flowered bushes to stir the butter-

flies into the air again. There were not as many as when we had first arrived. They clung to the sodden bushes and flapped their wings slowly in the sun, drying them out. A few took to the sky one last time, and Ren waited patiently while I watched. I sighed as we began the trek back to the highway where Mr. Kadam was camped. Even though I hated hiking and camping, this place was special.

My tiger led the way as usual, and I traipsed along behind, trying to avoid his muddy paw prints and walk on drier ground. To pass the time, I told Ren about how I'd talked to Kishan about palace life and of how he had carried a bag full of food in his mouth so that I wouldn't starve.

There were some things I did *not* share with Ren, especially the things Kishan had told me about Yesubai. I definitely didn't want Ren thinking about her, but also I felt Kishan needed to talk it out with Ren himself. Instead, I calmly babbled away about being bored in the jungle and watching the hunt.

Suddenly, Ren morphed into a man, grabbed my arms, and exploded, "You saw *what*?"

Confused, I repeated, "I saw the . . . the hunt. I thought you knew. Didn't Kishan tell you?"

Grinding his teeth, he said, "No, he didn't!"

I side-stepped around him onto a series of stones. "Oh. Well, it doesn't matter. I'm fine. I made my way back."

Ren grabbed my elbow, spun me into his arms, and then set me down in front of him.

"Kelsey, are you telling me that not only did you watch the hunt, but also that you hiked back to the campground by yourself?"

Ren was beyond angry.

I squeaked out, "Yes."

"The next time I see Kishan, I will *kill* him." He pointed his finger in my face. "You could have been killed or . . . or eaten! I can't even tell you all the dangerous things that live in the jungle. You are never leaving my sight again!"

He grabbed my hand and pulled me ahead on the trail. I could feel the tension radiating from his body.

"Ren, I don't understand. Didn't you and Kishan talk after your, uh . . . meal?"

He grumbled, "No. We went our separate ways. I came straight back to the camp. Kishan lingered over the . . . food, a bit longer. I must not have caught your scent because of the rain."

"Kishan might still be looking for me, then. Maybe we should go back."

"No. It would serve him right." He laughed spitefully. "Without a scent to track, it'll probably take him days to figure out we're gone."

"Ren, you really should go back and tell him we're leaving. He helped you on the hunt. It's the least you could do."

"Kelsey, we are not going back. He's a big tiger and he can take care of himself. Besides, I was doing fine without him."

"No, you weren't. I saw the hunt, remember? He helped you take down the antelope. Also, Kishan said that you hadn't hunted in more than three hundred years. That's why we went after you. He said he knew you'd need his help."

Ren scowled but said nothing.

I paused and put my hand on his arm. "It's not a sign of weakness to need help sometimes."

He grunted, dismissing my comment but tucked my hand under his arm and started walking again.

"Ren, what exactly happened to you three hundred years ago?"

Scowling, he didn't speak. I elbowed him and smiled encouragingly. The scowl slowly disappeared from his handsome face and the tension

melted from his shoulders. He sighed, ran a hand through his hair, and explained.

"It's a lot easier for a black tiger to hunt than a white tiger. I don't exactly blend into the jungle. When I got really hungry and frustrated in hunting wild game, I'd occasionally venture into a village and make off with a goat or a sheep. I was careful, but rumors soon spread of a white tiger, and the hunters came out in force. Not only were there farmers who wanted to keep me away, but big-game hunters wanted the thrill of capturing an exotic animal.

"They set traps for me all over the jungle, and many innocent creatures were killed. Whenever I found one, I'd disable it. One day, I happened upon a trap and made a stupid mistake. There were two traps right next to each other, but I focused on the obvious one, which was the standard meat-dangling-over-a-pit-trap.

"I was studying the pit, trying to figure out a way to get the meat, and I tripped a hidden wire. It triggered a shower of spikes and arrows that rained down on me from the tree above. I leapt to the side as a spear came down, but the dirt underfoot gave way and I fell into the pit."

"Did any of the arrows hit you?" I asked, on the edge of my seat.

"Yes. Several of them grazed me, but I healed quickly. Fortunately, the pit didn't have any bamboo stakes, but it was well made and deep enough that I couldn't get out."

"What did they do to you?"

"After a few days, the hunters found me. They sold me to a private collector who had a menagerie of interesting creatures. When I proved difficult, he sold me to another who sold me to another, and so on. Eventually, I ended up in a Russian circus and have been passed from circus to circus ever since. Whenever people became suspicious of my age or hurt me, I would cause enough trouble to inspire a quick sale."

It was a terrible, heart-breaking story. I stepped away from him to circle a log and when I moved back next to him, he twined his fingers in mine and kept walking.

"Why didn't Mr. Kadam just buy you himself and take you home?" I asked sympathetically.

"He couldn't. Something always happened to prevent it. Every time he tried to buy me from the circus, the owners refused to sell at any price. Once he sent people to try to purchase me, and that didn't work either. Mr. Kadam even hired people to try to steal me, but they were captured. The curse was in charge, not us. The more he tried to intervene, the worse my situation became. We eventually discovered that Mr. Kadam could send potential buyers with a genuine interest my way. He was able to influence good people to buy me, but only if he had no intention of getting me for himself.

"Mr. Kadam made sure I was moved around enough so people didn't notice my age. He visited me from time to time so that I knew how to contact him, but there was really nothing he could do. He never stopped trying to figure out a way to break the curse though. He spent all his time to researching solutions. His visits meant everything to me. I think I would have lost my humanity without him."

Ren swatted a mosquito on the back of his neck and reflected, "When I was first taken, I thought it would be easy to escape. I'd just wait for night to fall and pull the latch on the cage. But, once I was a captive, I was permanently in tiger form. I couldn't become a man again—not until you came along."

He held back a branch so I could pass under and I said, "What was it like, being in the circus all those years?"

I tripped over a stone, and Ren reached out to steady me. When I was standing firmly again, he slid his hands reluctantly from my waist and offered a hand to me again.

"It was boring mostly. Sometimes the owners were cruel and I was whipped, poked, and prodded. I was lucky, though, because I healed quickly and was smart enough to do the tricks other tigers refused to do. A tiger doesn't naturally want to jump through a flaming hoop or have a man's head in his mouth. Tigers hate fire, so the tiger has to be taught to fear the trainer more than he fears the flame."

"It sounds awful!"

"Circuses back then were. The animals were placed in cages much too small. Natural familial relationships were broken, and the babies were sold. In the early days, the food was bad, the cages were filthy, and the animals were beaten. They were trekked from city to city and left outdoors in places and climates they were not accustomed to. They didn't survive very long."

Thoughtfully, he went on, "Now, though, there's more study and effort to prolong the lives of the animals and better their quality of life. But, captivity is still captivity no matter how pretty the jail is.

"Being caged made me think long and hard about my relationships with other creatures, especially the elephants and horses. My father had thousands of elephants that were trained for battle or heavy lifting, and I had a favorite stallion once that I loved to ride. As I sat there in my cage day after day, I wondered if he felt like I did. I imagined him sitting in his stall, bored, just waiting for me hour after hour to come and let him out."

Ren squeezed my hand and changed back into a tiger again.

I got lost in my thoughts. How hard being caged up must have been. Ren had to endure centuries of that. I shuddered and kept hiking after him.

After another hour had passed, I spoke up again, "Ren? There's one thing I don't understand. Where was Kishan? Why didn't he help you get away?"

Ren leapt over a huge fallen log. At the height of his jump, he changed in midair, dropping to the ground on the other side, silently, on two feet. I reached out for his hand to help steady me as I began to climb over the log, but he ignored it, reached over the log, and put his hands around my waist.

Before I could even form the words to protest, he lifted me up and over the log as if I were as light as a down pillow. He cuddled me close to his chest before letting me go, which made me stop breathing entirely. He looked in my eyes, and a slow smile spread across his face. He set me down before reaching out his hand again. I placed my slightly shaky hand in his warm one, and we set off again.

"Back then, Kishan and I tried to avoid each other as much as possible. He didn't know what had happened until Kadam found him. By the time they'd figured it out, it was too late to do anything. Kadam had tried unsuccessfully to free me, so he persuaded Kishan to stay in hiding while he tried to figure out what to do. Like I said, he tried breaking me out, purchasing me, and hiring thieves for centuries. Not a single thing worked until you. For some reason, after you wished me free, I was able to call him."

Ren laughed. "When I changed into a man again for the first time in centuries, I asked Matthew to place a collect call for me. I told him that I'd been mugged and needed to get in touch with my boss. He helped me figure out how to use the phone, and Mr. Kadam flew in right away."

Ren changed back into a tiger again, and we continued. He stayed close beside me, so I kept a hand on the scruff of his neck.

After walking for several hours, Ren stopped suddenly and smelled the air. He sat on his haunches and stared at the jungle. I listened intently as something shook the bushes. First a black nose emerged, followed by the rest of the black tiger, from the undergrowth.

I smiled happily. "Kishan! You changed your mind. You're coming with us now? I'm so glad!"

Kishan approached me and held out a paw that changed into a hand.

"Hello, Kelsey. No, I haven't changed my mind. I am glad to find you safe though."

Kishan shot a nasty look down at Ren, who wasted no time morphing into human form himself.

Ren shoved Kishan's shoulder and shouted, "Why didn't you tell me she was out there! She saw the hunt, and you left her alone and unprotected!"

Kishan countered, poking Ren in the chest, "You left before I could say anything. If it makes you feel any better, I've been searching for her all night. You also packed up and left without telling me."

I stood between them and interjected, "Please calm down, both of you. Ren, I agreed with Kishan that it would be best for me to go with him, and he watched over me with great care. *I* was the one who decided to watch the hunt, and *I* was the one who chose to head back to camp alone. So if you're going to be mad at someone, be mad at me."

I turned to Kishan, "I'm so sorry that I made you search for me all night in a rainstorm. I didn't realize it was going to rain, or that it would hide my trail. I apologize."

Kishan grinned and kissed the back of my hand, while Ren growled menacingly. "Apology accepted. So, how did you like it?"

"You mean the rain or the hunt?"

"The hunt, of course."

"Umm, it was—"

"She had nightmares," Ren spat at his brother.

I grimaced and nodded, dipping my head in agreement.

"Well, at least my brother is well fed. It might have been weeks before he made a kill on his own."

"I was doing just fine without you!"

Kishan smirked. "No, you couldn't catch a limping turtle without me."

I heard the punch before I saw it. It was a hard, teeth-rattling punch, the kind that I thought only happened in the movies. Ren had moved me deftly to the side and then socked his brother.

Kishan stepped away while rubbing his jaw, but he stood up to face Ren with a smile.

"Try that again, big brother."

Ren scowled, saying nothing. He just took my hand and set off at a fast pace, pulling me along behind him through the jungle. I almost had to jog to keep up with him.

The black tiger whooshed past us and leapt into our path. Kishan changed to a man again and said, "Wait. I have something to say to Kelsey."

Ren frowned, but I put my hand on his chest and interjected, "Ren, please."

He shifted his gaze from his brother to me, and his expression softened. He let go of my hand, touched my cheek briefly, and moved off a few paces as Kishan approached me.

"Kelsey, I want you to take this," Kishan said, reaching around his neck to remove a chain tucked into his black shirt. After he attached the clasp around my neck, he said, "I think you know that this amulet will protect you in the same way Ren's protects Kadam."

I fingered the chain and pulled the broken charm up to look at it more closely. "Kishan, are you sure you want me to wear it?"

He grinned rakishly. "My lovely, your enthusiasm is infectious. A man can't be near you and remain aloof to your cause. And even though I will stay in the jungle, this will be my small contribution to your endeavors."

His expression turned serious. "I want to keep you safe, Kelsey. All we know for sure is that the amulet is powerful and may give the wearer a long life. But, that doesn't mean you can't be hurt or even killed, so keep your guard up."

He cupped my chin, and I looked into his golden eyes. "I wouldn't want anything to happen to you, *bilauta*."

"I'll be careful. Thank you, Kishan."

Kishan looked over at Ren, who inclined his head in a soft nod, and then Kishan turned back to me. He smiled, and said, "I'll miss you, Kelsey. Come visit me again soon."

I hugged him briefly and turned my cheek toward him for a kiss. At the last second, Kishan altered his stance and pecked me quickly on the lips.

I sputtered with shock, "You wily scoundrel!" Then I laughed and punched him lightly on the arm.

He just laughed and winked at me.

Ren clenched his fists and a dark expression stole across his handsome face, but Kishan ignored him and ran off toward the jungle. His laughter echoed back at us through the trees and became a gruff bark as he changed back into the black tiger.

Ren approached me, picked up the pendant, and rubbed it thoughtfully between his fingers. I put my hand on his arm, worried that he might still be angry about Kishan. He tugged on my braid, smiled, and pressed a warm kiss on my forehead.

Changing into a white tiger again, he led me through the jungle for another half hour until, with relief, I saw we'd finally reached the highway.

Waiting until there was no traffic, we hurried to the other side and disappeared into the verdant undergrowth. After following Ren's nose for a short distance, we finally came upon a military-style tent, and I ran up to hug the man who emerged from it.

"Mr. Kadam! I can't tell you how happy I am to see you!"

a beginning

Miss Kelsey!" Mr. Kadam welcomed warmly. "I'm glad to see you, too! I hope the boys took good care of you."

Ren snorted and found a shady spot to rest.

"Yes. They did. I'm fine."

Mr. Kadam led me to a log near his campfire. "Here, sit down and rest while I break camp."

I nibbled on a cookie as I watched Mr. Kadam shuffle around taking down his tent and packing up his books. His camp was as well organized as I expected it to be. He'd used the back of the Jeep to store his books and other study materials. A campfire was crackling merrily, and he had plenty of wood stacked alongside. His tent looked like something the United States military might house a general in if he were roughing it. It appeared to be expensive, heavy, and much more complicated to set up than mine. He even had a fancy fold-up writing desk covered with papers held down with smooth, clean river rocks.

I stood up and looked at the papers with curiosity. "Mr. Kadam, are these the translations of Durga's prophecy?"

I heard a grunt and a slight ping as Mr. Kadam pulled a heavy stake out of the ground. The tent suddenly folded in on itself and collapsed in a pile of heavy green canvas. He stood up to answer my question.

"Yes. I've begun working on the translation of the monolith. I am quite sure that we need to go to Hampi. I also have a better idea of what we're looking for."

"Hmm." I picked up his notes, most of which weren't in English. As I sipped my water, my hand came up to finger the amulet Kishan had given me.

"Mr. Kadam, Kishan gave me his piece of the amulet, hoping it will protect me. Does yours protect you? Can you still be hurt?"

He walked over and stowed the wrapped tent into the Jeep. He leaned on the bumper, and said, "The amulet helps protect me from serious injury, but I can still cut myself or fall and sprain my ankle."

Mr. Kadam rubbed his short beard thoughtfully. "I have become ill, but I have not experienced disease. My cuts and bruises have healed quickly, albeit not as quickly as Ren's or Kishan's would."

He picked up the amulet hanging around my neck and examined it carefully. "The different pieces may have different properties. We don't really know the extent of its power at this point. It's a mystery that I hope to solve one day. The bottom line, however, is to not take risks. If something looks dangerous, avoid it. If something chases you, run. Do you understand?"

"Got it."

He dropped the amulet and went back to stowing things in the Jeep. "I'm glad that Kishan agreed to give it to you."

"Agreed? I thought it was his idea."

"No, actually, getting the amulet was the reason Ren wanted to stop here in the first place. He wouldn't leave until he'd convinced Kishan to let you have it."

Puzzled, I said, "Really? I thought we were trying to convince Kishan to join us."

Mr. Kadam shook his head sadly. "We knew there was little hope of that. Kishan has been indifferent to any previous efforts I've made to conscript him for our cause. I've tried over the years to lure him out of the jungle and into a more comfortable life at the house, but he prefers to remain here."

I nodded. "He's punishing himself for Yesubai's death."

Mr. Kadam looked at me, surprised. "Did he speak of this to you?"

"Yes. He told me what happened when Yesubai died. He still blames himself. And not just for her death, but also for what happened to him and Ren. I feel very sad for Kishan."

Mr. Kadam sagely considered, "For such a young person, you're very compassionate and perceptive, Miss Kelsey. I'm glad Kishan was able to confide in you. There is hope for him yet."

I helped him gather up his papers and the fold up chair and table. When we were done, I patted Ren lightly on his shoulder to let him know we were ready to leave. He stood slowly, arched his back, twitched his tail, and then curled his tongue in a giant yawn. After rubbing his head against my hand, he followed me to the Jeep. I hopped into the passenger seat, leaving the back open for Ren to sprawl out in.

Driving back to the highway, Mr. Kadam seemed to actually enjoy weaving through the obstacle course of tree stumps, bushes, rocks, and potholes. The Jeep's shock absorbers were top of the line, but I still had to hold tightly onto the door handle and brace myself against the dashboard to keep from knocking my head on the roof. Finally, we were out onto the smooth highway again and heading southwest.

Mr. Kadam encouraged, "Tell me all about your week with two tigers."

I peeked at Ren in the backseat. He seemed to be napping, so I decided to start by telling him about the hunt first, and then I backtracked and talked about everything else. Well, almost everything else. I didn't talk about the kissing thing. It wasn't that I thought Mr. Kadam wouldn't have understood; in fact, I think he would have. I couldn't trust that Ren was actually asleep in the back, and I wasn't ready to share my feelings yet, so I skipped that part.

Mr. Kadam was most interested in hearing about Kishan. He'd been shocked when Kishan walked out of the jungle asking for more food for me. He said that Kishan hadn't seemed to care about anything or anyone since his parents had died.

I told him about how Kishan stayed with me for five days while Ren was hunting and that we talked about how he met Yesubai. I tried to keep my voice quiet and whisper about her so I didn't upset Ren. Mr. Kadam seemed puzzled at my need to encode everything I was saying, but he indulged me anyway. He nodded, carefully listening to my comments about you-know-what and the thing-that-happened-at-that-place.

I could tell he knew more and could have filled in a few blanks for me but he wouldn't divulge information loosely. Mr. Kadam was the type of man who kept confidences. That characteristic worked both for me and against me. Ultimately, I decided that it was a good thing and changed the subject to Ren and Kishan's childhood.

"Ah. The boys were their parents' pride and joy—royal princes with a knack for getting into trouble and charming their way out of it. They were given anything they desired, but they had to work to earn it.

"Deschen, their mother, was unconventional for India. She would take them out in disguise to play with the poor children. She wanted her children to be open to all cultures and religious practices. Her marriage to their father, King Rajaram, was a blend of two cultures. He loved and indulged her, not caring what anyone else thought. The boys were raised with the best of both worlds. They studied everything from politics and warfare to herding and crops. They were trained in the weapons of India, and also had access to the best teachers from all over Asia."

"Did they do other things? Like normal teenager stuff?"

"What types of things are you curious about?"

I twitched nervously. "Did they . . . date?"

Mr. Kadam quirked an eyebrow curiously. "No. Definitely not. The story you told me about," he winked, "you-know-what is the only time I have ever heard of either of them having a romantic escapade. Frankly, they had no time for that, and both boys were to have arranged marriages anyway."

I rested my head against the seat back after tilting it back a little. I tried to imagine what their lives were like. It must have been difficult having no choices, but then again they were privileged when others had much less. Still, having freedom of choice was something I treasured.

Soon, my thoughts became foggy, and my tired body nudged me into a deep sleep. When I woke up, Mr. Kadam handed me a wrapped sandwich and a large fruit juice.

"Go ahead and eat something. We'll stop at a hotel for the night so you can get a good night's rest in a comfortable bed for a change."

"What about Ren?"

"I picked a hotel that's near a small section of jungle. We can drop him there and pick him up on the way back."

"What about tiger traps?"

Mr. Kadam laughed softly. "Told you about that, did he? Don't worry, Miss Kelsey. He's not likely to make the same mistake twice. There aren't any big animals in this area so the townsfolk won't look for him. If he keeps his head low there shouldn't be any trouble."

An hour later, Mr. Kadam pulled over near a dense part of the jungle at the outskirts of a small town and let Ren out. We continued on to a village that was bustling with vibrantly dressed people and colorful homes and pulled to a stop in front of our hotel.

"It's not a five star," Mr. Kadam explained, "but it does have its charms."

A polished square convenience store window displayed sale items. On top of the store, I saw a giant sign supported by a wood frame. It was painted pink and red and announced the store's name, which I couldn't read, and featured an old-fashioned cola bottle, which was universally recognizable no matter what language was printed on it.

Mr. Kadam approached the hotel's front desk while I wandered around, examining the interesting products for sale. I found American chocolate bars and sodas mixed in with unusual candies and frozen popsicles in exotic flavors.

Mr. Kadam got our keys and bought us two colas and two popsicles. He handed me a white one while he took the orange one. I pulled off the wrapper, warily smelling my frozen treat.

"It's not something like soy bean and curry is it?"

He grinned. "Take a bite."

I did and was surprised to find it was coconut flavored. *Not as good as Tillamook Mudslide, but not bad at all*, I mused.

Mr. Kadam bit off a hunk of his popsicle, held it up with a grin, and said, "Mango."

The two-story, mint-green hotel had a wrought iron gate, a concrete patio, and flamingo-pink trim. My room had a full-size bed set in the middle of the floor. A colorful curtain hid a small closet with a few wooden hangers. A basin and a pitcher of fresh water as well as a couple of earthenware mugs rested on a table. Instead of air conditioning, a ceiling fan circled lazily overhead, barely stirring the warm air. There was no bathroom. All tenants had to share the facilities on the first floor. The accommodations were sparse, but it still beat the jungle, hands down.

After seeing me settled and giving me my key, Mr. Kadam said he would come retrieve me to take me to dinner in three hours, and then he retreated, leaving me to my privacy.

He was barely out the door when a small Indian woman wearing a bright orange flowing shirt over a white skirt came to launder my dirty clothes. In no time at all, she returned with my washed clothes and hung them on the clothesline outside my door. They flapped quietly in the breeze, and I drowsed listening to the soothing domestic sound.

After a short nap and sketching a few new drawings of Ren as a tiger, I braided my hair and tied it with a red ribbon to match my red shirt. I'd just finished putting on my sneakers when Mr. Kadam knocked on the door.

He took me out to eat at what he said was the best restaurant in town, The Mango Flower. We took a small motorboat taxi across the river and walked to a building that looked like a plantation house that was surrounded by banana, palm, and mango trees.

He led me around the back, and we walked on a paved stone path that led to an amazing view of the river. Heavy wooden tables with smooth polished tops and stone benches were placed all around a patio. Decorated iron lanterns were set on the corner of each table and provided the only light. A brick archway to the right was covered in white jasmine that perfumed the evening air.

"Mr. Kadam, this is lovely!"

"Yes, the man at the front desk recommended it. I thought you would enjoy a good meal since you've been eating army rations for a week."

I let Mr. Kadam order for me since I had no idea what the menu said. We enjoyed a dinner of basmati rice, grilled vegetables, chicken *saag*, which turned out to be chicken cooked with creamed spinach, a flaky white fish with mango chutney, vegetable *pakora* fritters, coconut prawns, naan bread, and a kind of lemonade made with a dash of cumin and mint called *jal jeera*. I sipped the lemonade, found it was a bit too tangy for my taste, and ended up drinking a lot of water instead.

As we started our meal, I asked Mr. Kadam what more he'd learned about the prophecy.

He wiped his mouth with his napkin, took a sip of water, and said, "I believe what you are seeking is called the Golden Fruit of India." He leaned in a little closer and lowered his voice. "The tale of the Golden Fruit is a very old legend forgotten by most modern scholars. It was supposedly an object of divine origin given to Hanuman to watch over and protect. Shall I tell you the story?"

I sipped my water and nodded.

"India was once a vast wasteland, completely uninhabitable. It was full of fiery serpents, great deserts, and fierce beasts. Then the gods and goddesses came and the face of the land changed. They created man and gave mankind special gifts, the first one being the Golden Fruit. When it was planted, a mighty tree sprang up, and from the fruit that grew on the tree, seeds were gathered and spread all over India, changing it into a fertile land that would feed millions."

"But, if the Golden Fruit was planted, wouldn't it have disappeared or become the roots of the tree?"

"One fruit from that first tree ripened quickly and became golden, and that Golden Fruit was taken and hidden by Hanuman, the half-man, half-monkey king of Kishkindha. As long as the fruit is protected, India's people will be fed."

"So that's the fruit we have to find? What if Hanuman is still protecting it and we can't get to it?"

"Hanuman protected the fruit by placing it in his fortress and surrounding it with immortal servants who would watch over it. I don't know much about the kinds of barriers that would be set up to stop you. I'm guessing there will be more than one trap designed to pull you from your course. On the other hand, you are Durga's favored one, and you have her protection as well."

I rubbed my hand absentmindedly. It tingled. The henna drawing had faded, but I knew it was still there. I sipped my water.

"Do you really think we'll find anything? I mean, do you really believe in this stuff?"

"I don't know. I hope it's true so the tigers can be freed. I try to keep my mind open. I know there are powers that I can't discern and things that bend and shape us that we can't see. I shouldn't be alive, but somehow I am. Ren and Kishan are trapped in some kind of magic that I don't understand, and it's my duty to help them."

I must have looked worried because he patted my hand and said, "Don't fret. I have a strong feeling that everything will work out in the end. It's faith that keeps me focused on our goal. I have great confidence in you and Ren, and I believe, for the first time in centuries, that there is hope."

He clapped his hands and rubbed them together. "Now, shall we turn our attention to dessert?"

He ordered *kulfi* for both of us, which he explained was an Indian ice cream made from fresh cream and nuts. It was refreshing on a warm evening, though not as sweet or creamy as American ice cream.

After dinner, we strolled back to the boat and talked about Hampi. Mr. Kadam advised that we should visit a local temple of Durga before we ventured to the ruins to look for the gateway to Kishkindha.

As we strolled slowly through town to the market, Mr. Kadam and I caught sight of our mint-green hotel. He turned to me with a sheepish expression and said, "I hope you forgive me in choosing this somewhat modest hotel. I wanted to stay in the smaller town closer to the jungle in case Ren needed me. He can reach us here quickly if he needs to, and I felt safer being closer to him."

"I'm fine, Mr. Kadam. After staying in the jungle for a week, this feels luxurious."

He laughed and nodded his head. We browsed through the different

stalls, and Mr. Kadam bought some fruit we could share for breakfast and some type of rice cakes wrapped in banana leaves. They looked similar to the lunch Phet had made for me, but Mr. Kadam assured me they were sweet and not spicy.

After I got ready for bed, I fluffed my pillow and stuck it behind my back, pulled my freshly washed and dried quilt over my lap, and thought about Ren sitting in the jungle all alone. I felt guilty being here with him out there. I also missed him and felt lonely. I liked having him around. Sighing deeply, I pulled my hair out of my braid, wiggled down, and fell into a light sleep.

Sometime around midnight, a soft knock on my door woke me. I was hesitant to open it. It was late, and surely it couldn't be Mr. Kadam. I walked to the door, put my hand quietly against it, and listened.

There was a muffled tap again, and I heard a familiar voice whisper faintly, "Kelsey, it's me."

I unlocked the door and peeked out. Ren was standing there dressed in his white clothes, barefoot, with a triumphant grin on his face. I pulled him inside and hissed out thickly, "What are you doing here? It's dangerous coming into town! You could have been seen, and they'd send hunters out after you!"

He shrugged his shoulders and grinned. "I missed you."

My mouth quirked up in a half smile. "I missed you too."

He leaned a shoulder nonchalantly against the doorframe. "Does that mean you'll let me stay here? I'll sleep on the floor and leave before daylight. No one will see me. I promise."

I let out a deep breath. "Okay, but promise you'll leave early. I don't like you risking yourself like this."

"I promise." He sat down on the bed, took my hand, and pulled me down to sit beside him. "I don't like sleeping in the dark jungle by myself."

"I wouldn't either."

He looked down at our entwined hands. "When I'm with you, I feel like a man again. When I'm out there all alone, I feel like a beast, an animal." His eyes darted up to mine.

I squeezed his hand. "I understand. It's fine. Really."

He grinned. "You were hard to track, you know. Lucky for me you two decided to walk to dinner, so I could follow your scent right to your door."

Something on the nightstand caught his attention. Leaning around me, he reached over and picked up my open journal. I had drawn a new picture of a tiger—my tiger. My circus drawings were okay, but this latest one was more personal and full of life. Ren stared at it for a moment while a bright crimson flush colored my cheeks.

He traced the tiger with his finger, and then whispered gently, "Someday, I'll give you a portrait of the real me."

Setting the journal down carefully, he took both of my hands in his, turned to me with an intense expression, and said, "I don't want you to see only a tiger when you look at me. I want you to see me. The man."

Reaching out, he almost touched my cheek but he stopped and withdrew his hand. "I've worn the tiger's face for far too many years. He's stolen my humanity."

I nodded while he squeezed my hands and whispered quietly, "Kells, I don't want to be him anymore. I want to be me. I want to have a life."

"I know," I said softly. I reached up to stroke his cheek. "Ren, I—" I froze in place as he pulled my hand slowly down to his lips and kissed my palm. My hand tingled. His blue eyes searched my face desperately, wanting, needing something from me.

I wanted to say something to reassure him. I wanted to offer him comfort. I just couldn't frame the words. His supplication stirred me. I felt a deep bond with him, a strong connection. I wanted to help him, I wanted to be his friend, and I wanted . . . maybe something more. I tried to identify and categorize my reactions to him. What I felt for him seemed too complicated to define, but it soon became obvious to me that the strongest emotion I felt, the one that was stirring my heart, was . . . love.

I'd built a dam around my heart after my family died. I hadn't really let myself love anyone because I was afraid they'd be taken from me again. I purposefully avoided close ties. I liked people and had many friendly relationships, but I didn't risk loving. Not like this.

His vulnerability allowed me to let my guard down, and gently and methodically, he tore apart my well-constructed dam. Waves of tender feelings were lapping over the top and slipping through the cracks. The feelings flooded through and spilled into me. It was frightening opening myself up to feel love for someone again. My heart pounded hard and thudded audibly in my chest. I was sure he could hear it.

Ren's expression changed as he watched my face. His look of sadness was replaced by one of concern for me.

What was the next step? What should I do? What do I say? How do I share what I'm feeling?

I remembered watching romance movies with my mom, and our favorite saying was "shut up and kiss her already!" We'd both get frustrated when the hero or heroine wouldn't do what was so obvious to the two of us, and as soon as a tense, romantic moment occurred, we'd both repeat our mantra. I could hear my mom's humor-filled voice in my mind giving me the same advice: "Kells, shut up and kiss him already!"

So, I got a grip on myself, and before I changed my mind, I leaned over and kissed him.

He froze. He didn't kiss me back. He didn't push me away. He just stopped . . . moving. I pulled back, saw the shock on his face, and instantly regretted my boldness. I stood up and walked away, embarrassed. I wanted to put some distance between us as I frantically tried to rebuild the walls around my heart.

I heard him move. He slid his hand under my elbow and turned me around. I couldn't look at him. I just stared at his bare feet. He put a finger under my chin and tried to nudge my head up, but I still refused to meet his gaze.

"Kelsey. Look at me." Lifting my eyes, they traveled from his feet to a white button in the middle of his shirt. "*Look* at me."

My eyes continued their journey. They drifted past the golden-bronze skin of his chest, his throat, and then settled on his beautiful face. His cobalt blue eyes searched mine, questioning. He took a step closer. My breath hitched in my throat. Reaching out a hand, he slid it around my waist slowly. His other hand cupped my chin. Still watching my face, he placed his palm lightly on my cheek and traced the arch of my cheekbone with his thumb.

The touch was sweet, hesitant, and careful, the way you might try to touch a frightened doe. His face was full of wonder and awareness. I quivered. He paused just a moment more, then smiled tenderly, dipped his head, and brushed his lips lightly against mine.

He kissed me softly, tentatively, just a mere whisper of a kiss. His other hand slid down to my waist too. I timidly touched his arms with my fingertips. He was warm, and his skin was smooth. He gently pulled me closer and pressed me lightly against his chest. I gripped his arms.

He sighed with pleasure, and deepened the kiss. I melted into him. *How was I breathing?* His summery sandalwood scent surrounded me. Everywhere he touched me, I felt tingly and alive.

I clutched his arms fervently. His lips never leaving mine, Ren took both of my arms and wrapped them, one by one, around his neck. Then he trailed one of his hands down my bare arm to my waist while the other slid into my hair. Before I realized what he was planning to do, he picked me up with one arm and crushed me to his chest.

I have no idea how long we kissed. It felt like a mere second, and it also felt like forever. My bare feet were dangling several inches from the floor. He was holding all my body weight easily with one arm. I buried my fingers into his hair and felt a rumble in his chest. It was similar to the purring sound he made as a tiger. After that, all coherent thought fled and time stopped.

All the neurons were firing in my brain simultaneously and causing my system to go haywire and stop working. I had no idea kissing felt like this. Sensory overload.

At some point, Ren reluctantly let me down. He still supported my weight, which was good because I was ready to fall over. He cupped my cheek and ran a thumb slowly across my bottom lip. He stood close to me, keeping one arm wrapped around my waist. His other hand moved to my hair, and his fingers began to slowly twist the loose strands.

I had to blink my eyes a few times to clear my vision.

He laughed quietly. "Breathe, Kelsey." He had a very self-satisfied, smug grin on his face, which, for some reason, got my ire up.

"You seem very happy with yourself."

He raised an eyebrow. "I *am*."

I smirked back at him and said, "Well, you didn't ask for permission."

"Hmm, perhaps we should rectify that." He trailed his fingers up my arm, swirling little circles as he went. "Kelsey?"

I watched his progress and mumbled, distracted, "Yes?"

He stepped closer. "Do I—"

"Hmm?" I wiggled slightly.

"Have your—"

He started nuzzling my neck then moved up to my ear. His lips tickled me as he whispered, and I felt him smile, "Permission—"

Goose bumps broke out on my arms and I trembled.

"To kiss you?"

I nodded weakly. Standing on my tiptoes, I slipped my arms around

his neck showing him that I was definitely giving permission. He trailed kisses from my ear across to my cheek in achingly slow motion, grazing along a path of his choosing. He stopped, hovering just over my lips, and waited.

I knew what he was waiting for. I paused only a brief second before whispering faintly, "Yes."

Smiling victoriously, he crushed me against his chest and kissed me again. This time, the kiss was bolder and playful. I ran my hands from his powerful shoulders, up to his neck, and pressed him close to me.

When he pulled away, his face brightened with an enthusiastic smile. He scooped me up and spun me around the room, laughing. When I was thoroughly dizzy, he sobered and touched his forehead to mine. Shyly, I reached out to touch his face, exploring the angles of his cheeks and lips with my fingertips. He leaned into my touch like the tiger did. I laughed softly and ran my hands up into his hair, brushing it away from his forehead, loving the silky feel of it.

I felt overwhelmed. I didn't expect a first kiss to be so . . . life altering. In a few brief moments, the rule book of my universe had been rewritten. Suddenly I was a brand new person. I was as fragile as a newborn, and I worried that the deeper I allowed the relationship to progress, the worse it would be if Ren left. *What would become of us?* There was no way to know, and I realized what a breakable and delicate thing a heart was. *No wonder I'd kept mine locked away.*

He was oblivious to my negative thoughts, and I tried to push them into the back of my mind and enjoy the moment with him. Setting me down, he briefly kissed me again and pressed soft kisses along my hair-line and neck. Then, he gathered me into a warm embrace and just held me close. Stroking my hair while caressing my neck, he whispered soft words in his native language. After several moments, he sighed, kissed my cheek, and nudged me toward the bed.

"Get some sleep, Kelsey. We both need some."

After one last caress on my cheek with the back of his fingers, he changed into his tiger form and lay down on the mat beside my bed. I climbed into bed, settled under my quilt, and leaned over to stroke his head.

Tucking my other arm under my cheek, I softly said, "Goodnight, Ren."

He rubbed his head against my hand, leaned into it, and purred quietly. Then he put his head on his paws and closed his eyes.

Mae West, a famous vaudeville actress, once said, "A man's kiss is his signature." I grinned to myself. If that was true, then Ren's signature was the John Hancock of kisses.

The next morning, Ren was gone. I got dressed and knocked on Mr. Kadam's door.

The door opened and he smiled at me. "Miss Kelsey! Did you sleep well?"

I couldn't detect any sarcasm and guessed that Ren had chosen not to reveal his night escapade to Mr. Kadam.

"Yes, I slept just fine. A bit too long though. Sorry about that."

He gestured dismissively, handing me a rice cake wrapped in banana leaf, some fruit, and a bottle of water. "Not to worry. We will go retrieve Ren and drive to Durga's temple. There's no rush."

I headed back to my room and set down my breakfast. Slowly gathering a few personal items, I placed them in my small travel bag. I frequently caught myself daydreaming. I'd look in the mirror and touch my arm, my hair, and my lips, while remembering Ren's kisses. I had to constantly shake myself and refocus. What should have taken me ten minutes took an hour and a half.

At the top of my bag, I placed my journal and my quilt. I zipped my

bag shut, and then went in search of Mr. Kadam. He was waiting for me in the Jeep looking over maps. He smiled at me and seemed in good cheer, even though I'd made him wait so long.

We picked up Ren, who leapt out of the trees like a playful cub. When he reached the Jeep, I leaned out to pet him, and he reared up on his hind legs to nuzzle my hand and lick my arm through the open window. He hopped in the back seat, and Mr. Kadam got us back on the road.

Carefully following the map routes, he pulled off on a dirt road that led through the jungle, finally stopping at Durga's stone temple.

durga's temple

Mr. Kadam instructed us to wait in the car while he checked the temple for visitors. Ren nudged his head between the seats and butted my shoulder until I turned around.

"You'd better keep your head down. Someone may see you if you're not more careful," I said with a laugh.

The white tiger made a noise.

"I know. I missed you too."

After about five minutes, a young American couple exited the temple and drove off, and Mr. Kadam returned.

I hopped out and opened the door for Ren, who started brushing up against my legs like a giant house cat waiting to be fed. I laughed.

"Ren! You're going to knock me over." I kept my hand on his neck, and he contented himself with that.

Mr. Kadam chuckled, and said, "You two go ahead and check out the temple while I keep watch for more visitors."

The path to the temple was lined with smooth terracotta-colored stones. The temple itself was the same terracotta color mixed with striations of soft sepia, spicy pink, and pale oyster. Trees and flowers had been planted around the temple grounds, and various walking paths led off from the main entrance.

We climbed the short stone steps that led to the opening. The entry was open to the air and displayed tall carved pillars that supported the access way. The threshold was just high enough for a person of average height to walk through. On either side of the opening were amazingly detailed carvings of Indian gods and goddesses.

A notice, written in several languages, warned that we should remove our shoes. The floor was dusty, so I took off my socks too, and stuffed them into my tennis shoes.

Once inside, the ceiling expanded into a high dome carved with intricate images of flowers, elephants, monkeys, the sun, and gods and goddesses at play. The rock floor was rectangular, and four tall decorative columns connected by ornamental arches stood at each corner. The pillars showed carvings of people in various stages of life and occupations in the act of worshipping Durga. A likeness of the goddess was found at the top of each post.

The temple was literally carved out of a rocky hill. A series of stairs led up from the main floor in three directions. I picked the archway on the right and climbed the steps. The area beyond had been damaged. Crumbled, broken rocks were scattered all over the floor. I couldn't imagine from the state of the space what it might have been used for.

The next area housed a stone altar of sorts. A small broken statue, now unidentifiable, rested on top. Everything was coated with thick sepia powder. Particles of it twinkled and hung in the air like pixie dust. Beams of light descended from cracks in the dome and spotlighted the floor with narrow rays. I couldn't hear Ren but every move I made echoed through the empty temple.

The air outside was stifling, but inside, the temple was merely warm and even cool in some places, as if each step brought me to a different climate. I glanced at the floor and saw my footprints and Ren's paw prints and made a mental note to sweep the floor before we left. We wouldn't want people to think a tiger was prowling the grounds.

After searching the area and finding nothing of consequence, we entered the archway on the left, and I gasped in amazement. A hollowed-out recess in the rock sheltered a beautiful stone statue of Durga. She wore a towering headpiece and had all eight arms arrayed around her torso like peacock feathers. She clutched various weapons, one of which was raised in defense. I looked closer and saw that it was the *gada*, the club. Curled around her legs was Damon, Durga's tiger. His large claws were extended from a heavy paw and aimed at the throat of an enemy boar.

"I guess she had a tiger to protect her too, huh, Ren?"

I positioned myself directly in front of the statue, and Ren sat next to me. As we examined her, I asked him, "What do you think Mr. Kadam expects we will find here? More answers? How do we get her blessing?"

I paced back and forth in front of the statue while investigating the walls, poking my fingers gingerly into crevices. I was looking for something out of the ordinary—but being a stranger in a strange land, I wasn't quite sure what that might be. After a half hour, my hands were smudged, cobwebby, and coated with terracotta dust. What was worse was that I'd gotten nowhere. I wiped my hands on my jeans and plopped down onto the stone steps.

"I give up. I just don't know what we should be looking for."

Ren came over and rested his head on my knee. I stroked his soft back.

"What are we going to do next? Should we keep looking or head back to the Jeep?"

I glanced at the supporting column next to me. It showed a carving of people worshipping Durga. On this one, there were two women and one man who were offering food. I thought they must be farmers because there were different types of fields and orchards dominating the rest of the post. Herds of domestic animals and farming tools were also carved into the scene. The man carried a bunch of grain slung over his shoulder. One of the women carried a basket of fruit, and the other woman had something small in her hand.

I got up to take a closer look. "Hey, Ren, what do you think that is in her hand?"

I jumped. The prince's warm hand took mine and squeezed it lightly.

I scolded, "You really should warn me before you change form, you know."

Ren laughed and traced the carving with his finger. "I'm not sure. It looks kind of like a bell."

I traced the carving with my finger and muttered, "What if we made an offering to Durga like that?"

"What do you mean?"

"I mean, what if we offered something. Like fruit. And then rang a bell?"

He shrugged his shoulders. "Sure. Anything's worth a try."

We headed back to the Jeep and told Mr. Kadam our idea. He seemed enthusiastic about making an attempt.

"Excellent idea, Miss Kelsey! I don't know why I didn't think of it myself."

He dug through our lunch and pulled out an apple and a banana.

"As for a bell, I did not think to bring one with me, but I believe that in many of these old temples a bell was installed. The disciples rang them when guests arrived, when worshipping, and to call others to a meal. Why not search the shrine for such a bell. Perhaps you will find one, and we will not have to drive back into town to buy one."

Taking the apple and the banana, I said, "I sure hope this works, and she blesses us because I have absolutely no idea what I am doing.

I hope you're not expecting too much. Please don't get your hopes up, Mr. Kadam, because you're bound to be disappointed."

He reassured me that he could never be disappointed in me and shooed us on our way.

Back inside the temple, Ren searched the altar area while I started digging through the rubble in the other room.

After about fifteen minutes, I heard, "Kelsey, over here! I found it!"

I quickly joined Ren who showed me a narrow wall at the edge of the room that couldn't be seen from the doorway of the temple. Shallow stone shelves had been carved out like tiny alcoves. On the top shelf, far above my reach but still within Ren's, sat a tiny rusty bronze bell covered in cobwebs and dust. It had a little ring at the top so it could hang from a hook.

Ren took it off the shelf and used his shirt to clean it. Wiping off the grime and powdery rust, he shook it, and it emitted an airy tinkling sound. He grinned and offered his hand, walking with me back to the statue of Durga.

"I think you should be the one to make the offering, Kells." He brushed his hair away from his eyes. "You *are* the favored one of Durga, after all."

I grimaced. "Perhaps, but you forget that *I'm* a foreigner, and *you* are a prince of India. Surely, you know what you're doing more than I do."

He shrugged. "I was never a Durga worshipper. I don't really know the process."

"What did or do you worship?"

"I participated in the rituals and holidays of my people, but my parents wanted Kishan and me to decide for ourselves what we believed. They had a great tolerance for different religious ideology because they were from two different cultures. What about you?"

"I haven't gone to church since my parents died."

He squeezed my hand and proposed, "Perhaps we both need to find a path to faith. I do believe there's something more than just us, a good power in the universe that guides all things."

"How do you stay so optimistic when you've been stuck as a tiger for centuries?"

He swiped a spot of dust from my nose with the tip of his finger. "My current level of optimism is a relatively new acquisition. Come on."

He smiled, kissed my forehead, and pulled me away from the column.

We approached the statue, and Ren began dusting off the tiger. Cleaning the statue seemed like a good place to start. I unfolded the napkin Mr. Kadam had wrapped the fruit in and started to wipe years of dust off the statue. After we cleaned off all the dust and cobwebs from Durga and her tiger, including all eight of her arms, we dusted around the base and up the frame. At the base of the statue, Ren found a slightly hollowed-out rock that looked like a bowl. We decided that this may have been where people left their offerings.

I set the apple and banana in the bowl and stood directly in front of the statue. Ren stood next to me and held my hand. I stammered, "I'm nervous. I don't know what to say."

"Okay, I'll start and then you add what feels natural."

He rang the small bell three times. Its tinkling sound echoed and bounced around the cavernous temple.

In a loud, clear voice, he said, "Durga, we come to ask your blessing on our quest. Our faith is weak and simple. Our task is complex and mystifying. Please help us find understanding and strength."

He looked at me. I swallowed, tried to wet my dry lips, and added, "Please help these two princes of India. Restore to them what was taken. Help me be strong enough and wise enough to do what's necessary. They both deserve a chance to have a life."

I gripped Ren's hand firmly, and we waited.

Another minute passed, and another. Still nothing happened. Ren hugged me briefly and whispered that he had to change back into a tiger again. I kissed his cheek, and he began to change. The minute he was a tiger again, the room began to vibrate, and the walls began to shake. A booming thunder sounded in the temple, followed by several bursts of white lightning.

An earthquake! We'd both be buried alive!

Rocks and stones began falling from overhead, and one of the great pillars cracked. I fell to the ground. Ren leapt over me and stood over my body, protecting me from falling debris.

The quake gradually stopped, and the rumbling ceased. Ren moved away from me, as I staggered up slowly. I looked back at the statue in astonishment. A section of the stone wall had broken and slid to the floor, shattering into hundreds of pieces.

On the wall where the rock had been was an imprint of a hand. I walked closer, and Ren growled softly. I traced the handprint with my finger and looked back at Ren. Mustering my courage, I lifted my hand and placed it in the print. I felt the stone grow hot like in the Cave of Kanheri. My skin glowed as if someone held a flashlight under my hand. Fascinated, I stared at the blue veins appearing as my skin became transparent.

Phet's henna design surfaced vividly again and blazed bright red. Crackling sparks leapt from my tingling fingers. I heard a tiger growl, but it wasn't Ren. It was Damon, Durga's tiger!

The tiger's eyes gleamed yellow. The stone changed from hard rock to living flesh and orange and black fur. It bared its teeth as it growled at Ren. Ren backed up a step and roared as his fur bristled around his neck. Suddenly, the tiger stopped, sat down, and turned its face up to its owner.

I took my hand out of the print and began moving away. Slowly, I stepped backward until I was standing behind Ren. Chills shot down my spine, and I started quaking with fear. The rigid statue began breathing, and the pale oyster-colored stone melted away into flesh.

The goddess Durga was a beautiful Indian woman, but with skin of gold. Dressed in a blue silk robe, she shifted, and I heard the whisper of material as it slid down a dainty limb. Jewels of every kind adorned each arm. They sparkled and glittered. Reflections in every color of the rainbow filled the temple and bounced from place to place as she moved. I sucked in a breath and held it as she blinked open her eyes and lowered her eight arms. Durga folded two pairs across her chest and tilted her head as she regarded us.

Ren moved closer and brushed his side against me. It reassured me, and I was very grateful for his steady presence. I put my hand on his back and felt his muscles tense under my palm. He was ready to pounce, to attack, if it became necessary.

The four of us considered each other silently for a time. Durga seemed to be particularly interested in my hand, which was currently stroking Ren's back. Finally, she spoke.

One of her golden limbs stretched out and gestured toward us. "Welcome to my temple, daughter."

I wanted to ask her why I was her favored one and why she called me daughter. I wasn't even Indian. Phet had said the same thing, and the concept still baffled me, but I felt it was better to keep quiet.

She pointed to the bowl at her feet and said, "Your offering has been accepted."

I looked down at the bowl. The food shimmered, sparkled, and then disappeared. Durga patted her tiger on the head for a while, seeming to forget we were there.

I chose to say nothing and let her take her time.

She looked at me and smiled. Her voice echoed like a tinkling bell through the cavern. "I see you have your own tiger to aid you in times of battle."

My voice sounded weak and frail compared to her rich, melodic tone. "Umm, yes. This is Ren, but he is more than just a tiger."

She smiled at me, and I found myself entranced by her splendor.

"Yes. I know who he is and that you love him almost as much as I love my own Damon. Yes?"

She tugged on her tiger's ear affectionately while I mutely nodded in agreement.

"You have come to seek my blessing, and my blessing I will give. Come closer to me and accept it."

Still frightened, I shuffled slightly closer. Ren maneuvered his body between the goddess and me and kept his attention trained on the tiger.

Durga raised all eight arms and used them to beckon me closer still. I took a few more steps. Ren came nose to nose with Damon. They both sniffed loudly while wrinkling their faces to show their dislike of the position.

The goddess ignored them, smiled warmly at me, and announced, "The prize you seek is hidden in Hanuman's Kingdom. My sign will show you the gateway. Hanuman's realm has many dangers. You and your tiger must stay together to make it safely through. If you separate, there is great danger for you."

Her arms began moving, and I took a small step back. She attached a conch shell to her belt and then began rotating the weapons in her hands. Passing them from limb to limb, she inspected each one carefully. When she came to the one she wanted, she stopped. She looked at the weapon lovingly and ran a free hand down the side of it.

It was the *gada*. She held it out in front of her and indicated that I should take it. I reached out, wrapped my hand around the handle, and lifted it toward me. It looked to be made of gold, but, strangely, it wasn't heavy. In fact, I could easily hold it in one hand.

I ran a hand over the weapon. It was about the length of my arm. The handle was twisted and carved in a golden spiral. The hilt was a smooth, thin, gold bar two inches wide that ended with a heavy sphere about the size of a softball. Tiny crystal jewels dotted the entire surface of the orb. I was stunned to realize that they were probably diamonds.

I thanked Durga as she smiled benevolently at me. She raised an arm and pointed at the pillar, then nodded, encouraging me.

I pointed and asked, "You want me to go to the pillar?"

She indicated the *gada* in my hand and then looked at the pillar again.

I sucked in a breath. "Oh. You want me to test it out?"

The goddess nodded once and began petting her tiger's head.

I turned toward the pillar and lifted the *gada* like a baseball bat. "Okay, but, just so you know, I've always been terrible at sports."

I took a deep breath, closed my eyes, and swung weakly. I expected it to hit the stone, bounce off, and jar my arms painfully. I missed. Or, so I had thought.

It all happened in slow motion. A thunderous boom shook the temple, and a chunk of stone shot across the temple like a missile. The piece hit with an echo and shattered, exploding into a million pieces. I watched as gritty dust rained down on the pile of rubble. The pillar was left with a huge gouge in its side.

My mouth gaped open in amazement. I turned back to the goddess, who was smiling proudly at me.

"I guess I'll have to be really careful with this thing."

Durga nodded and explained, "Use the *gada* when necessary to protect yourself, but I expect it will mostly be wielded by the warrior at your side."

I briefly puzzled over how a tiger would use a *gada*, and then carefully set the weapon on the stone floor. When I looked up, Durga had extended another delicate arm adorned with a golden snake as alive as the goddess herself. The serpent's tongue darted in and out, and it hissed slightly as it curled around her bicep.

"This, however, is for you," Durga announced, and I watched with horror as the golden snake slowly unwound itself from her arm and traveled down the dais. It stopped there and raised its head, bringing half its body up off the floor. It flicked its tongue, sensing the air around it. The eyes looked like tiny emeralds. As it fanned out the sides of its neck into the telltale hood, I trembled, realizing it was a cobra. The normal markings of the cobra were still there, but instead of brown and black scales, the markings of the hood were beige, amber, and cream swirled on a golden background. The skin of the belly was buttermilk white and its tongue was ivory.

The snake wound its way closer to me. Ren backed up a few steps as it slithered between his paws.

I was terrified. My mouth was dry. My throat closed, and I felt as if a stiff wind could easily blow me over. I looked up at the goddess. She had a serene smile plastered on her face as she watched her pet draw nearer to me.

The snake approached my shoe, flicked its tongue again, and wound its head around my leg. It circled my calf and twisted its body around several times. I could feel its muscles clench my limb tightly as it undulated and slowly ascended. Around and around it went. My limbs were quaking, and I wavered like a flower in a hard rain. I heard myself whimper. Ren half-growled and half-whined, apparently not knowing what to do to help me. The snake reached the top of my thigh. My elbows were locked stiff, and my arms were quivering as I held them slightly out and away from my sides. The snake gripped

my thigh with the lower half of its body and stretched its head toward my hand.

I watched in rapt alarm as it reached my wrist and quickly shot over. Curling under my arm, it continued its slow progress and began climbing up that limb. The scales felt cool, smooth, and polished, like onyx disks slipping over my bare skin. The snake was gripping me in a powerful vise. As it squeezed my arm and moved up, my blood flow stopped, and then began pounding again, as if I'd wrapped a faulty tourniquet around the limb.

When most of its body was bound around my upper arm the snake stretched its head up to my shoulder and brushed against my neck. Its tongue shot out and tasted the salty perspiration on my throat, causing my lower lip to quiver. Beads of sweat trickled down my face as I breathed heavily. I could feel its head pass my neck, brush against my chin, and then, there it was, open hooded and looking right in my face with its jeweled eyes. Just when I thought I was going to pass out, it descended to my arm again, wrapped itself around two more times, and then froze, its head facing Durga.

I cautiously dropped my eyes to look at it and was awed to see that it had become jewelry. It looked like one of the snake armlets that ancient Egyptians wore. Its emerald eyes stared unblinkingly ahead.

I tentatively reached my other arm over to touch it. I could still feel the smooth scales, but it felt metallic, definitely not living flesh. I shuddered and turned toward the goddess.

Like the *gada*, the snake was relatively light. *If I have to wear a golden snake on my arm, at least it didn't weigh me down*, I thought. Now that I was brave enough to look more closely, I could see that the snake had shrunk. The large serpent had diminished in size to become a small wraparound piece of jewelry.

The goddess spoke, "She is called Fanindra, the Queen of the Serpents. She is a guide and will help you to find what you seek. She can conduct you on safe paths and will light your way through darkness. Do not be afraid of her, for she wishes you no harm."

The goddess reached out to stroke the snake's immobile head and counseled, "She is sensitive to the emotions of others and longs to be loved for who she is. She has a purpose, as do all of her children, and we must learn to accept that all creatures, however fearsome they may be, are of divine origin."

I bowed my head and said, "I will try to overcome my fear and give her the respect she deserves."

The goddess smiled and said, "That is all I ask."

As Durga gathered her arms and began to return them to their original positions, she gazed down at Ren and me. "Now, may I give you some advice before you leave?"

I demurred, "Of course, Goddess."

"Remember to stay by each other. If you get separated, do not trust your eyes. Use your hearts. They will tell you what is real and what is not. When you obtain the fruit, hide it well, for there are others who would take it and use it for evil and selfish purposes."

"But aren't we supposed to bring the fruit back to you as an offering?"

The hand stroking the tiger froze on his fur, and the flesh dulled until it became rough and gray. "You have made your offering. The fruit has another purpose, which you will understand in due time."

"What about the other gifts, the other offerings?" I was desperate to learn more, and it was obvious my time was running out.

"You may present the other offerings to me at my other temples, but the gifts you must keep until—"

Her red lips seized in midsentence, and her eyes dimmed and became sightless orbs once more. She, and her golden jewels and bright clothing, faded to become a rough sculpture once again.

I reached out and touched Damon's head, and then I dusted my

hands on my jeans after grazing over a gritty ear. Ren brushed up next to me, and I trailed my fingers over his furry back, deep in thought. The sound of pebbles falling brought me out of my reverie.

I hugged Ren around his thick neck, carefully picked up the *gada*, and walked with Ren to the entryway of the temple. He stood there for a minute while I grabbed a tree branch and dusted away all of his paw prints.

As we walked down the dirt path back to the Jeep, I was surprised to see the sun had traveled a long way across the sky.

We'd been in the temple a while, much longer than I'd thought. Mr. Kadam was parked in the shade with the windows down, napping. He sat up quickly and rubbed his eyes as we approached.

I asked, "Did you feel the earthquake?"

"An earthquake? No. It's been as quiet as a church out here."

He chuckled at his own joke. "What happened in there?"

Mr. Kadam looked from my face down to my new gifts and gasped in surprise. "Miss Kelsey! May I?"

I passed the *gada* to him. He tentatively reached out both of his hands and took it from me. He seemed to struggle a bit with its weight, which made me wonder if he was weaker than he looked in his old age. Pure delight and scholarly interest reflected on his face. "It's beautiful!" he exclaimed.

I nodded. "You should see it in action." I lay my hand on his arm. "You were right, Mr. Kadam. I would say that we definitely received Durga's blessing." I pointed to the snake wrapped around my arm. "Say hello to Fanindra."

He stretched a finger to the snake's head. I winced, hoping she wouldn't reanimate, but she remained frozen. He seemed transfixed by the objects.

I tugged on his arm. "Come on, Mr. Kadam, let's go. I'll tell you all about it in the car. Besides, I'm starving."

Mr. Kadam laughed, elated and jubilant. Carefully wrapping the *gada* in a blanket, he stowed it in the back of the car. Then he came around to my side of the Jeep and opened the door for me and Ren. We climbed in. I put my seatbelt on, and we drove off toward Hampi. Durga had spoken, and we had a golden fruit to obtain. We were ready.

hampi

On the ride back to the city, Mr. Kadam listened with rapt attention to every detail of our experience at Durga's temple. He rattled off dozens of questions. He asked for details that I hadn't even considered important at the time. For example, he wanted to know what the other three pillars in the temple showed, and I didn't think I even looked at them.

Mr. Kadam was so absorbed in the story that he drove straight to the hotel and forgot to drop Ren in the jungle. We doubled back, and I walked Ren out. Mr. Kadam was happy to stay in the Jeep and examine the *gada* more closely.

I walked through the tall grass with Ren all the way to the tree line, bent down, hugged him, and whispered, "You can stay in my room again at the hotel if you like. I'll save you some dinner." I kissed the top of his head and left him there staring after me.

For dinner, Mr. Kadam used the hotel kitchen to whip us up some veggie omelets with pan-fried toast and papaya juice. I was starving, and, looking at the other foods emerging from the kitchen, I felt very appreciative that Mr. Kadam liked to cook. Another guest was boiling something in a large pot, and the smell left something to be desired. For all I knew, she was boiling the laundry.

I ate a plate full and then asked Mr. Kadam for seconds to take back to my room, in case I got hungry that night. He was more than happy to oblige and luckily didn't ask questions.

I left the *gada* in Mr. Kadam's care, but discovered the snake armlet wouldn't budge from my arm, no matter how I tried to slip, pull, and yank it off. Mr. Kadam worried that people would try to steal it from me.

"Believe me," I said, "I would love to take Fanindra off. But if you saw the way she got on my arm, you'd want her to remain inanimate too."

Squelching that thought quickly, I chastised myself for forgetting that Fanindra was a gift and a divine blessing, and I whispered a quick apology to her.

When I returned to my room, I changed into my pajamas, which took some doing. Lucky for me, I had a short-sleeved top. I tucked the top of the sleeve into Fanindra's coil so her head wasn't covered and picked up my toothbrush. I looked at Fanindra in the mirror while I brushed my teeth.

Tapping the snake lightly on the head, I mumbled with my toothbrush in my mouth, "Well, Fanindra, I hope you like water because tomorrow morning I plan to take a shower, and if you're still on my arm, then you're going with me."

The snake remained frozen but her hard eyes glittered back at me from the mirror in the dim room.

After brushing my teeth, I clicked on the ceiling fan, set Ren's dinner on the dresser, and climbed into bed. The snake's body dug into my side, making it hard to get comfortable. I thought I'd never be able to sleep with that hard piece of jewelry wrapped around my arm, but, eventually, I drifted off.

I woke in the middle of the night to Ren's soft scratching on my door. Anxious to be close, he ate quickly and then wrapped his arms around me, and pulled me onto his lap. He pressed his cheek against my forehead and started talking about Durga and the *gada*. He seemed excited about what the *gada* could do. I nodded sleepily and shifted, resting my head against his chest.

I felt safe snuggled in his arms and enjoyed listening to the warm timbre of his voice as he spoke quietly. Later, he began humming softly, and I felt the strong beat of his heart keeping rhythm against my cheek.

After a while, he stopped and moved his arms while I issued a sleepy protest. Rearranging my limp body, he lifted me in his arms and cuddled me close. Half asleep, I mumbled that I could walk but he ignored me, placed me on my bed, and gently straightened my limbs. I felt him brush a kiss on my forehead and cover me with my quilt, and then I was out.

Sometime later, I opened my eyes with a start. The golden snake was gone! I rushed to turn on the light and saw her resting on the night-stand. She was still frozen, but now she was coiled up with her head resting on top of her body. I watched her suspiciously for a moment, but she didn't move.

I shuddered, thinking of a live snake slithering over my body while I slept. Ren lifted his tiger head and looked at me with concern. I patted him and told him I was fine, and that Fanindra had moved during the night. I thought about asking Ren to sleep between the snake and me, but I decided that I needed to be brave. Instead, I turned on my side and rolled myself up in my quilt tightly to prevent any odd things from happening to my limbs without my knowledge.

I also mentioned to Fanindra that I would appreciate it if she wouldn't slither up and down my body when I wasn't aware of it and said that I would prefer it not to happen at all if she could help it.

She didn't move or blink a green eye.

Do snakes blink? Pondering that deep question, I rolled back on my side and fell asleep easily.

The next morning, Ren was gone and Fanindra hadn't moved, so I decided it was the perfect time for a shower. I was back in my room, towel-drying my hair, when I noticed that Fanindra had changed shape again. This time, she was twisted in loops as before, ready to be placed on my arm.

I picked her up gently and slid her unyielding body up the length of my arm where she fit comfortably. This time, when I tried to pull her off, she slipped down easily.

Pushing her back up, I said, "Thank you, Fanindra. It will be much easier if I can take you off when I need to."

I couldn't be sure, but I thought that I saw her emerald eyes glow softly for a moment.

I was just finishing plaiting my hair and tying it with a green ribbon to match Fanindra's eyes when I heard a knock. Mr. Kadam was standing outside the door with freshly washed hair and a trimmed beard.

"Ready to go, Miss Kelsey?" he asked, taking my bag.

We checked out of our hotel and drove over to the wooded area to pick up Ren. We waited for several minutes, then finally he shot out of the trees and ran up to meet the car. I laughed nervously.

"Overslept a little today, did you?"

He had probably just run the entire way back. I gave him a meaningful glance, hoping he understood my you-really-should-have-left-earlier look.

On the way to Hampi, we stopped at a fruit stand and got a smoothie, called a *lassi*, and a grainy breakfast bar for each of us. When I was halfway done with my drink, I offered it to Ren. He stuck his head between the front seats and lapped up the rest of my smoothie. His long tongue slurped out what was left of my shake and he also made sure to lick my hand "accidentally" every other lick.

I laughed. "Ren! Thanks a lot. Now my hands are all sticky."

He leaned over and started licking my hands with more enthusiasm, swirling his pink tongue between my fingers.

"Okay! Okay! That tickles. Thanks, but that's enough."

Mr. Kadam laughed heartily, then reached over to open the glove box and handed me a travel pack of antibacterial hand wipes.

As I wiped the tiger saliva off my hands, I threatened, "See if I ever share a milkshake with *you* again."

I heard a *harrumph* come from the back seat. When I looked back at him a moment later, he was the picture of an innocent tiger, but I knew better.

Mr. Kadam indicated that we were nearing Hampi and pointed to a large structure in the distance. He explained, "That tall, conical structure you see ahead is called the Virupaksha Temple. It's the most prominent building in Hampi, which was originally settled two thousand years ago. We'll be passing Sugriva's cave soon, where it is said the jewels of Sita were hidden."

"Are the jewels still there?"

"The jewels were never discovered, which is also one of the reasons the city has been sacked so often by treasure hunters," Mr. Kadam stated, pulled off to the side of the road, and let Ren out. "There will be too many tourists on the site during the day, so Ren can wait here while we walk the grounds and look for clues. We will return for him in the early evening."

We parked in front of the gate. Mr. Kadam led me to the first and largest structure, the Virupaksha Temple. It was about ten stories tall and resembled a giant upside-down waffle cone. Pointing ahead, he illustrated its architecture.

"This temple has courtyards, shrines, and gateways in all of those side buildings. Inside, there is an inner sanctum with pillared halls and cloisters, which are long, arched corridors open to a central courtyard. Come, I will show you."

As we wandered the temple, Mr. Kadam reminded that we were looking for a passageway to Kishkindha, a world ruled by monkeys.

"I'm not sure what it will look like, but perhaps there will be another hand print marking. Durga's prophecy also mentioned snakes."

More snakes, I thought, cringing. *A doorway to a mythical world? Things just keep getting stranger and stranger the deeper I get into this adventure.*

As the day progressed, I became so dazzled by the ruins that I completely forgot our purpose in being there. Everything I saw was amazing. We stopped at another structure called the Stone Chariot. It was a stonework carving of a miniaturized temple set on wheels. The chariot's wheels were shaped to look like lotus flowers and could even rotate like normal tires.

Another building, called the Vithala Temple, had beautiful statues of women dancing. We listened in on a tour guide who explained the significance of the temple's fifty-six pillars. He said, "When struck, the pillars vibrate and produce sounds exactly like musical notes. A truly skilled musician could even play a song on them."

We stood still for a moment to listen to the columns hum and vibrate as he softly tapped the stone. The magical musical tones thrummed through us, lifted into the air, and slowly faded into nothing. The sound disappeared long before the vibrations stopped.

We stopped at another building called the Queen's Bath. Mr. Kadam pointed out its features. "The Queen's Bath was a place the king and his wives could relax. There used to be apartments surrounding the center. Balconies jutted out from the rectangular buildings, and the women would sit, look over the bathing pool, and relax. An aqueduct pumped

water into the brick pool, and there used to be a small flower garden off to the side, over here, where the women could lounge and have picnics.

"The pool was about fifty feet long and six feet deep. Perfume was poured into the water to make it more fragrant, and flower petals were strewn across the surface. Lotus-shaped fountains surrounded the pool as well. You can still see a few of them. A canal surrounded the entire structure and the building was heavily guarded so that only the king could enter and frolic with the women. All other would-be suitors were kept out."

I frowned at him. "Umm, if the king was the only man to enter, then how is it that you know so many details about the ladies' pool?"

He stroked his beard and grinned.

Shocked, I whispered, "Mr. Kadam! You didn't break into the king's harem, did you?"

He shrugged his shoulders lightly. "It was a rite of passage for a young man to try to break into the Queen's Bath, and several died trying. I happen to be one of the brave few who lived through the experience."

I laughed. "Well, I have to say, my whole opinion of you has changed. Breaking into a harem! Who would've thought?" I walked a few more steps and then spun around. "Wait a minute. A rite of passage, did you say? Did Ren and Kishan—?"

He paused and raised his hands. "It might be better if you asked them yourself. I wouldn't want to say the wrong thing."

I grunted, "Hmm. That question has definitely moved to the top of my list for Ren."

We moved on to tour the House of Victory, the Lotus Mahal, and the Mahanavami Dibba, but we didn't see anything particularly interesting or outstanding there. The Noblemen's Palace was a place for diplomatic meetings and high-ranking officials to be wined and dined. The King's Balance was a building used by the kings to weigh gold, money, and grains in trade, and was also used to distribute goods to the poor.

My favorite place was the Elephant Stables. A long, cavernous structure, it had housed eleven elephants in its heyday. Mr. Kadam explained that those elephants were not used for battle, but for ritual. They were the king's private stock—highly trained and used for various ceremonies. Often, they were dressed in golden cloth and jewels, and their skin was painted. The building had ten domes of different sizes and shapes that rested on the top of each elephant's apartment. He explained that other elephants were kept also to do menial labor and construction, but that the private stock would have been special.

A large statue of Ugra Narasimha was the last thing that we saw. When I asked Mr. Kadam what he represented, he didn't respond. He walked around the structure, looking at it from many different angles while thinking and mumbling quietly to himself.

I shaded my eyes and studied the top of it. Trying to get Mr. Kadam's attention, I repeated, "Who is he? He's a pretty ugly fellow."

This time, Mr. Kadam replied, "Ugra Narasimha is a half-man, half-lion god, though he can assume other forms as well. He was supposed to look frightening and impressive. He is most famous for slaying a powerful demon king. What's interesting is the demon king could not be killed either on earth or in space, during day or night, not inside or outside, by neither human nor animal, nor by any object that was dead or alive."

"You sure seem to have a lot of unslayable demons running around in India. So how did he kill the demon king?"

"Ah, Ugra Narasimha was very clever. He picked up the demon king, placed him on his lap, and then killed him at twilight, on a door-step, with his claws."

I laughed. "Sounds like Miss Scarlett, in the conservatory, with a candlestick."

Mr. Kadam chuckled. "Indeed, it does."

"Hmm, day or night, that's twilight, inside or outside was the door-step, and he was half human and half lion, so that covers animal/human requirement. Not on earth or space is on his lap . . . what was the other one?"

He answered, "He could not be killed by an object that was dead or alive, specifically, animate or inanimate, so he used his claws."

"Huh. That *is* pretty clever."

"I'm impressed, Miss Kelsey. You figured out most of those on your own. If you look closely, you can see that he is sitting on the coils of a seven-headed snake, and their heads are arching above him, hoods open, to provide shade for his head."

I grimaced. "Uh-huh, those are snakes alright." I twitched my arm uncomfortably and peeked over at my golden snake. Fanindra was still a hard piece of jewelry.

Mr. Kadam started muttering to himself again and spent a long time examining the Ugra Narasimha statue.

"What are you looking for, Mr. Kadam?"

"Part of the prophecy says 'let serpents guide you.' Before, I thought it might only mean your golden snake, but perhaps the plural is important."

I joined him in looking for a secret doorway or a handprint like the one I found before, but didn't see anything. We tried to be as casual as the other tourists as we studied the statue.

Finally giving up, Mr. Kadam said, "I think it might be a good idea if you and Ren return here this evening. I have a suspicion that the entrance to Kishkindha might be here by this statue."

We brought a picnic dinner to Ren. I tore off pieces of Tandoori chicken for him, which he carefully nibbled from my hand, and told him about the different buildings we'd investigated at the temple.

Mr. Kadam explained to us that the ruins were closed to visitors at sundown unless there was a special event taking place.

"Most evenings, guards are standing watch, looking out for treasure hunters. In fact," he elaborated, "treasure hunters are responsible for much of the destruction you see in the ruins now. They seek gold and jewels, but those things were taken from Hampi long ago. The treasures of Hampi now are the very things they are destroying."

Mr. Kadam felt that it would be best if he dropped us off at a location on the other side of the hills because there were no roads leading into Hampi, and it wasn't guarded as well.

"But if there aren't any roads, then how will we get there?" I asked, fearing Mr. Kadam's answer.

He grinned. "Off-roading is one of the reasons I bought the Jeep, Miss Kelsey." He rubbed his hands together animatedly. "It will be exciting!"

I groaned and muttered, "Fantastic. I feel nauseous already."

"You will need to carry the *gada* in your backpack, Kelsey. Do you think you can manage?"

"Sure. It's not that heavy, really."

He stopped what he was doing and looked at me, puzzled.

"What do you mean it's not heavy? It is actually quite heavy." He pulled it free from its wrapping and hefted it with two hands, straining his muscles to hold it.

Puzzled, I mumbled, "That's weird. I remember it being light for its size." I walked over and took the *gada* from him, and we were both shocked that I could easily lift it with one hand. He took it back and tried to lift it with one hand, and he again faltered under its weight.

"To me it feels like fifty pounds."

I took it back again. "For me it feels like maybe five to ten pounds."

"Amazing," he marveled.

Shocked, I added, "I had no idea it actually weighed that much."

Mr. Kadam took the weapon from me again, wrapped it in a soft blanket, and then placed it into my backpack. We hopped back into the

Jeep, and he drove us along a back road, which changed to a dirt road, which changed to gravel, which changed to two lines in the dust, and then disappeared altogether.

He let us out and set up a mini-camp, assuring me that Ren would be able to find his way back. He also gave me a small flashlight, a copy of the prophecy, and then he included a warning: "Don't use the flashlight unless you have to. Be sparing because there are security guards walking through the ruins at night. Be alert. Ren can smell them coming, so you should be alright. Also, I would suggest that Ren stay in tiger form as much as possible in case you should need him for something later."

He squeezed my shoulders and smiled. "Good luck, Miss Kelsey. Remember that you might not find anything at all. We might have to start all over again tomorrow night, but we have plenty of time. Don't fret. There's no pressure."

"Okay. Well, here goes nothing!"

I began trailing after Ren. The moonless night allowed the stars to glisten with extra brilliance in the black, velvety sky. Beautiful though it was, I wished the moon were out. Fortunately, Ren's white hide was easy to follow. Pits and holes dotted the terrain, and I had to be extra careful. It would be bad timing to trip and break my ankle. I didn't even want to think about what kinds of creatures had made those holes.

After a few minutes of stumbling, a greenish light began to softly glow in front of me. I looked around and finally figured out that the light was coming from Fanindra's jeweled eyes. She lit the dark countryside for me, providing a special kind of night vision. Everything was clearly outlined, but it still felt creepy, like I was walking across alien terrain on some weird green planet.

After almost an hour of walking, we arrived at the outskirts of the ruins. Ren slowed and smelled the air. A cool breeze wafted over the hills and freshened the warm evening. He must have decided the coast was clear because he continued forward quickly.

We made our way through the ruins, striking a path toward the Ugra Narasimha statue. The ruins that had been stunning during the day now hovered over me, casting dark shadows. Beautiful archways and pillars that I had admired were now gaping black maws waiting to devour me. The gentle breeze I had appreciated earlier whistled and moaned as it wound through passageways and doors as if ancient ghosts were announcing our presence.

Hair on the back of my neck prickled as I imagined eyes watching us and demons lurking in hazy hallways. When we finally neared the statue, Ren started investigating, sniffing, and searching out hidden crevices.

After an hour of searching and finding nothing, I was ready to give up, head back to Mr. Kadam, and get some sleep.

"I'm exhausted, Ren. Too bad we don't have an offering and a bell. Maybe the statue would come alive. Hmm?"

He sat next to me, and I patted his head for a moment. I looked up at the statue, and an idea popped into my head. I mumbled, "A bell. I wonder—"

I got up and ran to the Vithala Temple with its musical columns. Guessing what to do, I lightly tapped on one three times hoping that no guards would hear it, and ran back to the statue. The eyes on the seven-headed snake were now glowing red, and a small carving of Durga had appeared on the side of the statue.

"This is it! The sign of Durga! Okay, we're doing something right. What do we do next? An offering?" I moaned in frustration. "But we don't have anything to offer!"

The mouth of the half-man, half-lion statue opened, and wispy, gray mist started pouring out of it. Puffs of the cold, smoky vapor rolled down the statue's body, spilled over the ground, and began to expand in all directions. Red snake eyes were soon the only thing I could still make out. I kept my hand on Ren's head for reassurance.

I decided to climb the stone carving and search the head of the statue for some sign. Ren growled an objection, but I ignored him and began climbing up. It didn't matter because I still found nothing to lead us further. As I hopped down from the statue, I misjudged the distance to the ground and tripped. Ren was at my side instantly. I wasn't hurt except for a broken fingernail, but being encompassed by the swirling fog was chilling.

Just then, as I stared at my fingernail, I remembered Mr. Kadam's story about Ugra Narasimha. I thought for a minute.

"Ren, maybe if we repeat Ugra Narasimha's actions, the statue will lead us to the next step. Let's try to reenact Ugra Narasimha's famous task."

He brushed against my hand in the darkness.

"Okay, there are five parts. The first thing we need is an animal/human, so that's you. Here, stand next to me. You can be Ugra Narasimha, and I'll be the demon king. Next, we need to stand somewhere that isn't inside or outside, so let's look for some steps or a doorway."

I felt around the statue. "I think there was a little doorway here, near the statue." I stretched out my hand and felt the stone door frame. We both stepped under it.

"The third part was neither day nor night. It's too late for dusk or twilight. I guess I can try using my flashlight." I clicked my little flashlight on and off, hoping that would be enough. "Then there was the part about claws. You do have those. Umm, I think you have to scratch me. The story says kill, but I think scratching me might work."

I flinched. "You might need to draw blood though."

I heard his chest rumble in protest.

"It's okay. Just do a small scratch. It's no big deal."

He growled again softly, lifted his paw, and set it gently on my arm. I'd seen him hunt from a distance and had also seen his claws during his fight with Kishan. As the flashlight shined on his extended claws, I couldn't help but feel a little scared. I closed my eyes and heard a soft grunt as he moved, but I didn't feel anything.

I shone the flashlight all over my legs and didn't see any blood. I knew he'd done something, though, because I'd heard his claws tear through flesh. Immediately, I had a suspicion and aimed the flashlight on his white body, searching for where he'd hurt himself.

"Ren! Let me see. How bad is it?"

He lifted his leg, and I saw vicious rips where his claws had raked through his fur to the flesh. Blood was freely dripping on the ground.

I was angry. "I know you can heal fast, but really, Ren. Did you have to wound yourself so deeply? You know it might not work anyway if I don't bleed. I appreciate your sacrifice, but I still want you to slash me. I'm the one representing the demon king, so cut me . . . preferably not as deep as that."

He wouldn't lift his paw. I had to bend over and actually lift his heavy paw myself. When I finally positioned it over my arm, he retracted his claws.

I begged, "Ren. Please, *please* cooperate. This is hard enough as it is."

He allowed his claws to peek out halfway, and he lightly scratched my arm, barely leaving a mark at all.

"Ren! Do it, please. Now would be good."

He growled softly in disapproval and scratched me harder. The scratch marks left angry red welts down the length of my forearm. Two of the scratches bled lightly.

"Thanks." I flinched. I adjusted my flashlight to see his scratches again, which were almost healed already. Satisfied, I moved on to the last item.

"Now, the last one was that the demon king can't stand either in heaven or on the earth. Ugra set the demon on his lap, which means I guess I'll have to . . . sit on your back."

Awkward. Even though Ren was a big tiger and it would be like riding a small pony, I was still conscious that he was a man, and I didn't feel right about turning him into a pack animal. I took off my back-pack and set it down wondering what I could do to make this a bit less embarrassing. Mustering the courage to sit on his back, I'd just decided that it wouldn't be too bad if I sat sidesaddle, when my feet flew out from under me.

Ren had changed into a man and swept me up in his arms. I wiggled for a minute, protesting, but he just gave me a look—the don't-even-bother-coming-up-with-an-argument look. I shut my mouth. He leaned over to pick up the backpack, let it dangle from his fingers, and then said, "What's next?"

"I don't know. That's all that Mr. Kadam told me."

He shifted me in his arms, walked over to stand in the doorway again, then peered up at the statue. He murmured, "I don't see any changes."

He held me securely while looking at the statue and, I have to admit, I totally stopped caring about what we were doing. The scratches on my arm that had been throbbing a moment ago didn't bother me at all. I let myself enjoy the feeling of being cuddled up close to his muscular chest. *What girl didn't want to be swept up in the arms of a drop-dead gorgeous man?* I allowed my gaze to drift up to his beautiful face. The thought occurred to me that if I were to carve a stone god, I'd pick Ren as my subject. This Ugra half-lion and half-man guy had nothing on Ren.

Eventually, he realized I was watching him, and said, "Hello? Kells? Breaking a curse here, remember?"

I just smiled back stupidly. He quirked an eyebrow at me.

"What were you thinking about just now?"

"Nothing important."

He grinned. "May I remind you that you are in prime tickling position, and there's no escape. Tell me."

Gads. His smile was brilliant, even in the fog. I laughed nervously.

"If you tickle me, I'll protest and struggle violently, which will cause you to drop me and ruin everything that we are trying to accomplish."

He grunted, leaned close to my ear, and then whispered, "That sounds like an interesting challenge, *rajkumari*. Perhaps we shall experiment with it later. And just for the record, Kelsey, I wouldn't drop you."

The way he said my name made goose bumps rise all over my arms. When I looked down to quickly rub them, I noticed the flashlight had been turned off. I switched it on, but the statue remained the same. Giving up, I suggested, "Nothing's happening. Maybe we need to wait till dawn."

He laughed throatily while nuzzling my ear and declared softly, "I'd say that something *is* happening, but not the something that will open the doorway."

He trailed soft, slow kisses from my ear down my neck. I sighed faintly and arched my neck to give him better access. With a last kiss, he groaned and reluctantly raised his head.

Disappointed that he'd stopped, I asked, "What does *rajkumari* mean?"

He laughed quietly, carefully set me down, and said, "It means princess. Let's find a good place to sleep for a couple of hours, shall we? I'll run back and tell Mr. Kadam that we're planning to wait till dawn to try again."

He took my hand and led me to a grassy spot hidden from view.

Once I was settled, he left. I bunched my quilt up under my head and attempted to sleep. Restless until Ren returned, I gratefully snuggled against his tiger back and fell asleep.

I awoke to find myself moving, nestled in Ren's arms. He was carrying me back to the doorway. I sleepily mumbled, "You don't have to carry me. I can walk."

He smiled. "You were tired, and I didn't have the heart to wake you. Besides, we're here already."

It was still dark outside, but the eastern horizon was just starting to lighten. The statue was the same as we'd left it—with red snake eyes glowing and mist seeping out from the mouth. We stood in the doorway for a moment. I immediately felt something twist and move. It was Fanindra. She suddenly came alive, swelled to her normal size, and unwound herself from my arm.

Ren lowered me closer to the ground so she could drop delicately to the dirt below. She wound her way toward the statue and found a way to climb up to the top where the snake heads were resting.

We watched from the steps as she weaved over and under the seven snakes. As she passed them, they too came alive and writhed back and forth. We could see the coils that the statue was sitting on slowly change to scaly flesh.

Fanindra made her way back down and slithered over to Ren and me. Winding her body into loops, she stiffened and shrunk back to her golden armlet form. Ren set me down and walked over to pick her up. He slid her carefully up my arm, smiled at me, then traced the scratches on my arm lightly and frowned. He brushed a light kiss on the tender skin and changed back into a tiger.

We approached the statue where the wriggling snake torso was now moving and shifting. The snake coils lifted and slowly raised the statue

higher and higher in the air, until a black void opened up underneath. It raised high enough that there was space for Ren and me to step down into the opening.

Peering into the hole, I saw a series of stone steps that disappeared down into the darkness. The mouth of the statue suddenly stopped emitting fog, and, instead, began to draw it back in. Fog swept back toward us, up into the mouth of the statue, and dropped down into the pit below. I gulped and turned my flashlight toward the steps. We stepped between the thick snake coils, and Ren and I descended into a fog of nebulous shadow.

We had found the entrance to Kishkindha.

20

trials

We walked carefully down the stone steps, totally dependent on the weak illumination of my tiny flashlight. When we reached the bottom, Fanindra's eyes began to glow and gave the tunnel an eerie, viridian illumination.

I stopped Ren and reread Durga's prophecy out loud.

For protection, seek her temple
And take hold of Durga's blessing.
Travel west and search Kishkindha
Where simians rule the ground.
Gada strike in Hanuman's realm;
And hunt the branch that's bound.
Thorny dangers grasp above;
Dazzling dangers lie below,
Strangle, ensnare, the ones you love—
And trap in brackish undertow.
Lurid phantoms thwart your route
And guardians wait to bar your way.
Beware once they begin pursuit

> Or embrace their moldering decay.
> But all of this you can refute
> If serpents find forbidden fruit
> And India's hunger satisfy . . .
> Lest all her people surely die.

At the bottom of the page were Mr. Kadam's handwritten notes in his usual, neat script. I also read it aloud:

> Miss Kelsey,
> There are several trials you must face when you enter Kishkindha, so be wary. I have also included the warnings from Durga as you described them. She said that you should try to stay near Ren. If for some reason you get separated, there will be great danger. She also said do not trust your eyes. Your hearts and your souls will tell you the difference between fantasy and reality. The last thing she said was that when you obtain the fruit, hide it well.
>
> Bhagyashalin!
> May you be endowed with luck!
> Anik Kadam

I mumbled, "I have no clue what these dangers might be. Hopefully the thorny ones are some kind of plant."

We started walking, and I babbled along the way about what kind of animals might have thorns.

"Let's see. There are stegosaurus. No, stegosauruses. Hmm, maybe it's stegosauri. Well, however you say the plural, there are those kinds

of dinosaurs. Then there are dragons, porcupines, and we can't forget horny toads. If I had to pick a thorny animal, that would be my number one choice. Oh! But what if the horny toads are giant sized with huge gaping mouths? They could swallow us whole. Maybe we should get the *gada* out of the backpack, huh?"

I stopped and took it out. The hiking would probably be bad enough without hauling around the club but it made me feel better to have it in hand.

The tunnel soon turned into a stony path, and the farther we walked, the brighter it became. Fanindra's eyes dimmed and her light went out. Her eyes became mere glittering emeralds again. Something strange was going on. My weirdness meter had expanded considerably in the last few weeks, but this was weird even for me.

I couldn't really tell where the light was coming from. It seemed to filter in from ahead. Literally, we were following a light at the end of the tunnel. I felt like I was in one of my nightmares in which it wasn't bright, but it wasn't dark either. A lurking evil permeated my subconscious and a powerful force chased me, thwarted my progress, and hurt those I cared about.

The rolling mist seemed to follow us. As we walked, it surged slightly ahead to hinder our view of the path. When we stopped, it gathered itself and circulated around us like small nebulous clouds in orbit. The cold, gray mist explored our skin with icy fingers as if looking for an Achilles' heel.

The corridor began to feel different. Instead of walking on stone, my feet sunk slightly into moist ground, and I could hear the crunch my shoes made on stubby grass. The walls became mossy, then grassy, and soon were covered with small fern-like plants. I wondered how they could survive in this humid, dim environment.

The walls grew farther apart, until I couldn't make them out

anymore. The ceiling opened up to a gray sky. There was no depth to
it, and yet I couldn't see an end. It reminded me of a biosphere dome,
but it wasn't manmade. It was like we'd stepped onto another planet.

Our path turned downward, and I had to focus on my feet in front of
me. We entered a forest full of strange plants and trees. They rocked on
their roots as if the wind was pushing them, but I didn't feel even a hint
of a breeze. The trees were so close together and the brush was so thick
that the path became difficult to see, and then it disappeared altogether.

Ren stayed in front and tore a trail with his body. The trees had
long branches that drooped to the ground like weeping willows. Their
tendrils were feathery and tickled my skin as I passed. I reached up to
scratch my neck and found it wet.

I must be sweating. Strange, I don't feel *overworked. Maybe water fell
from the branch.* Something was smeared on my hand. The greenish light
gave the liquid a brown appearance. *What is that? Tree sap? No! Blood!*

I plucked a feathery leaf to get a closer look. When I examined it,
I was surprised to find tiny needles lining the underbelly. I reached out
a finger to touch one, and the needles swelled out toward my finger. I
moved my finger back and forth, and the needles shifted, following my
finger like a magnet.

"Ren, stop! The branches are scratching us. They have needles underneath that follow our movements. They're the thorny grasping dangers!"

When he stopped, feathery branches slowly slithered down from
above and wrapped around his neck and tail. He jumped away and tore
them viciously from the tree.

"We'll have to run or they'll ensnare us!" I shouted.

He doubled his effort to break through the undergrowth. I jogged
after him. The forest seemed to go on forever with no sign of the trees
thinning. After another fifteen minutes, I slowed, feeling extremely
tired. I just couldn't run anymore.

Panting, I wheezed, "Ren, I'm slowing you down. Go on ahead without me. Break through the tree line. You can make it." He stopped, turned around, and raced quickly back to my side. The branches started snaking down and began to wrap their curly tendrils around his body.

He roared and rolled, then slashed at the branches with his claws, which made them retreat for a moment. I felt one twisting its way around my arm and knew that this was it for me. Tears welled up in my eyes, and I knelt to stroke Ren's cheek.

I begged, "Ren, go. *Please* leave me."

He shifted form and placed his hand over mine. "We have to stay together, remember? I won't leave you, Kelsey. I'll never leave you." He smiled sadly.

I swallowed and nodded as he gently removed the curly branch from my arm and batted away another one that was reaching out for my neck.

"Come on."

He grabbed the *gada* out of my hand and started beating it against the branches, but they just tried to wrap their sharp green fingers around the weapon, unaffected by its power. Then he moved to a trunk and beat it severely.

Immediately, the tree gathered into itself. Branches folded inward and wrapped around the trunk protectively. Ren stepped in front of me and cautioned me to wait by the injured tree. He walked ahead a few paces and swung the *gada*.

He thrashed the tree trunks, leaving gaping, pulpy wounds as he went. I followed a length behind as he made slow progress through the forest. The branches seemed to know what he was up to and tore at him viciously, but Ren seemed to have an endless amount of energy.

I winced as I watched the cuts and scrapes appear across every bare patch of his skin. His back was soon lacerated, his shirt torn and bloody. He looked like he'd been brutally whipped with a cat-o'-nine-tails.

At last, we reached the edge of the needle forest and stopped in a clearing. He pulled me out of the reach of the branches and allowed his body to collapse to the ground. He bent over, sweating and winded from his exertion. I took some water out of my backpack and offered it to him. He drank the entire bottle in one gulp.

I leaned over and inspected his bloody arm. His body was slippery with blood and sweat. I got out another water bottle and an old T-shirt and began cleaning the dirt from his cuts and bruises. I pressed the cool, wet cloth to his face and back. He started to relax and breathe slower as I continued my ministrations. His cuts quickly began to heal, and as my worry over Ren diminished, I realized something.

"Ren! You've been a man now for much longer than twenty-four minutes. Are you okay—well aside from the scratches?"

He rubbed his hand on his chest. "I feel . . . fine. I don't feel the need to change back."

"Maybe this is all we need to do. Maybe we've broken the curse!"

He considered for a minute. "No, I don't think so. I have a feeling that we need to move on."

"Why don't you test it? See if you can become a tiger or not."

He changed into a tiger and back and his bloody torn clothes were immediately replaced with clean white cloth.

"Perhaps it's just the magic of this place that allows me to be human."

My face must have appeared crestfallen. Ren laughed and kissed my fingers.

"Don't worry, Kells. I'll be fully human soon, but for now I'll take this gift as long as I can keep it."

He winked at me and grinned, and then he leaned over to pull me closer so he could have a turn at examining my injuries. He inspected my arms, legs, and neck. He swiped the wet cloth down my arms and cleaned my cuts with healing tenderness. I knew that his injuries were much more severe than mine, so I tried to dissuade him, but he wouldn't have it.

He declared, "Everything checks out okay. You have one wicked scratch on your neck, but I think it'll heal fine." He bathed the back of my neck with the towel and pressed it there for a moment. Then he tugged at the collar of my T-shirt with his finger. "Are there, ah, any *other* places you want me to check out for you?"

I batted his hand away. "No, thank you. Those *other* places I can check for myself."

He laughed good-naturedly, and then stood and helped me up. He slipped on my backpack and hefted the *gada* over one shoulder. After offering me his hand, we began walking.

We passed more of the needle trees, but they were spaced much farther apart and were mixed in with some normal, non-killer types of trees, so we were able to stay out of their range. Ren twined his fingers through mine.

"You know, it's nice just to walk with you and not be worried about how much time I have left."

"Hmm, yes," I agreed shyly.

Ren seemed happy despite our situation. I thought about how hard it must be for him, knowing that he had very little time each day to be a man and trying to make the most of each and every minute. He felt like this creepy place was a gift. His cheerful mood eventually affected me too.

I knew that worse challenges probably awaited us, but walking alongside Ren, I didn't care. I let myself enjoy my time with him.

We found a dirt path again and started to follow it. The path led

toward some hills and a large tunnel that we assumed led through them. There was no other place to go, so we entered slowly, keeping a careful watch of our surroundings. Lit torches lined the stone walls, and many other tunnels led off from the main one. I jumped as I saw something pass by in a side passage.

"Ren! I saw something in there."

"I saw something too."

It seemed we were in a vast honeycomb of tunnels, and figures kept appearing at the edge of our vision. I pressed my body close against Ren, and he draped an arm around my shoulders.

I heard a voice, a woman's voice, cry softly, "Ren? Ren? Ren? Ren?" It echoed from tunnel to tunnel.

"I'm here, Kells! Kells! Kells!"

Ren looked at me apprehensively and squeezed my shoulder. The voices were ours. He let go of me and pulled the *gada* out to a ready position in front of him. Walking warily in front, he watched the other tunnels very carefully.

I heard screams and running footsteps, growling tigers, and screeches. I stopped walking for a moment and stood in front of one of the tunnels.

"Kelsey! Help me!" Ren appeared in the side tunnel. He was fighting a group of monkeys that were scratching and biting him. He changed to a tiger, sunk his teeth into them, and ripped them apart. It was gruesome!

I took a step backward, feeling afraid. Then I froze and remembered Durga's warning about staying together. I turned around and saw two other tunnels that hadn't been there before. Two Rens were walking straight ahead with the *gada* in front, one in each tunnel. *Which was the main tunnel? Which one was the real Ren?*

I heard running footsteps behind me and hastily chose the one

on the right. I hurried to catch up to him, but it seemed the closer I got, the farther away he was. I knew I'd chosen the wrong path. I called out to him, "Ren!"

He didn't turn toward me. I stopped and looked in two other tunnels for a sign of him. I saw Kishan and Ren fighting as tigers in one tunnel. Mr. Kadam was in a swordfight with a man who looked like my nightmare guy in another.

I hurried from tunnel to tunnel. Several passageways flashed scenes of my life. My grandma beckoned me to help her plant flowers. My high school teacher was asking me questions. There was even one with my parents. They were calling out to me. I gasped, and tears filled my eyes.

I screamed aloud, "No, no, no! This can't be happening! Where's Ren?"

"Kelsey? Kelsey! Where are you?"

"Ren! I'm here!" I heard my voice, but I hadn't said anything.

I looked in another tunnel and saw Ren running up to approach . . . me. Only it wasn't me. I was me. Ren came close to the thing that looked like me, and stroked her face.

"Kelsey, are you okay?"

I heard it respond, "Yes. I'm fine." It turned its head and looked straight at me while Ren kissed its cheek. The image morphed, and with a sharp, shattering noise, the face melted into death. It smiled insidiously, and I shivered with revulsion as I looked at a smiling corpse pulsating with maggots.

I approached the tunnel entrance and yelled at Ren to stop, but he couldn't hear me. There was some kind of barrier blocking me so I couldn't enter. The corpse snickered at me and waved a hand. The image became obscure, and I could no longer make out its form.

Infuriated, I pounded on the barrier, but it had no effect. After a few

moments, the barrier disappeared, and I was staring into a long black tunnel lit with torches, just like the dozens of others that I'd passed by before.

I gave up and moved on. I passed a Ren who was cowering on the ground, forlorn and self-deprecating. He was sobbing and bemoaning his losses. He spoke of all the mistakes he'd made and how wrong he'd been about everything. He begged for forgiveness, but he could find no absolution. The things he mentioned having done were awful, ineffable, horrible things. Things that I knew Ren had never done and couldn't even imagine doing. His body was angular and broken, and it was indescribably heartbreaking.

I was indignant. This was too much! It was so awful to see someone I cared about broken down into nothing that I became furious. Someone or something was playing games with us, and I hated it. What was worse was knowing that the same things were happening to Ren somewhere in these tunnels. Who knew how they were representing me!

I moved on to another tunnel and saw an upright and proud Ren with his back turned to me. I called out cautiously, "Ren? Is that really you?"

He turned around and smiled his beautiful smile, and then he held out his arms to me and beckoned me closer.

"Kelsey! Finally! What took you so long? Where have you been?"

With great relief, I wrapped my arms around him as he pulled me close. He held me and rubbed my back.

Puzzled, I inquired, "Ren? Where's the backpack and the *gada*?" I pulled back and looked up into his handsome face.

"We don't need them anymore. Shh, now. Just stay here with me for a minute."

I moved back quickly and took a few steps away.

"You're not Ren."

He laughed. "Sure I am, Kelsey. What do I have to do to prove it to you?"

"No. Something's wrong. You're not him!"

I ran out of the tunnel and kept running until my lungs were about to explode but I got nowhere. I just passed tunnel after tunnel. Slowing to a stop, I breathed hard, trying to think about what I should do. Ren had the *gada* and the backpack. He would never discard them. So he still had them somewhere, and I had nothing. No, that wasn't true. I did have something! I pulled the paper out of my jeans pocket and read through the warnings again.

> If for some reason you get separated, there will be great danger. She also said to not trust your eyes. Your hearts and your souls will tell you the difference between fantasy and reality.

Do not trust my eyes? Well, that was obvious at this point. So my heart will help me tell the difference. Okay, follow my heart. How do I do that?

I decided to just continue walking and keep an open mind. At each tunnel, I stopped to watch for a minute and then closed my eyes and tried to feel if it was right. Usually, whatever or whoever was in there doubled their efforts. They talked and cajoled, trying to tempt me to go in after them. I continued in this way, passing several tunnels, and none of the places where I stopped felt right.

I came to another passageway and paused to examine the scene. I saw myself dead and lying on the ground with Ren kneeling beside me. He leaned over my inert body investigating. I heard him whisper, "Kelsey? Is it you? Kelsey, please. Talk to me. I need to know if it's really you."

He picked my body up and cradled it lovingly in his arms. I checked to make sure he had the *gada* and the backpack, which he did, but I'd been fooled before. Then he said, "Don't leave me, Kells."

I closed my eyes and listened to his voice begging me to live. My heart started thumping wildly, a different reaction than I'd had in the past visions. I took a step closer and hit a barrier again.

I spoke to him softly, "Ren? I'm here. Don't give up."

He raised his head as if he heard me.

"Kelsey? I can hear you, but I can't see you. Where are you?" He lowered me, or the body that looked like me, to the ground, and it disappeared.

I told him, "Close your eyes and feel your way to me." He stood slowly and closed his eyes.

I closed my eyes too, and tried to focus not on his voice but on his heart. I imagined my hand on his chest, feeling the strong thump of his heart beneath my fingers. My body seemed to move of its own volition, and I took several steps forward. I concentrated on Ren, his laugh, his smile, how I felt being near him, then, suddenly, my hand touched his chest, and I could feel his heart beating. He was there. I opened my eyes slowly and looked at him.

He reached out a hand to touch my hair, but then he pulled it back. "Is it really you this time, Kells?"

"Well, I'm no maggoty corpse, if that's what you mean."

He grinned. "That's a relief. No maggoty corpse would be that sarcastic."

I countered, "Well, how do I know it's really you?"

He considered my question for a moment and then ducked his head to kiss me. He tugged me flush up against his chest, pulling me closer than I even thought possible, and then his lips touched mine. His kiss started out warm and soft, but quickly turned hungry and demanding. His hands ran up my arms, to my shoulders, and then cupped my neck.

I wrapped my arms around his waist and luxuriated in the kiss. When he finally pulled back, my heart was pounding in response.

When the power of speech returned, I quipped, "Well, even if it isn't really you, I'll take this version."

He laughed and relief flooded both of us. "Kells, I think you'd better hold my hand the rest of the way."

I smiled gaily back at him. "No problem." Thrilled to have my Ren back, I was able to ignore the calls and beseeching inquiries coming from the side passages.

A light appeared at the far end of the tunnel, and we made our way there. Ren held my hand tightly until we emerged from the opening and stood well away from it. He stopped next to a meandering creek that curved off behind some trees.

It felt like noon here, wherever here was, so we decided to take a break and eat.

Munching on an energy bar, Ren said, "I'd prefer to avoid the trees and stay closer to the creek bed. I'm hoping that if we follow it a little farther, it'll lead us to Kishkindha."

I nodded in agreement and wondered what else was waiting for us around the next bend.

Feeling refreshed after our brief rest, we pushed on and followed the creek. The water was running ahead of us, which, according to Ren, meant we were walking downstream. The bank was pebbly and full of smooth river rocks.

Picking up a gray stone, I tossed it up and down as I walked and lost myself in thought. The weight and feel of the rock changed. I opened my hand and peered at it. It had transformed into a smooth, sparkling emerald. I stopped and looked down at the rocks underfoot. They were still gray and dull, but as they disappeared under the water, I saw shimmering jewels instead.

"Ren! Look there. Under the water." I pointed out the jewels glittering below. The farther out in the river I looked, the bigger the jewels were. "Do you see that? There's a ruby the size of an ostrich egg!"

I had just leaned over to pluck a large diamond from the water when I felt Ren wrap his arms around me from behind and pull me back several feet.

He whispered against my cheek while pointing to the river, "Look over there. There, out of the corner of your eye. What do you see?"

"I don't see anything."

"Use your peripheral vision."

Right next to the diamond, an image glimmered slightly beneath the water. It looked like a white monkey, but hairless. Its long arms were stretched up, reaching out toward me.

"It was trying to grab you."

I quickly tossed the emerald into the creek. The water swirled and hissed where it hit, then it quieted and calmed again to become as smooth as silk. When I looked directly at the jewels, that's all I could see, but when I looked out of the corner of my eye, I could see water monkeys everywhere, floating just under the surface. It looked like they used their tails to anchor their bodies to tree roots and underwater plants, just like sea horses.

Ren mumbled, "I wonder if they could be Kappa?"

"What are Kappa?"

"A demon from Asia my mother used to tell me about. They lurked in water, waiting to catch children and suck their blood."

"Vampire sea horse monkeys? Are you serious?"

He shrugged. "Apparently, they are real. Mother told me about them when I was young. She said that children in China were taught to show respect for their elders by bowing. They were told that if they didn't bow, the Kappa would get them. The Kappa have depressions on the tops of their heads that are full of water. They need water on their heads in order to survive. The only way to save yourself if one comes after you is to bow."

"How does bowing save you?"

"If you bow to a Kappa, it will bow back. When it does, the water spills out of the top of its head, which leaves them defenseless."

"Well, if they can come out of the water, why haven't they attacked?"

He pondered thoughtfully. "They usually attack only children, or so I was told. My mother told me that her grandmother used to carve the children's names into fruit or cucumbers and then toss them into the water before bathing. The Kappa would eat the fruit and be satisfied enough that they wouldn't hurt the bathing children."

"Did your mother follow that tradition?"

"No. First of all, we were royalty and had our baths drawn for us. Second, my mother didn't believe in the story. She just shared it with us so we would understand the point, which was that all people and things needed to be treated with respect."

"I'd like to learn more about your mother sometime. She sounds like a very interesting woman."

He replied softly, "She was. I would've liked for her to know you as well." He meticulously scanned the water and pointed out the waiting demon. "That one was grabbing for you, even though they're supposed to attack only children. These might be assigned to protect the jewels. If you'd taken one, they probably would've pulled you under."

"Why pull me under? Why not just jump out at me?"

"Kappa usually drown their victims before taking their blood. They stay in the water as much as possible to protect themselves."

I backed up putting Ren between me and the river. "So should we head for the trees again or stay by the creek bed?"

He ran a hand through his hair and shouldered the *gada* again,

keeping it ready for attack. "How about we stay somewhere in the middle. The Kappa seem content to stay in the water for the time being, but let's try to avoid the branches of the trees too."

We walked along for another couple of hours. We were able to skirt both the Kappa and the trees, though the latter did try their best to reach out and grab us. The creek curved in a long bend that brought us a bit too close for comfort to the trees, but Ren had the *gada* ready, and a few blows on the close trunks took care of any wayward branches.

Eventually, we came upon an enormous tree that was directly in our path. Its long, snaking branches stretched impossibly far out toward us, needles pricked forward. Ren crouched down. With an extraordinary burst of speed, he ran ahead and leapt up toward the trunk. The tree's leafy embrace immediately engulfed him.

I heard a big thump, and the tree quivered and released him. He emerged all scratched but walked up to me with a grin on his face. His expression quickly changed into a look of concern, however, because my mouth was gaping open as I looked over his head. The tree had been blocking our view, and now that it had folded in on itself, I could see the ghostly gray kingdom of Kishkindha ahead.

kishkindha

We moved past the giant needle tree's reach and stared at the city. It was actually more the size of a medieval castle than a city. The river ran down to its wall and split into two directions, circling it like a moat. The walls were built of light gray stone tinged with blue flecks of mica, giving it a sparkling smoky periwinkle color.

"We're losing our light, Kelsey. And it's been a hard day. Why don't we set up camp here, get some sleep, and enter the city tomorrow."

"Sounds good to me, I'm beat."

Ren went off to collect some wood and came back, muttering, "Even the old dead branches can scratch you."

He threw several branches into the stone ring I'd created and started a fire. I tossed him a bottle of water. Pulling out the little pot, he filled it with water and left it to boil.

He went off in search of more firewood while I bustled about setting up camp, which went rather quickly because I didn't have the tent this time. All I could do was clear the space of rocks and branches.

After the water was hot, I poured some into both of our dinner packets and waited for the freeze-dried food to rehydrate and become edible. He soon returned, grumbling about the wood, and sat down next to me. I handed him a dinner, and he stirred it quietly.

Between bites of hot pasta, I asked, "Ren, do you think those Kappa things will come after us during the night?"

"I don't think so. They've stayed in the water this whole time and, if the story is accurate, they're also afraid of fire. I'll just make sure to keep the fire going all night."

"Well, maybe we should stand watch. Just in case."

The corner of his mouth quirked up as he took another bite of his dinner. "Okay, who gets the first watch?"

"I do."

His eyes twinkled with mirth. "Ah, a brave volunteer?"

I glared at him and took another bite. "Are you making fun of me?"

He threw a hand over his heart, "No, ma'am! I already know you're brave. You have nothing to prove to me."

Ren finished his meal, and then hunkered down by the woodpile and threw more of the strange branches on. The fire was bright. The flames licking the wood started burning with a greenish hue at first, then sputtered and crackled like fireworks. The flame changed to a bright reddish-orange tinged with green around the burning kindling.

I set down my finished dinner packet and stared into the weird flames. He sat down beside me again and picked up my hand.

"Kells, I appreciate you volunteering to stand watch, but I want you to rest. This journey is harder on you than it is on me."

"You're the one getting all scratched up. I just follow along behind."

"Yes, but I heal fast. Besides, I really don't think there's anything to worry about. Tell you what, I'll take the first watch, and if nothing happens, we'll both sleep. Agreed?"

I frowned at him. He started playing with my fingers and turned my hand over so he could trace the lines of my palm. Firelight flickered across his handsome features. My eyes drifted to his lips.

"Kelsey?" He made eye contact, and I quickly looked away.

I wasn't used to dealing with him when camping like this. I usually got to make all my own decisions, and he just followed me around. Er, or I guess I followed him most places. But, at least when he was a tiger he didn't argue back. *Or distract me with thoughts of being wrapped in his arms kissing him.*

He smiled an amazingly white smile and stroked the inside of my arm. "Your skin here is so soft."

He leaned over to nuzzle my ear. My blood started pounding thickly and fogged my brain. "Kells, tell me you agree with my plan."

I shook myself free from the spellbinding fog and set my jaw stubbornly. "Fine, you win. I agree," I mumbled. "Even though you are coercing me."

He laughed and moved to look at me. "And how *exactly* am I coercing you?"

"Well, first of all, you can't expect me to have coherent thoughts when you're touching me. Second, you always know how to get your way with me."

"Is that right?"

"Sure. All you have to do is bat your eyes, or in your case smile and ask nicely, throw in a distracting touch, and then, before I know it, you get whatever it is you want."

"Really?" he teased quietly. "I had no idea I had that effect on you."

Reaching out a hand, he turned my face toward him. He trailed his fingers lightly from my jaw, down to the pulse at my throat, and then across my neckline. My pulse hammered as he touched the cord tied around my neck and followed its path down to the amulet; then he skimmed his fingers lightly back up to my neck, studying my face as he touched me. I swallowed thickly.

He leaned in close and threatened playfully, "I'll have to use it more to my advantage in the future."

I sucked in a breath, my skin tingled, and I quivered slightly, which seemed to make him even more pleased with himself. He went off to walk the perimeter of our camp one last time while I drew my knees up to my chin, wrapped my arms around them, and let my mind drift.

My throat tingled where Ren had touched me. I lifted my hand to the hollow at the base of my neck and fingered the amulet. Briefly, I thought about Kishan and how formidable he appeared to be on the surface. Inside, he was as harmless as a kitten. The dangerous brother was Ren. Innocent though the blue-eyed tiger appeared to be, he was a compelling predator. Utterly irresistible—like a Venus flytrap. So alluring, so tempting, so deadly. Everything he did was seductive and quite possibly hazardous to my heart.

He seemed much more intimidating to me than Kishan with his flirty and blatant comments. Both brothers were gorgeous and charming. They had old-fashioned chivalrous manners that any girl would swoon over. But the way they talked, the things they said were straightforward. It wasn't just a game to them. It wasn't just a way to pick up women. They were serious.

Kishan was equal to Ren in many ways. In that regard, I could understand Yesubai's choice, but what made Ren 100 percent more dangerous for me was that I had feelings for him—strong ones. I already loved the tiger part of him before I even knew he was a man. That bond made caring for the man that much easier.

But being with the man was so much more complicated than being with the tiger. I had to constantly remind myself that they were two sides of the same coin—literally heads and tails. There were so many reasons I *should* let myself fall completely for Ren. There was a definite connection between us. I was undeniably attracted to him. We had a lot in common. I enjoyed my time with him. I liked talking to him and listening to his voice. And, I felt like I could tell him anything.

But, there were also many reasons for me to be cautious. Our relationship felt so complex. Everything had happened so fast. I felt overwhelmed by him. We were from different cultures. Different countries. Different centuries. We were even from different species for most of the day.

Falling for him would be like cliff diving. It would be either the most exhilarating thing that ever happened to me or the stupidest mistake I'd ever make. It would make my life worth living or it would crush me against stony rocks and break me utterly. Perhaps the wise thing to do would be to slow things down. Being friends would be so much simpler.

Ren came back, picked up my empty dinner packet, and stowed it in the backpack. Sitting down across from me, he asked, "What are you thinking about?"

I kept staring glassily at the fire. "Nothing much."

He tilted his head and considered me for a moment. He didn't press me, for which I was grateful—another characteristic I could add to the pro relationship side of my mental list.

Pressing his hands together palm to palm, he rubbed them slowly, mechanically, as if cleaning them of dust. I watched them move, mesmerized.

"I'll take the first watch, even though I really don't think it'll be necessary. I still have my tiger senses, you know. I'll be able to hear or smell the Kappa if they decide to emerge from the water.

"Fine."

"Are you alright?"

I mentally shook myself. *Sheesh! I needed a cold shower! He was like a drug, and what did you do with drugs? You pushed them as far away as possible.*

"I'm fine," I said brusquely, then got up to dig through the back-pack. "You let me know when your spidey-senses start to tingle."

"What?"

I put my hand on my hip. "Can you also leap tall buildings in a single bound?"

"Well, I still have my tiger strength, if that's what you mean."

I grunted, "Fabulous. I'll add superhero to your list of pros."

He frowned. "I'm no superhero, Kells. The most important consideration right now is that you get some rest. I'll keep an eye out for a few hours. Then, if nothing happens," he said with a grin, "I'll join you."

I froze and suddenly became very nervous. Surely, he didn't mean what that sounded like. I searched his face for a clue, but he didn't seem to have any hidden agenda or be planning anything.

I fished out my quilt, purposefully moved to the other side of the fire, and tried to get comfortable on the grass. I rolled around, twisting in my quilt until I was mummy-wrapped to keep out the bugs. Tucking my arm under my head, I stared up at the starless black canopy.

Ren didn't seem to mind my defection. He found a comfortable spot on the other side of the fire and virtually disappeared into the darkness.

I murmured, "Ren? Where do you think we are? I don't think that's the sky up above us."

He replied softly, "I think we're deep underground somewhere."

"It feels almost like we've crossed over into another world." I shifted around, trying to find a soft piece of ground. After a restless half hour of wriggling, I sighed in frustration.

"What's wrong?"

Before I could stop myself, I mumbled, "I'm used to resting my head on a warm tiger-fur pillow is what's wrong."

He grunted, "Hmm, let me see what I can do."

Panicky, I squeaked out, "No, really. I'm okay. Don't bother."

He ignored my protests, scooped up my mummy-wrapped self, and set me down again on his side of the fire. He turned me on my side so I faced the fire, lay down behind me, and slid an arm under my neck to cradle my head.

"Is that more comfortable for you?"

"Uh, yes and no. My head can definitely rest better in this position. Unfortunately, the rest of me is feeling the complete opposite of relaxed."

"What do you mean? Why can't you relax?"

"Because you're too close for me to relax."

Bemused, he said, "Me being too close never bothered you when I was a tiger."

"The tiger you and the man you are two completely different things."

He put his arm around my waist and tugged me closer so we were spooned together. He sounded irritated and disappointed when he muttered, "It doesn't feel different to *me*. Just close your eyes and imagine I'm still a tiger."

"It doesn't exactly work like that." I lay stiffly in his arms, nervous, especially when he began nuzzling the back of my neck.

He said softly, "I like the smell of your hair." His chest rumbled against my back, sending massaging vibrations through my body as he purred.

"Ren, can you not do that right now?"

He lifted his head. "You like it when I purr. It helps you sleep better."

"Yes, well, that only works with the tiger. How can you do that as a man anyway?

He paused, said, "I don't know. I just can," then buried his face in my hair again and stroked my arm.

"Uh, Ren? Explain to me how you plan to keep watch like this."

His lips grazed my neck. "I can hear and smell the Kappa, remember?"

I twitched and shivered, with nerves, or anticipation, or something else, and he noticed. He stopped kissing my neck and lifted his head to peer at my face in the flickering firelight. His voice was solemn and calm, "Kelsey, I hope you know that I would never hurt you. You don't need to be afraid of me."

Rolling toward him, I lifted my hand and touched his cheek. Looking into his blue eyes, I sighed. "I'm not afraid of you, Ren. I trust you with my life. I've just never been close to someone like this before."

He kissed me softly and smiled. "I haven't either."

He shifted, lying down again. "Now, turn around and go to sleep. I'm warning you that I plan to sleep with you in my arms all night long. Who knows when, or if, I'll ever get to do it again. So try to relax, and for heaven's sake, don't wiggle!"

He pulled me back against his warm chest, and I closed my eyes. I ended up sleeping better than I had in weeks.

When I woke, I was nestled on top of Ren's chest. His arms were wrapped around me, and my legs were entwined with his. I was surprised I could breathe all night since my nose was smashed against his muscular torso. It had gotten cold, but my quilt covered both of us and his body, which maintained a warmer-than-average temperature, had kept me toasty all night.

Ren was still asleep, so I took the rare opportunity to study him. His powerful frame was relaxed and his face was softened by sleep. His lips were full, smooth, and utterly kissable, and for the first time, I noticed how long his sooty lashes were. His glossy dark hair fell softly over his brow and was mussed in a way that made him look even more irresistible.

So this is the real Ren. He doesn't seem *real.* He looked like an archangel who fell to the earth. I'd been with Ren night and day for the past four weeks, but the time he was a man was such a small fraction of each day that he seemed almost like a dream guy, a real life Prince Charming.

I traced a black eyebrow, following its arch with my finger, and lightly brushed the silky dark hair away from his face. Hoping not to disturb him, I sighed, shifted slowly, and tried to move away, but his arms tensed, restraining me.

He sleepily mumbled, "Don't even think about moving" and pulled me back to snuggle me close again. I rested my cheek against his chest, felt his heartbeat, and contented myself with listening to its rhythm.

After a few minutes, he stretched and rolled to his side, pulling me with him. He kissed my forehead, blinked open his eyes, and smiled at me. It was like watching the sun come up. The handsome, sleeping man was potent enough, but when he turned his dazzling white smile on me and turned his cobalt blue eyes on me, I was dumbstruck.

I bit my lip. Alarm bells started going off in my head.

Ren's eyes fluttered open, and he tucked some loose hair behind my ear. "Good morning, *rajkumari*. Sleep well?"

I stammered, "I . . . you . . . I . . . slept just fine, thank you."

I closed my eyes, rolled away from him, and stood up. I could deal with him a lot better if I didn't think about him much, or look at him, or talk to him, or hear him.

He wrapped his arms around me from behind, and I felt his smile as he pressed his lips to the soft spot behind my ear. "Best night of sleep I've had in about three hundred and fifty years."

He nuzzled my neck, and an image came to my mind of him beckoning me to jump off a cliff and then laughing as my body broke on the wet rocks below.

I mumbled something akin to, "Good for you," and pulled away from him. I wandered off to get myself ready for the day and ignored his puzzled expression.

We broke camp and headed toward the city. We were both very quiet. He seemed to be mulling over something in his mind; and as for me, I was trying to stop nervous flutterings from overwhelming me every time I glanced in his direction.

What is wrong with me? We have a job to do. We have to find the Golden Fruit and I'm acting . . . twitterpated!

I was annoyed with myself. I had to keep reminding myself that this was just Ren, the tiger, and not some teenage crush. Being close to the man for this long was making me come to grips with reality and the first thing I had to do was to get a handle on my emotions. As we walked, I pondered the problem that was our relationship and chewed my lip as I thought.

He'd probably fall in love with any girl who was destined to save him. Plus, there's just no way a guy like him would ever be attracted to a girl like me. Ren was like Superman, and I had to grudgingly admit that I was no Lois Lane. When the curse is broken, he'll probably want to date supermodels. Also, I'm the first girl he's been around in more than three hundred years, give or take—and, although the time line is a bit different, he's the first man I've ever felt anything for. If I let myself dream about having forever with him when this is all over, I'm sure to be disappointed.

In truth, I had no idea what to do about Ren. I had never been in love with anyone before. I had never even had a boyfriend before, and these feelings were exciting and scary all at once. For the first time in my life, I felt out of control, and it was a feeling I wasn't sure I completely liked.

The problem was, the more time I spent with him, the more I wanted to be with him. And I was a realist. My brief moments with him now, though exhilarating, wouldn't guarantee me a happy ending. I knew from painful experience that happy endings weren't real. Now that the end of the curse loomed in the near future, I had to face facts.

Fact one: Once Ren is free, he'll want to explore the world and not settle down. Fact two: *Love is risky. If he decides that he doesn't love me, it would destroy me. It would be safer for me to head back to Oregon and my solitary, normal life there and forget all about him. Fact three: I just might not be ready for all of this.*

Some of my reasoning was circular, but the circles all led to one thing: *not* being with Ren. I swallowed a wave of sadness and tightened my fists in determination. I decided that, to protect my heart, it would be better if I nipped this relationship in the bud right now and save myself the pain and embarrassment of our eventual breakup.

I would just focus on the task ahead: get to Kishkindha. Then, when this was all over, he could go his way and I could go mine. I'd just do my part to help my friend and then let him go off and be happy.

For what seemed like the next several miles of hiking through the strange, mythical world, I formulated a plan and started sending subtle signals that put the romantic brakes on. Whenever he reached over to hold my hand, I found a reason to gently pull back. When he touched my arm or my shoulder, I stepped away. When he tried to put his arm around me, I shrugged it off or moved ahead. I didn't say anything or offer any explanations because I couldn't think of a way to broach the subject.

Ren tried to ask me what was wrong, but I just said, "Nothing," and he dropped it. At first, he was confused, then he was somber, then he started closing himself off and became angry. Clearly, I had hurt him. It didn't take long for him to stop trying, and I felt a wall as big as the Great Wall of China go up between us.

We arrived at a moat and found a drawbridge. Unfortunately, it was pulled up, but it did hang down slightly on one side as if broken. Ren walked down the creek bed on both sides and stared hard into the water.

"There are too many Kappa here. I wouldn't recommend swimming across."

"What if we dragged a log over and crossed on that?"

Ren grunted, "That's a good idea." He walked over to me and spun me around.

I mumbled nervously, "What are you doing?"

"Just getting out the *gada*." He continued sarcastically, "Don't worry, that's *all* I'm doing."

He took it out, zipped up the backpack quickly, and then he strode off stiffly toward the trees.

I winced. He was angry. I'd never seen him angry before except with Kishan. I didn't like it, but it was a natural side effect of the whole yanking-out-the-seedling-of-love-and-avoiding-the-jagged-rocks-below plan. It couldn't be helped.

I gave Fanindra a cursory glance to see if she approved of what I was doing, but her glittery eyes revealed nothing.

A minute later, a heavy boom sounded, and a tree quickly sucked in its branches. Another splintering boom, and the tree crashed through the canopy and fell to the ground with a hard crack. He began clubbing the branches off the trunk, and I walked over to help.

"Is there something I can do?"

He kept his back turned toward me. "No. We only have one *gada*."

Even though I already knew the answer, I asked, "Ren, why are you angry? Is something bothering you?" I grimaced, knowing that it was me that was bothering him.

He stopped and turned to look at me. His vivid blue eyes searched my face. I quickly averted my gaze and looked down at a quivering branch flexing its needles. When I looked back at him, his face was set in an unreadable mask.

"Nothing's bothering me, Kelsey. I'm fine."

He turned and continued whacking the branches off the tree. When he was finished, he handed me the *gada*, picked up one end of the heavy tree, and started dragging it toward the creek.

I hurried after him and bent down to pick up the other end.

He called back without even looking at me, "Don't."

When we got back to the creek, he dropped the trunk and started looking for a good place to set it. I was about to sit on the tree trunk when I noticed the needles. Even the trunk had thick, spiky needles that rose up to sink themselves into unsuspecting flesh. I walked up to the front end and saw Ren's blood in great drops coating the shiny black needles.

When he came back, I demanded, "Ren, let me see your hands and chest."

"Leave it alone, Kelsey. I'll heal."

"But, Ren—"

"No. Now stand back."

He moved to the back of the trunk and picked it up, cradling it against his chest. My mouth gaped open in amazement. *Yep, he still has tiger strength.* I winced as I imagined those hundreds of needles digging into the skin on his chest and arms. His biceps bulged as he walked the trunk to the edge of the creek.

A girl can still admire, can't she? Even those who can't afford to go in the store can still window-shop. Right?

It was like watching Hercules in action. I sucked in an appreciative breath and had to keep repeating the words, "He's not for me, he's not for me, he's not for me," to strengthen my resolve.

The far end of the trunk butted against the stone wall. He moved down the creek bank several more steps until he found the spot he wanted and then dropped it into place with a soft thud.

The needles had ripped jagged, deep scratches down his chest and torn the front of his white shirt to ribbons. I walked over to him and reached out to touch his arm.

He turned his back to me and said, "Now stay here." Changing to a tiger, he vaulted up and across the log, then leapt up to the crack where the drawbridge was hanging slightly open. He clawed his way in and disappeared.

I heard a metallic clang and then a whoosh as the heavy stone drawbridge lowered. It fell across the creek, hit the water with a big splash, and then settled itself deeply in its pebbly bed. I walked quickly across, fearful of the Kappa I spied in the water below. Ren was still a tiger and seemed content to stay that way.

I entered the stone city of Kishkindha. Most of the buildings were about two or three stories high. The smoky periwinkle stone of the outer walls was also used in the buildings. The hard stone was polished like granite and contained shiny pieces of mica that reflected the light. It was beautiful.

A giant statue of Hanuman stood in the center, and every nook and crevice of the city was covered with life-sized stone monkeys. Every building, every rooftop, and every balcony, had monkey statues. Ornate carvings of monkeys even covered the walls of the buildings. The statues represented several different species of monkeys and were often grouped together in twos and threes. In fact, the only kind of monkeys not included were the fictitious flying monkeys from *The Wizard of Oz* and *King Kong*.

When I passed the central fountain, I felt pressure on my arm. Fanindra came alive. I bent down to let her slide off my arm to the ground. She raised her head and tasted the air with her tongue several times. Then she started slithering through the ancient city. Ren and I followed her as she wove her slow path.

"You don't have to stay a tiger just because of me," I said.

He kept his eyes forward following the snake.

"Ren, it's a miracle that you can be a man at all. Don't do this to yourself, please. Just because you're ang—"

He switched back to a man and spun around to face me.

"I *am* angry! Why shouldn't I stay a tiger? You seem to be much more comfortable with *him* than you are with me!" His blue eyes clouded with uncertainty and hurt.

"I *am* more comfortable with him, but not because I like him more. It's too complicated to discuss with you right now." I turned away from him, hiding my red face.

Frustrated, he ran a hand through his hair and asked anxiously, "Kelsey, why have you been avoiding me? Is it because I've been moving too fast? You aren't ready to think of me in that way yet. Is that it?"

"No. It's not that. It's just," I wrung my hands, "I don't want to make a mistake or get involved in something that will lead to one or both of us getting hurt, and I don't really think this is the best place to talk about this."

I stared at his feet as I said these words. He was quiet for several minutes. I peeked at his face from under my lashes and found him assessing me. He continued to watch me patiently as I squirmed under his gaze. I looked at the stone pavers, Fanindra, my hands, anything except him. Finally, he gave up.

"Fine."

"Fine?"

"Yes, fine. Here, hand me the backpack. It's my turn to carry it for a while."

He helped me slip it off my back and then adjusted the straps to fit over his wide shoulders. Fanindra seemed ready to be on the move again, and she continued her journey, slinking through the monkey city.

We passed into dark shadows between buildings where Fanindra's golden body gleamed in the darkness. She slipped through tiny cracks beneath unwieldy doors that Ren had to throw his body up against to open. She took us on an interesting obstacle course from a snake's perspective, going under and through things that were impossible for

Ren and me to navigate. She disappeared under cracks in the floor, and Ren had to sniff her out to find her. Often, we had to backtrack and meet her on the other side of walls or rooms. We always found her coiled and resting, patiently waiting for us to catch up.

Eventually, she led us to a rectangular reflecting pool brimming with sea-green algae-filled water. The pool was waist high, and on each corner stood a tall stone pedestal. On top of each pedestal was a carved monkey, each one looking out in the distance, one for each point of the compass.

The statues were crouched down with hands touching the ground. Teeth were bared, and I could visualize them hissing, as if ready to pounce. Their tails curled up over their bodies, fleshy levers to increase the range of their attack. Under the pedestals, groups of evil-looking stone monkeys stared out of the shadows with grimaces and hollowed black eyes. Their long arms were stretched out, as if to grab and claw at whoever passed by.

Stone steps led up to the reflecting pool. We climbed up and peered into the water. With relief, I saw that no Kappa were lurking in the murky depths. At the edge of the pool on the stone border was an inscription.

"Can you read it?" I asked.

"It says *Niyuj Kapi* or 'choose the monkey.'"

"Hmm."

We walked around the four corners examining each statue. One had ears pricked forward and another had ears flat against its head. All four were of different species.

"Ren, Hanuman was half-man, half-monkey, right? What kind of monkey was the monkey half?"

"I don't know. Mr. Kadam would know. I can tell you that these two statues are not monkeys native to India. This one's a spider monkey. They come from South America. This one is a chimpanzee, which is technically an ape, not a monkey. They're often classified as monkeys because of their size."

I gaped at him. "How do you know so much about monkeys?"

He crossed his arms over his chest. "Ah, so am I to assume that talking about monkeys is an approved topic of conversation? Perhaps if I were a monkey instead of a tiger you might clue me in as to why you're avoiding me."

"I'm not avoiding you. I just need some space. It has nothing to do with your species. It has to do with other things."

"What other things?"

"Nothing."

"It's something."

"It can't *be* anything."

"What can't *be* anything?"

"Can we just get back to the monkeys?" I yelled.

"Fine!" he hollered back.

We stood there glaring at each other for a minute, both of us frustrated and angry. He went back to examining the various monkeys and ticking off a list of their traits.

Before I could stop myself, I shot off a sarcastic, "I had no idea that I was walking with a monkey expert, but, then again, you have eaten them right? So I guess that would be the difference between say, pork and chicken, to someone like me."

Ren scowled at me. "I lived in zoos and circuses for centuries, remember? And I don't . . . eat . . . monkeys!"

"Hmm." I crossed my arms over my chest and glared back at him. He threw me a look and then stomped over and crouched in front of another statue.

Irritated, he spat out, "That one's a macaque, which is native to India, and this hairy one is a baboon, also found here."

"So which one do I pick? It has to be one of the last two. The other two monkeys aren't from around here, so I'd guess one of these is right."

He ignored me, probably still offended, and he was looking at the monkey clusters under the pedestal when I declared, "Baboon."

He stood up. "Why choose him?"

"His face reminds me of the statue of Hanuman."

"Okay, so give it a try."

"Give what a try?"

He lost patience. "I don't know! Do that thing you do, with your hand."

"I'm not sure it works that way."

He gestured to the monkey. "Okay, then rub his head like a Buddha statue. We've got to figure out the next step."

I frowned at Ren, who was definitely frustrated with me, and then walked up to the baboon statue and tentatively touched its head. Nothing happened. I patted its cheeks, rubbed its belly, and tugged on its arms, its tail . . . nothing. I was squeezing its shoulders when I felt the statue move a bit. I pushed on one of the shoulders, and the top of the pedestal moved aside to reveal a stone box with a lever. I reached in and pulled on the lever. At first, nothing moved. Then I felt my hand grow hot. The symbols drawn into my hand boldly resurfaced, and the lever shifted, rose up, twisted, and popped out.

Rumbling shook the ground, and the water in the pool started to drain. Ren grabbed my arms and quickly yanked me against his chest while swiftly backing us away from the pool. He rested his hands on my upper arms while we watched the shifting stone.

The rectangular pool cracked and divided in two. Both halves began moving in opposite directions. The water spilled out and fell below, splashing against rock and stone as it tumbled into a gaping hole that opened up where the pool used to be.

Something began to emerge. At first, I thought it was just a reflection of light on the shiny wet stone, but the light grew increasingly brighter until I saw a branch poke out of the hole. It was covered with sparkling golden leaves. More branches emerged and then a trunk. It kept rising until the entire tree was standing before us. The leaves were shimmering, radiating a soft yellow light as if thousands of golden Christmas tree bulbs were threaded through the branches. The golden leaves quivered, as if a slight breeze shook the tree.

The tree was about twelve feet tall and covered with small white flowers that released a sweet fragrance. The leaves were long and thin, attached to delicate branches that led to thick, stronger ones and from there to a sturdy, compact trunk. The trunk sat in a large stone box that had ascended on a solid stone base. It was the most beautiful tree I'd ever seen.

Ren took my hand and led me cautiously toward the tree. He stretched out a hand to finger a golden leaf.

"It's beautiful!" I exclaimed.

He plucked a flower and smelled it. "It's a mango tree."

We both admired the tree. I was sure my face was as awestruck as his.

Ren's expression softened. He took a step toward me and lifted his hand to tuck the flower in my hair. I turned away from him, pretending not to see, and fingered a golden leaf.

When I glanced at him a moment later, his expression was stony and the white flower lay crushed and broken. My heart throbbed painfully when I saw the beautiful petals lying torn and forsaken in the dirt.

We walked around the base of the tree, examining it from all angles. Ren shouted, "There! Do you see up at the top? It's a golden fruit!"

"Where?"

He pointed to the top of the tree and, sure enough, a golden orb swung softly from a branch.

"A mango fruit," he mumbled. "Of course. It makes sense."

"Why?"

"Mangoes are one of the main exports of India. It's a staple for our country. It's possibly the most important natural resource we have. So the Golden Fruit of India is a mango. I should have guessed it before."

I gazed up at the tall branches. "How are we going to reach it?"

"What do you mean, 'How are we going to reach it?' Climb up on my shoulders. We need to do this together."

I laughed. "Uh, Ren, I think you'd better come up with another plan. Like maybe leap up as you super-tigers do and catch it in your mouth or something."

He smiled at me malevolently. "No. You," he touched my nose with his finger, "are going to sit on my shoulders."

I moaned, "Please stop saying that."

"Come here. I'll talk you through it. It's child's play."

He picked me up and set me on the stone edge of the reflecting pool. Then he spun around with his back to me. "Okay, climb on."

He held out his hands. I tentatively grabbed them and swung one leg over his shoulder, complaining the entire time. I almost lifted my leg back off, but he anticipated that I would chicken out and reached back with his arm to grab my other leg and hoist me up before I could retreat.

After I yelled at him to no effect, he held my hands and, easily balancing my weight, walked back to the tree. He took his time looking for the right place and then began instructing me.

"See that thick branch right above your head?"

"Yes."

"Let go of one of my hands and reach up to grab it."

I did and threatened, "Don't drop me!"

He bragged, "Kelsey, there is absolutely *no* danger of me dropping you."

I grabbed the branch and clung to it.

"Good. Now reach up with your other hand and grab the same branch. I'll be holding your legs, don't worry."

I reached up and got a good hold of the branch, but my palms were sweaty, and if he hadn't been supporting me, I was sure I would have fallen.

"Hey, Ren, this was a great idea and all, but I'm still a good foot or two away from the fruit. What do you expect me to do now?"

In response, he laughed and said, "Hold on a sec."

"What do you mean, 'hold on a sec'?"

He yanked my tennis shoes off my feet and then said, "Hold on to the branch and stand up."

Frightened, I yelped and strangled the branch for dear life. Ren was pushing me up above the branch even higher. I glanced down and saw he was cupping my feet in his hands, supporting my entire body weight with his arms alone.

I hissed, "Ren, are you crazy? I'm too heavy for you."

He scoffed drolly, "Obviously not, Kelsey. Now pay attention. Keep your hold on the branch, and I want you to step from my hand to my shoulder, first one foot, and then the other."

He lifted my right leg first, and I felt my heel bump against his upper arm. Carefully, I shifted my foot to rest it on his wide shoulder, and then did the same with the other one. I looked at the fruit, which was now hanging directly across from me and bouncing slightly up and down.

"Okay, I'm going to try and grab the fruit now. Hold on."

His hands had moved to the back of my calves, and he squeezed them tightly. I pushed off from the branch, which was now at my waist, and stretched my arm to reach the bobbing fruit. It was attached to a long, woody stem that shot off from the top of the tree.

My fingers grazed it, and it shifted away from me for a moment. When it swung back to me, I wrapped my hand around it and pulled gently.

It didn't want to move. I tugged a bit harder, careful not to damage the golden fruit. Surprisingly, it felt like a real mango with leathery smooth skin, even though it twinkled with dazzling golden light. I braced my body on the branch again, yanked firmly, and was finally able to pluck it from the stem.

All at once, my body iced over and became rigid, and my mind was carried away in a black vision. A burning heat seared my chest, and I stood in complete darkness. A ghostly figure started making its way toward me. The misty features swirled around a shape and solidified into a form. It was Mr. Kadam! He was clutching at his chest. When he removed his hand, I saw the amulet he was wearing was glowing red hot. I looked down and saw mine too, glowing in the same manner. I tried to reach out to him, and I spoke, but he couldn't seem to hear me or I him.

Another ghostly figure swirled up across from us and slowly took form. He was gripping a large amulet as well. When he became alert, he turned his eyes to Mr. Kadam. Immediately, he focused his attention on the amulet Mr. Kadam was wearing.

The man was dressed in expensive, modern clothing. His quick eyes showed intelligence, confidence, determination, and something else, something dark, something . . . evil. He tried to take a step forward, but a barrier of some kind prevented any of us from moving.

His expression tightened and twisted into a vile rage that, though quickly suppressed, continued to swirl like a stalking beast behind his eyes. Black, desperate fear congealed in my stomach as the man turned his attention to me. He clearly wanted something.

His eyes examined me carefully from head to toe and then settled on the glowing amulet around my neck. Gleaming malice and loathsome delight swept over his face. I looked at Mr. Kadam for support, but he was studying the man meticulously as well.

I was very afraid. I cried out for Ren, but even I couldn't hear my own voice.

The man pulled something from his pocket and started muttering words to himself. I tried to read his lips, but he seemed to be speaking in another language. Mr. Kadam's features were becoming transparent. He was becoming spectral again. I looked at my arm and gasped as the same thing started happening to me. My mind swirled dizzily. I felt like I was going to pass out. I couldn't stand anymore. I fell down . . . down . . . down.

escape

When I opened my eyes, I was staring up into Ren's face.

"Kelsey! Are you okay? You fell. Did you faint? What happened?"

"No, I didn't faint!" I then mumbled, "At least I don't think I did." He was holding me in his arms, cradling me close, and I liked it. I didn't *want* to like it, but I did.

"You caught me?"

He lectured, "I told you I wouldn't drop you."

I muttered sarcastically, "Thanks, Superhero. Now put me down, please. I can stand."

Ren set me down carefully and, to my great dismay, my legs still wobbled. He reached out a hand to steady me, and I howled, "I said I can stand! Back off a minute, would you?"

I had no idea why I yelled at him. He was just trying to be helpful, but I was frightened. Strange things were happening to me that I had no control over. I also felt embarrassed and was overly sensitive about him touching me. I couldn't think straight when he touched me. My brain got all fogged up like a mirror in a steamy bathroom, so I wanted to get away from him as soon as possible.

I sat down on the stone border of the pool and put my tennis shoes back on, hoping the dizziness would soon pass.

Ren crossed his arms over his chest and narrowed his eyes at me. "Kelsey, tell me what happened, please."

"I don't know exactly. I had a . . . a vision, I guess."

"And what did you see in this vision?"

"There were three people, Mr. Kadam, some scary man, and me. All three of us wore amulets, and they were glowing red."

He dropped his arms and his face became serious. He asked quietly, "What did the scary man look like?"

"He looked like . . . I don't know, a mob boss or something like that. The kind of guy that likes to be in control and kill things. He had dark hair and black, glittery eyes."

"Was he Indian?"

"I don't know. Maybe."

Fanindra had curled up at my feet in her jewelry position. I picked her up, slid her onto my arm, and then looked around desperately. "Ren? Where's the golden fruit?"

"It's here." He picked it up from where it had fallen at the base of the tree.

"We should hide it." I picked up my backpack and yanked out my quilt. I reached for the fruit and took it from Ren carefully, making sure our hands didn't touch, and then I wrapped it in my quilt and stowed it in the backpack. I guess I'd been a little bit too obvious in my desire to avoid touching him, because he was scowling at me when I looked up at him.

"What? You can't even touch me now? Nice to know I disgust you so much! Too bad you couldn't convince Kishan to come with you so you could avoid being with me altogether!"

I ignored him and yanked my shoelaces into double knots.

He gestured toward the city and smiled mockingly, "Whenever you feel recovered enough, *rajkumari*."

I glared and poked him in the chest. "Maybe Kishan would have been less of a jerk. And for the record, Mr. Sarcastic, I don't like you very much right now."

He narrowed his eyes at me. "Welcome to the club, Kells. Shall we proceed?"

"Fine." I turned my back to him, adjusted the straps on the backpack, and marched off on my own.

He threw up his hands in exasperation, *"Fine!"*

I hollered back, "FINE!" and walked stiffly back to the city with him following silently behind me, fuming.

When we passed the first building, the ground started shaking. We stopped and turned to look at the golden tree. It was sinking back into the ground, and the two pool halves were moving back together. There was a strange glow coming from inside the four monkey statues.

"Uh, Kells? I think it might be wise to exit the city as soon as possible."

We double-timed our pace and jogged briskly between the buildings. I heard a hiss and a screech, followed by several more. Monkey statues were glowing and coming to life. Something moved overhead.

Small black and brown figures leapt across buildings following us. The screeches became cacophonous, and the noise level was incredible.

I yelled over at Ren as I ran, "Perfect! Now we're being chased by hoards of monkeys! Perhaps you would care to name their species as we're attacked, just so I can appreciate the special traits of said monkey as it kills me!"

He ran along beside me. "At least when the monkeys are harassing you, you don't have any time to harass *me*!"

The monkeys were getting close. I almost tripped over one as it darted in front of my legs. Ren leapt over a fountain with his tiger power. *Show-off.*

"Ren, you're holding back. Just get out of here! Take the backpack and go."

He laughed acerbically as he ran ahead of me; then, he turned to look at me while jogging backward, "Ha! You wish you could get rid of me that easily!"

He ran a bit farther ahead of me and switched to the tiger. Then he barreled back toward me and actually leapt over my running body into the throng of monkeys to slow them down.

I shouted back at him while still running, "Hey! Careful where you jump, Mister! You almost took my head off!"

I kept on course, pumping my legs as fast as they would go. I heard terrible noises behind me. Most of the monkeys had switched to full-on attack mode. Ren was biting, slashing with his claws, and roaring thunderously. I looked back over my shoulder. Brown, gray, and black monkeys covered his body and clung to his fur. A dozen or so monkeys were still chasing me, including the huge baboon from the reflecting pool.

I turned a corner and finally saw the drawbridge. A monkey leapt and latched itself onto my leg, slowing me down. I tried to shake it off as I ran.

Batting at him ineffectually, I hollered, "Stu-pid mon-key . . . get . . . off!" In response, he bit my knee.

"Owww!" I shook my leg harder as I ran and stomped my foot down hard to make the ride as jarring as possible for the little hitchhiker. Just then, Fanindra animated the top half of her body. She hissed and spat at the monkey, who screeched and immediately let go of my leg.

"Thanks, Fanindra." I patted her head as she settled back down on my arm again.

I reached the gate, crossed the bridge, and stopped on the other side. Ren was bouncing toward me trying to shake monkeys off his back.

Several monkeys were storming toward me. I kicked at them viciously, quickly threw off my backpack, and took out the *gada*.

I started swinging the *gada* like a baseball bat at the monkeys. I hit one with a sickening smack, and it whimpered and hightailed it back to the city. The problem was that I was able to hit a monkey only every third try or so. One jumped on my back and started pulling my hair. Another attached itself to my leg. I continued swinging the *gada* back and forth in front of me, and eventually ended up being able to get rid of most of them.

Ren ran down the drawbridge with about fifteen monkeys clinging to his fur. He bounced over, leapt into the trees, and banged his body up against the trunks, first on one side and then the other. He leapt up high to rub his back on a branch and scrape the remaining monkeys off.

The needle trees came alive, shot leafy tendrils down to ensnare the malicious simians by their legs and tails, and then pulled their shrieking bodies up into the branches. They were too lightweight to fight back and soon disappeared into the treetops.

Meanwhile, I swung the *gada* at the gray baboon but he darted around to avoid being hit. He was too fast for me and chattered at me violently. He swung his long arms and hammered my body at every opportunity. He was strong enough to make his blows hurt. Each pound from his monkey arms battered against my already tired muscles. I felt like I was being tenderized. A tiny monkey sat on my shoulder and tugged on my braids so hard that it brought tears to my eyes.

Free of monkeys, Ren jogged over, detached the monkey's fingers from my braids, plucked the tiny monkey off my shoulder, and threw him hard back through the city gate. The tiny monkey bounced, rolled on the ground, and then got up, hissed at us, and disappeared. Ren took the *gada* from my hand and raised it to threaten the baboon. The baboon must have realized that Ren's aim was better than mine because he shrieked loudly and headed back to the city too.

I sat down hard on the ground panting. The city became eerily quiet. Not a monkey hiss or screech could be heard.

Ren turned around to look at me. "Are you okay?"

I waved my hand at him dismissively. He crouched down, touched my cheek, looked me up and down, and then smirked.

"That was a pygmy marmoset, by the way. Just in case you were wondering."

I wheezed. "Thank you, oh Walking Monkey Dictionary."

He laughed and got out bottled water for both of us, then handed me an energy bar.

"Aren't you going to eat one?"

He put a hand on his chest and scoffed. "What, me? Eat an energy bar when the jungle is full of delicious monkeys? No thanks. I'm not hungry."

I nibbled my energy bar in silence and checked the Golden Fruit to make sure it wasn't bruised. It was still safely wrapped up in my quilt.

Between bites, I said, "You know, all in all, we made it out of the city fairly unscathed."

His mouth fell open. "Unscathed? Kelsey, I have monkey bites all over my back and in other places that I don't even want to think about!"

"I said *fairly*."

He grunted at me.

After a quick meal and rest, we started the walk back on the pebbly path between the trees and the creek. Ren banged the trees extra hard as we passed. I started to feel guilty about the way I'd been treating him. I watched his stiff shoulders as he paced angrily in front of me.

This was hard. I missed his friendship. Not to mention all the other things.

I was almost ready to apologize when I realized that Kappa were sticking the tops of their heads out of the water and were watching us.

"Uh, Ren? We have company."

Looking at them only seemed to empower them to more action. They slowly raised their heads out even farther and followed our progress with inky black eyes. I couldn't stop staring at them. They were horrible! They stank like a fetid swamp, and when they blinked, their lids moved sideways like a crocodile's.

Their flesh was pale, almost diaphanous, and their pulsing black veins could be seen under their clammy skin. I increased my pace. Ren moved between the creek and me, raising the *gada* as a warning.

"Try bowing to them," I suggested.

We both started dipping our heads and bowing as we passed, but they ignored us and rose up farther out of the water. They were now standing up and moving forward slowly, mechanically, as if they'd just awakened from a deep sleep. The water currently came up to their chests, but they were getting closer. I turned around and did a deep curtsy type of bow, but it still didn't work.

"Keep going, Kelsey. Move faster!"

We started jogging. I knew I wouldn't have the stamina to keep up this pace for long, even with Ren taking on the extra weight of the backpack. More Kappa emerged from the water, several feet in front of us. They had long arms and webbed hands. One of them smiled at me, and I saw sharp, jagged teeth. A shiver tore down my spine, and I ran a little faster.

Now I could see their legs. I was surprised that they had legs like humans. Ridges ran down their backs like a fish spine. Their powerful, muscular legs were covered in brine and pond scum, and their long tails curled like a monkey's, but ended in a transparent caudal fin. The Kappa swung back and forth menacingly, pulling their feet out of the muck with loud sucking noises while they made their way to the river bank.

The Kappa were careful to keep their heads level, which made their bodies disjointed. The head stayed in one place while the torso bobbed

and swayed, zombie-like. They were about a foot shorter than Ren and I, and they moved quickly, picking up speed while shifting awkwardly forward on webbed feet. It was eerie seeing their bodies accelerate while their heads remained virtually still.

"Faster, Kelsey. Run faster!"

"I can't go any faster, Ren!"

A horde of white Kappa vampires descended upon us, closing the distance quickly.

Ren shouted, "Keep running, Kelsey. I'll try to slow them down!"

I ran ahead a good distance then turned and jogged backward to see how Ren was faring. He had stopped to try bowing to them again. They paused to assess his action, but contrary to Ren's mother's story, the Kappa didn't bow in return. Gills on the sides of their necks opened and closed, and they opened their mouths to bare their teeth. Viscous black droplets trickled from their mouths as an insipid gurgle turned into a piercing squeal. They surged toward Ren, closing in on their prey.

He swung the *gada* mightily at the nearest one and sunk it deep into the creature's chest. The monster sprayed filthy dark fluid from its mouth and fell to the creek bank. The other creatures didn't even notice their fallen comrade. They just closed in on Ren.

He whacked several more, then spun around and ran in my direction again. He waved at me. "Keep running, Kelsey! Don't stop!"

We were able to keep ahead of them, but I was tiring quickly. We stopped for just a moment to catch our breath.

I gasped for air. "They're going to catch us. I can't keep running. My legs are giving out."

Ren was breathing heavily too. "I know. But we have to keep trying." Taking a big swig of water, he handed me the rest of the bottle he had taken from my backpack, and grabbed my hand, leading me to the trees. "Come on. Follow me. I have an idea."

"Ren, the needle trees are awful. If we go back there, we'll have two things trying to kill us instead of just one."

"Just trust me, Kells. Follow my lead."

When we entered the needle trees, the branches immediately began reaching for us. Ren pulled me along as we raced through. I seriously didn't think I could keep going, but somehow I did. I could feel the thorns whipping my back and ripping my shirt.

After several minutes of running, Ren stopped, told me to stand still, and beat the trees all around me with the *gada*.

He leaned over, panting. "Sit down. Rest for a while. I'm going to try to get the Kappa to chase me into the trees. I hope it works on them as well as it did with the monkeys."

Ren changed into a tiger, left me with the *gada* and backpack, and then leapt back into the waving branches. I listened carefully and heard the trees moving, trying to snag him as he passed. Then it became deathly quiet. The only sound was my jagged breathing. I sat on the mossy ground as far away from the trees as I could and waited.

I strained my ears to listen but heard nothing, not even birds. Eventually, I lay down and rested my head on my backpack. My sore body and muscles throbbed, and the scratches on my back stung. I must have drifted to sleep because a noise startled me awake. I heard a strange shuffling noise near my head. A sallow grayish-white shape lunged out of the trees toward me, and before I could even get up, it grabbed my arms and jerked me up to a sitting position. It leaned over me and drooled black spittle on my face.

I swung my arms wildly, beating on its chest, but it was more powerful than I was. Its torso was covered with cuts oozing murky droplets; the trees had torn off pieces of its flesh. Alien eyes blinked several times as it pulled me up closer, bared its teeth, and sunk them into my neck.

It grunted and suckled at my neck, and I kicked my legs hard, trying to escape its clutches. I screamed and thrashed, but my energy quickly waned. After a moment, I couldn't feel it any longer. It was almost as if it were happening to someone else. I could still hear the monster, but a strange lethargy stole through my frame. My vision fogged up, and my mind drifted until I felt a dreamy peace.

I heard a crash, followed by a very angry roar. Then I saw a warrior angel rise up above me. He was magnificent! I felt a slight tugging on my neck, and then a weight lifted off my body. There was a juicy splat, and the handsome man knelt beside me. Although he seemed to be speaking urgently to me, I couldn't understand his words. I tried to respond, but my tongue wouldn't work.

Gently, he brushed the hair away from my face and touched my neck with cool fingers. His dreamy eyes filled with tears, and a sparkling diamond drop fell to my lips. I tasted the salty tear and closed my eyes. When I opened them, he smiled. The warmth of that smile enveloped me and wrapped me in a blanket of soothing tenderness. The warrior carefully lifted me in his arms, and I slept.

When I regained consciousness, it was dark, and I was lying in front of a green-and-orange tinged fire. Ren sat nearby staring into it, looking broken, exhausted, and forlorn. He must have heard me move because he came directly to me and lifted my head to give me water. My throat suddenly burned as if I had swallowed the campfire. The heat moved deeper into my body until it exploded in my core. I was on fire from the inside out, and I whimpered from the terrible pain.

Ren set my head down gently and picked up my hand to stroke my fingers.

"I'm so sorry. I should *never* have left you alone. This should have happened to me, not to you. You don't deserve this."

He stroked my cheek. "I don't know how to fix this. I don't know

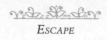

what to do. I don't even know how much blood you lost or if the bite is lethal." He kissed my fingers and whispered, "I can't lose you, Kelsey. I won't."

The burning in my blood overtook me until pain clouded my vision. I started writhing. The pain was beyond anything I'd ever felt before. Ren bathed my face with a cool wet towel, but nothing could distract me from the fire burning through my veins. It was excruciating! After a moment, I realized that mine was not the only body writhing.

Fanindra freed herself from my arm and coiled next to Ren's knee. I didn't blame her for wanting to get away from me. She raised her head and opened her hood. Her mouth gaped open wide, and she struck! She bit me on the neck, sinking her fangs deep into the ripped tissue.

She pumped her own venom in me, drew back, and then bit me again and again and again. I groaned, touched my neck, and then pulled back my hand to see oozing pus. Golden juices that had dribbled out of the fang punctures dotted my hand as well. I watched a golden drop trickle from my finger to meet some of the pus on my palm. It steamed and hissed. Fanindra's venom coursed through my body. It felt like ice as it shot through my limbs and entered my heart.

I was dying. I knew it. I didn't blame Fanindra. She was a snake, after all, and she probably just didn't want me to suffer anymore.

Ren lifted the bottle of water to my lips again, and I swallowed gratefully. Fanindra had turned inanimate and remained coiled at his side. Ren cleaned my wounded neck gently, washing off all the hissing black blood that had dribbled out.

At least the pain was gone. Whatever Fanindra had done numbed me. I became sleepy and knew that I needed to say good-bye. I wanted to tell Ren the truth. I wanted to say that he was the best friend I'd ever had. That I was sorry about the way I had treated him. I wanted to tell him . . . that I loved him. But I couldn't say anything. My throat was closed up, probably swollen from snake venom. All I could do was look at him as he knelt over me.

That's okay. Looking at his gorgeous face one last time is enough for me. I'll die a happy woman.

I was so tired. My eyelids were too heavy to keep open. I closed my eyes and waited for death to come. Ren cleared a space and sat down near me. Pillowing my head on his arm, he pulled me onto his lap and into his arms. I smiled.

Even better. I can't open my eyes to see him anymore, but I can feel his arms around me. My warrior angel can carry me in his arms up to heaven.

He squeezed me closer to his body and whispered something in my ear that I couldn't make out. Then darkness overtook me.

Light hit my eyelids, forcing me to crack them open painfully. My throat still burned, and my tongue felt thick and fuzzy.

"This is too painful for heaven; I must be in hell."

An annoyingly happy voice admonished, "No. You're not in hell, Kelsey."

As I tried to move, my sore, cramped muscles protested. "I feel like I lost a boxing match."

"You did a lot more than that. Here."

He crouched beside me and helped me to gingerly sit up. He examined my face, my neck, my arms, and then sat behind me to prop up my back against him and held a water bottle to my lips. "Drink," he commanded. He held the bottle for me and tipped it back slowly, but I couldn't swallow fast enough, and some of the water dribbled from my slack mouth down my chin, and then dripped down to my chest.

"Thanks, now I have a wet T-shirt."

I felt his smile on the back of my neck. "Perhaps that was my intention."

I snorted and lifted a hand to my face. I poked my cheek and arm.

The skin tingled and felt a little numb at the same time. "It feels like my whole body was shot full of Novocain and I'm just getting the feeling back. Here, hand me the bottle. I think I can lift it myself now."

Ren let go of the water bottle and snaked both arms around my waist, pulling me back to rest fully against his chest. His cheek grazed mine, and he murmured quietly, "How are you feeling?"

"Alive, I guess, though I sure could use some aspirin."

He laughed softly and retrieved the pills from the backpack. "Here," he said, handing me two aspirin. "We're at the entrance to the caves. We still have to go through the caves and the trees, and then climb back up to Hampi."

"How long have I been out of commission?" I asked groggily.

"Two days."

"Two days! What happened? The last thing I remember is Fanindra biting me and me dying."

"You didn't die. You were bitten by a Kappa. He was making quick work of you when I found you. He must have followed you there. They are nasty things. I'm glad most of them were done in by the trees."

"The one that found me was scratched and bloody, but he didn't seem to care."

"Yes, most of the ones that followed me were torn apart by the trees. Nothing seemed to halt their pursuit."

"Didn't any of them follow you here?"

"They stopped chasing me once I got near the cave. They must be frightened of it."

"I don't blame them. Did you . . . carry me the whole way? How did you whack the trees and hold me at the same time?"

He sighed. "I slung you over my shoulder and banged the trees until we cleared them. Then I stowed the *gada*, put on your pack, and hiked up here, carrying you in my arms."

I drank deeply from the water bottle and heard Ren let out a deep breath.

Quietly, he said, "I've experienced a lot in my life. I've been in bloody battles. I've been with friends who were killed. I've seen terrible things done to man and beast, but I've never felt afraid.

"I've been troubled. I've also been uneasy and tense. I've been in mortal danger, but I've never experienced that cold-sweat kind of fear, the kind that eats a man alive, brings him to his knees, and makes him beg. In fact, I always prided myself on being above that. I thought that I'd suffered through and seen so much that nothing could scare me anymore. That nothing could bring me to that point."

He brushed a brief kiss on my neck. "I was wrong. When I found you and saw that . . . that thing trying to kill you, I was enraged. I destroyed it without hesitation."

"The Kappa were terrifying."

"I wasn't afraid of the Kappa. I was afraid . . . that I'd lost you. I felt an unquenchable, gut-wrenching, corrosive fear. It was unbearable. The most agonizing part was realizing that I didn't want to live anymore if you were gone and knowing there was nothing I could do about it. I would be stuck forever in this miserable existence without you."

I heard every word he said. It pierced through me, and I knew I would have felt the same way if our places had been reversed. But I told myself that his heartfelt declaration was just a reflection of the tense pressure we'd been under. The little love plant in my heart was grasping at each wispy thought, absorbing his words like sweet drops of morning dew. But I chastised my heart and shoved the tender expressions of affection elsewhere, determined to be unaffected by them.

"It's okay. I'm here. You don't need to be afraid. I'm still around to help you break the curse," I said, trying to keep my voice even.

He squeezed my waist and whispered softly, "Breaking the curse didn't matter to me anymore. I thought you were dying."

I swallowed and tried to be flippant. "Well, I didn't. See? I lived to argue with you another day. Now don't you wish it had gone the other way?"

His arms stiffened, and he threatened, "Don't ever say that, Kells."

After a second of hesitation, I said, "Well, thank you. Thank you for saving me."

He pulled me closer, and I allowed myself a minute, just a minute, to lie back against him and enjoy it.

I had almost died after all. I deserved some kind of reward for surviving, didn't I?

After my minute was up, I wiggled forward and out of his grasp. He reluctantly let me go, and I turned around to face him with a nervous smile. I tested my legs, which felt strong enough for me to walk on.

When I thought I was dying, I wanted to tell Ren that I loved him, but now that I knew I'd survived, it was the last thing on earth I wanted to do. The strong resolve to keep him at a distance returned, but the temptation to allow myself to rest wrapped in his arms was strong, powerfully strong. I turned my back to him, squared my shoulders, and picked up the backpack.

"Come on, Tiger. Let's get a move on. I feel healthy as a horse," I lied.

"I really think you should take it easy and rest a bit more, Kells."

"No. I've been sleeping for two days already. I'm ready to hike another umpteen miles."

"At least wait until you've eaten something."

"Toss me an energy bar, and I'll eat on the way."

"But, Kells—"

My eyes locked briefly with his cobalt blue ones, and I said softly, "I need to get out of here."

I turned and started gathering our things. He just sat immobile, watching me closely, his eyes burning into my back. I *was* desperate

to get out of there. The longer we were together, the more my resolve wavered. I was almost to the point of asking him to stay there with me forever and live among the needle trees and the Kappa. If I didn't get the tiger part of him back soon, I'd lose myself to the man forever.

Finally, he said slowly, almost sadly, "Sure. Whatever you say, Kelsey." He stood up, stretched, and then put out the fire.

I walked over to Fanindra, who was spiraled into an arm cuff, and stared down at her.

"She saved your life you know. Those bites healed you," Ren explained.

I reached up and touched my neck where the Kappa had bitten me. The skin was smooth, without a pucker or a scar. I crouched down.

"I guess you saved me again, huh, Fanindra? Thanks."

I picked her up and positioned her on my upper arm, grabbed my backpack, and then walked ahead a few steps.

I spun around, "You coming, Superman?"

"Right behind you."

We entered the mouth of the black cavern. Ren held out his hand. I ignored it and began walking into the tunnel. He stopped me and held out his hand again, staring at it pointedly. I sighed and gripped a couple of his fingers in mine. I smiled sheepishly and was again too obvious in my attempt to avoid physical contact. He groaned in disgust, took my elbow, and yanked my body up next to his, settling his arm around my shoulders.

We walked through the tunnels quickly. The other Rens and Kelseys moaned and beckoned even more aggressively than before. I closed my eyes and let Ren lead me through. I gasped when the figures approached and tried to lay ghostly hands on us.

Ren whispered, "They can't become corporeal unless we pay attention to them."

We walked through as quickly as possible. Evil shapes and familiar forms clamored for us to notice them. Mr. Kadam, Kishan, my parents, my foster family, even Mr. Maurizio all shouted, begged, demanded, and coerced.

We made it through the tunnel much faster than the first time. Ren still held my hand in his warm grip after we emerged, and I tried to gently and inconspicuously free my hand from his. He looked at me and then at our entwined hands. He raised an eyebrow and grinned maliciously. I started tugging harder, but he merely tightened his grip. I finally had to wrench it away to get him to let go.

So much for subtlety.

He smirked at me knowingly while I glared back.

It wasn't long before we faced the needle tree forest again and Ren headed boldly toward the treeline. Striking with the *gada*, he moved slowly forward creating a path that I could walk through safely. The branches abused him violently and ripped his shirt to shreds. He pushed the branches away and I found myself staring in fascination first at the rippling muscles of his arms and back and then at his cuts as they healed before my eyes. Soon he was soaked with sweat and, and I couldn't watch anymore. I kept my eyes on my feet and followed along silently.

He moved steadily through the trees. Banging on them with the *gada*, we skirted through the prickly forest without further incident.

In no time at all, we were climbing the rocks leading to the cavern, heading back toward the Ugra Narasimha statue in Hampi. When we reached the long tunnel, Ren started to say something several times but stopped himself. I was curious, but not curious enough to start a conversation.

I pulled out my flashlight, angled my stride to put distance between us, and ended up hugging the other side of the cavern. He looked over at me once, but he allowed me to maintain my distance. Eventually, the tunnel narrowed enough that we had to walk side by side again. Every time I glanced at Ren, I saw that he was watching me.

When we finally reached the end of the tunnel and saw the stone steps that led to the surface, Ren stopped.

"Kelsey, I have one final request of you before we head up."

"And what would that be? Want to talk about tiger senses or monkey bites in strange places maybe?"

"No. I want you to kiss me."

I sputtered, "What? Kiss you? What for? Don't you think you got to kiss me enough on this trip?"

"Humor me, Kells. This is the end of the line for me. We're leaving the place where I get to be a man all the time, and I have only my tiger's life to look forward to. So, yes, I want you to kiss me one more time."

I hesitated. "Well, if this works, you can go around kissing all the girls you want to. So why bother with me right now?"

He ran a hand through his hair in frustration. "Because! I don't want to run around kissing all the other girls! I want to kiss *you!*"

"Fine! If it will shut you up!" I leaned over and pecked him on the cheek. "There!"

"No. Not good enough. On the lips, my *prema.*"

I leaned over and pecked him on the lips. "There. Can we go now?"

I marched up the first two steps, and he slipped his hand under my elbow and spun me around, twisting me so that I fell forward into his arms. He caught me tightly around the waist. His smirk suddenly turned into a sober expression.

"A kiss. A *real* one. One that I'll remember."

I was about to say something brilliantly sarcastic, probably about him not having permission, when he captured my mouth with his. I was determined to remain stiff and unaffected, but he was extremely patient. He nibbled on the corners of my mouth and pressed soft, slow kisses against my unyielding lips. It was so hard not to respond to him.

I made a valiant struggle, but sometimes the body betrays the mind. He slowly, methodically swept aside my resistance. And, feeling he was winning, he pressed ahead and began seducing me even more skillfully. He held me tightly against his body and ran a hand up to my neck where he began to massage it gently, teasing my flesh with his fingertips.

I felt the little love plant inside me stretch, swell, and unfurl its leaves, like he was pouring *Love Potion # 9* over the thing. I gave up at that point and decided what the heck. I could always use a rototiller on it. And I rationalized that when he breaks my heart, at least I will have been thoroughly kissed.

If nothing else, I'll have a really good memory to look back on in my multi-cat spinsterhood. Or multi-dog. I think I will have had my fill of cats. I groaned softly. *Yep. Dogs for sure.*

I opened myself up to the kiss and kissed him back with enthusiasm. Putting all my secret emotions and tender feelings into the embrace, I wound my arms around his neck and slid my hands into his hair. Pulling his body that much closer to mine, I embraced him with all the warmth and affection that I wouldn't allow myself to express verbally.

He paused, shocked for a brief instant, and then quickly adjusted his approach, escalating into a passionate frenzy. I shocked myself by matching his energy. I ran my hands up his powerful arms and shoulders and then down his chest. My senses were in turmoil. I felt wild. Eager. I clutched at his shirt. I couldn't get close enough to him. He even smelled delicious.

You'd think that several days of being chased by strange creatures and hiking through a mysterious kingdom would make him smell bad. In fact, I wanted him to smell bad. I'm sure I did. I mean, how can you expect a girl to be fresh as a daisy while traipsing through the jungle and getting chased by monkeys. It's just not possible.

I desperately wanted him to have *some* fault. *Some* weakness. Some . . . *imperfection.* But Ren smelled amazing—like waterfalls, a warm summer day, and sandalwood trees all wrapped up in a sizzling, hot guy.

How could a girl defend herself from a perfect onslaught delivered by a perfect person? I gave up and let Mr. Wonderful take control of my senses. My blood burned, my heart thundered, my need for him quickened, and I lost all track of time in his arms. All I was aware of was Ren. His lips. His body. His soul. I wanted all of him.

Eventually, he put his hands on my shoulders and gently separated us. I was surprised that he had the strength of will to stop because I was nowhere near being able to. I blinked my eyes open in a daze. We were both breathing hard.

"That was . . . enlightening," he breathed. "Thank you, Kelsey."

I blinked. The passion that had dulled my mind dissipated in an instant, and my mind sharply focused on a new feeling. Irritation.

"Thank you? Thank you! Of all the—" I slammed up the steps angrily and then spun around to look down at him. "No! Thank *you*, Ren!" My hands slashed at the air. "Now you got what you wanted, so leave me alone!" I ran up the stairs quickly to put some distance between us.

Enlightening? What was that about? Was he testing me? Giving me a one-to-ten score on my kissing ability? Of all the nerve!

I was glad that I was mad. I could shove all the other emotions into the back of my mind and just focus on the anger, the indignation.

He leapt up the stairs two at a time. "That's *not* all I want, Kelsey. That's for sure."

"Well, I no longer *care* about what you want!"

He shot me a knowing look and raised an eyebrow. Then, he lifted his

foot out of the opening, placed it on the dirt, and instantly changed back into a tiger.

I laughed mockingly. "Ha!" I tripped over a stone but quickly found my footing. "Serves you right!" I shouted angrily and stumbled blindly along the dim path.

After figuring out where to go, I marched off in a huff. "Come on, Fanindra. Let's go find Mr. Kadam."

23

six hours

It was early dawn. The sun was just peeking over the horizon. I stormed off through the buildings of Hampi and allowed the momentum of my anger to carry me halfway back to Mr. Kadam's camp.

Ren followed along behind me somewhere quietly. I couldn't hear him, but I knew he was there. I was acutely aware of his presence. I had an intangible connection with him, the man. It was almost as if he were walking next to me. *Almost as if he were touching me.*

I must have started walking down the wrong path because he trotted ahead, pointedly moving in a different direction. I muttered, "Show-off. I'll walk the wrong way if I want to." But, I still followed after him.

After a while, I made out the Jeep parked on the hill and saw Mr. Kadam waving at us.

I walked up to his camp, and he grabbed me in a brief hug. "Miss Kelsey! You're back. Tell me what happened."

I sighed, set down my backpack, and sat on the back bumper of the Jeep. "Well, I have to tell you, these past few days have been some of the worst of my life. There were monkeys, and Kappa, and rotted kissing corpses, and snakebites, and trees covered with needles, and—"

He held up a hand. "What do you mean a few days? You just left last night."

Confused, I said, "No. We've been gone at least," I counted on my fingers, "at least four or five days."

"I'm sorry, Miss Kelsey, but you and Ren left me last night. In fact, I was going to say you should get some rest and then try again tomorrow night. You were really gone almost a week?"

"Well, I was asleep for two of the days. At least that's what tiger boy over there told me." I glared at Ren who stared back at me with an innocuous tiger expression while listening to our conversation.

Ren appeared to be sweet and attentive, as harmless as a little kitten. He was about as harmless as a Kappa. I, on the other hand, was like a porcupine. I was bristling. All of my quills were standing on end so I could defend my soft belly from being devoured by the predator who had taken an interest.

"Two days? My, my. Why don't we return to the hotel and rest? We can try to get the fruit again tomorrow night."

"But, Mr. Kadam," I said and unzipped the backpack, "we don't have to come back. We got Durga's first gift, the Golden Fruit." I pulled out my quilt and unfolded it, revealing the Golden Fruit nestled within.

He gently picked it up out of its cocoon. "Amazing!" he exclaimed.

"It's a mango." With a smirk, I added, "It only makes sense. After all, mangoes are very important to Indian culture and trade."

Ren huffed at me and rolled onto his side in the grass.

"Indeed, it does make sense, Miss Kelsey." He admired the fruit for another moment, and then carefully rewrapped it in my quilt. Mr. Kadam clapped his hands together. "This is very exciting! Let's break camp then and head home. Or perhaps it would be better to go to a hotel so you can rest, Miss Kelsey."

"Oh, it's okay. I don't mind getting back on the road. We can stay in a hotel tonight. How many days will it take for us to get home?"

"We will need to stay over two more nights in a hotel on our trip home."

Momentarily alarmed, I glanced at Ren. "Okay. Umm, I was thinking that maybe this time if you don't mind, we could check out one of those bigger hotels. You know, something that has more people around. With elevators and rooms that lock. Or even better, a nice high-rise hotel in a big city. Far, far, *far* away from the jungle?"

Mr. Kadam chuckled. "I'll see what I can do."

I graced Mr. Kadam with a beatific smile. "Good! Could we please go now? I can't wait to take a shower." I opened the door to the passenger side then turned and hissed in a whisper aimed at Ren, "In my nice, upper-floor, inaccessible-to-tigers hotel room."

He just looked at me with his innocent, blue-eyed tiger face again. I smiled wickedly at him and hopped in the Jeep, slamming the door behind me. My tiger just calmly trotted over to the back where Mr. Kadam was loading the last of his supplies and leapt up into the back seat. He leaned in the front, and before I could push him away, he gave me a big, wet, slobbery tiger kiss right on my face.

I sputtered, "Ren! That is *so* disgusting!"

I used my T-shirt to swipe the tiger saliva from my nose and cheek and turned to yell at him some more. He was already lying down in the back seat with his mouth hanging open, as if he were laughing. Before I could really lay into him, Mr. Kadam, who was the happiest I'd ever seen him, got into the Jeep, and we started the bumpy journey back to a civilized road.

Mr. Kadam wanted to ask me questions. I knew he was itching for information, but I was still fuming at Ren, so I lied. I asked him if he could hold off for a while so I could sleep. I yawned big for dramatic effect, and he immediately agreed to let me have some peace, which made me feel guilty. I really liked Mr. Kadam, and I hated lying to people. I excused my actions by mentally blaming Ren for this uncharacteristic behavior. Convincing myself that it was his fault was easy. I turned to the side and closed my eyes.

I slept for a while, and when I woke up, Mr. Kadam handed me a soda, a sandwich, and a banana. I raised my eyebrow at the banana and thought of several good monkey jokes I could annoy Ren with, but I kept quiet for Mr. Kadam's sake. Instead, I immediately dug into my sandwich and drained my soda in one long drink.

Mr. Kadam laughed and handed me another one. "Are you ready to tell me about what happened, Miss Kelsey?"

"Sure, I guess so."

It took the better part of two hours to tell him about the tunnel, the needle forest, the cave, the Kappa, and Kishkindha. I spent a long time talking about the golden tree and the monkeys coming to life. I ended with the Kappa attack and Fanindra biting me.

I never mentioned that Ren was a man the whole time. In fact, I downplayed his presence in Kishkindha altogether. Whenever Mr. Kadam asked me how this or that was accomplished, I answered vaguely, or said lucky we had Fanindra, or lucky we had the *gada*. That seemed to satisfy most of his questions.

When he asked for more details about the Kappa attack, I just shrugged my shoulders and repeated my mantra, "Lucky I had Fanindra." I didn't want to answer any weird questions about Ren. I knew he'd probably tell his side of the story when he became a man again, but I didn't care. I kept my version of the trip factual, unemotional, and, more importantly, *Renless*.

Mr. Kadam said we'd be stopping at a hotel soon, but he wanted to find a good place to leave Ren first. I demurred, "Of course," and smiled a sickly sweet smile back at the attentive tiger.

Mr. Kadam worried, "I hope our hotel won't be too far away for him."

I patted Mr. Kadam's arm and reassured him, "Oh, don't worry

about him. He's *very* good at getting what he wants. I mean . . . taking care of his needs. I'm sure he'll find his long night alone in the jungle extremely *enlightening*." Mr. Kadam shot me a puzzled glance, but he eventually nodded and pulled over near a forested area.

Ren got out of the Jeep, came around to my side of the car, and stared at me with icy blue eyes. I just turned my body away so I wouldn't have to look at him. When Mr. Kadam got back in the Jeep, I peeked out my window again, but Ren was gone. I reminded myself that he deserved it and sat back against the seat with my arms folded over my chest and an intense expression on my face.

Mr. Kadam spoke softly, "Kelsey, are you alright? You seem very . . . tense, since I last saw you."

I muttered under my breath, "You have no idea."

"What was that?"

I sighed and smiled at him weakly. "Nothing. I'm fine, just drained from the trip is all."

"There's something else I've been meaning to ask you. Did you have any strange dreams while in Kishkindha?"

"What kind of dreams?"

He glanced at me, worried. "Perhaps a dream about your amulet?"

"Oh! I totally forgot to tell you! When I plucked the fruit, I fainted and had a vision. It was of you, me, and some evil guy."

Mr. Kadam grew visibly worried. He cleared his throat. "Then the vision was real—for all of us. I was afraid of that. The man you saw was Lokesh. He's the same dark wizard who put the curse on Ren and Kishan."

My mouth gaped open in shock. "He's still alive?"

"It seems he is. It also appears that he has at least one part of the amulet. I suspect, however, that he has *all* of the other pieces."

"How many pieces are there?"

"There are rumored to be five altogether, but no one really knows for sure. Ren's father had one piece, and his mother brought another piece into the family because she was the only offspring of a powerful warlord who also had one. That's how Ren and Kishan both ended up with a segment."

"But what does it have to do with me?"

"That's just it, Kelsey. You are helping Ren break the curse. The amulet connects the three of us, and I'm worried that Lokesh knows about us. About you, in particular. I was hoping that something had happened to him, that he wasn't alive anymore after all these years. I've been searching for him for centuries. Now that he's seen us, I'm worried that he will come after you and the amulet."

"You really think he's that ruthless?"

"I know he is." Mr. Kadam paused, and then suggested softly, "Perhaps it is time for you to return home."

"What?" I panicked.

Return home? Home to what? Home to whom? I had no life at home. I hadn't even thought about what would happen after we broke the curse. I guess I'd just assumed that there was so much to do that I'd be stuck here for a couple of years.

Dismayed, I inquired, "You really want me to go home now?"

He saw my face and patted my hand. "Not at all! I didn't mean to imply that I wanted you to leave us. Don't worry. We'll figure something out. I'm just speculating for now. I have no immediate plans to send you home. And, of course, if and when you do go, you may always return whenever you wish. Our home is yours. We just need to proceed with extreme caution now that Lokesh is back in the picture."

I felt my panic subside, but only halfway. *Maybe Mr. Kadam is right. Maybe I should go home. It would be much easier to forget Mr. Superhero if I were on the other side of the planet, right? Heck, he's the only young male*

I've been around for weeks, not counting Kishan. It would be healthier for me to get out and meet other guys anyway. Maybe if I did that, I'd realize this whole emotional connection I feel with him isn't really that strong.

Maybe my mind is playing tricks on me. I've just been isolated, that's all. When all you have is Tarzan and some monkeys, Tarzan looks pretty good, right?

I'll just get over him. I'll just go home and date a nice, normal computer geek who'd never leave me. I'll forget all about old what's-his-name.

I continued this line of thought, listing my reasons for staying away from Ren, and stubbornly rededicated myself to avoiding him. The only problem was my rebellious, weak mind kept drifting back to how safe I felt when he held me. And what he'd said when he thought I was dying. And the warm tingle that lingered on my lips after he kissed me. Even if I ignored his beautiful face, which was next to a Herculean task, there were many other dazzling qualities for my mind to dwell on, and those thoughts kept me occupied for the rest of the trip.

Mr. Kadam pulled into the smooth driveway of a fabulous five-star hotel. I felt frumpy in my week-old, ripped, torn, and bloody clothes. Mr. Kadam seemed nonchalant and was happy as a clam when he handed over the keys to a valet and accompanied me into the hotel. I kept my backpack close, but our other two bags were taken up to our rooms by hotel staff.

Mr. Kadam filled out the necessary forms and spoke quietly with the lady at the front desk in Hindi. Then he gestured for me to follow.

As we passed, I leaned over and asked, "Just out of curiosity, you don't allow pets. Am I right?"

She seemed confused and looked at Mr. Kadam, but shook her head no.

"Great. Just checking." I smiled back at her. Mr. Kadam tilted his head in puzzlement but said nothing.

He must think I'm off my rocker. I grinned and followed him to the elevator. The bellhop inserted a card key into the slot at the top of the elevator button pad, which automatically closed the door, and selected our floor. We got out and stepped directly into our room, the penthouse suite.

The staff person left us, and the elevator doors shut. Mr. Kadam told me that he'd be staying in the bedroom to the left and that I would have the suite on the right. He left me to myself with the admonishment that I rest and eat in whatever order I chose and that food would be delivered soon.

I walked into my beautiful suite with a king-sized bed and laughed giddily. A huge hot tub was set in the middle of my private bathroom. I quickly kicked off my dirty tennis shoes and decided to shower first and then soak in the hot tub. Stepping into the hot shower, I soaped my hair four times and then applied conditioner and let the silky liquid soak in while I scrubbed my skin raw. I dug my fingernails into a bar of soap and wiggled them back and forth to get the dirt out and paid special attention to my feet. My poor, knobby, blistered, sore feet. *Oh well, maybe Mr. Kadam will spring for a pedicure later.*

After I felt thoroughly clean, I wrapped a towel around my hair, and slipped into a robe. Filling the hot tub with hot water, I poured in bubble bath that was conveniently provided, and started the jets. The scent of juicy pears and just-picked berries rose into the air. Its smell reminded me of Oregon.

Sinking into that tub was the best feeling in the whole world. *Well, the second best feeling.* I was annoyed that the memory of kissing Ren popped into my mind, and I quickly dismissed it, or tried to. The more I relaxed in the tub, the more my mind seemed to dwell on it. It was like a song that got stuck in my head, and, no matter what I did, it kept coming back to me.

The kiss played over and over. Despite my best efforts to eradicate it, I felt myself smile at the memory. *Ugh! What's that about?* I shook myself out of my daydream angrily, and reluctantly climbed out of the tub. After I dried off and pulled on a pair of shorts and a clean T-shirt, I sat down to brush out my hair. It took a long time to get all the tangles out. The brushing was soothing. It reminded me of my mom. I sat back on my king-sized bed and just enjoyed the feel of pulling my hairbrush through clean, wet hair.

Later, I ventured to the sitting room and found Mr. Kadam reading a newspaper.

"Hello, Miss Kelsey. Are you feeling refreshed?"

"I feel so much better; I can't even begin to tell you."

"Good. There's a late dinner under the cover over there. I took the liberty of ordering for you."

I lifted the lid and found turkey, cornbread stuffing, cranberry relish, peas, and mashed potatoes.

"Wow! How did you get them to do this?"

He shrugged. "I thought you might like something American for a change, and that's about as American as it gets. There's even apple pie for dessert."

I picked up my dinner plate and the glass full of icy lemon water that he knew I liked and sat down next to him with my legs tucked under me to eat.

"Did you eat already?"

"Yes, an hour or so ago. Don't worry about me. Enjoy your dinner."

I dug in and was pleasantly stuffed before I'd even had the apple pie. I swirled a piece of roll in my gravy and said, "Mr. Kadam? I want to tell you something. I feel guilty about not telling you before, but I think you should know."

I took a deep breath and went on. "Ren was a man the whole time we were in Kishkindha."

He set down his newspaper. "That's interesting. But why couldn't you tell me this before?"

I shrugged a shoulder and hedged, "I don't know. Things weren't exactly . . . smooth between us these past few days."

His eyes twinkled as he laughed with understanding. "Now things make sense. I wondered why you were acting differently around him. Ren can be . . . difficult, if he chooses."

"Stubborn, you mean. And demanding. And," I looked out the window at the nighttime city lights and muttered, "lots of other things."

He leaned forward and took one of my hands in his. "I see. Don't fret, Miss Kelsey. I'm surprised that you've accomplished so much in such a short time. It's hard enough to undertake a perilous journey, let alone with someone you are just getting to know and are not sure if you can trust. Even the best of companions can have falling-outs when under such great duress as you two have been. I'm sure that this is just a temporary setback in your friendship."

Our friendship was not exactly the issue. Still, Mr. Kadam's words gave me some comfort. Maybe, now that we were out of that situation, we could talk it out and apply good ol' common sense to the problem. Perhaps I could be the bigger person. After all, Ren was just starting to communicate with people again. If I could just explain to him how the world worked, I was sure he would understand and be able to move on to a place where we could still be friends.

He continued, "It's remarkable that he was able to maintain human form the entire time there. Perhaps it has something to do with time stopping."

"Do you really think time stopped in Kishkindha?"

"Perhaps time just moves differently there, but I do know that you were gone in our time for only a short while."

I nodded, agreeing with his assessment. Feeling better after talking and also happy that I had told Mr. Kadam the truth, I said that I was going to read for a while and then go sleep for a long time with a soft pillow. He nodded and asked me to place all my clothing in the laundry bag so it could be cleaned overnight.

Heading back to my suite, I began to gather my things. I threw in my clothes and tennis shoes too. Also, I carefully unrolled my quilt, removed the Golden Fruit, and wrapped it in a small towel. I picked up my sad-looking, filthy quilt and popped it into the laundry bag as well.

Placing the laundry bag outside my door, I hopped into the huge bed, luxuriating in the soft, plush sheets. I sunk into the goose-down pillows, and fell into a deep, relaxing sleep.

The next morning, I smiled and stretched out all my limbs as far as they could go and still didn't even reach the edge of the bed. I brushed out my hair again and pulled it up into a loose ponytail.

Mr. Kadam was just sitting down to a breakfast of hash browns, toast, and Spanish omelets. I joined him, sipped my orange juice, and chatted about how exciting it was to be heading back home.

Our laundry was brought back pressed and folded as if brand new. Taking some clothes out of the pile to wear, I transferred all the rest of the folded clothing to my other bag. When I got to my quilt, I stopped for a moment to smell the lemony soap they'd used and inspected it carefully for damage. Faded and old as it was, it was still holding together well. I sent a silent thanks to my grandmother. *They don't make them anymore like you did, Gran.*

I placed my folded quilt on the bottom of my backpack and put the *gada* on the side standing straight up. I'd taken the *gada* out to clean the night before, but I was surprised to find it shiny and spotless, as if it had never been used. Next, I set Fanindra carefully on top of my quilt

and put the Golden Fruit right in the middle of her coils. Then I zipped it up, leaving just a part open so Fanindra could breathe. I didn't know if she actually breathed, but it made me feel better anyway.

Soon it was time to leave. I felt happy, refreshed, and perfectly content until we pulled up to the side of the road, and I saw *him* and he wasn't a tiger. Ren had been waiting for us, wearing his usual white clothing and a toothy grin. Mr. Kadam walked over and hugged him. I could hear their voices, but I couldn't make out what they were saying. I did hear Mr. Kadam laugh as he clapped Ren on the back rather loudly. He was obviously very happy about something.

Then Ren changed back into a tiger and jumped into the car. He curled up for a nap in the back while I pointedly ignored him and selected a book to keep myself occupied on the long drive.

Mr. Kadam explained that we would have to stop at another hotel on the way back and that we would be driving all day. I told him that it was fine with me. I had plenty of books to read because Mr. Kadam had bought me a couple of novels at the hotel bookstore as well as a travel book of India.

I napped on and off during the day between chapters. I finished the first novel by early afternoon and was nearing the end of the second book by the time we drove into the city. The car was unusually quiet. Mr. Kadam seemed in high spirits, but he wasn't sharing, and Ren slept the day away in the back.

After the sun went down, Mr. Kadam announced that we were near our destination. He indicated that he would drop me off first and then we would have dinner in the hotel restaurant to celebrate.

Inside my new hotel room, I lamented over what to wear because all I had were jeans and T-shirts in my bag. As I was rifling through the same three items for the third time, I heard a knock at the door and shuffled over in my robe and slippers. A maid handed me a zipped garment bag and a box. I tried to talk to her, but she didn't understand English. She just kept saying, "Kadam."

I took it, thanked her, and unzipped the garment bag to find a gorgeous dress inside. The fitted black velvet bodice had a sweetheart neckline, and the capped sleeves and skirt were made of a pearlescent plum dupioni silk. The dress's snug fit made me look curvier than I really was. It tapered down to my hips and settled over the full plum, knee-length skirt. A belt, made of the same soft material as the skirt, was knotted on the side and pinned with a sparkling broach to emphasize my waist.

The dress was beautifully made, fully lined, and probably expensive. When I moved in the light, the material shimmered, reflecting several different shades of purple. I'd never worn something so lovely, except for the beautiful blue Indian dress I had back at the house. I opened the box and found a pair of strappy black heels with diamond buckles and a matching lily clip for my hair. A dress like this required makeup, so I headed to the bathroom and finished getting ready. I clipped the lily into my hair just over my left ear and finger-combed through my wavy hair. Then I slipped on my shoes and waited for Mr. Kadam.

He soon knocked on my door and admired me with fatherly appreciation. "Miss Kelsey, you look beautiful!"

I swirled my skirt for him. "The *dress* is beautiful. If I look good, it's all your doing. You picked out something fabulous. Thank you. You must have known that I wanted to feel like a lady for a change, instead of a camper Jane."

He nodded. His eyes seemed thoughtful, but he smiled at me, held out his arm, and escorted me out to the hotel elevator. We rode down the elevator and laughed about monkeys, as I told him about Ren running around with about twenty of them attached to his fur.

We walked into a candlelit restaurant with white linen tablecloths and napkins. The hostess guided us to a section with floor-to-ceiling windows overlooking the lights of the city below. Only one of the tables in this section of the restaurant was occupied. A man was dining alone. He was sitting with his back turned toward us as he looked out at the lights.

Mr. Kadam bowed and said, "Miss Kelsey, I will leave you to your dining companion. Enjoy your dinner." Then he walked out of the restaurant.

"Mr. Kadam, wait. I don't understand."

Dining companion? What is he talking about? Maybe he's confused.

Just then, a deep, all-too-familiar voice behind me said, "Hello, Kells."

I froze, and my heart dropped into my stomach, stirring up about a billion butterflies. A few seconds passed. Or was it a few minutes? I couldn't tell.

I heard a sigh of frustration. "Are you still not talking to me? Turn around, please."

A warm hand slid under my elbow and gently turned me around. I raised my eyes and gasped softly. He was breathtaking! So handsome, I wanted to cry.

"Ren."

He smiled. "Who else?"

He was dressed in an elegant black suit and he'd had his hair cut. Glossy black hair was swept back away from his face in tousled layers that tapered to a slight curl at the nape of his neck. The white shirt he wore was unbuttoned at the collar. It set off his golden-bronze skin and his brilliant white smile, making him positively lethal to any woman who might cross his path. I groaned inwardly.

He's like . . . like James Bond, Antonio Banderas, and Brad Pitt all rolled into one.

I decided the safest thing to do would be to look at his shoes. Shoes were boring, right? Not attractive at all. *Ah. Much better.* His shoes were nice, of course—polished and black, just like I would expect. I smiled wryly when I realized that this was the first time I'd ever seen Ren in shoes.

He cupped my chin and made me look at his face. *The jerk.* Then it was his turn to appraise me. He looked me up and down. And not a quick look. He took it all in *slowly.* The kind of slow that made a girl's face feel hot. I got mad at myself for blushing and glared at him.

Nervous and impatient, I asked, "Are you finished?"

"Almost." He was now staring at my strappy shoes.

"Well, hurry up!"

His eyes drifted leisurely back up to my face and he smiled at me appreciatively, "Kelsey, when a man spends time with a beautiful woman, he needs to pace himself."

I quirked my eyebrow at him and laughed. "Yeah, I'm a regular marathon alright."

He kissed my fingers. "Exactly. A wise man never sprints . . . in a marathon."

"I was being sarcastic, Ren."

He ignored me and tucked my hand under his arm then led me over to a beautifully lit table. Pulling the chair out for me, he invited me to sit.

I stood there wondering if I could sprint for the nearest exit. *Stupid strappy shoes, I'd never make it.*

He leaned in close and whispered in my ear, "I know what you're thinking, and I'm not going to let you escape again. You can either take a seat and have dinner with me like a normal date," he grinned at his word choice, "or," he paused thoughtfully then threatened, "you can sit on my lap while I force-feed you."

I hissed, "You wouldn't dare. You're too much of a gentleman to force me to do anything. It's an empty bluff, Mr. Asks-For-Permission."

"Even a gentleman has his limits. One way or another, we're going to have a civil conversation. I'm hoping I get to feed you from my lap, but it's your choice."

He straightened up again and waited. I unceremoniously plunked down in my chair and scooted in noisily to the table. He laughed softly and took the chair across from me. I felt guilty because of the dress and readjusted my skirt so it wouldn't wrinkle.

I glared at him as our waitress came over. She set my menu down quickly, and I had to watch as she took an extra long time giving him his menu. She stood near his shoulder and pointed out several choices while leaning over his arm. After she finally left, I rolled my eyes in disgust.

Ren took his time perusing the menu and seemed to be thoroughly enjoying himself. I didn't even pick my menu up. He shot me meaningful glances while I sat silently, trying to avoid making eye contact. When she came back, she spoke to him briefly and gestured to me.

I smiled, and in a syrupy sweet voice, said, "I'll have whatever will get me out of here the fastest. Like a salad, maybe."

Ren smiled benignly back at me and rattled off what sounded like a banquet of choices, which the waitress was more than happy to take her time writing down. She kept touching him and laughing with him too. Which I found very, *very* annoying.

When she left, he leaned back in his chair and sipped his water.

I broke the silence first and hissed at him quietly, "I don't know what you're playing at, but you only have about two minutes left, so I hope you ordered the steak tartar, Tiger."

He grinned mischievously. "We'll see, Kells. We'll see."

"*Fine*. No skin off my nose. I can't wait to see what happens when a white tiger runs through this nice establishment creating mayhem and havoc. Perhaps they will lose one of their stars because they put their patrons in danger. Maybe your new waitress girlfriend will run away screaming." I smiled at the thought.

Ren affected shock, "Why, Kelsey! Are you jealous?"

I snorted in a very unladylike way, "No! Of course not."

He grinned. Nervously, I played with my cloth napkin. "I can't believe you convinced Mr. Kadam to play along with you like this. It's shocking, really."

He opened his napkin and winked at the waitress when she came to bring us a basket of rolls.

When she left, I challenged, "Are you winking at her? Unbelievable!"

He laughed quietly and pulled out a steaming roll, buttered it, and put it on my plate. "Eat, Kelsey," he commanded. Then he sat forward. "Unless you are reconsidering seeing the view from my lap."

Angrily, I tore apart my roll and swallowed a few pieces before I even noticed how delicious they were—light and flaky with little flecks of orange rind mixed into the dough. I would have eaten another one, but I wouldn't give him the satisfaction.

The waitress returned shortly with two helpers, and they piled dish after dish on our table. Sure enough, he had ordered a smorgasbord. There was not one inch left on our table. He took my plate and piled it high with aromatic, mouth-watering selections. After placing it in front of me, he began filling his own. When he was finished, he set his plate down, looked at me, and raised an eyebrow.

I leaned forward and whispered angrily, "I am *not* going to sit on your lap, so don't get your hopes up, Mister."

He still waited until I picked up a fork and took a few bites. I speared a bite of macadamia nut crusted ruby snapper and said, "Whew. Time's up. Isn't it? The clock is ticking. You must be sweating it, huh? I mean, you could turn any second."

He just took a bite of curried lamb and then some saffron rice and sat there chewing as cool as a cucumber.

I watched him closely for a full two minutes and then folded up my napkin.

"Okay, I give up. Why are you acting so smug and confident? When are you going to tell me what's going on?"

He wiped his mouth carefully and took a sip of water. "What's going on, my *prema*, is that the curse has been lifted."

My mouth dropped open. "What? If it was lifted, why were you a tiger for the last two days?"

"Well, to be clear, the curse is not completely gone. I seem to have been granted a partial removal of the curse."

"Partial? Partial meaning what, exactly?"

"Partial, meaning a certain number of hours per day. Six hours to be exact."

I recited the prophecy in my mind and remembered that there were four sides to the monolith, and four times six was . . . "Twenty-four."

He paused, "Twenty-four what?"

"Well, six hours makes sense because there are four gifts to obtain for Durga and four sides of the monolith. We've only completed one of the tasks, so you only get six hours."

He smiled. "I guess I get to keep you around then, at least until the other tasks are finished."

I snorted. "Don't hold your breath, Tarzan. *I* might not need to be *present* for the other tasks. Now that you're a man part of the time, you and Kishan can resolve this problem yourselves, I'm sure."

He cocked his head and narrowed his eyes at me. "Don't under-estimate your level of . . . involvement, Kelsey. Even if you weren't needed anymore to break the curse, do you think I'd simply let you go? Let you walk out of my life without a backward glance?"

I nervously began toying with my food and decided to say nothing. That was exactly what I'd been planning to do.

Something had changed. The hurt and confused Ren that made me feel guilty for rejecting him in Kishkindha was gone. He was now supremely confident, almost arrogant, and very sure of himself.

He kept his eyes on my face while he ate. When he finished all the food on his plate, he filled it again, scooping up at least half of every dish on the table.

I squirmed under his gaze and played with my food. He looked like the cat that had the canary or the student who had all the answers to the test before the teacher even told the class about it. He was disgustingly pleased with himself, and I sensed that there was much more to his newfound confidence than just getting time back as a man.

He seemed to know all my secret thoughts and feelings. His confidence set me on edge. I felt like I was backed into a corner.

"The answer to that question is . . . I won't. You belong with me. Which leads me to the discussion I wanted to have with you."

"Where I belong is for me to decide, and though I may listen to what you have to say, that doesn't mean I will agree with you."

"Fair enough." Ren pushed his empty plate to the side. "We have some unfinished business to take care of."

"If you mean the other tasks we have to do, I'm already aware of that."

"I'm not talking about that. I'm talking about *us*."

"What about us?" I put my hands under the table and wiped my clammy palms on my napkin.

"I think there are a few things we've left unsaid, and I think it's time we said them."

"I'm not withholding anything from you, if that's what you mean."

"You are."

"*No.* I'm not."

"Are you refusing to acknowledge what has happened between us?"

"I'm not refusing anything. Don't try to put words in my mouth."

"I'm not. I'm simply trying to convince a stubborn woman to admit that she has feelings for me."

"If I *did* have feelings for you, you'd be the first one to know."

"Are you saying that you *don't* feel anything for me?"

"That's not what I'm saying."

"Then what *are* you saying?"

"I'm saying . . . *nothing!*" I sputtered.

Ren smiled and narrowed his eyes at me.

If he kept up this line of questioning, he was bound to catch me in a lie. I wasn't a very good liar.

He sat back in his chair. "Fine. I'll let you off the hook for now, but we *will* talk about this later. Tigers are relentless once they set their minds to something. You won't be able to evade me forever."

Casually, I replied, "Don't get your hopes up, Mr. Wonderful. Every hero has his Kryptonite, and you don't intimidate me." I twisted my napkin in my lap while he tracked my every move with his probing eyes. I felt stripped down, as if he could see into the very heart of me.

When the waitress came back, Ren smiled at her as she offered a smaller menu, probably featuring desserts. She leaned over him while I tapped my strappy shoe in frustration. He listened attentively to her. Then, the two of them laughed again.

He spoke quietly, gesturing to me, and she looked my way, giggled, and then cleared all the plates quickly. He pulled out a wallet and handed her a credit card. She put her hand on his arm to ask him another question, and I couldn't help myself. I kicked him under the table. He didn't even blink or look at me. He just reached his arm across the table, took my hand in his, and rubbed the back of it absentmindedly with his thumb as he answered her question. It was like my kick was a love tap to him. It only made him happier.

When she left, I narrowed my eyes at him and asked, "How did you get that card, and what were you saying to her about me?"

"Mr. Kadam gave me the card, and I told her that we would be having our dessert . . . later."

I laughed facetiously. "You mean *you* will be having dessert later by *yourself* this evening because I am done eating with you."

He leaned across the candlelit table and said, "Who said anything about eating, Kelsey?"

He must be joking! But, he looked completely serious. *Great! There go the nervous butterflies again.*

"Stop looking at me like that."

"Like what?"

"Like you're hunting me. I'm not an antelope."

He laughed. "Ah, but the chase would be exquisite, and you would be a most succulent catch."

"Stop it."

"Am I making you nervous?"

"You could say that."

I stood up abruptly as he was signing the receipt and made my way toward the door. He was next to me in an instant. He leaned over.

"I'm not letting you escape, remember? Now, behave like a good date and let me walk you home. It's the least you could do since you wouldn't talk with me."

Ren took my elbow and began to guide me out of the restaurant. I was acutely aware of him, and the thought that he was walking me back to my room and would most likely try to kiss me again sent shivers down my spine. For self-preservation purposes, I had to get away. Every minute I spent with him just made me want him more. Since merely annoying him wasn't working, I'd have to up the ante.

Apparently, I needed him not only to fall out-of-like with me, but to hate me as well. I'd frequently been told that I was an all-or-nothing kind of girl. If I were going to push him away, it was going to be so far away that there would be absolutely no chance of him ever coming back.

I tried to wrench my elbow out of his grasp, but he just held on more tightly. I grumbled at him, "Stop using your tiger strength on me, Superman."

"Am I hurting you?"

"No, but I'm not a puppet to be dragged around."

He trailed his fingers down my arm and took my hand instead. "Then you play nice, and I will too."

"Fine."

He grinned. *"Fine."*

I hissed back. *"Fine!"*

We walked to the elevator, and he pushed the button to my floor.

"My room is on the same floor," Ren explained.

I scowled and then grinned lopsidedly and just a little bit evilly, "And umm, how exactly is that going to work for you in the morning, Tiger? You really shouldn't get Mr. Kadam in trouble for having a rather large . . . pet."

Ren returned my sarcasm as he walked me to my door. "Are you *worried* about me, Kells? Well, don't. I'll be fine."

"I guess there's no point in asking how you knew which door belonged to me, huh, Tiger Nose?"

He looked at me in a way that turned my insides to jelly. I spun around but awareness of him shot through my limbs, and I could feel him standing close behind me watching, waiting.

I put my key in the lock, and he moved closer. My hand started shaking, and I couldn't twist the key the right way. He took my hand and gently turned me around. He then put both hands on the door on either side of my head and leaned in close, pinning me against it.

I trembled like a downy rabbit caught in the clutches of a wolf. The wolf came closer. He bent his head and began nuzzling my cheek. The problem was . . . I *wanted* the wolf to devour me.

I began to get lost in the thick sultry fog that overtook me every time Ren put his hands on me.

So much for asking for permission . . . and so much for sticking to my guns, I thought as I felt all my defenses slip away.

He whispered warmly, "I can always tell where you are, Kelsey. You smell like peaches and cream."

I shivered and put my hands on his chest to push him away, but I ended up grabbing fistfuls of shirt and held on for dear life. He trailed kisses from my ear down my cheek and then pressed soft kisses along the arch of my neck. I pulled him closer and turned my head so he could really kiss me. He smiled and ignored my invitation, moving instead to the other ear. He bit my earlobe lightly, moved from there to my collarbone, and trailed kisses out to my shoulder. Then he lifted his head and brought his lips about one inch from mine and the only thought in my head was . . . *more*.

With a devastating smile, he reluctantly pulled away and lightly ran his fingers through the strands of my hair. "By the way, I forgot to mention that you look beautiful tonight." He smiled again then turned and strolled off down the hall.

Tiny quakes vibrated through my limbs like aftershocks following an earthquake. I couldn't steady my hand as I twisted the key. I shoved open the door to my dark room, entered, and shakily closed it behind me. Leaning back against the door, I let the darkness envelop me.

endings

The next morning, I quickly packed up all my things and waited for Mr. Kadam. I sat in the easy chair, nervously tapping my foot back and forth. Last night had convinced me that I needed to do something about Ren. His presence was overwhelming.

I knew that if I spent any more time with him, he would persuade me to become serious about him, and I absolutely could not allow that.

I would end up crushed. Oh, it would be great for a while. Really, *really* great. But, it would never last. He was an Adonis, and I was no Helen of Troy. We'd never make it. I had to be realistic and to take control of my life again. I decided that when we got back to the house, he and I would have a woman-to-tiger talk.

Then, if he still wouldn't give up, I'd just go home as Mr. Kadam had suggested. Maybe distance would help. Maybe Ren just needed time apart from me to realize that a relationship between us would be a mistake. With that resolve, I braced myself to see him again as we left the hotel.

I waited a long time for Mr. Kadam. I was almost ready to call his room, when, finally, there was a knock at the door. Mr. Kadam stood there alone.

"Are you ready, Miss Kelsey? I'm sorry that we're getting such a late start."

"It's okay. Mr. Wonderful was probably taking his sweet time, right?"

"No, it was actually my fault this morning. I was busy with . . . paperwork."

"Oh. Well, that's alright. Don't worry about it. What kind of paperwork?"

He smiled. "Nothing important."

Mr. Kadam held the door for me, and we walked out into an empty hallway. I was just starting to relax at the elevator doors when I heard a hotel room door close. Ren walked down the hall toward us. He'd purchased new clothes. Of course, he looked wonderful. I took a step back from the elevator and tried to avoid eye contact.

Ren wore a brand new pair of dark-indigo, purposely faded, urban-destruction designer jeans. His shirt was a long-sleeved, buttoned-down, crisp, oxford-style and was obviously of high quality. It was blue with thin white stripes that matched his eyes perfectly. He'd rolled up the sleeves and left his shirt untucked and open at the collar. It was also an athletic cut, so it fit tightly to his muscular torso, which made me suck in an involuntary breath in appreciation of his male splendor.

He looks like a runway model. How in the world am I going to be able to reject that? The world is so unfair. Seriously, it's like turning Brad Pitt down for a date. The girl who could actually do it should win an award for idiot of the century.

I again quickly ran through my list of reasons for not being with Ren and said a few "He's not for me's." The good thing about seeing his mouthwatering self and watching him walk around like a regular person was that it tightened my resolve. Yes. It would be hard because he was so unbelievably gorgeous, but it was now even more obvious to me that we didn't belong together.

As he joined us at the elevator, I shook my head and muttered under my breath, "Figures. The guy is a tiger for three hundred and fifty years and emerges from his curse with expensive taste and keen fashion sense too. Incredible!"

Mr. Kadam asked, "What was that, Miss Kelsey?"

"Nothing."

Ren raised an eyebrow and smirked.

He probably heard me. Stupid tiger hearing.

The elevator doors opened. I stepped in and moved to the corner hoping to keep Mr. Kadam between the two of us, but unfortunately, Mr. Kadam wasn't receiving the silent thoughts I was projecting furiously toward him and remained by the elevator buttons. Ren moved next to me and stood too close. He looked me up and down slowly and gave me a knowing smile. We rode down the elevator in silence.

When the doors opened, he stopped me, took the backpack off my shoulder, and threw it over his, leaving me with nothing to carry. He walked ahead next to Mr. Kadam while I trailed along slowly behind, keeping distance between us and a wary eye on his tall frame.

In the car, Mr. Kadam did enough talking for all three of us. He was so excited that Ren could be a man again. It must have been a great relief for him. In a way, Mr. Kadam was just as cursed as Ren and Kishan. He couldn't ever have a life of his own. Focusing his time and attention on serving the brothers had become his only purpose in life. He was as much of a slave to the tigers as they were to the curse.

The thought occurred to me that I was in danger of becoming a slave to a tiger as well. *Hah! I'd probably like it too.* I rolled my eyes at the thought. *I disgust myself. I'm so darn weak!* I hated the idea that all he'd have to do was crook his finger at me, beckon me to come to him, and I probably would. The fiercely independent side of me flared up. *That's it! No more! I'm going to talk it all out with him when we get back and hope that we can still be friends.*

This was pretty much my line of thought for the entire trip home.

I'd daydream and then stop, lecture myself, and repeat my stubborn mantra. I tried to read, but I kept rereading the same paragraph over and over. Eventually, I gave up and napped a little.

We finally got back late in the evening. I took one look at Ren's beautifully lit-up dream home and sighed deeply. It felt like home to me. It would be very hard to leave it when the time came, and I had a sinking feeling that the time would come all too soon.

Even though I had napped some during the ride, I figured that I should try to get some rest. I forced myself to stop agonizing over my choice and brushed my teeth and changed into my pajamas. I carefully took Fanindra out of my backpack. Placing a small pillow on the night-stand, I arranged Fanindra's hard, coiled body as comfortably as I could with her head facing the view of the pool. If I were a frozen snake, that would be what I'd like to look at.

Next, I took out the *gada* and the Golden Fruit. Wrapping the Golden Fruit in a soft towel, I put it and the *gada* in my dresser drawer. Looking at the fruit, I realized that I was hungry. I wanted a midnight snack, but I was too lazy to go downstairs to get one. I tucked the fruit in the drawer. I'd have to remember to ask Mr. Kadam to lock up the Fruit and the *gada* with Ren's family Seal, wherever that was. We needed to be sure it was safe.

As I crawled into bed, I noticed a small plate of crackers and cheese with sliced apples on the nightstand next to Fanindra. I hadn't noticed it before.

Huh. Mr. Kadam must have snuck the plate in when I was in the bathroom.

Grateful for his thoughtfulness, I ate my snack and then turned out the lights. Sleep wouldn't come. My mind wouldn't let me rest. I was afraid to face Ren the next day. I was afraid that I couldn't say what needed to be said. I finally drifted off at about four in the morning and slept till noon.

I took my time getting up, which turned out to be the next afternoon. I knew I was avoiding Ren and our discussion, but I didn't care. I took my time showering and dressing. By the time I mustered the courage to go downstairs, my stomach was grumbling from hunger pains.

I crept down the stairs and heard someone puttering in the kitchen. Relieved that it must be Mr. Kadam, I turned the corner and, to my dismay, found Ren, all alone, trying to make a sandwich. He had sandwich fixings spread all over the kitchen. Every vegetable in the refrigerator and almost every condiment were set out on the counter. He was standing there, deep in thought, trying to figure out if he should use ketchup or chili sauce on his turkey and eggplant sandwich. He had tied on one of Mr. Kadam's aprons, and it was smeared with mustard. Despite my attempt to be quiet, I giggled.

He smiled but kept his attention on his sandwich. "I heard you get up. Took your sweet time coming downstairs. I thought you might be hungry and came down to make you a sandwich."

I laughed acerbically, "Ugh, not one of those. I'll take a peanut butter."

"Okay. Umm, which one of these jars is peanut butter?"

He pointed to a group of condiments. He'd separated all the bottles, placing the ones labeled in English to one side and keeping everything else near him.

Bemused, I approached him. "You can't read English, can you?"

He scowled. "No. I can read about fifteen other languages and speak about thirty, but I can't figure out what these bottles are."

I smirked at him. "If you smelled it, you'd probably figure it out, Tiger Nose."

He looked up, grinned, then set down both bottles, walked over to me, and kissed me right on the mouth.

"See? That's why I need to have you around. I need a smart girlfriend."

He went back to his sandwich and started opening bottles and smelling them.

I sputtered, "Ren! I am *not* your girlfriend!"

He just grinned at me in response, located the peanut butter, and made me the thickest peanut butter sandwich I'd ever seen. I took one bite and couldn't open my mouth. "Weenn, hobouutssomme mlkk uff datte?"

He laughed. "What?"

"Ilkk, illlkk!" I mimed drinking something.

"Oh, milk! Okay, hold on a sec."

He had to open every cupboard in the kitchen to locate a cup, and, naturally, they were in the last cupboard he chose. He poured me a frothy glass, and I drained half of it immediately to clear the sticky peanut butter out of my mouth. Pulling the slices of bread apart, I chose the one with the least amount of peanut butter, folded it in half, and ate that instead.

Ren sat down across from me with the biggest, strangest looking sandwich on the planet and dug in. I blinked at it and laughed. "You're eating a Dagwood."

"What's a Dagwood?"

"A giant sandwich named after a comic strip character."

He grunted and took another big bite. I decided it was a good time to talk when he couldn't talk back.

"Umm, Ren? We have something important we need to discuss. Meet me on the veranda at sundown, okay?"

He froze with his sandwich halfway to his mouth. "A secret rendezvous? On the veranda? At sundown?" He arched an eyebrow at me. "Why, Kelsey, are you trying to seduce me?"

"Hardly," I dryly muttered.

He laughed, "Well, I'm all yours. But be gentle with me tonight, fair maiden. I'm new at this whole being human business."

Exasperated, I threw out, "I am *not* your fair maiden."

He ignored my comment and went back to devouring his lunch. He also took the other half of my discarded peanut butter sandwich and ate that too, commenting, "Hey! This stuff's pretty good."

Finished, I walked over to the kitchen island and began clearing away Ren's mess. When he was done eating, he stood to help me. We worked well together. It was almost like we knew what the other person was going to do before he or she did it. The kitchen was spotless in no time. Ren took off his apron and threw it into the laundry basket. Then, he came up behind me while I was putting away some glasses and wrapped his arms around my waist, pulling me up against him.

He smelled my hair, kissed my neck, and murmured softly in my ear, "Mmm, definitely peaches and cream, but with a hint of spice. I'll go be a tiger for a while and take a nap, and then I can save all my hours for you this evening."

I grimaced. He was probably expecting a make-out session, and I was planning to break up with him. He wanted to spend time with a girlfriend, and my intention was to explain to him how we weren't meant to be together. Not that we were ever officially together. Still, it felt like a break up.

Why does this have to be so hard?

Ren rocked me and whispered, "'How silver-sweet sound lovers' tongues by night, Like soft music to attending ears.'"

I turned around in his arms, shocked. "How did you remember that? That's *Romeo and Juliet!*"

He shrugged. "I paid attention when you were reading it to me. I liked it."

He gently kissed my cheek. "See you tonight, *iadala*," and left me standing there.

The rest of the afternoon, I couldn't focus on anything. Nothing held my attention for more than a few minutes. I rehearsed some sentences in front of the mirror, but they all sounded pretty lame to me: "It's not you, it's me," "There are plenty of other fish in the sea," "I need to find myself," "Our differences are too big," "I'm not the one," "There's someone else." Heck, I even tried "I'm allergic to cats."

None of the excuses I came up with would work with Ren. I decided the best thing to do was be straightforward with him, and tell him the truth. That's who I was. I faced things, got on with the hard parts, and moved on with life.

Mr. Kadam was gone all day. The Jeep was missing. I was hoping that he'd be around to distract me a little bit, maybe give me some advice, but he was MIA.

Sundown came too quickly, and I nervously headed upstairs. I walked in the bathroom, took out my braids, and brushed out my hair until it fell down my back in loose waves. I put on some lip gloss and eyeliner and then searched through my closet for something nicer to wear than a T-shirt. Apparently, someone had been adding designer clothing to my wardrobe. I came out with a mulberry, small-scale, plaid, cotton blouse trimmed in black silk, and some slim-leg black pants cropped at the ankles.

The charitable thing to do would be to make myself as homely looking as possible, which would probably make it much easier on him, but I didn't want his parting memories of me to be that I was a frumpy mess dressed in tomboy clothes.

I do have some feminine pride after all. I still want him to squirm. At least a little.

Satisfied with my appearance, I passed Fanindra, patted her head, and asked her to wish me luck. I slid open the glass door and stepped outside. The air was warm and fragrant with the scent of jasmine and the woodsy aroma of the jungle. I watched the sun dip down below the horizon, leaving the sky carnation pink and clementine orange. The pool and fountain lights clicked on below as I sat back on the cushioned patio loveseat and rocked gently, enjoying the balmy, sweet-smelling breeze as it wafted over my skin.

I sighed and spoke aloud, "The only thing missing is one of those fruity, tropical drinks with pineapple, cherries, and an umbrella." Something fizzed next to me on a side table. It was a curved, frosty glass containing a cold red-orange fruit drink, complete with umbrella and cherries! I picked it up to see if it was real. It was. I sipped it cautiously, and the bubbly sweet juice was perfect.

Something weird is going on. Nobody else is here, so how did this drink get here?

Right then, Ren appeared, and I forgot all about my mysterious beverage. He was barefoot, dressed in a black slacks with a thin belt and a sea-green silk shirt. His hair was damp, and he'd brushed it back away from his face. He sat down beside me on the loveseat and snuck his arm around my shoulders. He smelled fantastic. That warm summery sandalwood scent of his mixed with the jasmine.

That's got to be what heaven smells like.

Ren propped his foot up on a side table and started to rock us back and forth. He seemed content to just sit, relax, and enjoy the breeze and sunset, so we stayed that way for a while, sitting comfortably together for several minutes. It was nice. Maybe we could still be friends like this afterward. I hoped so. I liked his companionship.

He reached over and took my hand, lacing his fingers through mine. He toyed with my fingers for a while, then brought my hand up to his lips and kissed them slowly, one by one.

"What did you want to talk about tonight, Kelsey?"

"Uh . . ." *What the heck did I want to talk about? For the life of me, I couldn't remember. Oh yeah.* I shook off my reaction to him and braced myself.

"Ren, I would kind of prefer it if you would sit across from me so I can see you. You're a little less distracting from over there."

He laughed at me. "Okay, Kells. Whatever you say."

He slid a chair across from me and then sat down. Leaning over, he picked up my foot and brought it up to his lap.

I twitched my leg. "What are you doing?"

"Relax. You seem tense." He began massaging my foot. I started to protest, but he just gave me a look.

He twisted my foot one way and then another. "You have blisters all over your feet. We need to get you better shoes if you're going to be hiking in the jungle this often."

"The hiking boots gave me blisters too. It probably doesn't matter what shoes you get me. I've been hiking more in the last few weeks than I have my entire life. My feet aren't used to it."

He frowned and softly traced my arch with his finger, which shot tingly sensations up my leg. Then he wrapped his hands around my foot and started massaging, being careful to avoid any tender places. I was going to object again, but it felt good. Besides, it could be a good distraction during an uncomfortable conversation, so I let him continue. I glanced at his face. He was studying me curiously.

What was I thinking? I thought him sitting across from me would make it easier. Stupid me! Now I have to stare right at the warrior archangel and try to stay focused. I closed my eyes for a minute. *Come on, Kells. Focus. Focus. You can do this!*

"Okay, Ren, there really is something that we need to discuss."

"Alright. Go ahead."

I blew out a breath. "You see, I can't . . . reciprocate your feelings. Or your, umm, affections."

He laughed. "What are you talking about?"

"Well, what I mean is, I—"

He leaned forward and spoke in a low voice, full of meaning, "Kelsey, I *know* you reciprocate my feelings. Don't pretend anymore that you don't have them."

When did he figure all this out? Maybe when you were kissing him like an idiot, Kells. I'd hoped that I'd fooled him, but he could see right through me. I decided to play dumb and pretend I didn't know what he was talking about.

I waved my hand in the air. "Okay! Yes! I admit that I'm attracted to you."

Who wouldn't be?

"But it won't work out," I finished. *There, it was out.*

Ren looked confused. "Why not?"

"Because I'm too attracted to you."

"I don't understand what you're saying. How can your being attracted to me be a problem? I would think that's a good thing."

"For *normal* people . . . it is," I stated.

"So I'm not normal?"

"No. Let me explain it this way. It's like this . . . a starving man would gladly eat a radish, right? In fact, a radish would be a feast if that's all he had. But if he had a buffet in front of him, the radish would never be chosen."

Ren paused a moment. "I don't get it. What are you saying?"

"I'm saying . . . I'm the radish."

"And what am I? The buffet?"

I tried to explain it further. "No . . . you're the man. Now . . . I don't really want to be the radish. I mean, who does? But I'm grounded enough to know what I am, and I am *not* a buffet. I mean, you could be having chocolate éclairs, for heaven's sake."

"But not radishes."

"No."

"What . . ." Ren paused thoughtfully, "if I like radishes?"

"You don't. You don't know any better. I'm also really sorry that I've been so rude to you. I'm not normally. I don't know where all the sarcasm comes from."

Ren raised an eyebrow.

"Okay. I have a cynical, evil side that is normally hidden. But when I'm under great stress or extremely desperate, it comes out."

He set down my foot, picked up the other one, and began massaging it with his thumbs. He didn't say anything, so I continued, "Being cold-hearted and nasty was the only thing I could do to push you away. It was kind of a defense mechanism."

"So you admit you were trying to push me away."

"Yes. Of course."

"And it's because you're a radish."

Frustrated, I said, "*Yes!* Now that you're a man again, you'll find someone better for you, someone who complements you. It's not your fault. I mean, you've been a tiger so long that you just don't know how the world works."

"Right. And how *does* the world work, Kelsey?"

I could hear the frustration in his voice but pressed on. "Well, not to put too fine a point on it, but you could be going out with some supermodel-turned-actress. Haven't you been paying attention?"

Angrily, he shouted, "Oh, yes, indeed I *am* paying attention! What you are saying is that I should be a stuck-up, rich, shallow, *libertine* who cares only about wealth, power, and bettering my status. That I should date superficial, fickle, pretentious, brainless women who care more about my connections than they do about me. *And* that I am not wise enough, or up-to-date enough, to know *who* I want or *what* I want in life! Does that about sum it up?"

I squeaked out a small, "*Yes.*"

"You truly feel this way?"

I flinched. "Yes." Ren leaned forward. "Well, you're wrong, Kelsey. Wrong about yourself and wrong about me!"

He was livid. I shifted uncomfortably while he went on.

"I know what I want. I'm not operating under any delusions. I've studied people from a cage for centuries, and that's given me ample time to figure out my priorities. From the first moment I saw you, the first time I heard your voice, I knew you were different. You were special. The first time you reached your hand into my cage and touched me, you made me feel alive in a way I've never felt before."

"Maybe it's all just a part of the curse. Did you ever think of that? Maybe these aren't your true feelings. Maybe you sensed that I was the one to help you, and you've somehow misinterpreted your emotions."

"I highly doubt it. I've never felt this way about anyone, even before the curse."

This was not going the way I wanted it to. I felt a desperate need to escape before I said something that would screw up my plans. Ren was the dark side, the forbidden fruit, my personal Delilah—the ultimate temptation. The question was . . . could I resist?

I gave his knee a friendly pat and played my trump card . . . "I'm leaving."

"You're *what*?"

"I'm going home to Oregon. Mr. Kadam thinks it will be safer for me anyway, with Lokesh out there looking to kill us and all. Besides, you need time to figure out . . . stuff."

"If you're leaving, then I'm going with you!"

I smiled at him wryly. "That kind of defeats the purpose of me leaving. Don't you think?"

He slicked back his hair, let out a deep breath, then took my hand and looked intently into my eyes. "Kells, when are you going to accept the fact that we belong together?"

I felt sick, like I was kicking a faithful puppy who only wanted to be loved. I looked out at the pool.

After a moment, he sat back scowling and said menacingly, "I won't let you leave."

Inside, I desperately wanted to take his hand and beg him to forgive me, to love me, but I steeled myself, dropped my hands in my lap, then implored, "Ren, please. You have to let me go. I need . . . I'm afraid . . . look, I just can't be here, near you, when you change your mind."

"It's not going to happen."

"It might. There's a good chance."

He growled angrily. "There's *no* chance!"

"Well, my heart can't take that risk, and I don't want to put you in what can only be an awkward position. I'm sorry, Ren. I really am. I do want to be your friend, but I understand if you don't want that. Of course, I'll return when you need me, if you need me, to help you find the other three gifts. I wouldn't abandon you or Kishan in that way. I just can't stay here with you feeling obligated to pity-date me because you need me. But I'd never abandon your cause. I'll always be there for you both, no matter what."

He spat out, "*Pity*-date! *You*? Kelsey, you can't be serious!"

"I am. Very, *very* serious. I'll ask Mr. Kadam to make arrangements to send me back in the next few days."

He didn't say another word. He just sat back in his chair. I could tell he was fuming mad, but I felt that, after a week or two, when he started getting back out in the world, he would come to appreciate my gesture.

I looked away from him. "I'm very tired now. I'd like to go to bed." I got up and headed to my room. Before I closed the sliding door, I asked, "Can I make one last request?"

He sat there tight-lipped, his arms folded over his chest, with a tense, angry face.

I sighed. *Even infuriated he was beautiful.*

He said nothing so I went on, "It would be a lot easier on me if I didn't see you, I mean as a man. I'll try to avoid most of the house. It *is* yours after all, so I'll stay in my room. If you see Mr. Kadam, please tell him I'd like to speak with him."

He didn't respond.

"Well, good-bye, Ren. Take care of yourself." I tore my eyes away from him, shut the door, and drew the curtains.

Take care of yourself? That was a lame good-bye. Tears welled in my eyes and blurred my vision. I was proud that I'd gotten through it without showing emotion. But, now, I felt like a steamroller had come along and flattened me.

I couldn't breathe. I went into the bathroom and turned on the shower to drown out any sounds. I closed the door, which trapped all the steam inside, and sobbed. Gut-wrenching spasms shook my body. My eyes, nose, and mouth all leaked simultaneously as I allowed myself to feel the empty despair of loss.

I slumped to the floor and then slid down even farther until I was sprawled out on it with my cheek resting on the cool marble. I let my emotions overtake me until I was completely spent. My limbs felt lifeless and dull, and my hair frizzed up and stuck to the wet tears on my face.

Much later, I got up slowly, turned off the now-cold shower, washed my face, and climbed into bed. Thoughts of Ren ran through my mind again, and silent tears started streaming once more. I actually thought about putting Fanindra on my pillow and cuddling her. That was how desperate I was for comfort. I cried myself to sleep, hoping that I would feel better the next day.

I again slept in late the next day and got up feeling hungry and numb. I was emotionally exhausted. I didn't want to risk going downstairs to get something to eat. I didn't want to run into Ren. I sat on the bed, pulled my knees up to my chest, and wondered what to do.

I decided to write in my journal. Pouring all my jumbled thoughts and emotions onto its pages helped me feel a bit better. My stomach growled.

I wish I had some of Mr. Kadam's berry crepes.

Something moved at the corner of my vision. I turned and saw a breakfast laid out for me on the little table. I walked over to inspect it. Crepes with triple berries! My mouth fell open in shock.

That's just too convenient.

I suddenly remembered that fizzing juice that I had tasted last night. When I wanted something to drink, it had appeared.

I decided to test these strange phenomena. I said out loud, "I would also like some chocolate milk." A tall cold glass of chocolate milk materialized out of nowhere. This time, I decided to try to think something.

I wish I had a new pair of shoes.

Nothing happened. I voiced, "I wish I had a new pair of shoes." Still nothing.

Maybe it only works with food. I thought, *I would like a strawberry milkshake.*

A tall glass appeared, full to the brim with a thick strawberry milkshake topped with whipped cream and a sliced strawberry.

What is doing this? The gada? Fanindra? Durga? The Fruit? The Fruit! The Golden Fruit of India! Mr. Kadam had said that through the Golden Fruit, the people of India would be fed. The Golden Fruit provided food! I took the fruit out of the drawer and held it in my hand as I wished for something else.

"A . . . radish, please."

The fruit shimmered and glowed like a golden diamond, and a radish

appeared in my free hand. I examined it thoughtfully and then chucked it in my trash can.

I mumbled ironically, "See? Even *I* don't want a radish."

I immediately wanted to share this exciting news with Ren and ran for the door. I twisted the knob, but then I hesitated. I didn't want to undo all the things I'd said last night. I meant it about staying friends with him, but, ironically, I was the one who couldn't be his friend right now. I needed time to get over him.

I decided to wait for Mr. Kadam to come back; then, I would tell Ren about the Fruit.

I dug into my crepes and enjoyed my meal—all the more special because it was magical. Then I got dressed and decided to read in my room. After awhile, someone knocked on my door.

"May I come in, Miss Kelsey?" It was Mr. Kadam.

"Yes. The door's open."

He entered, shutting the door behind him and sat down on one of the easy chairs.

"Mr. Kadam, stay right there. I have something to show you!" I got up excitedly and ran to the dresser. Pulling out the Golden Fruit, I unwrapped it and set it carefully on the table. "Are you hungry?"

He laughed. "No. I just ate."

"Well, wish for something to eat anyway."

"Why?"

"Just try it."

"Alright." His eyes twinkled. "I wish for a bowl of my mother's stew."

The fruit twinkled, and a white bowl appeared in front of us. The tangy aroma of an herbed lamb stew filled the room.

"What is this?"

"Go on, Mr. Kadam, wish for something else. Food, I mean."

"I wish for a mango yogurt."

The fruit sparkled again, and a small dish of mango yogurt appeared.

"Don't you see? It's the fruit! It *feeds* India. Get it?"

He picked up the fruit carefully. "What an amazing discovery! Have you shared this with Ren?"

I blushed guiltily. "No, not yet. But you go ahead."

He nodded, stunned, and turned the fruit in his hands, looking at it from all angles.

"Umm . . . Mr. Kadam? There's something else I wanted to talk with you about."

He set the fruit down carefully and gave me his full attention. "Of course, Miss Kelsey. What is it?"

I let out a deep breath. "I think it's time . . . for me to go home."

He sat back in his chair, steepled his fingers, and looked at me thoughtfully for a moment. "Why do you believe so?"

"Well, like you said, there's the Lokesh thing, and there are also other . . . things."

"Other things?"

"Yes."

"Such as?"

"Such as . . . well, I don't want to take advantage of your hospitality forever."

He scoffed, "Nonsense. You are a member of the family. We owe you an eternal debt, one that can never be repaid. This house is as much yours as it is ours."

I smiled at him gratefully. "Thank you. It's not only that, though, it's also . . . Ren."

"Ren? Can you tell me about it?"

I sat on the edge of the couch and opened my mouth to say that I didn't want to talk about it, but the whole thing came spilling out. Before I knew it, I was crying, and he was sitting next to me patting my hand and comforting me as if he were my grandfather.

He didn't say a word. He just let me spill out all of the hurt, confusion, and tender new feelings. When I was done, he patted my back while I hiccupped with tears dropping onto my cheeks. He handed me an expensive cloth handkerchief, smiled, and wished for a cup of chamomile tea to give me.

I laughed wetly at his delighted expression as he handed me the tea; then, I blew my nose and calmed down. I was horrified that I had confessed everything to him. *What must he think of me?* Then another thought pierced my despair: *Will he tell Ren?*

As if reading my thoughts, he said, "Miss Kelsey, don't you feel bad about what you have told me."

I begged, "Please, *please* don't tell Ren."

"Rest assured, I will never break your confidence." He chuckled. "I am very good at keeping secrets, my dear. Don't despair. Life often seems hopeless and too complicated to hammer out a happy result. I only hope I can offer you some of the peace and harmony that you have given to me."

He sat back and thoughtfully stroked his short beard. "Perhaps it *is* time for you to go back to Oregon. You are right that Ren needs time to learn how to be a man again, although not quite in the way you believe. Plus, I have a lot more research to do before we set off looking for Durga's second gift."

He paused for a moment. "Of course I will arrange for you to go back. Never forget, though, that this home is yours too, and you can always call me at a moment's notice, and I will bring you back. If it's not too forward of me, I consider you a daughter." He laughed. "Or perhaps, granddaughter would be more accurate."

I smiled at him tremulously, threw my arms around his neck, and sobbed anew on his shoulder. "Thank you. Thank you so much. You are like family to me too. I will miss you terribly."

He hugged me back. "And I will miss you. Now, enough tears. Why

don't you go out for a swim and get some fresh air while I make the arrangements."

I swiped a sparkling tear from my eye. "That's a good idea. I think I will."

He squeezed my hand and left the room, quietly closing the door behind him.

I decided to take his advice, changed into my bathing suit, and headed for the pool. I swam laps for a while, trying to put my energy into something other than my emotions. When I got hungry, I tried wishing for a club sandwich and one appeared next to the swimming pool.

This sure comes in handy! I don't have to even be in the same room! I wonder what the range on that thing is.

I ate my sandwich and lay out on a beach towel until my skin got hot, then I hopped back in the pool and floated lazily for a while to cool off.

A tall man walked up and stood by the pool directly in front of the sun. Even shading my eyes, I couldn't see his face, but I knew who it was.

I scowled, "Ren! Can't you leave me alone? I don't want to talk to you right now."

The man stepped out of the sun, and I squinted up at him.

"You don't want to see me? And after I came all this way?" He clicked his tongue, "Tsk, Tsk, Tsk. Someone needs to teach you some manners, Miss."

I gasped, "Kishan?"

He grinned, "Who else, *bilauta*?"

I squealed, darted up the pool steps, and rushed over to him. He opened his arms to me and laughed as I gave him a big wet hug.

"I can't believe you're here! I'm so glad."

He looked me up and down with his golden eyes, so different from

Ren's, "Well, if I knew that this was the kind of welcome I'd be getting, I would have come here a lot sooner."

I laughed. "Stop teasing me. How did you get here? Did you get six hours back too? You have to tell me all about it!"

He raised his hand and chuckled. "Hold on, hold on. First of all, who's teasing? And secondly, why don't you go get changed, and we can sit down for a long talk."

"Okay." I smiled at him then faltered, "But can we meet out here by the pool?"

He cocked his head, confused, but smiled. "Sure, if you want to. I'll just wait for you right here."

"Alright. Don't move. I'll be right back!"

I ran up the back steps to my room and quickly showered, got dressed, and brushed out my hair. I also ordered two root beer floats, courtesy of the Golden Fruit, and carried them down with me.

When I got to the pool, he had moved two deck chairs over into the shade and was sitting back and relaxing with his hands behind his head and his eyes closed. He was wearing a black T-shirt with jeans, and his feet were bare. I sunk down into the other chair and handed him a root beer float.

"What's this you've brought me?"

"It's called a root beer float. Try it."

He took a sip and coughed. I laughed. "Did the bubbles go up your nose?"

"I believe they did. It's good though. Very sweet. It reminds me of you. Is it from your country?"

"Yes."

"If I want to answer your questions before nightfall, I guess I'd better get started."

He took another sip of his root beer and continued, "First, you

asked me if I got six hours back. The answer is yes. You know, it's strange. I've been content being a tiger for centuries, but after you and Dhiren visited, I've felt uncomfortable in my black hide. For the first time in a long time, I wanted to be alive again, not as an animal but as myself."

"I understand. How did you figure out you had six hours, and how did you get here?"

"I'd been changing to a man every day and had also started sneaking into nearby villages to watch people and see what the modern world offers." He sighed sadly. "The world has changed much since I was last a part of it."

I nodded, and he went on, "One day, about a week ago, I'd changed to a man and was watching the children play in the village square. I knew my time was almost up, so I moved back into the jungle and waited for the tremors that come before a change. They didn't come.

"I waited one hour, then two, and still no change. I knew that something had happened. I walked back through the jungle and waited until I felt the pull of the tiger take over again. I tested myself the next day, and the next, and the time was the same every day.

"That's when I knew that you and Ren had been at least partially successful. After that, I returned to the village as a man and asked some people to help me place a call to Mr. Kadam. Someone finally figured out how to reach him, and he drove out to pick me up."

"So that's where Mr. Kadam was for the last couple of days."

Kishan looked me up and down then leaned back and sipped his float appreciatively. He raised his glass to me. "I have to say, I had no idea what I was missing."

He smiled at me and stretched out his long legs in front of him, crossing them at the ankles.

I said, "Well, I'm glad you're here. This is your home, and you belong here."

He looked off soberly in the distance. "I guess it is. For the longest time, I felt I had no spark of humanity in me. My soul was dark. But, you, my dear," he reached over, took my hand, and kissed it, "have brought me back into the light again."

I put my hand lightly on his arm. "You just missed Yesubai. I don't believe your soul was dark or that you had lost your humanity. It just takes time to heal when your heart's been broken like that."

His eyes twinkled. "Perhaps you are right. Now, tell me of your adventures! Mr. Kadam filled me in on the basics, but I want to hear details."

I told him about Durga's weapons, and he expressed a keen interest in the *gada* in particular. He laughed when I shared the tale of the monkeys attacking Ren and looked at me in horror when I described the Kappa that had almost eaten me. It was easy talking to him. He listened with interest, and I didn't have any of the nervous butterflies I felt when I talked with Ren.

When I got to the end of the story, I stared at the pool, while Kishan carefully studied my face.

"There's something else I'm curious about, Kelsey."

I smiled at him. "Sure, what else do you want to know?"

"What exactly is going on between you and Ren?"

A vise clamped down on my chest, but I tried to play it cool. "What do you mean?"

"I mean, are you two more than just traveling companions? Are you together?"

I clipped off a fast, "No. Definitely not."

He grinned. "Good!" He grabbed my hand and kissed it. "Then that means you're free to go out with me. No girl in her right mind would want to be with Ren, anyway. He's very . . . stuffy. Cold, as far as relationships go."

My mouth hung open for a minute, shocked, and then I felt anger shove the shock aside and take over. "First of all, I am not going to be with either one of you. Second, a girl would have to be crazy not to want Ren. You're wrong about him. He's not stuffy or cold. In fact, he's considerate, warm, drop-dead gorgeous, dependable, loyal, sweet, and charming."

He raised an eyebrow and measured me thoughtfully for a minute. I squirmed under his gaze, knowing that I had spoken too quickly and said way too much.

He ventured carefully, "I *see*. You may be right. The Dhiren I know has surely changed in the past couple of hundred years. However, despite that and your insistent claim that you will not be with either one of us, I would like to propose that we go out and celebrate tonight, if not as my . . . what is the correct word?"

"The word is date."

"Date. If not as my date . . . then, as my friend."

I grimaced.

Kishan continued, pressing his point, "Surely, you won't leave me to fend for myself on my first night back in the real world?"

He smiled at me, encouraging my acceptance. I did want to be his friend, but I wasn't sure what to say to his request. And for just a moment, I wondered how Ren would feel about it and what the consequences might be.

I questioned, "Where exactly do you want to go to celebrate?"

"Mr. Kadam said there's a nightclub in town nearby with dinner and dancing. I thought we could celebrate there, maybe get something to eat, and you can teach me how to dance."

I laughed nervously. "This is my first time in India, and I don't know a thing about the dancing or the music here."

Kishan seemed even more delighted by that news. "Fantastic! Then we will learn together. I won't take no for an answer." He jumped up to rush off.

I yelled, "Wait, Kishan! I don't even know what to wear!"

He shouted back over his shoulder, "Ask Kadam. He knows everything!"

As soon as he disappeared into the house, I sunk glumly into a depression. The last thing I wanted to do was try to be happy when I was emotionally wrung dry. I was pleased that Kishan was back and in high spirits though.

In the end, I decided that, although I really didn't feel like celebrating, I didn't want to dampen Kishan's newfound enthusiasm for life. I leaned over to pick up our discarded root beer glasses and found that they'd disappeared.

How awesome was that? Not only did the Golden Fruit provide food, it also did the dishes!

I got up to head back into the house and sensed something. Goose bumps stood out on my arms. I looked around but didn't see or hear anything. Then I felt an electric sizzle shoot through my body. Something tugged at me and pulled my eyes up to the balcony. Ren was standing there, leaning against a pillar with his arms folded across his chest watching me.

We looked at each other for a minute, not saying anything, but I could feel the air between us shift. It became thick, sultry, and tangible—like when the air changes right before a storm. I could feel its power envelop me as it brushed across my skin. Even though I couldn't see it, I knew a storm was coming.

The sultry air pulled on me like a riptide, trying to suck me back into the vacuum of power Ren had stirred between us. I felt like I had to physically yank myself away from it. I closed my eyes and ignored it, continuing on.

When it finally let me go, a horrible ripping feeling occurred within me, and I spun out into a void alone. As I dragged myself to my room and closed the door behind me, I could feel his eyes still on me, burning a fiery hole between my shoulder blades. I stiffly entered my dark room, trailing the torn threads of disconnection along behind me.

I stayed in my room for the rest of the afternoon. Mr. Kadam visited me and expressed his delight that I would be going out for the evening with Kishan. He suggested that a celebration was indeed in order and that we should all go.

I asked, "So you and Ren want to come too?"

"I don't see why not. I will ask him."

"Mr. Kadam, it might be better for you to just have a guys' night out. I'd just get in the way."

"Nonsense, Miss Kelsey. We all have something to celebrate, and I will make sure that Ren is on his best behavior."

He turned to leave, and I said, "Wait! What should I wear?"

"You may wear whatever you wish. You can wear modern clothes or dress in more traditional fashions. Why don't you wear your *sharara* dress?"

"You don't think I'd be out of place?"

"No. There are many women who wear them for celebrations. It would be perfectly acceptable."

My face fell, and he added, "If you don't wish to wear it, you can wear your regular clothes instead; either choice is appropriate."

He left and I groaned. Being alone and trying to celebrate with Kishan was bad enough, but at least he didn't make me feel like I was drowning in emotional turmoil. Now, Ren would be there. It would be miserable.

I felt stressed about going out. I wanted to wear regular clothes, but I knew the boys would probably be wearing Armani or something like

that, and I didn't want to stand next to them in jeans and sneakers, so I opted for my *sharara* dress.

I pulled the heavy skirt and top out of the closet, ran my hand over the beading, and sighed. It was so beautiful. I spent some time doing my hair and makeup. Playing up my eyes with more mascara and liner than I usually did, I also smudged some purple-gray shadow over my lids and used a flat iron to straighten my hair. The feel of smoothing it out in long strokes was very therapeutic and helped me to relax.

By the time I was finished, my golden-brown hair was sleek and shining and hung in a curtain down my back. I carefully slipped the purple-blue bodice over my head and then picked up the heavy skirt. I centered it on my hips and aligned the glittering folds, liking the weighty feel of it. Fingering the intricate pattern of teardrop pearls, I couldn't help but smile.

I was just lamenting that the Golden Fruit could not create foot-wear when a knock sounded at my door. Mr. Kadam was waiting for me.

"Are you ready to go, Miss Kelsey?"

"Well, not exactly. I don't have any shoes."

"Ah, perhaps Nilima has something in her closet you can borrow."

I followed him to Nilima's room, where he opened her closet and pulled out a pair of golden sandals. They were a little big, but I laced them tight and they worked fine. Mr. Kadam offered me his arm.

"Wait just a second. I forgot something." I ran back to my room and grabbed my dupatta scarf, wrapping it around my shoulders.

He smiled at me and offered his arm again. We walked outside to the front drive where I expected to see the Jeep, but parked there instead was a glossy platinum Rolls-Royce Phantom. He held the door open for me as I sank into a luxurious smoke-gray leather interior.

"Whose car is this?" I asked, rubbing my hand across the polished dashboard.

"Oh, this? This, is my car." Mr. Kadam beamed with obvious

love and pride for his vehicle. "Most cars in India are very small and economical. In fact, only about one percent of the population owns a car. When you compare automobiles of India to American vehicles . . ."

He rattled off several more automobile facts before turning the key while I grinned and sank back in my seat listening with rapt attention.

When he finally started the car, the engine didn't roar to life, it purred. *Very nice.*

"Kishan is on his way down, and Ren . . . has opted not to come."

"I see."

I should have been glad, but I was surprisingly disappointed. I knew it was better if we didn't spend time together until this crush, or whatever it was, went away, and he was probably just honoring my wish to not see him, but there was still a part of me that wanted to be with him at least this one last time.

I bit back my emotion and smiled at Mr. Kadam. "That's okay. We'll still have fun without him."

Kishan darted out the door. He wore a lightweight burgundy V-neck sweater over pressed khaki slacks. His hair had been trimmed to a shorter length and was cut in angled, choppy layers that had been styled to give him a dramatic fall-in-your-face Hollywood look. The thin sweater showed off his muscular build. He looked very handsome.

He opened the back door to the car and hopped in. "Sorry I took so long."

He leaned up between the front seats. "Hey, Kelsey, did you miss—" He whistled. "Wow, Kelsey! You look amazing! I'm going to have to beat the other guys off with a stick!"

I blushed. "Please. You won't even be able to get near me what with the crowds of women that will be surrounding you."

He grinned at me and leaned back in his seat. "I'm glad Ren decided to back out. More of you for me that way."

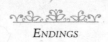
"Hmm." I turned around in my seat and buckled the seatbelt.

We pulled up outside a nice restaurant with an outdoor wraparound porch, and Kishan rushed forward to open the door for me. He offered me his arm while smiling at me disarmingly. I laughed and took it, determined to enjoy my evening.

We were seated at a table in the back of the place. The waitress came by, and I took the liberty of selecting cherry colas for me and Kishan. He seemed happy to let me make suggestions of food choices for him.

We had a fun time looking through the menu together. He asked me what my favorite foods were and what he should try. He translated what the menu said, and I offered my opinions. Mr. Kadam ordered some herbal tea and sat quietly, sipping it as he listened to our discussion. After we ordered our food, we sat back and watched couples swaying on the dance floor.

The music was soft and slow, timeless classics, but in a different language. I let melancholy sweep over me and fell quiet. When the food arrived, Kishan dug into it with relish and then happily finished mine when I gave up trying to eat. He seemed fascinated with everything—the people, the language, the music, and especially the food. He asked Mr. Kadam thousands of questions like "How do I pay?" "Where did the money come from?" "How much money do I give the server?"

I listened and smiled, but my thoughts were far away. Once our plates were taken away we sipped refills of our drinks and watched the people around us.

Mr. Kadam cleared his throat. "Miss Kelsey, may I have this dance?"

He stood up and held out his arm. His eyes were twinkling, and he was smiling at me. I looked up at him with my own watery smile and thought about how much I would miss this kind man.

"Of course you may, kind sir."

He patted my hand on his arm and led me to the dance floor. He was a very good dancer. I'd only danced with high school boys at dances before, and they usually just moved in a circle until the song was over. It was nothing interesting or exciting, but dancing with Mr. Kadam was much more exhilarating. He led me all around the dance floor spinning me in circles that made my skirt fan out. I laughed and enjoyed my time with him. He twirled me out and then brought me back deftly each time. His skill made me feel like I was a good dancer.

When the song was over, we walked back to the table. Mr. Kadam acted as if he was old and winded, but I was actually the one breathing hard. Kishan was thumping the floor impatiently with his foot, and as soon as we returned, he immediately stood up, grabbed my hands, and led me back out to the dance floor.

This time, the song was faster. Kishan seemed to be a quick-study as he carefully watched and copied the moves of the other dancers on the floor. He had good rhythm, but he was trying too hard to look natural. We had a good time, though, and I laughed through the entire song.

The next song was a slow love song, and I started to walk back to our table, but Kishan grabbed my hand and said, "Wait a minute, Kelsey. I want to try this."

He watched another couple near us for a few seconds; then, he placed my arms around his neck while he encircled my waist with his. He kept his eyes on the other couples for only a few more seconds and then looked at me with a rakish smile.

"I can definitely see the benefit of this kind of dancing." He pulled me a bit closer and mumbled, "Yes. This is very nice."

I sighed and let my thoughts drift for a moment. A sound suddenly vibrated through my body. A deep rumble. No. A soft growl. Barely

heard over the music. I looked up at Kishan, wondering if he'd heard it too, but he was staring at something over my head.

A quiet but indomitable voice behind me said, "I believe this is *my* dance."

It was Ren. I could feel his presence. The warmth of him seeped into my back, and I quivered all over like spring leaves in a warm breeze.

Kishan narrowed his eyes and said, "I believe it is the lady's choice."

Kishan looked down at me. I didn't want to cause a scene, so I simply nodded and removed my arms from his neck. Kishan glared at his replacement and stalked angrily off the dance floor.

Ren stepped in front of me, took my hands gently in his, and placed them around his neck, bringing my face up achingly close to his. Then he slid his hands slowly and deliberately over my bare arms and down my sides, until they encircled my waist. He traced little circles on my exposed lower back with his fingers, squeezed my waist, and drew my body up tightly against him.

He guided me expertly through the slow dance. He didn't say anything, at least not with words, but he was still sending lots of signals. He pressed his forehead against mine and leaned down to nuzzle my ear. He buried his face in my hair and lifted his hand to stroke down the length of it. His fingers played along my bare arm and at my waist.

When the song ended, it took both of us a minute to recover our senses and remember where we were. He traced the curve of my bottom lip with his finger then reached up to take my hand from around his neck and led me outside to the porch.

I thought he would stop there, but he headed down the stairs and guided me to a wooded area with stone benches. The moon made his skin glow. He was wearing a white shirt with dark slacks. The white made me think of him as the tiger.

He pulled me under the shadow of a tree. I stood very still and quiet, afraid that if I spoke I'd say something I'd regret.

He cupped my chin and tilted my face up so he could look in my eyes. "Kelsey, there's something I need to say to you, and I want you to be silent and listen."

I nodded my head hesitantly.

"First, I want to let you know that I heard everything that you said to me the other night, and I've been giving your words some very serious thought. It's important that you understand that."

He shifted and picked up a lock of hair, tucked it behind my ear, and trailed his fingers down my cheek to my lips. He smiled sweetly at me, and I felt the little love plant bask in his smile and turn toward it as if it contained the nourishing rays of the sun. "Kelsey," he brushed a hand through his hair, and his smile turned into a lopsided grin, "the fact is . . . I'm in love with you, and I have been for some time."

I sucked in a deep breath.

He picked up my hand and played with my fingers. "I don't want you to leave." He began kissing my fingers while looking directly into my eyes. It was hypnotic. He took something out of his pocket. "I want to give you something." He held out a golden chain covered with small tinkling bell charms. "It's an anklet. They're very popular here, and I got this one so we'd never have to search for a bell again."

He crouched down, wrapped his hand around the back of my calf, and then slid his palm down to my ankle and attached the clasp. I swayed and barely stopped myself from falling over. He trailed his warm fingers lightly over the bells before standing up. Putting his hands on my shoulders, he squeezed, and pulled me closer.

"Kells . . . *please*." He kissed my temple, my forehead, and my cheek. Between each kiss, he sweetly begged, "Please. Please. Please. Tell me you'll stay with me." When his lips brushed lightly against mine, he said, "I need you," then crushed his lips against mine.

I felt my resolve crumbling. I wanted him, wanted him badly. I needed him too. I almost gave in. I almost told him that there was nothing in the world I wanted more than to be with him. That I didn't think I was capable of leaving him. That he was more precious to me than anything. That I'd give up anything to be with him.

But then he pressed me close and spoke softly in my ear, "Please don't leave me, *priya*. I don't think I could survive without you."

My eyes filled up with tears, and shiny wet drops spilled down my cheeks. I touched his face.

"Don't you see, Ren? That's exactly why I have to go. You need to know that you can survive without me. That there's more to life than just me. You need to see this world that's opened up to you and know that you have choices. I refuse to be your cage.

"I could capture you and keep you selfishly to indulge my own desires. Regardless of whether you're willing or not, it would be wrong. I helped you so that you could be free. Free to see and do all of the things that you missed out on all these years." My hand slipped from his cheek to his neck. "Should I put a collar on you? Chain you up so you spend your life connected to me out of a sense of obligation?" I shook my head.

I wept openly now. "I'm sorry, Ren, but I won't do that to you. I can't. Because . . . I love you too."

I kissed him quickly one last time. Then, I gathered up my skirts and ran back to the restaurant. Mr. Kadam and Kishan saw me enter, looked at my face, and immediately rose to leave. Thankfully, the men were quiet on the way home while I cried softly and brushed the flowing tears away with the back of my hand. When we arrived, a sober Kishan briefly squeezed my shoulder, got out, and went into the house. I took a deep breath and told Mr. Kadam that I'd like to fly home in the morning.

He nodded silently, and I ran up to my room, closed the door, and fell onto my bed. I dissolved into a broken puddle of weeping despair. Eventually, sleep overcame me.

The next morning, I got up early, washed my face, and plaited my hair, tying the end with a red ribbon. I put on jeans, a T-shirt, and my tennis shoes, and I packed my things into a large bag. Reaching out a hand to touch the *sharara* dress, I decided that it held too many memories to bring with me, so I left it in the closet. I wrote a note for Mr. Kadam, which told him where the *gada* and the Fruit were and asked him to store them in the family vault and to let Nilima have my *sharara* dress.

I decided to take Fanindra with me. She felt like a friend to me now. Carefully placing her on top of my quilt, I picked up the delicate golden anklet that Ren had given me. The little bells tinkled as I brushed my finger across them. I had intended to leave it on the dresser, but I changed my mind at the last minute. It was probably a selfish thing to do, but I wanted it. I wanted to have something from him, a keepsake. I dropped it in my bag and zipped the bag closed.

The house was quiet. Silently, I walked down the stairs and passed the peacock room where I found Mr. Kadam sitting and waiting for me. He took my bag and walked with me out to the car, then he opened my door, and I slid in to the seat and buckled my seatbelt. Starting the car, he circled the stone driveway slowly. I turned to take one last look at the beautiful place that felt like home. As we started down the tree-lined road, I watched the house until the trees blocked my view.

Just then, a deafening, heartrending roar shook the trees. I turned in my seat and faced the desolate road ahead.

EPILOGUE

shadow

the immaculately dressed man stood at his penthouse office window. He gazed upon the city lights far below and clenched his fist.

He lived in a city of twenty-nine million people, the most densely populated city in the world, but the generations rose and fell like so many waves upon the beach, and he stood alone, a rocky, unmovable sentinel, letting the waves of humanity pass him by, hardly noticing them at all.

How do you find one small person in a city of millions, let alone a world of billions?

After all these centuries, the other pieces of the Damon Amulet had resurfaced—and with it, a girl. He hadn't felt this surge of energy in a long, long time.

A quiet chime announced his returning assistant who entered and bowed. He stood and said only three words, the words his employer had been longing to hear from the moment he had seen the vision and caught a glimpse of an old foe and a mysterious girl.

"We found her."

ACKNOWLEDGMENTS

I'd like to thank my early reading group. My family—Kathy, Bill, Wendy, Jerry, Heidi, Linda, Shara, Tonnie, Megan, Jared, and Suki. And my friends—Rachelle, Cindy, Josh, Nancy, and Linda.

Hand claps for Jared and Suki who helped me brainstorm cover designs for the *Tiger* series books and for also organizing my author photos and the website.

Special thanks for my editor from India, Sudha Seshadri. Her enthusiasm and guidance in the language and culture of India was invaluable. She patiently and kindly advised me, going above and beyond the duties of an editor. I'm sure I would have offended many people without her. If there are any discrepancies, cultural or linguistic, they are entirely my own, and I apologize in advance for anything aberrant. Rest assured, it was not my intention. My hope is that I've shown India's people and culture respect, and have depicted the beauty of their land and the rich mythology of their people in an appropriate way.

I am always appreciative of my husband, who went through countless edits. He waded through pages of meager novice scribbling and helped shape my first book into what it is today. His enthusiasm kept me writing. Even though he's lived on sandwiches and leftovers for a year he's never complained and brags about his author wife to anyone willing to lend an ear and even to some who won't.

Thanks to my friend Linda who gave me great feedback on every chapter. Many of the paragraphs in *Tiger's Curse* are thanks to her requests for more detailed information. Her tireless support and excitement kept me motivated to write every day and I always look forward to talking about my tigers with her.

Thanks to my sister Linda who is my confidant, hair stylist, personal chef, housekeeper, and cookie baker. Without her, there would be no double chocolate chip peanut butter cookies. She kept my household running so I could write my first book. When she moved away I was crushed and overwhelmed. There's no replacement for her. Everyone should have such a sister . . . such a friend.

I would also like to express my gratitude to Tina Anderson, the Manager of the Polk County Fairgrounds and to my editors—Rhadamanthus, Gail Cato, Mary Hern, and especially Cindy Loh. Cheers for my agent Alex Glass, who gently coaxed me through my post-traumatic-rejection-letter syndrome as well as patiently explained all the business parts of the writing industry, and thanks for all the help from his team at Trident Media.

Thank you to all the people at Booksurge who got my self-published version on the market. I'd like to give my undying gratitude to Judi Powers and all the people at Sterling who joined Team Tiger with a level of excitement that was entirely unexpected. I feel extremely humbled and grateful that they were willing to give my tigers and this new author a chance.

Thanks to Raffi Kryszek who was the first in the mainstream world of books and movies to embrace my story. He's a fellow Trekkie with a wide grin that never leaves his face, whose energy for my series, and tigers in general, matches and perhaps surpasses my own. And thanks to his eleven-year-old niece who gave him the book in the first place.

Extra special hugs for my nieces and nephews who lent me their names—Michael, Matthew, Sarah, Rebecca, Sammy, Joshua, M. Cathleen, D. Andrew, and Madison. I promise I'll work the rest of you in later.

Will Kelsey be reunited with her beloved Ren?

Or will she discover a new love?

Will Ren and Kishan be freed from
the tiger's curse once and for all?

Their true destiny awaits
as the *Tiger's Curse* series continues with . . .

tiger's quest

going home

I clung to the leather seat and felt my heart fall as the private plane ascended into the sky, streaking away from India. If I took off my seatbelt, I was sure I would sink right through the floor and drop thousands of feet, freefalling down to the jungles below. Only then would I feel right again. I had left my heart in India. I could feel it missing. All that was left of me was a hollowed-out shell, numb and empty.

The worst part was . . . I did this to myself.

How was it possible that I had fallen in love? And with someone so . . . complicated? The past few months had flown by so quickly. Somehow I had gone from working at a circus to traveling to India with a tiger—who turned out to be an Indian prince—to battling immortal creatures to trying to piece together a lost prophecy. Now, it was all over, and I was alone.

It was hard to believe just a few minutes ago, I had said good-bye to Mr. Kadam. He hadn't said much. He just gently patted my back as I'd hugged him hard, not letting go. He pried my arms from the vise I'd locked him in, muttered some reassurances, and turned me over to his great-great-great granddaughter, Nilima, and we were off.

Thankfully, Nilima left me alone on the plane. I didn't feel like company. She brought me lunch, but I could not even think about eating. I'm sure it was delicious, but I felt like I was skirting the edge of a pit of quicksand. Any second I could be sucked down into an abyss of despair. The last thing I wanted was food. I felt spent and lifeless, like crumpled-up wrapping paper after Christmas.

Nilima removed the meal and then tried to tempt me with my favorite drink: ice-cold lemon water. But I just left it on the table. I stared at the glass for who knows how long, watching the moisture bead up on the outside and slowly dribble down, pooling around the bottom.

I tried to sleep and forget about everything at least for a few hours—but the dark, peaceful oblivion eluded me. Thoughts of my white tiger and the centuries-old curse that trapped him raced through my mind, and I ended up staring into space. I looked at Mr. Kadam's empty seat across from me. I stared out the window and watched a blinking light on the wall. I gazed down at my hand, tracing over the spot where Phet's henna design had faded away.

Nilima returned and brought me an MP3 player with thousands of songs. Several were Indian musicians, but most of them were American. I scrolled through and found the saddest break-up songs I could find. Putting the plugs in my ears, I selected play.

I unzipped my backpack and retrieved my grandmother's quilt, remembering only then that I had wrapped Fanindra inside it. Pulling back the edges of the blanket, I spied her golden body and set the serpent next to me on the armrest. The enchanted piece of jewelry was coiled up, resting, or at least I assumed she was. Rubbing her smooth, scaly head, I whispered, "You're all I've got now."

Spreading out my quilt over my legs, I leaned back in the reclined chair, stared at the ceiling of the airplane, and listened to a song called

"One Last Cry." Keeping the volume soft and low, I placed Fanindra on my lap and stroked her gleaming coils. The snake's jeweled eyes softly illuminated the cabin of the plane, and the green glow comforted me as I let the music fill the empty place in my soul.

1

YOU

the plane finally landed several mind-numbing hours later at the airport in Portland, Oregon. When my feet hit the tarmac, I shifted my gaze from the terminal to the gray, overcast sky. I closed my eyes and let the cool breeze blow over me. I could smell the forest and feel a soft, dewy sprinkle settle on my bare arms. It must have rained recently. It felt good to be home.

Taking a deep breath, I felt Oregon center me. I was a part of this place, and it was a part of me. I belonged here. It was where I grew up and spent my whole life. My roots were here. My parents and grandma were buried here. Oregon welcomed me like a beloved child, enfolded me in her cool arms, shushed my turbulent thoughts, and promised peace through her whispering pines.

Nilima had followed me down the steps and waited quietly while I absorbed the familiar environment. I heard the hum of a fast engine, and a cobalt blue convertible pulled around the corner. The sleek sports car was the exact color of *his* eyes.

Mr. Kadam must have arranged for the car. I rolled my eyes at his expensive taste. Mr. Kadam thought of every last detail—and he always did it in style. *At least the car's a rental,* I mused.

I stowed my bags in the trunk and read the name on the back:

Porsche Boxster RS 60 Spyder. I shook my head and muttered, "Holy cow, Mr. Kadam, I would have been just as happy to take the shuttle back to Salem."

"What?" Nilima asked politely.

"Nothing. I'm just glad to be home."

I closed the trunk and sank down into the two-toned blue and gray leather seat. We drove in silence. Nilima knew exactly where she was going, so I didn't even bother giving her directions. I just leaned my head back and watched the sky and the green landscape zip by.

Cars full of teenage boys passed us and whistled. They were admiring either Nilima or the nice car. I'm not sure which inspired the cat-calls, but I knew they weren't for me. Older men cruised past us slowly, too. They didn't whistle, but they definitely enjoyed the view. Nilima just ignored them, and I tuned them out, thinking, *I must look as awful as I feel.*

When we entered downtown Salem, we passed the Marion Street Bridge, which would take us over the Willamette River and onto Highway 22 heading for the farmlands of Monmouth and Dallas. I tried to tell Nilima she missed a turn, but she merely shrugged and said we were taking a short cut.

"Sure," I said sarcastically, "what's another few minutes on a trip that lasts for days?"

Nilima tossed her beautiful hair, smiled at me, and kept driving, maneuvering into the traffic headed for South Salem. I'd never been this way before. It was definitely the long way to Dallas.

Nilima was driving toward a large hill that was covered with forest. We wound our way slowly up the beautiful tree-lined road for several miles. I saw dirt roads leading into the trees. Houses poked through here and there, but the area was largely untouched. I was surprised that the city hadn't annexed it and started building there. It was quite lovely.

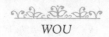

Slowing down, Nilima turned onto one of the private roads and followed it even higher up. The tree line was thick. Although we passed a few winding driveways, I didn't see any houses. At the end of the road, we stopped in front of a duplex. The home was nestled in the middle of a pine forest.

Both sides of the duplex were identical, mirror images of each other. Each had two floors with a garage and a small shared courtyard. A large bay window looked out over the trees. The house's wood siding was painted cedar brown and midnight green, and the roof was covered with grayish-green shingles. In a way, it kind of resembled a ski cabin.

Nilima glided smoothly into the garage and stopped the car. "We're home," she announced.

"Home? What do you mean? Aren't you taking me to my foster parents' house?" I asked, even more confused than I already was.

Nilima smiled understandingly. She told me gently, "No. This is your house."

"My house? What are you talking about? I live in Dallas. Who lives here?"

"You do. Come inside and I'll explain."

We walked through a laundry room to the kitchen, which was small but had brand new stainless steel appliances, lemon yellow curtains, and walls decorated with lemon stencils. Nilima grabbed a couple of sodas from the fridge.

I plopped my backpack down and said, "Okay, Nilima, now tell me what's going on."

She ignored my question. Instead, she offered me a soda which I declined, and then told me to follow her.

Sighing, I slipped off my tennis shoes so I wouldn't mess up the duplex's plush carpeting and followed her to the living room, which was small and cute. We sat down on a beautiful chestnut leather sofa. A

tall library cabinet full of classic hardbound books that probably cost a fortune beckoned invitingly from the corner, while a large, flat-screen television mounted above a polished cabinet and a sunny window also vied for my attention.

Nilima began rifling through papers left on a coffee table.

"Kelsey," she began. "This house is yours. It's part of your payment for your work in India this summer."

"It's not like I was really working, Nilima."

"What you did was the most vital work of all. You accomplished much more than any of us even hoped. We all owe you a great debt and this is a small way to reward your efforts. You've overcome tremendous obstacles and almost lost your life. We are all very grateful."

Embarrassed, I teased, "Well, now that you put it that way—wait! You said this house is *part* of my payment? You mean there's more?"

With a nod of her head, Nilima said, "Yes."

"No. I really can't accept this gift. An entire house is way too much—never mind anything else! It's much more than we agreed on. I just wanted some money to pay for books for school. He shouldn't do this."

"Kelsey, he insisted."

"Well, he will have to un-insist. This is too much, Nilima. *Really.*"

She sighed and looked at my face which was set with steely determination. "He really wants you to have it, Kelsey. It will make him happy."

"Well, it's impractical! How does he expect me to catch the bus to school from here? I plan to enroll in college now that I'm back home, and this location isn't exactly close to any bus routes."

Nilima gave me a puzzled expression. "What do you mean catch the bus? I guess if you really want to ride the bus, you could drive down to the bus station."

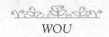
"Drive down to the bus station? That doesn't make any sense."

"Well, *you* aren't making any sense. Why don't you just drive your car to school?"

"My car? What car?"

"The one in the garage, of course."

"The one in the . . . *Oh, no!* No way! You have *got* to be kidding me!"

"No. I'm not kidding. The Porsche is for you."

"*Oh, no, it's not!* Do you know how much that car costs? No way!"

I pulled out my cell phone and searched for Mr. Kadam's phone number. Right before I pressed SEND, I thought of something that stopped me in my tracks. "Is there anything else I should know?"

Nilima winced. "Well . . . he also took the liberty of signing you up for Western Oregon University. Your classes and books have already been paid for. Your books are on the counter next to your list of classes and a map of the campus."

"He signed me up for WOU?" I asked, incredulous. "I had been planning on attending the local community college and working—not going to WOU."

"He must have thought a university would be more to your liking. You start classes next week. As far as working goes, you may if you wish, but it will be unnecessary. He has also set up a bank account for you. Your new bank card is on the counter. Don't forget to endorse it on the back."

I swallowed. "And . . . uh . . . exactly how much money is in that bank account?"

Nilima shrugged. "I have no idea, but I'm sure it's enough to cover your living expenses. Of course, none of your bills will be sent here. Everything will be mailed straight to an accountant. The house and the car are paid for, as well as all of your college expenses."

She slid a whole bunch of paperwork my way and then sat back and sipped her soda.

Shocked, I sat completely still for a minute and then remembered my resolve to call Mr. Kadam. I opened my phone and searched for his number again.

Nilima interrupted, "Are you sure you want to give it all back, Miss Kelsey? I know that he feels very strongly about this. He wants you to have these things."

"Well, Mr. Kadam should know that I don't need his charity. I'll just explain that community college is more than adequate and I really don't mind staying in the dorm and taking the bus."

Nilima leaned forward. "But, Kelsey, it wasn't Mr. Kadam who arranged all of this."

"What? If it wasn't Mr. Kadam, then who . . . *Oh!*" I snapped my phone shut. There was no way I was going to call *him*, no matter what. "So *he* feels strongly about this, does he?"

Nilima's arched eyebrows drew together in pretty confusion, "Yes, I would say he does."

It almost tore my heart to shreds to leave him 7,196.25 miles away in India, and somehow he still manages to have a hold on me.

Underneath my breath, I grumbled, "Fine. He always gets what he wants anyway. There's no point in trying to give it back. He'll just engineer some other over the top gift that will only serve to complicate our relationship even further."

A car honked outside in the driveway.

"Well, that's my ride back to the airport." Nilima rose and said, "Oh! And I almost forgot. This is for you, too." She pressed a brand new cell phone in my hand and hugged me quickly before walking to the front door.

"But, wait! Nilima!"

"Don't worry, Miss Kelsey. Everything will be fine. The paperwork you need for school is on the kitchen counter. There's food in the

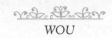

fridge, and all of your belongings are upstairs. You can take the car and visit your foster family later today if you wish. They are expecting your call."

She turned, gracefully walked out the door, and climbed into the airport shuttle. She waved gaily from the passenger seat. I waved back morosely and watched her until the shuttle drove out of sight. Suddenly, I was all alone in a strange house surrounded by quiet forest.

Once Nilima had gone, I decided to explore the place that I was now going to call home. Opening the fridge, I saw that the shelves were indeed fully stocked. Twisting a bottle cap off, I sipped a soda and peeked in the cupboards. There were glasses and plates, as well as cooking utensils, silverware, and pots and pans. On a hunch, I opened the bottom drawer of the refrigerator—and found it full of lemons. Clearly, this part was Mr. Kadam's doing. The thoughtful man knew drinking lemon water would be a comfort to me.

Mr. Kadam's interior design touch didn't end in the kitchen, though. The downstairs half bath was decorated in sage green and lemon. Even the soap in the dispenser was lemon-scented.

I placed my shoes in a wicker basket on the tiled floor of the laundry room beside a brand new front-loading washer and dryer set and continued on to a small office.

My old computer sat in the middle of the desk, but right next to it was a brand new laptop. A leather chair, file drawers, and a shelf with paper and other supplies completed the office.

Grabbing my backpack, I headed upstairs to see my new bedroom. A lovely queen bed with a thick ivory down comforter and peach accent pillows was nestled against the wall, and an old wooden trunk sat at the foot. Cozy peach-colored reading chairs sat in the corner facing the window overlooking the forest.

There was a note on the bed that lifted my spirits right up:

Hi, Kelsey!
Welcome home. Call us ASAP!
We want to hear all about your trip!
All of your things are stored away.
We love your new home!
        Love,
        Mike and Sarah

Reading Mike and Sarah's note in addition to being back in Oregon grounded me. Their lives were normal. My life with them was normal, and it would be nice to be around a normal family and act like a normal human being for a change. Sleeping on jungle floors, talking to Indian goddesses, falling in love with a . . . tiger—well, none of that was normal. Not by a long shot.

I opened my closet and saw that my hair ribbon collection and all my clothes had indeed been moved from Mike and Sarah's. I fingered through some things I hadn't seen in a few months. When I opened the other side of the closet, I found all the new clothes that had been purchased for me in India as well as several new items still in garment bags.

How on earth did Mr. Kadam get this stuff here before me? I left all this in my closet back in India. I closed the door on the clothes and my memories, determined not to open that side of the closet.

Moving to the dresser, I pulled open my top drawer. Sarah had arranged my socks exactly the way I liked them. Each pair of black, white, and assorted colored socks was wound into a neat ball and placed in a row. But opening the next drawer wiped the smile off my face. I found the silky pajamas I had purposely left in India.

My chest burned as I ran my hand over the soft cloth and then resolutely shut the drawer and moved onto the bathroom, which was

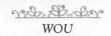

white and soft, powdery blue with glistening tiles. Turning to leave the bright, airy room, a detail suddenly hit me, causing my face to flush scarlet red. My bedroom was peaches and cream.

He *must have picked these colors*, I surmised. *He'd once said that I smelled like peaches and cream. Figures he'd find a way to remind me of him even from a continent away. As if I could forget . . .*

I threw my backpack on the bed and instantly regretted it, realizing that Fanindra was still inside. After taking her out carefully and apologizing, I set her on top of a white pillow with peach embroidery. I stroked her golden head for a minute and then set to work putting away my traveling clothes.

When that was done, I lay back on the bed and pulled my new cell phone out of my jeans pocket. Like everything else, the phone was expensive and totally unnecessary. It was designed by Prada. I turned the phone on and expected *his* number to show up first, but it didn't. There weren't any messages either. In fact, the only numbers stored on the phone were Mr. Kadam's and my foster parents'.

Various emotions raced through my head. At first I was relieved. Then I was puzzled. Then I was disappointed. A part of me pondered, *It would have been nice of him to call. Just to see if I arrived okay.*

Annoyed with myself, I called my foster parents and told them I was home, tired from the flight, and that I would come over for dinner the next night. Hanging up, I grimaced, wondering what kind of tofu surprise would be in store for me. Whatever the health food meal turned out to be, I was happy to sit through it as long as I got a chance to see them.

I wandered downstairs and made myself a snack of apple slices with peanut butter and started rifling through the college papers on the counter. Mr. Kadam had chosen international studies as my major, with a minor in art history.

I looked through my schedule. Somehow, Mr. Kadam had managed to get me, a freshman, into 300- and 400-level classes. Not only that, but he had also booked my classes for both the fall *and* the winter terms—even though winter registration wasn't available yet.

WOU probably received a big, fat donation from India, I thought, smirking to myself. *I wouldn't be surprised to see a new building going up on campus this year.*

KELSEY HAYES, STUDENT ID 69428L7
WESTERN OREGON UNIVERSITY

FALL TERM

College Writing 115 (4 credits). *Introduction to thesis writing.*

First Year Latin 101 (4 credits). *Introduction to Latin.*

Anthropology 476 D: Religion and Ritual (4 credits). *A study of the religious practices around the world. Delineates religious observance as seen through anthropology, while focusing on particular topics including: spirit possession, mysticism, witchcraft, animism, sorcery, ancestor worship, and magic. Examines the blending of major world religions with local beliefs and traditions.*

Geography 315: The Indian Subcontinent (4 credits). *An examination of South Asia and its geography, with emphasis on India. We will evaluate the economic relationship between India and other nations; study patterns, issues, and challenges specifically related to geography; and explore the ethnic, religious, and linguistic diversity of its people historic and modern.*

WINTER TERM

Art History 204 A: Prehistoric through Romanesque (4 credits). *A study of all art forms of that time period with specific emphasis on historical and cultural relevance.*

History 470: Women in Indian Society (4 credits). *An examination of women in India, their belief systems, their cultural place in society, and associated mythology, past and present.*

College Writing II 135 (4 credits). *Second-year class expanding research-based document writing and skills.*

Political Science 203 D: International Relations (3 credits). *Comparison of global issues and the policies of world groups with similar and/or competing interests.*

All of the courses sounded interesting, especially religion and magic. Mr. Kadam's selections were subjects I probably would have picked for myself, other than Latin. I wrinkled my nose. I'd never been too good with languages. Too bad WOU didn't offer an Indian language. It would be nice to learn Hindi, especially if I'm going back to India at some point to tackle the remaining three tasks outlined on Durga's prophecy that will break the tiger's curse. But Latin would be good for me, too.

I still had a week until classes started, but I thought it might be a good idea to look around campus. All of my classes were located in the Humanities and Social Sciences building, which would be convenient. I set aside my course schedule, pulled out a map of the campus, and found the HSS building. It looked like I could park in Lot F, which was right next to it.

Grabbing the keys and my new credit card, I slid into the convertible, pushed the garage door button, and waited for it to clear. The Porsche was terribly expensive, which made me feel extremely paranoid. My plan was to eventually return it or sell it, so I backed out carefully and drove like a grandma down the hill, wincing every time I passed a tree branch that came too close.

Parking in a visitor spot, I easily found the HSS building and walked to the bookstore where there was already a line of new students waiting to get their ID cards. I waited with them and got my ID. Then I suited up like every other WOU freshman by buying a red hooded sweatshirt which had the school mascot, a western wolf, printed on the front.

I followed the cashier's directions to the administration building for

a student parking permit. When I got to the front of the line, I told the lady my name. She said that someone had already issued a parking pass in my name. *Of course they did.*

On the drive home, I found the parking pass in the glove box and tried out the satellite radio stereo system. I turned the button to Lite Pop. My hand was on the dial in an instant when a love song belted out. I switched to Top 40, just in time to pick up a breakup song, skipped right over Love, and landed on New Country.

I should have known better. Carrie Underwood's "I Told You So" blared from the high-tech speakers. I couldn't seem to shake sad love songs, no matter how many stations I tried. *Maybe the universe was sending me a message? Well, if that's the case, then bring it on.*

The song was about a girl who realized she made a mistake leaving the man she loved. If she returned to him, would he laugh and say, "I told you so," or would he send her packing? Would he admit he'd been lonely without her or would he have moved on? I couldn't have picked a better song to beat myself up with if I tried. *Perfect. Thank you, Carrie Underwood. I hope YOUR guy took YOU back.* I chewed my bottom lip and my vision became blurry.

The wind whipped through my hair as the words whipped my heart. Brushing a tear away from my eye, I considered that *he* probably *would* find somebody new very soon. I wouldn't take me back if I were him. Letting myself think about him for even a minute was too painful. I tucked away my memories and folded them into a tiny wedge of my heart. Then I shoved a whole bunch of new thoughts in place of the painful ones. I thought about school, my foster family, and being back in Oregon. I stacked those thoughts like books, one on top of the other, to try to suppress everything else.

For now, thinking about other things and other people was an effective distraction. But I could still feel his ghost hovering in the quiet,

dark recess of my heart, waiting for me to be lonely or to let my guard down, so that he could fill my mind again with thoughts of him.

I'll just have to stay busy, I decided. *That will be my salvation. I'll study like mad and visit people and . . . and date other guys. Yes! That's what I can do. I'll go out with other people and stay active and then I'll be too tired to think about him.*

By the time I headed for bed, it was late and I was tired. Patting Fanindra, I slipped under the sheets and slept.

The next day, I studied my new text books for five hours and then took a break by going shopping in Salem. At a toy store, I bought two orange and black stuffed animal tigers, which seemed appropriate. As I headed toward the checkout counter, my eye drifted upward.

Hanging over the top shelf was a large, stuffed white tiger. Its bright blue eyes stared down at me.

The salesclerk saw me gape at it. "Would you like to see it?" she asked hopefully, bringing over a stepstool. "Here, let me get it down for you."

The tiger was half as big as she was. The clerk set it on the counter, and I mumbled, "How much?"

"Two hundred and forty dollars, but this is a high-end product. It's made to look lifelike. It looks almost real, don't you think?"

"Yes, it's pretty real looking, alright," I admitted and thought sadly, *I should know.*

The woman smiled at me. "Would you like to add it to your purchase today?"

I nodded, and before I knew it, she had placed a small bag over my wrist and pressed the white tiger into my arms. I grabbed the tiger around the middle and buried my face in the fur. It was soft but didn't smell right. *He* smelled wonderful, like sandalwood and waterfalls. This

stuffed animal was just a disparate replica. Peeking out from the side, I thanked the woman and walked out to my car.

Back in the driver's seat, I looked over at my new passenger, who was staring at me with glassy blue eyes. *His* eyes were bright cobalt. This poor thing's were an imitation, a lifeless, dull blue. And its stripes were different.

What on earth is wrong with me? I shouldn't have bought it. It was just going to make forgetting him that much harder.

I drove home, dragged my stuffed tiger upstairs, and threw it on my bed. Then I pulled out a change of clothes and got ready to visit my foster family.

As I drove through town, I went the long way around so I could avoid the Polk County Fairgrounds and more painful memories. When I pulled up in front of Mike and Sarah's house, the door opened wide. Mike hurried toward me . . . but couldn't resist getting a better look at the Porsche and ran past me to the car.

"Kelsey! May I?" he asked sweetly.

"Knock yourself out," I said and laughed. *Same old Mike*, I thought and tossed him the keys so he could drive himself around the block a few times.

Sarah put her arm around my waist and guided me toward the house. "We're so glad to see you! Both of us are!" She yelled and frowned at Mike who waved happily while backing out of the driveway.

"We were worried when you first left for India because we didn't get too many calls from you, but Mr. Kadam phoned every other day and explained what you were doing and told us how busy you were."

"Oh? And what did he say, exactly?" I asked, curious to know what story he had made up.

"Well, it's all very exciting, isn't it? Let's see. He talked about your new job and about how you will be interning every summer and working with him on various projects from time to time. I had no idea that you

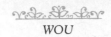

were interested in international studies. That is a wonderful major. Very fascinating. He also said that when you graduate, you can work for his company full time. It's a fantastic opportunity!"

I smiled at her. "Yes, Mr. Kadam's great. I couldn't ask for a better boss. He treats me more like a granddaughter than an employee, and he spoils me terribly. I mean, you saw the house and the car, and then there's school, too."

"He did speak very fondly of you over the phone. He even admitted to us that he's come to depend on you. He's a very nice man. He also insists that you are . . . how did he say it . . . 'an investment that will have a big payoff in the future.'"

I shot Sarah a dubious look. "Well, I hope he's right about that."

She laughed and then sobered. "*We* know you're special, Kelsey. And you deserve great things. Maybe this is the universe's way of balancing the loss of your parents. Though I know nothing will ever take the place of them."

I nodded. She was happy for me. And knowing that I would be financially secure enough to live comfortably on my own was probably a big relief to them.

Sarah hugged me and pulled a strange-smelling dish out of the oven. She placed it on the table, and said, "Now, let's eat!"

Feigning enthusiasm, I asked, "So . . . what's for dinner?"

"Tofu and spinach whole wheat organic lasagna with soy cheese and flax seed."

"Yum, I can't wait," I said and wrestled a half-smile to my face. I thought fondly of the magical Golden Fruit that I had left behind in India. The divine object could make the most delicious food appear instantly. In Sarah's hands, maybe even a healthy meal would taste good. I snuck a bite. *Then again . . .*

Rebecca, six years old, and Samuel, four years old, ran into the room

and bounced up and down trying to get my attention. I hugged them both and directed them to the table. Then I went to the window to see if Mike was back yet. He had just pulled up in the Porsche and was walking backward to the front door, staring at the car.

I opened the door. "Umm, Mike, it's time for dinner."

He replied over his shoulder, never taking his eyes off the car, "Sure, sure. Be right there."

Sitting between the kids, I scooped up a wedge of lasagna for each of them and took a tiny piece for myself. Sarah raised her eyebrow, and I rationalized it by saying that I'd had a big lunch. Mike finally came in and started chatting animatedly about the Porsche. He asked if he could take Sarah on a date and borrow the car some Friday night.

"Sure. I'll even come over and babysit for you."

He beamed while Sarah rolled her eyes. "Are you planning on taking me out or the car?" she asked.

"You, of course, my dear. The car is just a vehicle to showcase the beautiful woman sitting at my side."

Sarah and I looked at each other and snickered.

"Good one, Mike," I said.

After dinner, we retired to the living room where I gave the kids their orange tigers. They squealed in delight and ran around growling at each other. I felt bad about buying them here, but the tag still said *Made in India*, and they didn't seem to mind.

Sarah and Mike asked me all kinds of questions about India, and I talked about the ruins of Hampi and Mr. Kadam's house. Technically, it wasn't his, but they didn't need to know that. Then they asked me about how the tiger was adapting to his new home.

I froze, but only for an instant, and told them that he was doing fine and that he seemed very happy there. Thankfully, Mr. Kadam had explained that we were often out exploring Indian ruins and cataloging

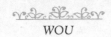
artifacts. He'd said my job was to be his assistant, keep records of his findings, and take notes, which wasn't too far from the truth. It also explained why I was going to minor in art history.

Being with them was fun, but it also wore me out because I had to make sure I didn't slip up and tell them anything too weird. They'd never believe all the things that had happened to me. I had a hard time believing it myself sometimes.

Knowing they went to bed early, I gathered my things and said goodnight. I hugged them all good-bye and promised to visit again the next week.

When I got home, I spent a couple of more hours studying and then took a hot shower. Climbing into bed in my dark room, I gasped quietly as my hand brushed against fur. Then I remembered my purchase, shoved the stuffed tiger to the edge of the bed, and tucked my hand under my cheek.

I couldn't stop thinking about *him*. I wondered what he was doing right now and if he was thinking of me or if he even missed me at all. I felt like I was playing whack-a-mole with my thoughts. Every time I punched one thought down, another one would surface in a different place. I couldn't win; they kept popping up from my subconscious. Sighing, I reached over, grabbed the leg of the stuffed tiger, and pulled it close. Wrapping my arms around its middle, I buried my nose in its fur and fell asleep on its paw.

READ ALL THE BOOKS
IN THE BESTSELLING
tiger's curse SERIES

KELSEY'S RECIPES

ULTIMATE HOT CHOCOLATE

- 12 oz milk chocolate
- 4 tsp butter
- 1 tsp vanilla
- ¼ tsp salt
- 2 cups cream
- 2 cups milk
- whipped cream
- maraschino cherries
- chocolate syrup
- ¼ cup chocolate chips

Melt chocolate chips, butter, vanilla, and salt over low heat. Whisk until smooth. Slowly add the cream and the milk. Keep heat on low and bring up to the desired temperature. Continue whisking to prevent the chocolate from burning.

Pour into two large mugs. Top with whipped cream and cherries. Drizzle chocolate syrup over it and sprinkle with chocolate chips.

REN'S COOKIES

- 2 sticks of butter
- ¾ cup sugar
- ¾ cup brown sugar
- 2 eggs
- 1 ½ tsp vanilla
- ¼ tsp salt
- ¾ cup dark cocoa powder
- 2 cups flour
- ½ tsp baking powder
- ½ tsp baking soda
- 1 bag of chocolate chips
- ¾ cup smooth peanut butter
- ½ cup brown sugar

Cream the butter then add sugars. When it's light and fluffy, add eggs and vanilla. Sift the next 5 dry ingredients and mix with the wet until thoroughly combined. Add one package of chocolate chips (or as many as you like!) to the dough. Mix together the next 2 ingredients to make the peanut butter filling. Then place a spoonful of the chocolate dough on a baking sheet, top with some peanut butter filling, and cover with some more chocolate dough. Bake at 350° for 12-20 minutes depending on cookie size.

BISCUITS AND GRAVY

Part 1—Biscuits
- 4 cups flour
- 1 tsp sugar
- 1 tbsp baking powder
- 1 tsp baking soda
- 1 tsp salt
- 1 cup shortening or butter
- 1 ½ cups buttermilk

Combine dry ingredients. Then cut in shortening and add the buttermilk a little at a time, continually mixing until the dough comes together. Knead dough a few times. If it's too sticky, add a bit more flour. If it's too dry, add a bit more buttermilk. Roll out into a log shape and slice to desired thickness. Place biscuits on a buttered baking sheet and brush with melted butter. Bake at 450° for 15-20 minutes depending on how thick you've made your biscuits.

BISCUITS AND GRAVY

Part 2—Gravy
- ½ pound of ground beef
- ½ pound of sausage
- ¼ cup flour
- 3 cans evaporated milk
- Salt and pepper to taste

Brown the ground beef and sausage, then set meat aside reserving ¼ cup of grease in the pan. If you don't have enough grease, then add a few tbsp of butter. Whisk in flour and heat until smooth and bubbly. Then add milk slowly and bring to a boil. Reduce heat and simmer for five minutes or so until your gravy reaches the desired thickness. Add your meat back in and stir. Serve over hot biscuits.

A DISCUSSION GUIDE TO
Tiger's Curse

1. Do you think it was fate that led Kelsey to the Circus Maurizio—or just chance?

2. Should Mr. Kadam have told Kelsey the real reason he wanted her to travel to India before she left home?

3. Mr. Kadam finds that his aging process has been slowed so that he can care for Ren and Kishan. However, he has also watched his beloved wife and generations of their descendents age and die. Would you accept the price that Mr. Kadam must pay in exchange for superhuman longevity?

4. *Tiger's Curse* takes sibling rivalry to the ultimate level. Should Ren have forgiven Kishan after three hundred years, or was his brother's betrayal too great?

5. While flirting with Kelsey, Ren pretends that he is the predator and she is his prey: "He was tracking me, hunting me. His eyes locked on mine and pinned me to the spot where I was standing" (p. 179). How is romance like a hunt? What are the ways in which it should never be like one?

6. The broken Damon amulet is named after the Goddess Durga's tiger. Why hasn't Lokesh tried to capture Mr. Kadam and Kishan's pieces before? What powers do you imagine it might offer once it is whole?

7. Kelsey is jealous when Mr. Kadam tells her that Ren and Kishan had once broken into their father's harem. Is it fair to feel jealous about something your girlfriend/boyfriend did before you even met?

8. Houck uses a lot of Hindi words and phrases. Does their presence enhance or detract from the story?

9. Ren tells Kelsey how "being caged made me think long and hard about my relationships with other creatures, especially the elephants and horses" (p. 231). How do you think human behavior would change if everyone had to spend time in an animal's body?

10. After the brothers' confrontation with Lokesh, Ren was turned into a white tiger and Kishan into a black tiger. Kishan's darker coloring allowed him to survive more easily in the wild, while Ren became easy prey for angry villagers. Is Ren meant to symbolize good and Kishan evil?

11. Is Kishan just flirting with Kelsey to annoy his brother?

12. Kelsey decides that she can't lose her heart to Ren because he's too perfect, and she fears he'll think she's not good enough for him. Can you relate to Kelsey's dilemma? Have you ever chosen safety over risk? Did you regret your decision or not?

13. How much did you know about Indian mythology before reading *Tiger's Curse*? Discuss its similarities and differences compared to the folklore and mythology of other cultures.

Author photo by Gabriel Boone

COLLEEN HOUCK's *New York Times* bestselling Tiger's Curse series has received national praise. Colleen is a lifelong reader whose literary interests include action, adventure, science fiction, and romance. She has worked as a nationally certified American Sign Language interpreter for nearly twenty years. Colleen lives in Salem, Oregon, with her husband and a huge assortment of plush tigers.

To find out more, visit
www.tigerscursebook.com.